The Blazing World

Siri Hustvedt

W F HOWES LTD

This large print edition published in 2015 by
W F Howes Ltd
Unit 4, Rearsby Business Park, Gaddesby Lane,
Rearsby, Leicester LE7 4YH

1 3 5 7 9 10 8 6 4 2

First published in the United Kingdom in 2014
by Sceptre

A CIP catalogue record for this book is available
from the British Library

ISBN 978 1 47129 483 9

Typeset by Palimpsest Book Production Limited,
Falkirk, Stirlingshire
Printed and bound by
www.printondemand-worldwide.com of Peterborough, England

EDITOR'S INTRODUCTION

'**A**ll intellectual and artistic endeavors, even jokes, ironies, and parodies, fare better in the mind of the crowd when the crowd knows that somewhere behind the great work or the great spoof it can locate a cock and a pair of balls.' In 2003, I ran across this provocative sentence in a letter to the editor that was published in an issue of *The Open Eye*, an interdisciplinary journal I had been reading faithfully for several years. The letter's author, Richard Brickman, did not write the sentence. He was quoting an artist whose name I had never seen in print before: Harriet Burden. Brickman claimed that Burden had written him a long letter about a project she wanted him to make public. Although Burden had exhibited her work in New York City in the 1970s and '80s, she had been disappointed by its reception and had withdrawn from the art world altogether. Sometime in the late nineties, she began an experiment that took her five years to complete. According to Brickman, Burden engaged three men to act as fronts for her own creative work. Three solo shows in three New York galleries,

1

attributed to Anton Tish (1998), Phineas Q. Eldridge (2002), and the artist known only as Rune (2003), had actually been made by Burden. She titled the project as a whole *Maskings*, and declared that it was meant not only to expose the antifemale bias of the art world, but to uncover the complex workings of human perception and how unconscious ideas about gender, race, and celebrity influence a viewer's understanding of a given work of art.

But Brickman went further. He argued that Burden insisted that the pseudonym she adopted changed the character of the art she made. In other words, the man she used as a mask played a role in the *kind* of art she produced: 'Each artist mask became for Burden a "poetized personality," a visual elaboration of a "hermaphroditic self," which cannot be said to belong to either her or to the mask, but to "a mingled reality created between them."' As a professor of aesthetics, I was immediately fascinated by the project for its ambition, but also for its philosophical complexity and sophistication.

At the same time, Brickman's letter puzzled me. Why hadn't Burden published her own statement? Why would she allow Brickman to speak for her? Brickman claimed that the sixty-page letter Burden called 'Missive from the Realm of Fictional Being' had arrived unannounced in his mailbox and that he had no knowledge of the artist beforehand. The tone of Brickman's letter is also curious: It alternates between condescension and admiration. He criticizes Burden's letter as hyperbolic and unsuited for publication in an academic journal but then quotes other passages he attributes to her with seeming approval. I was left with a muddled impression of the letter, as well as a feeling of irritation with Brickman, whose commentary effectively smothers Burden's original text. I immediately looked up the three exhibitions, *The History of Western Art* by Tish, *The Suffocation Rooms* by Eldridge, and *Beneath* by Rune, each of which was visually distinct from the other two. Nevertheless, I gleaned what I would call a 'family resemblance' among the three. The Tish, Eldridge, and Rune shows Burden had allegedly invented were all compelling as art, but I was especially intrigued by Burden's experiment because it resonated with my own intellectual concerns.

My teaching schedule was heavy that year. I had duties as temporary chair of my department, and I wasn't able to satisfy my curiosity about *Maskings* until three years later, when I took a sabbatical leave to work on my book *Plural Voices and Multiple Visions*, in which I discuss the work of Søren Kierkegaard, M. M. Bakhtin, and the art historian Aby Warburg. Brickman's description of Burden's project and her *poetized personalities* (the latter expression is Kierkegaard's) meshed perfectly with my own thoughts, so I decided to track Brickman down through *The Open Eye* and hear what he had to say for himself.

Peter Wentworth, the editor of the journal, retrieved e-mail correspondence from Brickman to him – several short, dry, business-related notes. When I tried to contact Brickman, however, I discovered the address was defunct. Wentworth produced an essay Brickman had published in the journal two years before his letter in *The Open Eye*, which I belatedly remembered having read: an abstruse paper critiquing the ongoing debates about concepts in analytical philosophy, a subject remote from my own interests. According to Wentworth, Brickman had earned a PhD in philosophy from Emory University and was an assistant professor at St Olaf College in Northfield, Minnesota. When I contacted St Olaf, however, it turned out that no person named Richard Brickman was teaching or had ever taught in that department. Needless to say, Emory University had no records of a PhD candidate by that name either. I decided to go straight to Harriet Burden, but by the time I tracked her down in New York through her daughter, Maisie Lord, Burden had been dead for two years.

The idea for this book was born during my first telephone conversation with Maisie Lord. Although she knew about Brickman's letter, she was surprised to hear that its author was not the person he had purported to be, if indeed he was anyone at all. She assumed her mother had been in touch with him but knew nothing about the particulars of their connection. Harriet Burden's artworks had all been catalogued and stored by the time I spoke to Maisie, and she had been at work on a documentary film about her mother for several years. The film includes voice-over excerpts from the twenty-four private journals her mother began keeping after her husband, Felix Lord, died in 1995, each one labeled with a letter of the alphabet. As far as Maisie knew, none of the diaries mentioned Brickman. (I found two references to R.B., presumably Richard Brickman, but nothing more revealing than that.) Maisie, however, felt sure her mother had left a number of 'clues' inside the journals, not only to her pseudonymous project but also to what she called 'the secrets of my mother's personality.'

Two weeks after our phone call, I flew to New York, where I met with Maisie, her brother, Ethan Lord, and Burden's companion, Bruno Kleinfeld, all of whom spoke to me at great length. I viewed hundreds of artworks Burden had never shown anywhere, and her children informed me that her work had just been taken by the prestigious Grace Gallery in New York City. The Burden retrospective mounted in 2008 would garner the respect and recognition the artist had so desperately longed for, essentially launching her career posthumously. Maisie showed me rushes from her unfinished film and, most crucially, gave me access to the notebooks.

While reading the hundreds of pages Burden had written, I found myself by turns fascinated, provoked, and frustrated. She kept many journals simultaneously. She dated some entries, but not others. She had a system of cross-referencing the notebooks that was sometimes straightforward but at other times appeared byzantine in its complexity or nonsensical. In the end, I gave up trying to decode it. Her handwriting shrinks into illegibility on some pages and on others grows so large that a few sentences take up an entire page. Some of her texts are obscured by drawings that intrude into the written passages. A few of the notebooks were full to bursting and others contained only a few paragraphs. Notebook A and Notebook U were mostly autobiographical, but not entirely. She kept elaborate notes on artists she loved, some of whom take up many pages of a notebook. Vermeer and Velázquez share V, for example. Louise Bourgeois has her own notebook under L, not B, but L contains digressions on childhood and psychoanalysis. William Wechsler, Notebook W, contains notes on Wechsler's work but also lengthy asides on Lawrence Sterne's *Tristram Shandy* and Eliza Heywood's *Fantomina*, as well as a commentary on Horace.

Many of the journals are essentially notes on her reading, which was voluminous and darted in and out of many fields: literature, philosophy, linguistics, history, psychology, and neuroscience. For unknown reasons, John Milton and Emily Dickinson shared a notebook labeled G. Kierkegaard is in K, but Burden also writes about

Kafka in it, with several passages on cemeteries as well. Notebook H, on Edmund Husserl, has pages on Husserl's idea about 'the intersubjective constitution of objectivity' and the consequences of such an idea on the natural sciences, but also tangents on Maurice Merleau-Ponty, Mary Douglas, and a 'Fantasy Scenario' on artificial intelligence. Q is devoted to quantum theory and its possible use for a theoretical model of the brain. On the first page of Notebook F (for *female*, apparently), Burden writes, 'Hymns to the Fair Sex.' Page after page of quotations follow. A small sample will suffice to give the flavor. Hesiod: 'Who trusts a woman, that man trusts a swindler.' Tertullian: 'You [woman] are the devil's gateway.' Victor Hugo: 'God became man, granted. The devil became a woman.' Pound (Canto XXIX): 'The female / Is an element, the female / Is chaos, an octopus / A biological process.' Along with these examples of blatant misogyny, Burden had stapled dozens of newspaper and magazine articles onto a single page with the word *suppressed* written on it. There was no common theme to these miscellaneous pieces, and I wondered why they had been lumped together. And then it dawned on me that what they shared were lists. Every article included a list of contemporary visual artists, novelists, philosophers, and scientists, in which no woman's name appeared.

In V, Burden also quotes scholarly books, with and without citation. I found this quotation: 'The

7

"woman-as-monster" image – with women depicted as snakes, spiders, extraterrestrials, and scorpions – is very common in boys' literature, not only in the United States but also in Europe and Japan (see T, p. 97).' The parenthetical reference is to Burden's own Notebook T, for *teratology*, the study of monsters, which, as Burden explains on its first page, is 'the category that is not a category, the category to hold what can't be held.' Burden was preoccupied by monsters and collected references to them in both science and literature. On page 97 of Notebook T, Burden quotes Rabelais, whose comic monsters changed the face of literature, noting that Gargantua is not born through the usual orifice: 'Thanks to this unfortunate accident there took place a weakening of the uterus; the child leapt up through the Fallopian tubes to a hollow vein and, scrambling across the diaphragm to the upper arm where this vein divides in two, he left the fork and crawled out through the left ear' (Book I, Chapter 6). Immediately after this, she writes, 'But the monster is not always a Rabelaisian wonder of hearty appetites and boundless hilarity. She is often lonely and misunderstood (see M and N).'

Two densely filled notebooks (M and N) treat the work of Margaret Cavendish, the Duchess of Newcastle (1623–1673), and the materialist organicism she developed as a thinker in her maturity. These two notebooks, however, also discuss the work of Descartes, Hobbes, More, and Gassendi. Burden links Cavendish to contemporary philosophers such

8

as Suzanne Langer and David Chalmers, but also to the phenomenologist Dan Zahavi and the neuroscientist Vittorio Gallese, among others. After reading the passages in question, a colleague of mine in neurobiology, Stan Dickerson, who had never heard of either Burden or Cavendish, declared Burden's argument 'a bit wild but cogent and learned.'

Despite the fact that Cavendish lived in the seventeenth century, she served Harriet Burden as an alter ego. During her lifetime, the Duchess of Newcastle published poetry, fiction, and natural philosophy. Although a few people defended and admired her work at the time – most notably her husband, William Cavendish – the duchess felt brutally constricted by her sex and repeatedly articulated the hope that she would find readers and acclaim in posterity. Snubbed by many with whom she would have liked to engage in dialogue, Cavendish created a world of interlocutors in her writing. As with Cavendish, I believe that Burden cannot be understood unless the dialogical quality of her thought and art is taken into consideration. All of Burden's notebooks may be read as forms of dialogue. She continually shifts from the first person into the second and then to the third. Some passages are written as arguments between two versions of herself. One voice makes a statement. Another disputes it. Her notebooks became the ground where her conflicted anger and divided intellect could do battle on the page.

Burden complains bitterly about sexism in the culture, the art world in particular, but she also laments her 'intellectual loneliness.' She broods on her isolation and lashes out at her many perceived enemies. At the same time, her writing (like Cavendish's) is colored by extravagance and grandiosity: 'I am an Opera. A Riot. A Menace,' she writes in an entry that directly discusses her spiritual kinship to Cavendish. Like Cavendish, Burden's desire for recognition in her lifetime was ultimately transmuted into a hope that her work would finally be noticed, if not while she was alive, then after her death.

Burden wrote so much and so broadly that my dilemma as an editor turned on the crucial question: What do I put in and what do I leave out? Some of the notebooks contain esoteric material unintelligible except to those well versed in the history of philosophy or science or art history. I found myself stumped by some of her references, and even after I had traced them, their meanings in the context of her writing often remained obscure to me. I have focused my attention on *Maskings* and included only passages that directly or indirectly relate to the pseudonymous project. The first excerpts from Burden's journals in this volume were taken from Notebook C (*Confessions? Confidences?*), the memoir Burden began writing sometime in early 2002 after her sixty-second birthday, but which she appears to have abandoned to return to her other notebooks and a more fragmentary style.

Nevertheless, I found it expedient to try to construct a story of sorts out of the diverse material Burden left behind. Ethan Lord suggested I gather written or oral statements from people close to his mother to give additional perspectives to *Maskings*, and I agreed. I then decided to solicit information from those who knew about or had somehow been involved in the pseudonymous project.

Since the Grace exhibition, interest in Harriet Burden's work has grown exponentially, despite the fact that controversy still surrounds her 'masks,' especially her involvement with the last and by far the most famous artist of the three, Rune. Although there is a consensus that Burden made Tish's *The History of Western Art* as well as Eldridge's *Suffocation Rooms*, there is little agreement about what actually happened between her and Rune. There are those who believe Burden is not responsible for *Beneath* or contributed very little to the installation, and others who are convinced that Burden created it without Rune. Still others argue that *Beneath* was a collaborative effort. It may not be possible to determine absolutely who generated that work, although it is clear that Burden felt betrayed by Rune and turned against him. She also became convinced he had stolen four works from her studio, although no one can explain how the theft could have happened. The building was locked and protected by an alarm system. *Windows*, a series of twelve pieces, was sold as artwork by Rune. The dozen boxes resemble constructions made by Burden and it is at least possible that four of them were hers, not Rune's.

Rune's version of events could not be included in this anthology. His widely publicized death in 2004, which may or may not have been suicide, became a sensational media story. Rune's career has been extensively documented. His work was widely reviewed, and there are also many critical articles and several books on him and his work available to anyone who is interested. Nevertheless, I wanted Rune's view to be represented in this collection, and I asked Oswald Case, a journalist as well as a friend and biographer of Rune, to contribute to the volume. He graciously accepted. Other contributors include Bruno Kleinfeld; Maisie and Ethan Lord; Rachel Briefman, a close friend of Burden's; Phineas Q. Eldridge, Burden's second 'mask'; Alan Dudek (also known as the Barometer), who lived with Burden; and Sweet Autumn Pinkney, who worked as an assistant on *The History of Western Art* and knew Anton Tish.

Despite Herculean efforts on my part, I was unable to contact Tish, whose account of his involvement with Burden would have been invaluable. A short interview with him, however, is part of this collection. In 2008, I wrote to Rune's sister, Kirsten Larsen Smith, asking her for an interview about her brother's involvement with Burden, but she demurred, saying that she was not able to talk about her brother because she was too distressed about his untimely death. Then, in March 2011, after I had compiled and edited all the materials for the book, Smith called me and explained that she had decided to accept my request for an interview. My conversation with her has now been added to the book. I am deeply grateful for her courage and honesty in speaking about her brother.

I have included a short essay by the art critic Rosemary Lerner, who is currently working on a book about Burden; interviews with two of the art dealers who showed Burden's 'masks'; and a couple of brief reviews that were published after the opening of *The Suffocation Rooms*, an exhibition that received far less attention than the other two shows that are part of the *Maskings* trilogy. Timothy Hardwick's article, published after Rune's death, was added to the anthology because it addresses Rune's views on artificial intelligence, a subject that interested Burden as well, although her notes on the subject suggest that the two of them were not in agreement.

I feel obliged to touch upon the question of mental illness. Although, in an essay on Burden in *Art Lights*, Alison Shaw called the artist 'a paragon of sanity in an insanely biased world,' Alfred Tong, in an article for *Blank: A Magazine of the Arts*, takes the opposite position:

Harriet Burden was rich. She never had to work after she married the renowned art dealer and collector Felix Lord. When he died in 1995, she suffered a complete *mental breakdown and was treated by a psychiatrist. She remained in his care the rest of her life. By all accounts, Burden was eccentric, paranoid, belligerent, hysterical, and even violent. Several people watched her physically attack Rune in Red Hook near the water. One of the eyewitnesses told me personally that Rune left the scene bloody and bruised. I am hard pressed to understand why anyone would believe that she was even close to stable enough to produce* Beneath, *a rigorous, complicated installation that may be Rune's greatest work.*

In the excerpts from the journals that follow, Burden writes about her suffering after her husband's death, and she writes about Dr Adam Fertig, to whom she felt indebted. Tong is right that she continued to see Fertig, a psychiatrist and psychoanalyst, for the eight remaining years of her life. She went to him for psychotherapy twice a week. It is also true that she punched Rune in front of a number of witnesses. The conclusions Tong draws from these facts, however, are largely unfounded. The author of the notebooks is sensitive, tormented, angry, and, like most of us, prone to neurotic blind spots. For example, Burden often seems to forget that it was *her* decision to leave the art world. She exhibited her work behind at least two, if not three, male masks, but she refused

14

to show the art she had amassed over many years to a single dealer, a fact that more than hints at self-sabotage.

My careful reading of the twenty-four notebooks, along with the texts and statements of those who knew her well, has provided me with a nuanced view of Harriet Burden, the artist and the woman; but while I worked on this book intermittently over the course of six years – interpreting her handwriting, doing my best to track down her references and cross-references, and trying to make sense of her multiple meanings – I confess I sometimes had the uncomfortable feeling that the ghost of Harriet Burden was laughing over my shoulder. She referred to herself several times in her journals as a 'trickster,' and she seems to have delighted in all kinds of ruses and games. There are only two letters missing from Burden's alphabet of notebooks: I and O. The letter *I* is, of course, the first-person pronoun in English, and I began to wonder how Burden could have resisted keeping a notebook under that letter and whether she hadn't hidden it somewhere, if only to tease people like me, whom she had obviously hoped would eventually take notice of her and her work. There appear to be two parenthetical references to *I*, although she may have meant the number 1 instead. As for *O*, it is a number as well as a letter, a nullity, an opening, a void. Perhaps she purposely left that letter out of her alphabet. I don't know. And Richard Brickman?

There are hundreds of Richard Brickmans in the United States, but my guess is that Brickman was another of Burden's pseudonyms. When Ethan told me his mother had published at least one critical work in 1986, using the preposterous name Roger Raison, I began to feel quite sure of my hypothesis, although I have no evidence to substantiate it whatsoever.

The best policy may be to let the reader of what follows judge for him- or herself exactly what Harriet Burden meant or didn't mean and whether her account of herself can be trusted. The story that emerges from this anthology of voices is intimate, contradictory, and, I admit, rather strange. I have done my best to assemble the texts into a reasonable order and to provide notes for Burden's writing when needed for clarification, but the words belong to the contributors, and I have let them stand with only minor editorial intervention.

Finally, I must add a few words about the title of this volume. In Notebook R (possibly for *revenant*, *revisit*, or *repetition* – all three words appear multiple times), after twenty pages on ghosts and dreaming, there is a blank space followed by the words *Monsters at Home*. This served as my working title until I had received all the texts, organized them into the present order, and read them through. I decided that the title Burden borrowed from Cavendish and gave to the last work of art she was able to complete before her death was better suited to the narrative as a whole: *The Blazing World*.

I. V. Hess

Postscript

Just as this book was going to press, I was contacted by Maisie and Ethan Lord, who reported that they had just recovered another notebook: Notebook O. The entries in O provide further information on Harriet Burden's relationship with Rune and reveal that Richard Brickman is, as I had guessed, a pseudonym for Burden herself. The most significant pages from that notebook have been added to this volume, but as they have not fundamentally altered my view of the artist, I have not revised my introduction. If at some point there is a second edition of this text, and if Notebook I (which I now feel certain exists) is discovered, I may well have to return to my text and change it accordingly.

(I. V. H.)

HARRIET BURDEN
Notebook C (memoir fragment)

I started making them about a year after Felix died – totems, fetishes, signs, creatures like him and not so like him, odd bodies of all kinds that frightened the children, even though they were grown up and didn't live with me anymore. They suspected a version of grief-gone-off-the-rails, especially after I decided that some of my carcasses had to be warm, so that when you put your arms around them you could feel the heat. Maisie told me to take it easy: Mom, it's too much. You have to stop, Mom. You're not young, you know. And Ethan, true to his Ethan self, expressed his disapproval by naming them 'the maternal monsters,' 'the Dad things,' and 'pater horribilan.' Only Aven, wondrous grandbabe, approved of my beloved beasties. She was not yet two at the time and approached them soberly and with great delicacy. She loved to lay her cheek against a radiant belly and coo.

But I must back up and circle around. I am writing this because I don't trust time. I, Harriet Burden, also known as Harry to my old friends and select new friends, am sixty-two, not ancient, but well on my way to THE END, and I have too much left to do before one of my aches turns out to be a tumor or loss-of-a-name dementia or the errant truck leaps onto the sidewalk and flattens me against the wall, never to breathe again. Life is walking tiptoe over land mines. We never know what's coming and, if you want my opinion, we don't have a good grip on what's behind us either. But we sure as hell can spin a story about it and break our brains trying to get it right.

Beginnings are riddles. Ma and Da. The floating fetus. *Ab ovo*. There are multiple moments in life, however, that might be called originating; we just have to recognize them for what they are. Felix and I were eating breakfast, back in the old apartment at 1185 Park Avenue. He had cracked his soft-boiled egg, as he did every morning with a smart smack of his knife to the shell, and he had brought the spoon with its white and running yellow contents to his mouth. I was looking at him because he appeared to be on the brink of speaking to me. He looked surprised for just an instant, the spoon fell to the table, then to the floor, and he slumped over, his forehead landing on a piece of buttered toast. The light from the window shone weakly on the table with its blue-and-white cloth, the discarded knife lay at an angle on the saucer of the coffee cup; the green salt and pepper shakers stood inches from his left ear. I couldn't have registered that image of my husband collapsed over his plate for more than a fraction of a second, but the picture was scored into my mind, and I still see it. I see it even though I leapt up and lifted his head, felt for his pulse, called for help, breathed into his mouth, prayed my muddled, secular prayers, sat in the back of the ambulance with the paramedics and listened to the siren scream. By then I had become a stone woman, an observer who was also an actor in the scene. I remember it all vividly, and yet a part of me is still sitting there at the small table in the long, narrow kitchen near the window, looking at Felix. It is the fragment of Harriet Burden that never stood up and went on.

I crossed the bridge and bought a building in Brooklyn, a scruffier borough in those days than it is now. I wanted to flee the Manhattan art world, that incestuous, moneyed, whirring globule composed of persons who buy and sell aesthetic *objets*. In that effete microcosm, it is fair to say Felix had been a giant, dealer to the stars, and I, Gargantua's artist wife. Wife outweighed artist, however, and with Felix gone the inhabitants of that beau monde cared little whether I stayed or left them for the remote region known as Red Hook. I had had two dealers; both had dropped me, one after the other. My work had never sold much and was little discussed, but for thirty years I served as hostess to the lot of them – the collectors, the artists, and the art writers – a mutually dependent club so ingrown and overgrown that their identities seemed to merge. By the time I bid goodbye to it all, the 'hot' new properties, fresh from art school, had begun to look alike to me, with their film or performance art and their pretentious patter and garbled theoretical references. At least the kids were hopeful. They took their cues from the hopeless – those morons who wrote for *Art Assembly*, the hermetic rag that regularly served up the cold leftovers of French literary theory to its eager, equally ignorant readers. For years, I worked so hard to hold my tongue, I nearly swallowed it. For years, I had slid around the dining room table in various costumes of the bright, eccentric variety, opposite the Klee, directing traffic with deft signals and smiling, always smiling.

Felix Lord discovered me standing in his gallery late one Saturday afternoon in SoHo, contemplating an artist who has long since vanished but had a moment of glory in the sixties: Hieronymous Hirsch.* I was twenty-six. He was forty-eight. I was six-two. He was five-ten. He was rich. I was poor. He told me my hair made me look like a

---

* There is no documentary evidence of an artist by that name. Why Burden twists the name of the fifteenth-century Flemish painter Hieronymous Bosch (ca. 1450–1516), thereby fictionalizing an autobiographical story, is unknown. In Notebook G, writing about *The Garden of Earthly Delights*, Burden comments: 'perhaps the greatest artist of corporeal borders and their dreamlike meanings. He and Goya.'

person who had survived an electrocution and that I should do something about it.

It was love.

And orgasms, many of them, in soft damp sheets.

It was a haircut, very short.

It was marriage. My first. His second.

It was talk – paintings, sculptures, photographs, and installations. And colors, a lot about colors. They stained us both, filled our insides. It was reading books aloud to each other and talking about them. He had a beautiful voice with a rasp in it from the cigarettes he could never quit smoking.

It was babies I loved looking at, the little Lords, sensuous delights of pudgy flesh and fluids. For at least three years I was awash in milk and poop and piss and spit-up and sweat and tears. It was paradise. It was exhausting. It was boring. It was sweet, exciting, and sometimes, curiously, very lonely.

Maisie, maniacal narrator of life's stream, the piping voice of boomin', buzzin' confusion. She still talks a lot, a lot, a lot.

Ethan, child of method, first one foot, then the other, in a parquet square, the rhythmic ambulatory contemplation of the hallway.

It was talks about the children late into the night and the smell of Felix, his faint cologne and herbal shampoo, his thin fingers on my back. 'My Modigliani.' He turned my long, homely face into an artifact. *Jolie laide*.

Nannies so I could work and read: fat Lucy and muscular Theresa.

In the room I called my microstudio, I built tiny crooked houses with lots of writing on the walls. Cerebral, said Arthur Piggis, who once bothered to look.* Gelatinous figures hovered near the ceiling, held up by nearly invisible wires. One gripped a sign that said: *What are these strangers doing here?* I did my writing there – the exclamations nobody read, the wildnesses even Felix didn't understand.

Felix to the airport. His rows of suits in the closet. His ties and his deals. His collection.

Felix the Cat. We await you in Berlin next week, madly, hotly. Love, Alex and Sigrid. Inside pocket of the suit jacket on its way to the cleaners. His negligence, Rachel said, was a way to tell me about them without telling me. *The Secret Life of Felix Lord.* It could be a book or a play. Ethan, my author boy, could write it if he knew that his father had been in love with a couple for three years. Felix with the distant eyes. And hadn't I also loved his illegibility? Hadn't it drawn me in and seduced me the way he seduced the others, not with what was there but with what was missing?

First my father's death, then my mother's death, within a year of each other, and all the sick dreams, floods of them, all night, every night – the flashes of teeth and bone and blood that leaked from under countless doors that took me down hallways into rooms I should have recognized but didn't.

* See Arthur Piggis, *Notes on Artists, 1975–1990* (New York: Dreyfus Press, 1996).

Time. How can I be so old? Where's little Harriet? What happened to the big, ungainly frizz-head who studied so hard? Only child of professor and wife – philosopher and helpmeet, WASP and Jew – wedded not always so blissfully on the Upper West Side, my left-leaning, frugal parents, whose only luxury was doting on me, their cause célèbre, their oversized hairy burden who disappointed them in some ways and not in others. Like Felix, my father dropped dead before noon. One morning in his study after he had retrieved *Monadology* from its home on the shelf across from his desk, his heart stopped beating. After that, my once noisy, bustling mother became quieter and slower. I watched her dwindle. She seemed to shrink daily until I could hardly recognize the tiny figure in the hospital bed who in the end called out, not for her husband or for me, but for her mama – over and over again.

I was an agitated mourner for all three of them, a big, restless, pacing animal. Rachel says that no grief is simple, and I've discovered that my old friend, Dr Rachel Briefman, is mostly right about the strange doings of the psyche – psychoanalysis is her calling – and it's true that my first year of living without Felix was furious, vengeful, an implosion of misery about all I had done wrong and all I had wasted, a conundrum of hatred and love for us both. One afternoon I threw away heaps of expensive clothes he had bought for me from Barneys and Bergdorf's, and poor Maisie with her bulging belly looked into the closet and blubbered about saving Father's presents and how could I be so cruel, and I regretted the stupid act. I hid as much as I could from the children: the vodka that put me to sleep, the sense of unreality as I wandered among the rooms I knew so well, and a terrible hunger for something I couldn't name. I couldn't hide the vomiting. I ate, and the food came blasting up and out of me, splattering the toilet and walls. I couldn't stop it. When I think of it now, I can feel the smooth, cool surface of the toilet seat as I grip it, the gagging, wrenching paroxysms of throat and gut. I'm dying, too, I thought, disappearing. Tests and more tests. Doctors and more doctors. Nothing to be found. Then the very last stop for the so-called functional ailment, for a possible conversion reaction, for a body that usurps speech: Rachel referred me to a psychiatrist-psychoanalyst. I wept and talked and wept some more. Mother and Father, the apartment on Riverside Drive, Cooper Union. My old and flattened ambitions. Felix and the children. What have I done?

And then, one afternoon, at three ten, just before the session ended, Dr Fertig looked at me with his sad eyes, which must have seen so much sadness other than mine, no doubt so much sadness worse than mine, and said in a low but emphatic voice: There's still time to change things, Harriet.

There's still time to change things.

The vomiting disappeared. Don't let anyone say there aren't magic words.

CYNTHIA CLARK

(interview with former owner of the Clark Gallery, NYC, April 6, 2009)

Hess: Do you remember the first time you met Harriet Burden?

Clark: Yes, Felix brought her around to the gallery. He was divorced from Sarah by then, and he walks in with this gigantic girl, big as a house, really, and va-va-va-voom shapely, but with a long, peculiar face. They used to call her the Amazon.

Hess: Were you familiar with her work then?

Clark: No, but to be honest, no one was familiar with her work. I've seen it now, the early pieces, but the truth is nobody in the art world would have picked it up back then. It was too busy, too off the beaten track. It didn't fit into any schema. There were a lot of art wars, you know, in the late sixties, early seventies. She wasn't Judy Chicago either, making a feminist statement. And I guess Felix was a problem for her, too. He couldn't represent her, after all, it would have been nepotism.

Hess: Is there any other impression of her, besides her appearance, that you noted and would like to share for the book?

Clark: She made a scene once at a dinner. It was years ago, around eighty-five, I think. She was talking to Rodney Farrell, the critic – he faded, but he had some power then – anyway, something he said must have set her off, and this woman, who we all thought of as very quiet, burst out and rattled on about philosophy, art, language. She was very loud, lecturing, unpleasant. I don't think anyone had the slightest idea what she was saying. Frankly, I thought it might have been gibberish. Everyone stopped talking. And then she started laughing, crazy, nutty laughter, and left the table. Felix was upset. He hated scenes.

Hess: And the pseudonyms? Did you suspect anything?

Clark: Absolutely not. After Felix died, she disappeared. No one talked about her.

Hess: Weren't you surprised by the sophistication of Anton Tish's work? He was only twenty-four at the time, seemed to come out of nowhere, and in interviews he was strikingly inarticulate and seemed to have only superficial thoughts about his own work.

Clark: I've shown many artists who weren't able to say what they were about. I've always believed that the work is supposed to speak and that the pressure put on artists to explain themselves is misplaced.

Hess: I agree with you, and yet *The History of Western Art* is a complex joke about art, full of references, quotations, puns, and anagrams. There is an allusion to Diderot on a Chardin canvas shown at the Academy's annual Salon show, taken from the French edition. That particular essay had not been translated into English. The boy did not speak French.

Clark: Listen, I've said this before. It's all very well and good to look back now and ask how on earth we could have been taken in. You can cite all the examples you want. I wasn't pondering how he did it. He gave me the work. It caused a stir. It sold. I visited his studio and there were works in progress all over the place. What would you have thought?

Hess: I'm not sure.

Clark: There's nothing cut-and-dried about this, you know. One can easily argue that the posing, the performance, was part of the work itself, that it all goes together, and as you well know, pieces from that show signed by Anton Tish command high prices. I don't regret for a second that I showed them.

Hess: I think the real question is: Would you have shown them if you had been aware of who had really made them?

Clark: I believe I would have. Yes, I think I would have.

MAISIE LORD
(edited transcript)

After she moved to Brooklyn, my mother collected strays – human strays, not animals. Every time I went to visit her, there seemed to be another 'assistant,' poet, drifter, or just plain charity case living in one of the rooms, and I worried they might take advantage of her, rob her, or even kill her in her sleep. I worry too much; it's chronic. I became the worrier in the family – my job. The man who called himself the Barometer lived with Mother for a long time. He had spent two weeks in Bellevue not long before he landed on her doorstep. He rattled on about the words of the winds and made peculiar gestures to lower the humidity. When I mentioned my anxiety about him to my mother, she said, 'But, Maisie, he's a gentle person, and he draws very well.' She was right about him, as it turned out. He became the subject of one of my films, but there were other, more fleeting and unsavory characters who kept me up at night until Phineas came along and put her affairs in order, but that was later. My mother's place was immense, an old warehouse building. She had two floors, one to live in and one to work in. When she renovated the place, she made sure there were several bedrooms for 'all my future grandchildren,' but I think she also had a fantasy about supporting young artists directly, putting them up, giving them space to work in. My father had his foundation. My mother had her ad hoc Red Hook artists' colony.

Not long after she moved, my mother said to me, 'Maisie, I can fly.' Her energy was up, to say the least. I read somewhere about hypomania, and I asked myself if my mother might not be hypomanic. Mourning can be complicated by all kinds of nervous ups and downs, and she was really sick after my father died. She was so weak and thin, she could hardly move, but after she recovered, she didn't stop. My mother worked long hours in her studio every day, and after that she read for two or three hours, one book after another, novels, philosophy, art, and science. She kept journals and notebooks. She bought herself one of those big, heavy punching bags and hired a woman named Wanda to give her some boxing lessons. Sometimes I felt limp just looking at her. She'd always had a streak of fierceness in her – she could explode suddenly over a trivial incident. Once when she had asked me to brush my teeth and I dawdled – I must have been about seven – she lost it. She yelled and screamed and pressed an entire tube of toothpaste into the sink. But most of the time she was a patient mother to me and my brother. She was the one who read to us and sang to us, who made up long stories that satisfied both me and Ethan, not an easy task, because I wanted fairies and goblins, and he wanted vehicles that released various weapons and robots, so she would make a hybrid. For a whole year, she told us a long saga about the Fervidlies, who lived in a country called Fervid. Lots of magic and fights and elaborate weaponry. She helped us with our homework all through high school. I'd call her from college, too, and ask her questions about my classes or papers. My mother was interested in everything, and she seemed to have read everything. She was the one who attended our games, recitals, and plays. My father came when he could, but he traveled a lot. Sometimes, when I was little, I would go in and sleep with my mother when he was gone. She talked in her sleep. I don't know why I remember, but once she yelled out, 'Where's Felix now?'

Children are selfish. I knew my mother was an artist who made intricate houses filled with dolls and ghosts and animals she sometimes let me touch, but I never thought of her work as a job. She was my mother. My father called her his Madonna of the Mind. It's awful when I think about it, but it never occurred to me that my mother was frustrated or unhappy. The endless rejection must have hurt her, the injustice of it, but I can't say I felt it when I was a child. She liked to hum and sway when she worked on one of her constructions, and she'd waggle her fingers over a figure before she touched it. Sometimes she sniffed the materials and sighed.

She'd close her eyes from time to time and liked to say that there was no art for her without the body and the rhythms of the body. Of course, when I was a teenager, I found these gestures and tics excruciating, and I tried to make sure none of my friends witnessed them. When I was seventeen she once said to me, 'Maisie, you're lucky you didn't get my breasts. Big breasts on a little woman are fetching; big breasts on a big woman are scary – to men, that is.' It hit me that she felt her womanliness, her body, her size had somehow interfered with her life. This was long before the pseudonyms, and I was busy making my first little film in high school, a visual diary, I called it – very pretentious, lots of long, moody shots of my friends walking down the street or sitting in their rooms at home in states of existential anguish, that sort of thing. What did my breasts have to do with it?

Much, much later, when it came out, I had the sickening thought that she had been right. Of course, by then I was an adult and had run into my share of belittlement and prejudice with my own work. I believed she used those men as fronts to prove a point, and she did, at least in part, but when I read the fragment of her memoir and the journals, I saw how complicated her involvements with them had been and that the masks were real, too. She's been terribly misunderstood. She was not a calculating beast exploiting people right and left. I don't think anybody really knows when she first started thinking about pseudonyms. She published one dense art review under the name Roger Raison in a magazine in the eighties, dumping on the Baudrillard craze, demolishing his simulacra argument, but few people paid attention. I remember when I was fifteen, our family was in Lisbon, and she went over and kissed the statue of Pessoa. My mother told me to read him, and, of course, he was famous for what he called his heteronyms. She was also deeply influenced by Kierkegaard. No doubt her urge to be other people went back to her childhood. My mother's best friend, Rachel Briefman, is a psychiatrist and a psychoanalyst. She is probably right that psychotherapy unleashed a Harriet Burden none of us had ever seen before, as well as a number of other characters or personas she had been sitting on for quite some time. I don't mean as in multiple personalities but as in protean artist selves, selves that popped out and needed bodies. I could never have said any of this even a year ago, but slowly I've come to see my mother in a different light, or maybe, I should say, several different lights.

But that's happened over the years. When I first saw *Memorial Dream*, I was unprepared. It shocked me. One Sunday I brought my daughter, Aven, to Red Hook for brunch. My husband, Oscar, didn't come along. I can't remember why. He probably had to write a report on one of the kids he works with. (He has a PhD in psychology and sees private patients, but he also spends time with foster children in the system, for which he is paid next to nothing.) If Mother had any strays at the time, none of them was around. Aven had just started to walk then, so it must have been the spring of 1996, and we had an eventful meal because my daughter spent every minute walking, or rather walking and falling, walking again and falling again. My mother clapped and laughed, and Aven was delighted, showing off more and more until she exhausted herself, sobbed, and I settled her in for a nap on a sofa surrounded by pillows to keep her from falling off. My mother had many pillows, in both muted and bright colors. She used to talk about color and meaning. Color, she said, has corporeal meaning. Before we can name the color we're seeing, it's in us.

Where was I? When Aven woke up, my mother told me she wanted to show me something she had been working on, and she took me to the far end of her studio space, which was still under construction at the time. She had built a little room with translucent glass walls the color of milk. I could see a figure through the wall and all at once I understood I was looking at my father seated in a chair. The likeness must have been in the figure's posture, because when Mother pushed open a nearly invisible door, the soft stuffed body that had looked so much like Father had only blunt features, but it was wearing one of my father's suits and *Don Quixote* was open in its lap, the book my father loved most. When I looked down, I saw that the floor was plastered with papers, Xeroxes, memoranda, notes my father had taken, and that my mother's own handwriting was scrawled on the red linoleum squares. And there were three miniature stairways that jutted upward and ended against the three walls. Five doors had been crudely drawn onto one of the walls. I burst into tears. Then Aven started crying, and my mother tried to repair the situation. 'I'm sorry, I'm so sorry.' That was typical. She couldn't bear to see people distressed. It affected her physically. She would clutch her rib cage as if someone had hit her.

We all recovered, but before I left in a car service with Aven, my mother looked me in the eyes. It was a severe look, not cold but strict, the way she sometimes looked at me when I was small and had lied or cheated or hit Ethan.

I remember it because I felt guilty, although I wasn't sure why. She closed her eyes, then she opened them, and in a calm low voice said, 'I'm sorry you were unsettled, Maisie, but I'm not sorry I made him. There are more dreams, I'm afraid, and they must out.' She smiled sadly and escorted us down to the waiting car.

I can still see her as she turned away from us. I wish I had filmed her then. It's beautiful out there by the water with the view of the Statue of Liberty, but it was desolate, too, bleaker then than it is now, and the sight of my mother striding away from us toward the brick building under a big cloudy sky made me feel that I was losing her. I used to feel that way after I said goodbye to her at my summer camp. And then – it was just a minor thing – I noticed that she was letting her hair grow, and it looked like a small wild bush on top of her head.

HARRIET BURDEN
Notebook C

Where did they come from? The penis with wings, his penis, the empty suit jackets and pants aloft and running with Felix paraphernalia – reading glasses, cologne, gleaming nail file (file X), a blank canvas (hope) – the giant Felix squashed into one of my rooms like Alice, the tiny Felixes lined up in a row, clad in various outfits, husband dolls, I called them. Somehow my father began to come in, too. The book man sleeping on a page of Spinoza, skipping over Leibniz (he loved Leibniz), a small daddy *Luftmensch* hovering just above a flight of stairs, words inscribed all over his two-piece suit. The elusive one, my elusive ones, began to mingle in the drawings and the sculptures, their faces and their clothes, mergings of desire, maddening beloveds mixed up in Harry's mind. And anger, too, at their power over me. That's why they grew and shrank.

I didn't know how to make my mother. That would come later. There was some problem rendering a person I had once been inside.

I did not have to chase her.

I chased the men howling *Look at me!*

Nonexistent, impossible, imaginary objects are in our thoughts all the time, but in art they move from the inside to the outside, words and images cross the border. I read a lot of Husserl in those days, lying on the sofa in the big room with the long windows and the view of the water: The cogitationes are the first absolute data. Husserl loved Descartes, and he had his streams of consciousness, like William James (whom he read), and they run by and past and through one another, and he knew that empathy was a deep form of knowledge.*
Husserl's student Edith Stein is the best philosopher on the subject, and she lived it, lived her words.† Philosophy is hard to picture. I began to

* Edmund Husserl (1859–1938). German philosopher who founded phenomenology, the study of the structures of consciousness from a first-person perspective. In Notebook H, Burden writes about the 'affinities of mind' between Descartes and Husserl, their love of mathematics and logical certainties, and their shared radical doubt. 'Husserl's doubt,' she writes, 'is not Descartes' doubt. Descartes' cogito is bedrock for deduction, which rises up from within the mental cave. Husserl's *cogito me cogitare* is consciousness as relation to and toward the world.' Husserl was influenced by William James's idea of consciousness as a stream, and he understood empathy as the path to intersubjectivity. See Dan Zahavi, *Husserl's Phenomenology* (Stanford, Calif.: Stanford University Press, 2003).
† Edith Stein (1891–1942) wrote her doctoral dissertation under Husserl, but her ideas depart from his and in

wonder if I could represent empathy, for example, build an empathy box. I doodled possible forms for the inside. I made notes. I hummed. I listened to the *St Matthew Passion* a lot. I understood that my freedom had arrived. There was nothing and no one in my way except the burden of Burden herself. The wide-open future, the great yawn of absence, made me dizzy, anxious, and, occasionally, high, as if I had doped myself, but I hadn't. I was the ruler of my own little Brooklyn fiefdom, a rich widow woman, long past babies and toddlers and teenagers, and my brain was fat with ideas.

But then came the loneliness at night, the restless wanting that reminded me of my years alone in my first apartment in the city when I was at Cooper Union. I was hurled back to my young self – the solitary girl artist with vague cravings for a future that somehow involved both fame and love. I began to understand that the feelings I had

---

certain instances resemble the work of Maurice Merleau-Ponty, whom Burden quotes extensively in the notebooks. See Edith Stein, *On the Problem of Empathy*, trans. Waltraut Stein (Washington, D.C.: ICS Publications, 1989). Stein edited Volume 2 of Husserl's *Ideas* for publication. She was born a Jew, but she had a conversion experience after reading St Theresa of Avila's autobiography, converted to Catholicism, and became a Carmelite nun. Although she moved to the Netherlands to escape the Nazi threat, she was deported to Auschwitz and died there in 1942. In 1987, she was beatified by the Catholic Church.

assigned to my youth were not really about that time of life. The agitation I felt after a long day of work was the same disquiet I had felt as a person who had barely emerged from childhood. I pined for a Someone, a potential personage to fill up the remaining hours. Felix, old friend and interlocutor, delicate, evasive, acerbic, philandering, kind Felix was gone. You've driven me to my wits' end! (I had been a sometime screamer.) But that end had never been reached. My wits had stayed, and so had his, and we had repaired the damage to them regularly. There was no fixing anymore. No fixing. No Felix. I struggled to comprehend the void, and the fact that I had begun to register it as real took the form of that empty other being, a lacuna, a hole in the mind, but it was not the hole named Felix.

And so I'd walk over to Sunny's Bar, where I'd sit and look at the people and listen to them talk, a balm of voices. Sometimes there was music. Once I heard a poetry reading and afterward talked to the poet, who had big eyes and red lipstick, much younger even than Ethan, and, although I found her poems terrible, I rather liked her. She called herself April Rain, an idea I supposed had come to her while writing. The girl had a large duffel bag with a gaping zipper, and she had tied a couple of sweaters and a hat on to it, and when she picked up the load and began to walk, I told her she looked like an immigrant staggering off the pier in 1867, and she explained to me that she

41

was sleeping on a friend's sofa because she was 'between places,' and I took her home.

April Rain, little white girl with bird tattoos on her lower arms and quantities of shattered glass in her poems that occasionally caused bleeding, was my first artist in residence. She didn't stay more than a week. One night she found a disheveled beau at Sunny's and never returned, but while she lasted, I liked having her around, and her presence staved off the jostling pains of evening. While looking at Ms Rain's soft pale face and plump cheeks as we ate our lentils or roasted vegetables (she was vegetarian) and chatted about Hildegard of Bingen or Christopher Smart, I forgot what I looked like. I forgot that I had wrinkles, breasts that needed a mighty brassiere to hold them up, and a middle-aged gut that protruded like a melon. This amnesia is our phenomenology of the everyday – we don't see ourselves – and what we see becomes us while we're looking at it. One night after saying good night to my twenty-two-year-old bardess, I looked in the mirror before bed, surprised myself with my own face, and burst into tears. Felix loved this aging mug, I thought. He praised it and stroked it. There's no one to love it now.

It may have been self-pity – the sense that I had grown too ugly to warm up any man's bed – that lay behind the idea that some of my constructed beings needed to have a bit of heat. My mother had had a penchant for electric mattress pads that toasted her through the night; the problem, as she explained it, was her circulation and ossified feet. *My blood doesn't run; it crawls, and it seems never to arrive at my toes.* My parents' pad had two settings, one for each side of the bed. She would set hers on six and make sure my father's side was turned off so he didn't cook in his sleep. After he died, she raised her level to ten, but she left his side cold, a memorial chill. No extra technology was required for my carcasses, although I fiddled with the wiring before I was truly happy with it. I began with a life-size effigy of Felix; it was an idea of him, not a likeness, his slender stuffed form covered with material I painted in blues and greens with a little yellow and dabs of red, man as canvas, but I added short white hair on the top of his head. When I plugged him in, his soft body ran a fever.

The pleasure this gave me was ludicrous. I couldn't say then why the hot creature filled me with joy, but it did. I touched his colored sides gingerly to feel his warmth. I put my arms around him. I sat him next to me on the sofa. I called him my transitional object. Aven adored him. Ethan hated him. Maisie tolerated him. Rachel was both amused by and serious about him and the others. She wanted me to try for a gallery again, to go out like Willie Loman and hawk my wares and get attention, attention. But hadn't they given their verdict over and over again? No one wanted Mrs Lord's handicrafts and dollies. Who was I, St Sebastian?

43

I was telling Dr Fertig about my heating mechanism for the bodies when the obvious reason for my elation came to me. Anima. Animate.

And the Lord God formed man of the dust of the ground and breathed into his nostrils the breath of life; and man became a living soul.

It was preposterous. Harry Burden, demigod of the studio, trying to resurrect her dead husband and father over and over again, the machinery of grief churning away as she sewed and stuffed and wired and sawed and molded and soldered, but it helped. It helped, and I had come to a pass where I accepted help in all forms.

After a year of frantic spousal and paternal or perhaps spouernal creation, I began to muse about the creatures that lived in my memory, not only actual persons, but those borrowed from my vast collection of books. I don't mean just characters but ideas, voices, shapes, figures, articulated thoughts, unarticulated feelings. I would call them metamorphs, and they would be cool or warm or hot or room temperature.

It may have been April Rain who told some of the other young stragglers around the neighborhood that I had rooms and beds to spare, but it's more likely that it was Edgar Holloway III, a refugee from the Upper East Side and musician friend of Ethan's, several years out of college, who sought work to supplement his rock 'n' roll dreams. Edgar became my construction assistant. A stocky boy with an upturned nose that looked too small for his face, he was strong, docile, and a quick study when it came to materials and building. He was remarkably dull when it came to conversation, however, but this liberated me from any need to entertain him or explicate the meanings of my rooms or the critters I was putting inside them. I wasn't sure what I was doing anyway.

What I did know was that I had been sitting on myself for years and that something had happened to me. Dr Fertig used the word *inhibition*. I had become less inhibited, untied and unfettered. I could thank all the vomiting. The symptom had prompted the talk and the turn. I had become Harriet Unbound, only fifty-five then, but counting, and I did wonder about other paths, the alternative existences, the other Harry Burden who might have, could have, should have unleashed herself earlier, or a Harry Burden who had looked like April Rain, petite and pinkish, or a Harry who had been born a boy, a real Harry, not a Harriet. I would have made a strapping young man with my height and wild hair. Hadn't I heard my mother bemoan all those inches wasted on a girl? The thought of another body, another style of being haunted me. Was this a form of regret? I wondered what my consciousness would feel like in Edgar's body. I certainly did not want Edgar's mind, filled to the brim with techno bands and run-on sentences with the word *man* popping up in them as continual, meaningless punctuation. The fantasy that began to take shape revolved around possible trajectories for me, an artist of multifarious shapes.

I suspected that if I had come in another package my work might have been embraced or, at least, approached with greater seriousness. I didn't believe that there had been a plot against me. Much of prejudice is unconscious. What appears on the surface is an unidentified aversion, which is then justified in some rational way. Perhaps being ignored is worse – that look of boredom in the eyes of the other person, that assurance that nothing from me could be of any possible interest. Nevertheless, I had hoarded my direct hits and humiliations, and they had made me gun-shy.

Not to my face: That's Felix Lord's wife. She makes dollhouses. Titters.

To my face: I heard that Jonathan took your work because he's a friend of Felix. Plus they needed a woman in the stable.

In a rag: *The show at Jonathan Palmer by Harriet Burden, wife of legendary art dealer Felix Lord, consists of small architectural works cluttered with various figures and texts. The work has no discipline or focus and seems to be an odd blend of pretentiousness and naïveté. One can only wonder why these pieces were deemed worthy of exhibition.**

Time had made the feelings worse, not better. Despite Rachel's prompting that I return to the

* Anthony Flood, 'A Muddy Aesthetic,' *Art Lights*, January 1979.

46

fray, I knew that youth was the desired commodity and that, despite the Guerrilla Girls, it was still better to have a penis.* I was over the hill and had never had a penis. It was too late for me to go as myself. I had disappeared for good, and the ease with which I had done so had made it clear to me how shallow my relations had been with all of them. They had come to the memorial service, or at least some of them had. By the time he died, Felix's heyday had passed. He had become historical, the dealer to P. and L. and T. of days gone by. His wife was ahistorical, but what if I could return as another person? I began to make up stories of ingenious disguise. Like a latter-day Holmes, I would dissolve into my costumes and fool even the children and Rachel with my clever personas. I drew images of possible Harrys: Superman Harry with cape; homeless, sexually ambiguous Harry hauling bottles; old man dandy Harry with short, neat white beard; Harry as male cross-dresser (quite convincing); Harry grinning with modest-size-in-the-Hellenic-tradition male genitalia. And I took some inspiration from the past:

* The organization was founded in 1985 in reaction to the Museum of Modern Art's exhibition *International Survey of Recent Painting and Sculpture*, showcasing 169 artists, only seventeen of whom were women. The Guerrilla Girls stage anonymous protests and actions to call attention to sexism and racism in the visual arts.

[An] His[toric]al and Phy[s]ic[al] Dissertation on the Case of Catherine Vizzani, containing the Adventures of a Young Woman, born at Rome, who for eight years passed in the Habit of a Man, was killed for an Amour with a young Lady; and being found on Dissection, a true Virgin, narrowly escaped being treated as a Saint by the Populace. With some curious and anatomical Remarks on the Nature and Existence of the Hymen. By Giovanni Bianchi, Professor of Anatomy at Sienna, the Surgeon who dissected her. To which are added, certain needful Remarks by the English Editor. (London: Meyer, 1751)

Not long after Professor Bianchi's treatise was published in England, translated and edited by John Cleland, the notorious author of *Fanny Hill*, Charles d'Eon de Beaumont, French diplomat, spy, and captain of the dragoons, began to appear in public wearing women's clothing. He explained that he had been raised as a boy but was in fact a woman. She published a memoir called *La Vie militaire, politique et privée de Madmoiselle d'Eon.* At her death, she was discovered to have male genitalia.

There was also the remarkable case of Dr James Barry, who entered medical school at the University of Edinburgh in 1809, passed his examination for the Royal College of Surgeons in England in 1813, became a surgeon in the military, traveled from post to post, and rose through the ranks. When his career ended, he was inspector general in charge of military hospitals in Canada. He died in London in 1865 from dysentery. It was then discovered that he had been a she. Barred from medicine by her sex, she had changed it.

Billie Tipton, successful jazz musician, born Dorothy Lucille Tipton in 1914, was denied a spot in her high school band because she was a girl, began performing as a man, and then moved entirely into a masculine life, had a long-term relationship with one Kitty Oakes, a former stripper, and adopted three sons with her. None of them knew until his death in 1989 that anatomically Billie had been a woman.

There are many stories and as many reasons for leaving the feminine behind and adopting the masculine, or dropping either one for the other, as was convenient. There were women who followed their husbands to war and fought to be near them, and women who fought purely from patriotic fervor and, after the battle, returned to being women. There were women who posed as men to inherit their fathers' fortunes and women who had lost everything – husbands and children and money – who felt too vulnerable to go on as women and turned themselves into men. Many of them had sympathetic mothers and fathers and siblings

49

and friends who kept their secret. Some garments, a name, a differently inflected voice, and the gestures to go with them were all that was required. After a time being a man became effortless. Moreover, it became real.

But was I interested in experimenting with my own body, strapping down my boobs and packing my pants? Did I want to live as a man? No. What interested me were perceptions and their mutability, the fact that we mostly see what we expect to see. Didn't the Harry I saw in the mirror change enough as it was? I often wondered if I could truly see myself at all. One day I found myself all-right-looking and relatively slim – for me, that is – and the next day I saw a sagging, bulbous grotesque. How could one account for the change except with the thought that self-image is unreliable at best? No, I wanted to leave my body out of it and take artistic excursions behind other names, and I wanted more than a 'George Eliot' as cover. I wanted my own indirect communications à la Kierkegaard, whose masks clashed and fought, works in which the ironies were thick and thin and nearly invisible. Where would I find a Victor Eremita, an A and a B, a Judge William, a Johannes de Silentio, a Constantin Constantius, a Vigilius Haufniensis, a Nicolaus Notabene, a Hilarius Bookbinder, an Inter et Inter, a Johannes Climacus, and an Anti-Climacus all my own?* How such transformations could be achieved in my case was fuzzy at best: no more than mental doodles, but I found them fertile.

Hadn't S.K., under his pseudonym Notabene, written a series of prefaces that were followed by no text?† What if I invented an artist who was all art criticism, all catalogue copy, and no work? How many artists, after all, had been catapulted into importance by drivel written by all those hacks who had taken the linguistic turn? Ah, *écriture*! The artist would have to be a young man, an *enfant terrible* whose emptiness generates page after page after page of text. Oh, the fun of it! I gave it a shot:

---

* In Notebook K, Burden devotes seventy-five pages to Kierkegaard's pseudonyms and his 'indirect communications.' From S.K.'s posthumously published *The Point of View for My Work as an Author: A Direct Communication, A Report to History*, Burden records the following quote: 'One can deceive a person out of what is true and – to recall old Socrates – one can deceive a person into what is true. Yes, only in this way can a deluded person actually be brought into what is true – by deceiving him' (*Kierkegaard's Writings*, vol. XXII, trans. Howard and Edna Hong [Princeton: Princeton University Press, 1989], 53). Burden writes, 'The path to the truth is doubled, masked, ironic. This is my path, not straight, but twisted!'
† Kierkegaard wrote eight satirical prefaces under the pseudonym Nicolaus Notabene. Søren Kierkegaard, *Prefaces, Writing Sampler*, ed. and trans. Todd W. Nichol (Princeton: Princeton University Press, 1987).

The aporia in the work of X is achieved through the processes of auto-induction into absence. The implied, hence invisible, autoerotic acts with a sexual origin facilitate an abysmal collapse, the phantasms of rupture and the withdrawal of the object of desire.

Dead end. I knew that manufacturing this pretentious, hackneyed prose would kill me.

I, Harriet Burden, hereby confess that my diverse fantasies were driven:

1. by a general desire for revenge against twits, dunderheads, and fools,
2. by an ongoing, wrenching intellectual isolation that resulted in loneliness because I roamed in too many books that no one could talk to me about,
3. by a growing sense that I had always been misunderstood and was madly begging to be seen, truly seen, but nothing I did made any difference.

In my frustration and misery I would wind myself up every day as if I were my old toy monkey with the cymbals, listen to myself crash them, and then, *nota bene*, I would cry and, when I cried, I would long for my mother, not the small dying mother in the hospital but the big mother of my childhood, who had held and rocked me and tutted and stroked and taken my temperature and read to me. Mommy's girl, except Mommy was not oversized but short and curvy and wore high heels. *Your father likes my legs in heels, you know.* But then, after I had wailed for a while, I would remember the wet shine of two fallen tears on my mother's shrunken cheeks and the IV in her blue-veined hand many years later. I did not say, You'll get well, Mommy, because she would not get well. *Who knows how long I'll last? Not long.* And yet in hospice, my mother fussed about the food, the sheets, her pajamas, the nurses. A week before she died, she asked me to open her purse and apply a little lipstick because she was too weak to do it herself, and when she lapsed into a morphine haze at the very end, I took out the gold tube and dabbed her thin mouth with the rose-colored stick.

Orphaned.

What I am trying to articulate is that my self-imposed exile in Red Hook was not uneventful from an internal point of view. Time was forever collapsing in on me. Dead and imaginary people played a larger part in my quotidian reality than the living did. I lurched backward to recover shreds of memory and forward to fashion an imaginary future. As for the actual breathing people in my life, I faithfully kept my weekly appointment with Dr Fertig, with whom I was making 'progress,' after which I would meet Rachel for tea or a glass of wine somewhere near her office on Park Avenue and Ninety-First, and the old intimacy between us never seemed to lessen even when we bickered and she accused me of being 'obsessive.' Maisie worried about me. I could see it in her eyes, and she worried aloud about Aven and about Oscar, and I worried in turn that she would give up too much for the family and her own work would suffer, and Ethan wrote stories in cafés and ran his very small magazine, *The Neo-Situationist Bugle*, with Leonard Rudnitzky, his good friend from Oberlin. My son talked a lot about commodification and the spectacle and alienation and the visionary Guy Debord, who served as his Romantic hero.* Ethan didn't seem to understand the man's hyperbole, only that

* Guy Debord (1931–1994), self-proclaimed leader of the Situationist International (SI), founded in 1957. This small group of Parisian artists and intellectuals (it never had more than twelve members) initially hoped to integrate art and life into an indistinguishable whole and eliminate the distinction between actor and spectator. By the 1960s, the group's anticapitalist critique, inspired by the anarchist movement, extended beyond art to society in general. In Debord's most famous work, *Society of the Spectacle*, published in 1967, he argues that images have come to dominate life, that they have become the 'currency' of a society that is continually creating 'pseudo needs' in its populace. The group disbanded in 1972 due to internal strife. In 1994, Debord committed suicide. Although the French press had largely ignored both the Situationists and Debord's work, after his death, he became a celebrity.

his thought had come true on the Internet: *Everything that was directly lived has moved into representation.* What about a stomachache?

My son, the revolutionary, was secretive about his private life (girls) and, I feared, a little angry at me for taking on a new life at my age, which I suspected he viewed as vaguely indecent and something of a betrayal of his father's memory, although he could not say it. He was, I'm afraid, alienated from himself. The little boy who used to hide in the closet with his stiff little figures and narrate their battles and truces had grown up. He could not remember his baby self and how his mother had walked him back and forth and jiggled and rocked him for hour after hour and had sung in his ear very softly because it had been so hard for him to settle into sleep. But then, none of us remembers infancy, that archaic age in the land of the mother giant.

Anton Tisch looked right. He was tall, almost my height, a skinny kid in loose jeans with a significant nose and searching eyes that seemed unable to fix on anything for long, which gave him a distracted air that could be interpreted as restless intelligence under the right circumstances. And he was an artist. I met him at Sunny's in early '97 on a very cold night. There was snow. I remember the rhythmic presence of cold air as the door opened and closed, the pounding of boots, and lamp-lit white beyond the window. I had the Barometer

55

with me, ambulatory weather vane and exquisite draftsman, whom I had harbored for some weeks. Not only did the Barometer register every incremental rise and drop in air pressure through his bodily instrument – his preternaturally sensitive head – at some juncture he had actually gained control over this aspect of the environment and would lower or raise it by a hectopascal or two. I knew nothing of hectopascals until the Barometer entered my life, but I loved the term, named after Blaise, that genius of the much and the many. The Barometer and I got along rather well, although the man lived in a cocoon of his own making, and dialogue – true back-and-forth exchanges – was nearly impossible.

By then I had become a Sunny's regular. In gratitude for services rendered and reliable camaraderie, I had presented the establishment with a framed ink drawing of the bar and some of its lurid and not-so-lurid characters, and the gift had been mounted on a wall. I mention this because Anton Tisch had paused in front of it. The vanity of the artist is such that I knew the identities of those who had even glanced at the small work in my presence – they were few indeed – and my happiness at the sight of the angular young man with short brown curls inspecting my rendition of Sunny's knew no bounds, well, perhaps a few bounds, but it definitely swelled.

Still, I was shy. The Barometer had been highly excitable because of the snow, but for some reason he, too, saw the young Tisch ogling the drawing and, in a voice quite unlike his own and in a manner entirely out of character, he shouted at the stranger: *Harry did it!* As I recall, it took a little time to establish that I was Harry, but once that business was cleared away, Anton Tisch, whom the Barometer took to calling 'Table' almost immediately, sat down with us and we settled in for an evening of alcohol and chitchat. The content of that talk has vanished. Over time, however, I learned that the boy had attended the School of Visual Arts, did not know who Giorgione was but considered Warhol the most important artist of all time, which must have explained his silk-screen obsession. Rather than celebrities, Tisch did silk screens of his friends, presumably because their proverbial fifteen minutes had or would come. He explained that his art referred directly to Warhol while also pointing to the phenomenon of reality TV, although it was difficult to glean this information from the banal images he showed me. He liked the term *conceptual* and used it a lot, not unlike the way Edgar used *man*. Anton was not a bad kid. He was just stupendously, heartbreakingly ignorant.

OSWALD CASE
(written statement)

To the gaudy denizens of Manhattan's nocturnal scene, I was known as the Crawler, as in night and club, but my column for *Blitz* was called 'Head Case,' a fitting tribute to Mr and Mrs Case, to whom I naturally owed everything. At the magazine I developed my gift for gossip and the art of innuendo, puffing up and smacking down the rich and vain and much-photographed, wheedling dirt out of bouncers and waiters and hangers-on who imagined that fame was a quality that could be rubbed off onto them, when in fact it only laid bare their puny bridge-and-tunnel lives, but I encouraged them in their idle daydreams and that's how the Crawler trawled them in.

It is a delicate job, penning gossip, a balancing act not to be underestimated, and it is easy to go too far. Mutual dependence must always be recognized, that they need you and you need them. I hit my stride in the late seventies, in the glory days of Studio 54, nibbling up delectable tidbits here and there about Bianca and Andy and Calvin, and I had a blast, those long nights of cocaine and ludes and plain old booze and blind sex in big, fashionably empty lofts, typing for dollars in the late afternoons after I had regained consciousness. I miss those days. They had a patina now lost. Yes, glamour is gone for good, Virginia. It disappeared the moment it became democratic, and every loser could be Googled or find himself a star on YouTube. There is always an exclusive scene in the city, of course. But isn't there something wearying about yet another celeb puking in a back room or punching a paparazzo or flashing a Brazilian wax job? Ennui set in, especially after I turned sober, the inevitable result of the decision to give up the wonders of intoxication to hold on to my liver and other body parts equally fragile.

I drifted into less taxing forms of journalism, supposedly more elevated, but I have found that the human primate varies little. Grasping and grubbing and knocking over those in your way are omnipresent characteristics of the species, and every little urban band has its own hierarchy and cycles of highly entertaining antics fueled by envy. I turned to New York's shrinking Culture Pages, strategically written for the declining numbers of middlebrow readers, and I pounded out articles on movies, art, books, and music as a freelancer. I reviewed, and I interviewed. As a writer, I knew that it was my tone that delivered the goods; that is what they wanted, a tone of boredom and superiority that mimicked my readers' fantasies of a posh British accent and assured them that I knew better, just as they did. I wrote to inflate them. This meant never, ever making a reference they might not understand; anything too highbrow was a no-no. The idea was to stroke their insecurities, not to bring them out.

As an interviewer, I quickly grasped that the key was to ingratiate myself with the subject, to be admiring, even humble, but not Heepish. (In an article, even *Heepish* would not be allowed to stand without explanation.) And then, after becoming suitably flattered and flaccid, the VIP might disgorge a verbal gem, a meaty indiscretion that could be used as a headline or a focus for my article, a word-for-word, wholly accurate quotation that caged the beast. I was a hunter for the media zoo. These techniques served me exceptionally well, and I found a niche for myself. I did my detective work, kept my sensitive auditory canals open and quivering, and familiarized myself with names, who was who and who was who to whom, and with my Crawler days long behind me, I found myself recognized as a cognoscente of the arts.

Culture in the big city is private business and much of its funding is in the hands of wealthy white women who, although they may not always have the dough themselves, vie for rising status as supporters of the arts. They gleam at benefit dinners, coiffed and perfumed and oiled and lifted, while their hubbies, exhausted from the rigors of deal-making, glance around them in confusion and snore through the rubber chicken. The worst must be the annual PEN dinner, where gloomy writers and gloomier publishers don ill-fitting, frayed tuxedos or dumpy dresses and hideous shoes to eye one another suspiciously as they mingle with the money. Whatever my circumstances, and, rest assured, they have often been close to dire, I am never anything less than well turned out. Hadn't Mrs Case, daughter of a plumber in Milwaukee, had a sharp eye for the 'right' clothes and good grammar? Hadn't she sacrificed to send her boy to the 'right' schools? Had I been a scholarship runt at Yale for nothing?

And then, through my contacts (and hard work, I might add), I landed the plum, writing articles for *The Gothamite* on salary. They never would have hired me in the WASPy days of reliably dull but oh-so-clubby self-congratulation, but those days had passed, and they wanted a writer with a squirt of venom when needed. I was their man. The positively nubile, fresh-from-his-undergraduate-studies Anton Tish had made a splash at the Clark Gallery with his installation, *The History of Western Art*, and I was asked to write a 'What's On About Town' piece, a nod to the buzz. Jeff Koons had unveiled his *Puppy* a few years earlier, and I was expecting yet another silky huckster – not that I have anything against Koons. He is the American Dream.

Like every good reporter, I did my research. As it turned out, the excitement had been caused not by 'Flashbulb! Giant topiary dog!' but by the kid's supposedly prodigious brain. He had made a puzzle that art wonks were trying to solve, and furthermore, he was mum about it, a buff little boy-genius, who insisted that all people had to do was look and read 'a little.' Yes, he admitted the gigantic sculpture of a woman spread out in the gallery was an overblown, three-dimensional allusion to Giorgione's painting of Venus, finished by Titian; she was in the same position, asleep, one hand behind her head, another at her crotch, red bolster, ochre draperies swimming beneath her nudity. The gimmick: Illustrated Woman. Her creamy body was covered with hundreds of minute reproductions, photographs and texts, some framed, some not, each one 'a thought': Greek vase with the classical male porno themes, *erestes* and *eromenos*, Madonna and Child, crucifixions, still lifes, a note that said 'Just the West, please.' RESTRICTED was etched on her thumb. PRIMITIVE was scrawled on her forehead. Some smart-ass from *Art Assembly* had written that the picture of a Brillo box on Venus's left buttock referred to the philosopher Arthur Danto, who had claimed that art came to an end with Warhol's Brillo. Quotes from Vasari and Diderot had been uncovered, as well as fragments of Goya's and Van Gogh's letters. The all-too-predictable feminist critics had zeroed in on a reproduction of a self-portrait by Sofonisba Anguissola, a Renaissance painter (whom, they claimed, Michelangelo had admired), in Venus's exposed armpit – a ha-ha about the dumped-on and ignored, women in art history. A photograph of the artist taking a piss in what looked like Duchamp's urinal, *Fountain*, complete with R. Mutt inscription, amused some. All this amounted to a tour de force.

There was lots of esoteric yammering about another sculpture in the room, a male mannequin dressed in a navy two-piece suit and red tie with his hands behind his back eyeing said naked lady. Deeply meaningful? Deeply unmeaningful? And what were those seven large wooden boxes scattered around her? The square crates were all numbered and had small barred windows, so curious visitors had to kneel and cut past one another to get a glimpse. Each 'story' was lit from the inside to create an 'eerie' light.

Story 1. Small girl figure stands on a chair looking out a window in a miniature bedroom with her arms raised and mouth open. On the floor is a nasty arrangement of dirty paper towels, rags, bits of lace, and yarn. Ugly brown, green, and yellow stains cover all. From under the bed a man's arm protrudes, its hand clenched in a fist.

Story 2. Another room with sofa, two chairs, coffee table, bookshelves. On the table is a torn piece of paper with *Don't* printed on it. Beside it: small wooden coffin with more words: *she/he/it*. Tiny painting hangs on wall. Portrait of figure looking much like girl in story 1 but boyish – arms raised, mouth open.

Story 3. Same room as story 2. Female figure,

disproportionately large for room, must bend head to fit under ceiling, stares down at chair. Message?

Story 4. Disturbing fuzzy mammal, something like a rabbit, but not a rabbit, with two heads, lies on floor of bedroom in story 1. Loose letters cut from construction paper are scattered on the bed: G R A T E L O O T Y.

Story 5. Bathroom. Disproportionately large figure from story 3 huddled on floor clutching portrait of child from story 2 to her chest. One leg sticks out doorway and through wall of box. Bathtub filled with mucky brown water. Aargh!

Story 6. Bathroom again. Tub drained but with dark ring. Floor piled with tiny books. One marked 'M.S. 1818' appears to be leaking unidentifiable embryonic gelatinous something.

Story 7. Bedroom, living room, bathroom from stories 1–6, with extra room, a study lined with books. The two-dimensional figures of a smiling man and a smiling woman that appear to have been cut out from the same old black-and-white photograph lie beside each other on a rug. Boy child stands in open doorway looking in, holding portrait of girl child up over his head.

And who was this enfant terrible, born and bred in Youngstown, Ohio, attended Chaney High, liked his parents, met lots of 'cool people' at the School of Visual Arts, thought New York was 'great'? He played the naïf perfectly, the Forrest Gump of visual art, befuddled by sudden success, but he knew enough to carry it off. Large brown eyes darting off here and there as he considered the question. Big grin when asked about influences. Mentions Goya, Malevich, Cindy Sherman. 'Basically, it's a conceptual thing, you know.' A boy who looked as if he had started shaving last week became an instant hit. Then, after that single show, he disappeared. Like Cady Noland before him, he stopped showing art.

I am as tickled by a good hoax as the next person, an Ern Malley, for instance, or David Bowie and William Boyd's Nat Tate, or David Cerny's *Entropa*, but a fiftyish woman who's been hanging around the art world all her life can't really be called a prodigy, can she? And the last of these ruses by the Queen of Deception went bad.

When she took credit for Rune's work, she went too far. I struck up a friendship with Rune when I interviewed him for a profile in *The Gothamite* in 2002. Not long after he committed suicide (yes, I believe it was intentional), on October 17, 2003, I began thinking about writing a book. I wanted the real story, to find out what actually happened to Rune. My book *Martyred for Art* (Mythrite Press, 2009) is Rune's story, and I stand behind it. I spent a couple of years on it, doing in-depth reporting – making interviews, chasing clues and documents. Read the book! It's at your local bookstore. Order it online.

Harriet Burden bought and paid for Tish and Eldridge. Without her bags of money, neither of them would have fallen in with her. That's a fact. Rune was a celebrity, an art star. His crosses were commanding millions. Rune didn't need her. Whatever he did with her, he did as a lark, an amusement, an aesthetic dalliance. No one can blame her for wanting to latch onto his fame. The problem in the end was that Rune turned out to be a lot more than she had bargained for. His genius as an artist far outstripped her fussy, pretentious work. The twelve Larsen windows are triumphs. I do not believe she made any of them. And, of course, he outmanipulated her with one stupendous gesture: his own corpse. The film he took of his death will last. In it, he revealed the alienated truth of what we have become in this postmodern, soon-to-be cyborgian age.

The first time I recall laying eyes on the woman was in Tish's studio when I traveled to Brooklyn to snatch a couple of quotes for the piece. She looked like a cartoon character, big bust and hips, huge – six-five, maybe – a galumphing jump-shot-sized broad with long, muscular arms and giant hands, an unhappy combination of Mae West and Lennie in *Of Mice and Men*. She lumbered around the studio with a tool belt, and when I asked her what she did there, she told me she was 'Anton's friend' who 'helps him out with things' – not inaccurate when you think about it now. Before I left, I shook her hand and said casually, 'And what's your opinion of Anton's work?' She practically bit my head off. 'There's the outside and the inside; the question is: Where is the border?' I didn't quote that obscurantist comment in the article, but I recorded it in my

66

notes. I have it on tape. She went on for some time, waving those meaty hands, barking at me, nodding.

She had one thing right. I don't think she would have gone over with dealers or collectors, although who knows? They can get used to anything if it's sold right. But whether they could have sold her without remodeling, I'm not convinced. She was too excited. She quoted Freud, big mistake – the colossal charlatan – and novelists and artists and scientists no one's ever heard of. She dripped with earnestness. If there's one thing that doesn't fly in the art world, it's an excess of sincerity. They like their geniuses coy, cool, or drunk and fighting in the Cedar Bar, depending on the era. Before I published the Tish article, I found out that the weird woman in the studio was Felix Lord's widow, and the story clicked: a flush widow and her protégé. He was a kept boy, if not for his adorable, slender hips, then for his talent.

What puzzled me was why I didn't recognize her. I must have seen her multiple times before that day with Tish. I was a regular at openings and, at least twice, I'd been to cocktail receptions uptown at the Lords' spacious digs – noisy, packed, stand-up dos with revolving hors d'oeuvres and snarky, competitive small talk. Still, I have a keen eye, and my ears can take in a suggestive sentence fragment from across the room, and yet Mrs Felix Lord had left no trace whatsoever. For all practical purposes, she had been invisible. Well, I guess she's having her fifteen minutes now – from the grave.

RACHEL BRIEFMAN
(written statement)

I agreed to contribute to this book only after long conversations with Maisie and Ethan Burden, as well as with Bruno Kleinfeld, the companion of Harriet's last years. I also corresponded with Professor Hess and became convinced that this book about my friend Harriet Burden would illuminate aspects of her life and art for the many people who have now discovered her work.

Harriet and I met in 1952 when we were twelve years old at Hunter High School. There were only girls at Hunter then. I sat beside Harriet in French class and, before I ever said a word to her, I watched her draw. Although she seemed to be wholly engaged in the class – always ready with a conjugation – she never stopped drawing. She drew faces, hands, bodies, machines, and flowers inside her notebooks, outside her notebooks, on bits of scrap paper, anywhere she could find a blank surface. Her hand appeared to move by itself, idly, but with uncanny precision. From a few lines sprang characters, scenes, still lifes. Who was this tall, solemn girl with the magic hand? I told her I was impressed, and she turned to me, waved her hand in the air, put on a faux-spooky voice, and said, 'The Beast with Five Fingers.' The horror movie starring Peter Lorre featured a musician's amputated hand that committed murders and played the piano.

Years later in medical school, I read about neurological patients with alien hand syndrome. Some brain-damaged people have found themselves with an upstart hand that does exactly the opposite of what she or he wills it to do: unbuttoning a shirt that has just been buttoned, turning off the water before the glass is full, even masturbating in public. In general, alien hands cause dismay and havoc. At least one rebellious hand in the medical literature tried to strangle its owner. After I had read about these limbs with minds of their own, I called Harriet to tell her, and she laughed so hard she came down with a fit of the hiccoughs. I mention this because the joke still resonates. Harriet, who soon became Harry to me, was smart, gifted, and exquisitely sensitive. She could sulk for hours in silence when we were together, and then, just when I couldn't tolerate it anymore, she would throw her arms around me and apologize. Although I wouldn't have said it at the time, her drawings and later her paintings and sculptures seemed to have been made by a person I didn't know, but whom she didn't know either. She needed the Beast with Five Fingers, a creative imp that broke through the restraints that bound her as surely as ropes or chains.

We studied together, and we daydreamed together. I imagined myself in a white coat with a stethoscope around my neck, marching down hospital corridors, ordering around nurses, and Harriet saw herself as a great artist or poet or intellectual – or all three. We were intimates as girls can be, unhampered by the masculine posing that plagues boys. We talked on the steps of the Metropolitan Museum when the weather was fine and often when it wasn't. We shared our torments and analyzed the girls in our class. We were pretentious children who read books we didn't understand and embraced politics we knew little about, but our pretenses protected us. We were a team of two against a hostile world of adolescent hierarchies. My mother once said to me, 'Rachel, all you really need is one good friend, you know.' I found that friend in Harriet.

Too much time has passed for me to recapture us as we were then. I have treated children and adolescents in my practice for many years now, and my knowledge of their stories, as well as my own analysis, has surely reconfigured my memories. Accumulated experience always alters perception of the past. The fact that I knew Harriet until she died in 2004 has also changed my understanding of our early friendship. I do know that the passionate girl became a passionate woman, an omnivore driven by an immense appetite for ingesting as much learning as she possibly could. That hunger never left her. There were other forces that impeded her path.

I have a photograph of us taken when we were twelve or thirteen in my parents' apartment on West Eighty-sixth Street. It requires no effort to return to the room. The apartment's spaces live in my bones, but I must work harder to penetrate the young strangers in the snapshot. Tall Harry stands beside short Rachel. We are wearing cotton dresses, cinched at the waist by matching belts, and saddle shoes with anklets. Harriet's hair is pulled back in a ponytail and mine is loose. Harriet's body is blooming; mine is just beginning to bud. Neither of us looks comfortable in front of the camera, but we have acquiesced to the command 'Cheese,' and the result is two strained, if not false, expressions. When I look at the picture now, I am struck by its banality, but also by how much it hides. As a vehicle of memory, it resists inner reality. The document of an instant, it records what we looked like then. The high feeling that ran between us, the secrecy of our confidences, the pact of friendship we made – all of that is missing.

Harriet and I were 'good girls,' high-achieving, cooperative students who might as well have had gold and silver stars plastered to our foreheads; but my best friend's character had a saintly streak I lacked, a rigid moral imperative that probably came from her Protestant father. I liked Professor Burden. Remote as he was, he was never less than kind to me, and when he talked to us, I remember that the corner of one side of his mouth would often move upward in an expression of amused irony, but he rarely showed his teeth. Unlike my expansive, loudmouthed father (who had his own problems), Harriet's father was physically awkward, prone to self-conscious pats of his daughter's arm or quick, hard hugs that were more like speeding collisions than expressions of affection. When he stood up from a chair, he seemed to rise for a long time, and when he was finally erect, he loomed over us, a rangy, thin, pale, balding being. He liked to expound to us on philosophy and politics in a language that was often beyond our comprehension, but Harriet would listen to him rapt, as if God himself were talking. I don't remember any self-righteousness in his speeches. He believed in tolerance and academic freedom, and, like my own parents, he railed against the monstrosity that was the Red Scare. But it is not what is said that makes us who we are. More often it is what remains unspoken. Even as a girl I felt the coiled-up tension in the man as he sat in his large chair, his long fingers curled around a martini with two olives. As far as I could tell, his thoughts were usually elsewhere.

As little children during the war, Harriet and I had lived without our fathers, and we remembered their return. My father never saw combat, but Professor Burden had been part of an intelligence unit in Europe. According to Harriet, he had never said a word to her about it, not one word. Once, when she asked him about those years, he picked up a book and began to read, as if the words had never come out of her mouth. Before he went off to war, he married, and Harriet knew that her father had alien-ated his family because the girl of his dreams was Jewish. It wasn't a permanent rift; the Burdens came to nominally accept Ruth Fine and their granddaughter, but the Burdens were snobs – pure and simple. No money, but heaps of old-money notions that included an unarticulated anti-Semitism. Although Harriet's father had rejected the pinched world of his parents, he was nevertheless its product. He worked long hours, was meticulous, dutiful, and self-punishing. Praise for his wife and daughter was meted out in small, grudging doses. I never saw him irritable or angry, but then, his self-restraint was so powerful it prevented all spontaneity. It was her father who came up with the nickname 'Harry.' As a psychoanalyst, it is hard for me not to see a wish parading openly in the 'pet' name.

I marveled at the absence of all bickering and banter in the Burden household. Ruth yelled at Harry from time to time, but never at her husband. My own parents were subject to regular melees followed by periods of standoff, and although their struggles often pained me terribly, I was more accustomed to conflict at home than Harriet was. (I also had two brothers who were masters of the choke hold.) A young person always extrapolates human reality from her own life. However anomalous that life may be to others, it is normal for the one who lives inside it every day.

At the same time, I envied the harmony in the Burden household. Ruth was affable, efficient, and appeared to believe in her wifely duties, not as a yoke but as a calling. She had a sharp sense of humor and was subject to fits of giggling, sometimes so extreme she found it hard to stop. Once, after she dropped a pot roast on the floor of the kitchen and watched it slide with its abundant juices across the floor and hit the leg of a stool, she laughed so hard the tears streamed down her face. After she recovered, Mrs Burden scooped up the chunk of beef, popped it back into the pan, and 'made a few repairs.' We ate the dinner without a word to the patriarch, but Ruth winked at Harry and me throughout the dinner, which gave me a wonderful feeling of conspiracy.

Because the pot roast chaos was an anomaly in the Burden household, it became an object of hilarity. My own mother, a translator from French and German, worked at our kitchen table. Before we ate dinner, she would shove her manuscripts to one side, and then, when she discovered drips of spaghetti sauce on her pages in the morning, she would yell, 'Am I raising pigs in this family?' I now think that Ruth Burden ordered her world to keep anxiety at bay and to preserve the quiescent surface of her husband, who was roiling underneath and drank his three martinis every evening to subdue the rising floods. I liked Mrs Burden's touch; it was warm and affectionate, and she lavished it on Harry and sometimes on me. When I spent the night, she would tuck us in, old as we were, and I liked the feel of her hand on my forehead, liked her perfume and the sweetness of her voice saying good night to us.

After Harriet had Maisie, those passionate maternal emotions, as well as a zeal for order, seemed to take possession of her. She threw herself into motherhood and domesticity in a way that, frankly, startled me. She became her mother, not so easy because she also desperately wanted to be her father – philosopher-king. Harry and I used to meet every week for tea after she had seen her psychotherapist, a colleague of mine, Adam Fertig. One afternoon she rushed in a few minutes late and, apologizing, sat down opposite me. 'Rachel,' she said, 'isn't it strange that we don't know who we are? I mean, we know so little about ourselves it's shocking. We tell ourselves a story and we go along believing in it, and then, it turns out, it's the wrong story, which means we've lived the wrong life.'

We talked about our stories that afternoon, about self-deception, and Harry's fury at her lot. Neither her family story nor cultural politics nor her temperament can explain what happened to her. There are clouds in all of us, and we give names to them, but the names make divisions that aren't always there. There were storms inside Harry, whirlwinds and tornadoes that went their various destructive ways. Her suffering ran deep, and her suffering did not begin as an adult. I remember her standing in front of the mirror, tears streaming down her face. She was probably fifteen or sixteen. 'I hate the way I look. Why did I turn out this way?'

The popular girls at Hunter bragged on Tuesday about having dates for Friday and Saturday nights. Harry and I pretended to keep ourselves aloof from such petty concerns, but what teenager doesn't want to be admired and loved? What person, for that matter? I suppose her appearance was the arena where the more pernicious aspects of America touched her – the sense that she was too big to be attractive to men. The truth is Harriet was striking. She had a beautiful, strong, voluptuous body. Men stared at her on the street, but she wasn't a flirt, and she wasn't socially graceful or prone to small talk. Harriet was shy and solitary. In company, she was usually quiet, but when she spoke, she was so forceful and intelligent, she frightened people, especially boys her own age. They simply didn't know what to make of her. Harry sometimes wished she were a boy, and I can say that had she been one, her route would have been easier. Awkward brilliance in a boy is more easily categorized, and it conveys no sexual threat.

Not long ago, I reread the book Harry loved best when we were in high school: *Frankenstein* by Mary Shelley. We often read the same novels, and the two of us had polished off *Jane Eyre*, *Wuthering Heights*, all of Austen, and much of Dickens by then, but *Frankenstein* became Harriet's archetypal text, a fable of the self, a scripture for the reality of Harry Burden. Although I was taken by the story as a foreboding myth about the developments of modern medicine, I did not read it again and again. Dr Frankenstein and the book's vapid female characters held little interest for Harry. The person she loved was the monster, and she used to quote long passages from his chapters by heart, declaiming them like an old-fashioned poet, which made me laugh, even though I was bewildered by her fanatical attachment to the Miltonic creature.

Reading the book again as an adult, however, I felt a door had been opened. I walked through it and found Harry. I found Harry in a novel that had been written by a nineteen-year-old girl on a bet. In 1816, Mary Shelley was spending the summer in Switzerland with her husband, their neighbor Lord Byron, and another person less celebrated whose name I cannot remember. The challenge was to write a ghost story for the pleasure of the others. Mary was the only one who fulfilled the bargain. In the preface, she writes that the story came to her in a 'waking dream,' as one image after another possessed her. She watched as a 'pale student of unhallowed arts' created a monster.

'Behold the horrid thing stands at his bedside opening his curtains and looking on him with yellow, watery, but speculative eyes.'

It is impossible to forget the novel's essential story. I knew the terrible being Frankenstein makes is so lonely and misunderstood that his very existence is cursed. I knew his awful isolation is transformed into vengeance, but I had forgotten, or probably had never felt before, the ferocity of his feeling – his fury, grief, and bloodlust. And then I came across these lines spoken by the monster in Chapter 15:

'My person was hideous and my stature gigantic. What did this mean? Who was I? What was I? Whence did I come? What was my destination? These questions steadily recurred, but I was unable to solve them.'

I felt as if Harry's ghost were speaking to me.

A COMPENDIUM OF THIRTEEN
*Characters, a Non Sequitur, a Confession,
a Riddle, and Memories for H.B.*

Ethan Lord

1. **H**ow did Gobliatron, hero of the Fervidlies, who inhabit a country far to the north of Nowhere, disentangle himself from the ice-cold clutches of the Bobblehead, a machine man who froze great lakes by looking at them? Bobblehead froze Gobliatron solid with a mere glance. So Gobliatron, stranded in mid-step on a field of ice, began to think hot. He thought so hot he gave himself a fever. The fever melted the ice, and the hero was free.

2. **A** word eludes a picture. How do you draw *whenever, but, and then,* or *last week*? Arrows.

3. **R**ed roosters all over pajamas purchased in France that Edward Boyle said belonged on girls. I took a pair of scissors, cut a hole in one leg, and threw the scrap in the garbage. The slashed

pajamas disappeared. This is a confession. I was eight.

4. **R**iddle: What is so fragile even saying its name can break it? Silence. . . . F.L., paterfamilias, asked me this riddle when I was nine. I could not answer him, but after he gave up the secret, I could not stop thinking about the answer. I lay in bed and said *Silence* again and again to hear it break. You asked me what I was doing, and I told you, and you smiled, but the smile went crooked, and I did not know exactly what it meant.

5. **I** remember the closet was my enemy. I remember there was something behind the door. I remember you put a flashlight inside the closet and that, when it burned out, you let me change the batteries.

6. **E**verything has a pattern or a rhythm that can be discerned through close attention, but whether those repetitions exist outside the mind is an open question. You and I did not see the same patterns.

7. 'Theory is good but it does not prevent things from happening.' You told me that one month, two days, and thirty-seven minutes before you died. It is a quote from a neurologist, Jean-Martin Charcot, who dressed in black, admired

paintings, and wrote the first descriptive analysis of multiple sclerosis.

8. **B**oredom never touched you, except when waiting for suitcases at the airport.

9. **U**nder the logical fallacy argumentum ad popular, the biggest brand is the best brand. This false reasoning is used by every cultural herd, however large or small. The herd runs to gape at the spectacle of whitening toothpaste. The herd runs to see the new hot gallery star. The herd thinks in unison. The herd is a collective voyeur, driven by received knowledge to see beauty, sophistication, cleverness in the shining thing, the empty vehicle of worth and wealth and glory. But the herd loves ugliness, too: humiliations, murders, suicides, and corpses – not actual corpses within reach, not corpses that stink, but the mediated dead, the dead and dying on screen. The familiar herd, our own herd, is mostly sanitary in its tastes. The herd reads *The Gothamite* to discover sanitary tastes that will not interfere with the spectacle of whitening toothpaste that brightens its collective Madison Avenue grin and will not sully its Wall Street suit. The herds, large and small, create varying identities through one or another commodity of choice,

80

their raison d'être. Images of the living as well as the dead are sold on the open market as delectable bodies. Their reality is exclusively of the third-person pronominal variety. The bodies have no inside because the first-person singular is not allowed. Value is determined within each herd by collective perception and the number of viewers.

10. **R**ubik's Cube: 43,252,003,274,489 856,000 permutations. You gave it to me because you knew its algorithms would haunt me. M.L., Maisie Lord, aka Twinkletoes, the tutus-and-Mad-Hatter's-tea-party sibling, did not understand that this was a hexahedral universe to be mastered by movement and color, that it was a cosmology, a separate reality, a place to be. She broke my Rubik's Cube. I cut off her ponytail. I held the ponytail over the toilet while she screamed. I flushed. The toilet did not want to digest the hair. You came, you looked, you yelled, and while you yelled, you waved your hands beside your ears. Then you brought towels, and you spoke to us about tolerance, but we were not interested in it, not interested in tolerance, that is. We were too old, you said, to be breaking Rubik's Cubes and flushing ponytails down toilets, and you were

dead tired of it – of us. I was eleven and Maisie was thirteen. And then you sat down on the bathroom floor (with the towel that had a beige stripe at one end) even though the floor was not dry. Your head flopped down onto your chest and a sound came from you – a choking sound and sniffs. I froze like Gobliatron. I could not move. Twinkletoes said to me, Now look what you've done! Now look what you've done! But my mouth was too tight and cold to answer.

11. **D**ebord, Guy. He invented the Game of War. It was a board game about the Napoleonic Wars. Guy Debord, Julien Sorel, Ethan Lord – all wanting to play the game, move the pieces. Tell me the rules. Men love games. You said that once to me. But you loved games, too.

12. **E**than Lord, only son of Harriet Burden and Felix Lord, product of afore-mentioned two persons in nuclear family arrangement, aspirant scribbler, puzzle-maker, neo-Situationist orphan, remembers his mother. I am trying to remember you, Mother, to find those brain scraps and turn them into more than a Humian bundle of impressions, as you would have said, Humian, after David Hume. Kantian and Hegelian, but not Spinozaian, perhaps Husserlian?

There is *Husserliana, Gesammelte Werke*. You would be glad to know that I've looked, read a few pages of him. He is difficult. You, too, could be difficult to understand.

13. Nobisa Notfinger lived in Paciland, a country beside Fervid where the inhabitants were well dressed and serene and followed the rules, but Nobisa had a temper, and she was a messy, dirty, chubby girl, and life was hard for her, and so she left to make her fortune in Fervid. You created Nobisa for Maisie, but you armed her for me. In her trusty brown suitcase she had a ray gun and a sword and a special ear-pincher given to her by the Fairy of Ill-Will and Malice that Nobisa could use only seven times. Maisie doesn't remember the stories as well as I do. Different patterns of mind.

HARRIET BURDEN
Notebook A

September 25, 1998, 10:00 p.m.

Vindication of the Rights of Harriet Burden! They have swallowed the Tish shit whole, gulped it down so readily I am dizzy with success, to quote that demon, Joseph Stalin. We have removed the *c* from his name to make the anagram work. Table no more! The little boy with a few fresh acne scars has whetted their appetites for more Wunderkind works, more smartass jokes with art historical flourishes, and the buffoons are pounding out their enthusiasm in reviews. They haven't found a tenth of my little witticisms, my references, my puzzles, but who cares? They've had little to say about the story boxes, but that only demonstrates their blindness, doesn't it? The other day one of their ranks showed up at Anton's, someone Case, a dwarf in a suit and bow tie with anachronistic hair pomade and a fake Brahmin accent that made me wince. He asked me for my 'views.' Poor, self-important little man.

★ ★ ★

After he left, Anton and I laughed so hard I had to sit down on the folding chair in the studio and rock back and forth. We are a team, I told him, a twosome deep in research on the nature of perception: Why do people see what they see? There must be conventions. There must be expectations. We see nothing otherwise; all would be chaos. Types, codes, categories, concepts. I put him in, didn't I? The fellow in the suit looking oh-so-seriously at immense naked woman. How quick they are to embrace and anoint the smiling young male artist with innocent air; look how knowledgeable, how sophisticated, how clever he is. Big Venus has made a big (little) buzz. I hear the sound of bees, and bees sting. I have told Dr Fertig that I hate the bees. *Hate* is not a word I use lightly. He knows that. He knows that the joke is also no joke. He wants to know when I will reveal my identity. The phrase itself is exciting. It makes me feel as if I am living in a thriller. When will I reveal my identity?

He asks about Anton, too.

But Big Venus belongs to Anton Tish, I said. Dear Dr Fertig, without Anton she would not exist. It is a work that came into being between him and me because it was made by a boy, an *enfant terrible*, not by me, old lady artist Harry Burden with two adult children and a grandchild and a bank account.

★   ★   ★

85

Dr Fertig pointed out that the money is rarely simple.

Anton gets the money from sales. That is the deal.

I close my eyes. I close my eyes. It is my time now. It is my time, and I will not let them take it away from me. The Greeks knew that the mask in the theater was not a disguise but a means of revelation. And now that I have started I can feel the winds behind me, not because Big Venus is so much – cynical fun – but because I see what they gobble down and with the right face I can do more. *Nota bene.*

And yet, Anton says she is beautiful in the gallery space asleep, that she is better than I imagine because we couldn't see her so well when we assembled her. I have not dared to go yet, but maybe I will peek in from outside and look through the window at my big doll, my first success.

Nobody knows but me and Anton and Dr Fertig. Edgar is suspicious. The other little assistants know that I paid for her, but they believe the lady is blown straight from Anton's imagination. One of them, with a preposterous name, Falling Leaves or Autumn Sunshine, no doubt the offspring of New Age fruitcakes, seems to have glued herself to Anton – an *unheimlich* little creature, very pretty with blond curls and poppy-colored lips, and strange, large, knowing blue eyes.

Speaking of winds, where is the Barometer? I looked in his room. He is usually curled up in his sleeping bag by now with his eye mask and earphones on to keep out the pressure so he can rest from his labors of feeling the weather. I hope the poor man hasn't burst and been taken to a hospital. Although Rachel insists medicine can help him, I know that he doesn't want the poison pellets the doctors give him, which mute his gift, and it is a gift, strange to say. Sometimes when I listen to him talk, I begin to feel the barometric variations myself – the ups and downs in my own bodily register – a hum in the system.

I have another guest: Phineas Q. Eldridge, not his real name. He was born John Whittier; he disavowed the name when he emerged from the closet. The new man disconcerted his sister and homophobic brother-in-law, but his mother, whom he e-mails often and visits once a year in North Carolina, has stayed true. Mother and sister come on the sly to see him at a hotel. Phineas is a performance artist; he performs in 'half drag,' half man, half woman, half white, half black, cut straight down the middle, and the two parts of him have conversations onstage.

His father was white; his mother is black, so he knows something about halves. The couple is mostly in conflict, apparently; it would not be entertaining otherwise, but they also blend at times, mingle and mix, which I find compelling. He has invited me to watch him next week, and I am excited about it and just a bit anxious as well because I hope he is good. Phineas Q. (the *Q*, he says, can stand for anything one desires – Quentin or Query or Querulous or Question or just Q) is highly articulate and, although I haven't seen him much because he works at night, I have come to hope he will saunter in and offer one of his tart comments about my work. He called my Felix dolls 'ambrosial runts.' He also said my Empathy Box could do with some empathy. That hurt me, but he was right. I have begun over with mirrors. He also made reference to the building as a 'flophouse' and advocates rules, organization, someone to run it. I can't just take in any drug addict or slea-zeball that knocks on my door. He is right about this. Last week I housed a girl in pigtails whose bum had been squeezed so tightly into a pair of red leather shorts, I thought of sausages in casing. It's possible she turned a couple tricks before I asked her to leave. There were two grim-faced men who came and went in a single night. If they had sex with Red Shorts, it wasn't happy sex.

There is sadness in Phineas, a wound that lies

beneath the brisk, bright persona. I don't know how old he is, mid-thirties maybe, but I am drawn to that doleful piece of him. In unguarded moments, a pensive expression changes his features. It never happens when he is looking at me, but when he pauses, when he turns away. Once I asked him, Are you okay?

And he said, No.

The *no* made me glad. Aren't we always saying, Yes, I'm fine?

Yes, and you?

Fine, fine.

We're all fine.

I wish I hadn't been so fine, so goddamned fine for so many years . . .

I waited politely for Phineas Q. to tell me why he wasn't fine, but he didn't, and I let it go because there is fear in me, a sickening reticence. For as long as I can remember it has been there, lying in wait – a fat, leaden, hideous thing. I don't want to wake it. If I wake it, the earth will rumble and the walls will crack and fall. Put your finger to your lips, Harry, put your finger to your lips and tiptoe around the thing. Make nice and fine, Harry, as nice and fine as you know how.

It was there with Felix, too, the thing, but it wasn't his fault. I understand that now. It was there long before Felix. Let him sleep. Walk softly. Defer. Don't upset him. He is fragile, fragile and somehow dangerous. Felix always deserves what you don't.

Why? Mysterious feelings: ingrown, automatic, thoughtless. Before words. Under words.

What is early memory, I ask you?

> *It is with considerable difficulty that I remember the original era of my being; all the events of that period appear confused and indistinct.* *

Mine, too.

> *The mind is its own place and in itself can make a heav'n of hell, a hell of heav'n.*†

Can I rely upon the pictures I see or are they reconfigured to a degree that obscures all sense?

> *My Life had stood – a Loaded Gun.*‡

I am wild on paper. I am bestial. And then I must hide and, with the thick black crayon, I rub

---

* The opening sentence of Chapter 11 of Mary Shelley's *Frankenstein*.

† John Milton, *Paradise Lost*, Book 1 (554–55). The words are Satan's. In Notebook G, Burden notes, 'Satan removes his mind from God. Heresy, of course. Hubris, of course. Modern, of course.'

‡ *The Complete Poems of Emily Dickinson*, ed. Thomas H. Johnson (New York: Little Brown and Co., 1960), no. 754, p. 369.

out every line. I blacken the page so they will never see what I have drawn, what I have done.

Why do I feel there is a secret I carry in my body like an embryo, speechless and unformed, beyond knowing? And why do I feel it might erupt in a great blast if not checked? It must be easy, so easy to fill in that damp, throttling unease with words, to write the disturbance, to write a story to explain the why of it.

I was in my crib.

I was standing on the floor.

The curtains were drawn, and I had to climb onto a chair to pull aside the fabric and look outside into the street.

I saw his feet in front of the door.

The memory begins to form itself from the cloud of unknowing. The shapeless takes shape and soon there is a smothered articulation – ominous and meaningful.

Shame arrives before guilt.

But there is no going back, Harry. The mind is its own place, and it bears us backward and forward. It has its own architecture of the past that comes from real rooms and real streets, but they are made over and over again in time and now reside within, not without. Once those places were filled with the noise of garbage trucks and sirens and the sentence fragments of chattering pedestrians and the odors of the moving seasons, but the dense visions and clamor and smells have been simplified into interior mental codes grown stiff with words. The future is made of that same stuff – elemental spaces we inhabit with wishes or fears. Why so many fears? There is no single story in that foggy region of childhood to explain you, Harry.

I think of Bertha, Bertha Pappenheim, alias Anna O.
   It is frightening what we imagine and what we make by imagination.

She, Anna O., receives Dr Breuer, the physician who has supposedly cured her, who has used the cathartic method, the first talking cure, but she, Bertha, named it, not he. She named it. In a letter to Stefan Zweig in 1932, Freud provided a coda. And when Breuer comes into the room, Bertha is clasping her belly and writhing in pain. What is the matter? he asks. What has happened? And she says, Now comes Dr B.'s child.

It is the thing they have made together. Look at it.

The good doctor runs in terror.

The good doctor does not run in terror. It is a myth.

They rewrote her.

She would rewrite them. In courage.*

* Bertha Pappenheim was the real name of Josef Breuer's patient Anna O., whose case figures in Freud and Breuer's *Studies on Hysteria* (1895). Her symptoms included tics, intense facial pain, loss of vision, memory lapses, and even a temporary inability to speak her mother tongue, German. Breuer's treatment, along with other methods, included letting his patient talk and tell him stories. Pappenheim coined the name *the talking cure* in English. In the case study, Anna O.'s story ends with her cure, but the truth is far more complicated. Breuer handed his patient over to a Swiss sanitarium. Pappenheim still suffered from hysterical symptoms, although they were less dramatic than before her treatment with Breuer, and she was addicted to both morphine and chloral hydrate. See A. Hirschmuller, *The Life and Work of Josef Breuer: Physiology and Psychoanalysis* (New York: New York University Press, 1970), 301–2, and D. Gilhooley, 'Misrepresentation and Misreading in the Case of Anna O.,' *Modern Psychoanalysis* 27, no. 1. After her release from the sanitarium, she was hospitalized three times over the course of the next five years.

In his letter to Zweig, Freud writes, 'What really happened with Breuer's patient I was able to *guess* later on, long after a break in our relations, when I suddenly remembered something Breuer had once told me . . . On the evening of the day all her symptoms had been disposed of, he was summoned to the patient again, found her confused and writhing with abdominal cramps. Asked what was wrong with her, she replied, "Now Dr B.'s child is coming!"' E.

I dream of Dr F.

The suppressed thing. The thing that comes up. She has named it: Dr B.'s child. It will out.

Where is the borderland between memory and hallucination?

*   *   *

Freud, ed., *The Letters of Sigmund Freud* (New York: Basic Books, 1960), 67, my italics. From this memory Freud conjectures that Anna O. suffered from a hysterical pregnancy and that the sexual character of those symptoms caused Breuer to flee in fear. Ernest Jones later corroborates this version of events in his biography of Freud, as does Peter Gay in his. These interpretations of the evidence are disputed, however, and Burden appears to be well acquainted with the controversy. 'They rewrote her. She would rewrite them. In courage' refers to Pappenheim's later life as a feminist activist. In 1888, Pappenheim left the haute bourgeois life she had led as an Orthodox Jew in Vienna and traveled throughout Eastern Europe, fighting for and publishing works about the rights of Jewish women. In 1904, she co-founded the League of Jewish Women, which organized health-care facilities, vacation retreats, and youth homes, and offered career training for women. The League was dissolved on November 9, 1938. Many of its leaders were murdered in the camps. Burden may be referring to Pappenheim's Last Will and Testament, in which she wrote: 'If you remember me, bring a little stone, as the silent promise and symbol of the establishment of the idea and mission of women's duty and women's joy in serving unceasingly and courageously in life.' E. Loentz, *Let Me Continue to Speak the Truth: Bertha Pappenheim as Author and Activist* (Cincinnati: Hebrew Union College Press, 2007).

We make images spontaneously. They will out.

For as long as I can remember they have come to me at night before I sleep. They used to frighten me, the horrors of that self-generated cinema, like dreams but not dreams, a threshold reality between waking and sleeping; a limen that should be named, but isn't. I am not inside the screen but outside, watching their exploits, and I have come to love them. Every night I wait for them. The brutes rise up, fierce and menacing, their teeth bared and their noses leaking pink snot as they lumber over brimming blue hills. They are never still but in constant metamorphosis, mouths become chins, eyes turn into welts, boobs and cocks drop to the ground and molt into new devils or vanish in festering heaps of color. Hair floats behind a disfigured head in curling knots or garlands, but I also see the innocent and the lackadaisical, sweet children and well-formed adults; two dancers fornicate while airborne, and I smile at their rhythmical hips. A tiny man leaps from a cliff, and pure geometries of hard green and red and yellow melt into a riot of running lava. I have seen us all, Maisie and Ethan and Felix and me and my parents and Rachel fleeing past my closed eyelids on the screen, barely recognized but there nevertheless among the parade, as if my mind had retained the reels of an old movie. If only I could transfer those hypnagogic muses into paint or film or little kinetic sculptures. Where do they come from? Why one image and not another? Is it memory transmuted? Where do hallucinations come from in the brain? No one can say.

I hear the Barometer wheezing in the hall. I'm glad he's back. I'm not sure where he goes for hours at a time. Proselytizing or schmoozing or just wandering? But I can hear his whistling tubes. Felix wheezed, too. And he coughed. My father coughed. Smokers all. Each man's cough had/has its own moist rumble or dry rattle. Isn't it odd that we can recognize a person's cough, that phlegm loosened in bronchia has an idiosyncratic sound? My madman wheezes and coughs and has begun to scratch imaginary sores, which, with scratching, become real. I offered him a salve. In his notebooks he draws cities on fire and dragons and dervishes and circle upon circle and cryptic symbols and clouds, of course, and rain and snow and hail of various sizes. He has little interest in fair weather; he is my foul-weather friend.

ROSEMARY LERNER
(written statement)

There is a pronounced tendency in all the arts to mythologize the dead, by which I mean the creation of reductive narratives to explain artists' lives and works. I have been an art writer for more than forty years and have witnessed this time and time again. The reasons for simplification are often ideological, but sensational biographies can also erase all nuance when they appear to fit a prefigured character and script – tragic hero or heroine, victim, genius. It is helpful to undermine these wooden scenarios. Harriet Burden was not nearly as obscure or unnoticed as she has been made out to be in the stories that are now circulating about her career. Her work was represented in no less than five group shows in the seventies and I, for one, singled her out in a review I wrote for *Art in New York* in 1976:

> *Harriet Burden's uncanny architectural piece with its slightly askew walls and floors, its emotionally charged figures, pastel palette, and dense use of text lingers in this reviewer's mind*

*as the work of a brilliant and strikingly inde-
pendent artist.*

Albeit a minority view, I was not alone. Archie
Frame, Beatrice Brownhurst, and Peter Grosswetter
all commented favorably on her two one-woman
shows, both at major New York galleries. Yes, both
dealers let her go, but this is hardly a unique fate.
It merely places Harriet Burden among the
numerous distinguished visual artists, male and
female, who were respected by other artists,
received mixed reviews, and didn't attract big
collectors to their work.

Reviewers of every ilk like to feel they are above
a work of art. If it puzzles them or if they are
intimidated, they are more than likely to trash it.
Many artists are not intellectuals, but Burden was,
and her work reflected her wide learning. Her
references spanned many fields and were often
impossible to track. There was also a literary,
narrative quality to her art that many resisted. I
am convinced that her knowledge alone acted as
an irritant to some reviewers. I once had a conversation with a man who had excoriated her first
one-woman show. When I brought up his review
and offered a defense of her work, he was hostile.
He was not a stupid man and had written well
on some artists I admired. He had attacked Burden's
work as confused and naïve, the very opposite,
in fact, of what it was. I realized that he had
been incapable of a fair-minded appraisal because,

although he prided himself on his sophistication, the multiple meanings of her carefully orchestrated texts had eluded him, and he had projected his own disorientation onto the work. His last words to me were 'I hated it, okay? I just hated it. I don't give a damn about what she was referring to.' That conversation has stayed with me, not as a story about Harriet Burden so much as a lesson for myself: Beware of the violent response and the sophisms you may use to explain it.

Then there is the question of sex. It has often taken women longer to gain a hold in the art world than men. The remarkable Alice Neel worked without much attention until she was in her seventies. Louise Bourgeois made a breakthrough with her show at MoMA in 1982. She was seventy. Like Burden, these women were not ignored but gained prominent recognition only late in their careers. During her lifetime the painter Joan Mitchell was known and admired, but it wasn't until after her death that her place among second-generation abstract expressionists began to grow enormously. Grace Hartigan was the only woman in MoMA's legendary *New American Painting* exhibition in 1958–1959. Eva Hesse, who was at Cooper Union only a few years before Burden, died in 1970 at age thirty-four of a brain tumor. She didn't live to see her star continue to rise or the power of her influence on younger artists. But when she was alive she complained that her work did not receive the serious attention given to the work of her male colleagues, and she was right. There were many reviewers who reviewed her life, not her art. Lee Krasner's work was subsumed by her husband's in the eyes of the art world. Jackson Pollock was and is deified as a Romantic hero. A year before Krasner died, a retrospective of her work was mounted, but by then, she said, it was 'too late.' Mostly, the art business has been about men. And when it has been about women, it has often been about correcting past oversights. It is interesting that not all, but many women were celebrated only when their days as desirable sexual objects had passed.

Although the number of women artists has exploded, it is no secret that New York galleries show women far less often than men. The figures hover around twenty percent of all one-person shows in the city, despite the fact that almost half of those same galleries are run by women. The museums that exhibit contemporary art are no better, nor are the magazines that write about it. Every woman artist faces the insidious propagation of a male status quo. With almost no exceptions, art by men is far more expensive than art by women. Dollars tell the story. After giving up on a public life as an artist, Burden decided to experiment with the perception of her work through the use of masculine personas. The results were striking. When presented as the work of a man, her art suddenly found an enthusiastic audience. Caution is in order, however. Art world trends are constantly changing. The raw is in one day, the cooked the next. And there is an ever-present hunger for youth, the latest ingénue or mangenue on the menu. Might a young woman have served Burden equally well? Probably not, but the story cannot simply be told as a feminist parable, even though it seems obvious that sexual bias played a determining role in the perception of Burden's work. And yet, each of her masks seemed to uncover a different aspect of her imagination, and it is not unfair to say that the trajectory of her artistic experimentation became a movement toward an increasing and almost sinister ambiguity.

Anton Tish, who has disappeared from the art world entirely, seems to have been little more than a puppet. Phineas Eldridge, on the other hand, brought his own searing charm to *The Suffocation Rooms* they worked on together. He, too, has retired from art but not from speaking out, and his letter to *Art Lights* remains, to my mind, not only a tribute to Burden, the woman, but a perspicacious reading of her work.

Burden's involvement with Rune is, at least to me, both sad and mysterious. The controversy over his apparent suicide and the antics of Oswald Case, whose book *Martyred for Art* turns Rune into the genius-celebrity of a new technological era, have only blurred the real issues. It is true that four of the window pieces cannot be absolutely attributed to Burden, and there are those who insist they belong to Rune. The final verdict has not been made, and the uncertainty may continue for quite some time, if not forever. Nevertheless, a black-and-white treatment of the Burden-Rune story is uncalled for. It leads to mythmaking at its worst: The wish supplants the evidence. It ignores Burden's autobiographical writings, which make a strong case for out-and-out theft of some of her pieces by someone, possibly Rune. In a notebook entry from September 12, 2003, she wrote, 'Four works have vanished from the studio overnight. I am desperate.' Why would she write this if it weren't true? Case's theory is that Burden framed Rune by leaving written records that strongly hint at his malfeasance and that she did it out of envy and spite. Case relies heavily on what Rune told him, and he had access to almost none of Burden's papers when he wrote his book. He quotes a single sentence taken from three pages of her writing that were published in the spring issue of *Dexterity* (2008), the year of her retrospective at Grace. 'It is so easy for Rune to shine. Where does that effortlessness come from? How do people acquire it? He is so light. I am earthbound, a Caliban to his Ariel.' This is hardly proof of some Machiavellian plan to poach another artist's career.

I have only one personal note to contribute. When I saw *The History of Western Art*, supposedly the work of Anton Tish, at the Clark Gallery, I was struck by a passage etched into Venus's inner thigh:

Have not girls done as much for the doll? – the
doll – yes, target of things past and to come?
The last doll, given to age, is the girl who should
have been a boy, and the boy who should have
been a girl! The love of that last doll was fore-
shadowed in that love of the first. The doll and
the immature have something right about
them, the doll because it resembles but does not
contain life, and the third sex because it contains
life but resembles the doll.

It is from *Nightwood* by Djuna Barnes, a difficult, strange little novel. To be honest, I am not at all sure what is meant by this meditation on dolls, but I do know that in not one but in three of the works in her second show, Burden included quotes from that particular book. No one has exclusive rights to quote from *Nightwood*. Still, it struck me as curious, and then, when I looked inside the boxes that circled the large Venus sculpture, the little scenes bore such strong similarities to Burden's early rooms with their small figures and oblique narratives that I felt sure Tish must have seen her pieces. Influences are normal, but these looked like the development of that earlier work, and I was bothered by the thought that he might have looted from works she had never shown. Not a single reviewer mentioned Burden.

Through the son of a friend who knew Burden's daughter, I got the artist's telephone number in Brooklyn and called her. I introduced myself, explained the nature of my call, and asked her if she had been to the gallery to see the show, to which she answered, 'No.' I discovered later that this was technically true. I then asked her if she was still making art. She said, 'Yes.' I waited for her to say something more, then elaborated further, saying that aspects of the work seemed so close to hers that I found it alarming. There was a long, awkward silence. I could hear her breathing. Finally, she cleared her throat and then said, 'Thank you. Thank you for calling. Goodbye.'

That was it. I had given her an opening. She didn't take it. Harriet Burden had allies. I count myself among them. I am convinced that had she looked for a dealer, she would have found one, but even if she hadn't, she could have taken another route. There are women's cooperatives that show artists who fail to receive recognition from mainstream venues. I have seen some very good work exhibited in those galleries. Burden wanted her experiment, and she wanted to remain hidden. I can't help but wish that she had been able to answer me then. At the same time, the masks must be considered as furthering what she did best – creating works of focused ambiguity.

BRUNO KLEINFELD
(written statement)

I met Harry during a dog-eared, smudged, scribbled-in-the-margins, stained, and torn chapter of my life. But that was a cosmetic problem, really. I am the proud owner of any number of tattered and beaten biographies that are still decipherable. Time creeps. Time alters. Gravity insists. As my mother used to say to me, 'After fifty, Bruno, it's just patch, patch, patch.' No, it wasn't my going-on-sixty carcass with receding hairline and basset-hound cheeks that made that chapter so bad. It was that I had lost me. I was no longer the hero of my own life. Instead, I was lurking in the proverbial shadows as some goddamned minor character with only a couple of lines of dialogue here and there. Imagine getting up in the morning and scouring the apartment for yourself, turning out drawers and rifling through closets and checking under the bed for yourself. Where had I mislaid him, that bright, curly-headed youth with prospects shining just over yonder hill? Whatever happened to Bruno Kleinfeld? You may well ask. My person seemed to have sidelined itself in ways that meant I was no longer I. The imposter,

Bruno Kleinfeld, the one who woke up in the morning in the ratty apartment in Red Hook, would have been a big surprise to the actual Bruno Kleinfeld, who was traveling boldly from one chapter to another in his fully authorized biography. But I simply couldn't lay my hands on that Bruno and found myself stuck with the former, a sad sack who regularly ate Spaghetti Os for dinner and twice in desperation descended to gourmet tidbits for the doggy set. You see, he couldn't pay his rent and had to go panhandling to his old friend Tip Barrymore in Park Slope, whose brownstone life looked far more like the one the genuine Bruno was living. Eyes. It's all in the eyes. Tip's eyes when he said he didn't need it back. 'I don't need it back, Brune.' Brune is the only way to shorten Brun-O. Pupils askance, furtive, not straight double-barreled, not man to man. Poor Brune. He didn't say it. Oh no. His eyes said it. Pity the bright boy of yonder hill? What the fuck? You've got the wrong guy, bub, the wrong Brun-O, old man. Take it on the chin. Take it in the gut. Garçon! Bring me a glass of the Fronsac and the steak frites *tout de suite*. With mayonnaise! Little dreams of meals. Little dreams of no roaches, of a smoothly working, rust-free toilet, of linoleum without chips and yellow stains. The sad little dreams of the poseur, that fake Kleinfeld of swollen proportions and disabled swing with no pop. Who was that guy that used to hit them over the fence, used to speed around the bases, used to be a schmooze artist, ladies' man, seducer, used to be husband to three women and father to three daughters, promising author of two books of poetry, published by a major press, major, not minor (verses in minor key but not of the minor leagues), with tributes from luminaries plastered on back covers with that significant word he had relished, chewed over, sucked on long and hard: *Whitmanian*? The kid's work is 'Whitmanian,' and there were no less than three exclamation marks that ended sentences inside those blurbs by notables of international reputation, emphatic punctuation for emphatically bright boy who raked in grant money on strength of looming hill yonder, young, handsome poet whippersnapper who begins epic poem, poem for the ages, the poem to end all American poems.

And he writes, and he writes, and he writes, and then he writes it again, and he cannot get it just the way he wants it. And as he writes it, the years pass; he marries and divorces, and he marries and divorces again and then again; children are born, and he is still writing the poem, and he cannot get it the way he wants it. Sometimes he can't see it anymore. He is under the poem, and it is threatening to crush him. He wants the bullshit out of it; don't you see? B.K. hopes to purify MS. of all B.S. and climb said hill, and he cannot get over it. There are days when he feels he is pushing the poem toward the top, and he can almost see the other side, but then, like Sisyphus, he cannot get it to roll over the summit.

And so one morning in October, the false Kleinfeld is gently easing a turd from his aged ass into poorly functioning toilet bowl in afore-mentioned rat hole with the window shade slightly raised for viewing traffic below and large warehouse building across the street, where renovations have been underfoot for quite some time, and he sees her again, the woman he has seen often, nearly every day for many months, and has heard tell about, the tall, striding woman with a pair of tits that make his heart stop. There she is again in another coat, a fern-green number with wide sleeves and some kind of built-in scarf that sweeps over her shoulder. Kleinfeld has an idea that the woman has a closet with nothing but coats in it and another for boots, since those changed, too. She is wrapped up daily, he thinks, in the magic of money, which means simply this: You can tell she isn't thinking about the coat or the boots; they just are. The poor wear their prizes – the gleaming new leather shoes, the just-off-the-rack sweater, the expensive gloves – with a stiff self-conscious air that gives them away. No, her mind is on greater things, he says to himself. You can tell by the little V between her eyebrows, a philosophical wrinkle, he believes, not a run-of-the-mill V carved in deep by sick worry about rent money and groceries. Hadn't he spied her once, quite by accident, on the remote F train reading Schelling? God help us, the woman was reading Friedrich von Schelling on the F as calmly as if she were gliding through the *Daily News*. The old Bruno, the speed demon, had looked into Schelling once as an undergraduate and had taken a bad fright, equaled only by his opening up the *Phenomenology of Spirit* by Georg Wilhelm Friedrich Hegel, who also scared the boy witless. This was not some regular dame. No, this was a doll with high tastes, with ideas dancing in her head like fireflies. The lady's hair was a jumble of curls and her eyes were big and wide and dark, and she had a long neck and wide, square shoulders, and that day, that October morning, as she crossed the street below him, just as she had crossed it many times before, he saw something vulnerable and hurt cross her face that came like a breeze and, as it blew, she suddenly looked very young. Her mouth, her brows, her eyes all contributed to the expression, which didn't last long, but it seemed to Kleinfeld's double, sitting there on the pot, boxers around his ankles, that the pain he had seen and she had felt had come and gone with a single grievous thought about someone.

That vision kicked him loose. It kicked loose the kid, the base stealer, the poet of pizzazz, of confidence, and that lost charmer, the original Kleinfeld, returned, at least for a moment, and I (for it was I, the Bruno Kleinfeld of old) wiped my ass hastily but thoroughly, grabbed the jeans and shirt lying in a heap before me, whisked my jacket off the hook near the door with its four locks, checked the pocket for keys, hurtled down the stairway, out the door into the street, and chased the lady like some half-cocked troubadour. I yelled, 'Stop!'

She stopped and turned. She wasn't my Harry yet. Oh no, she was the lady with the coats, who had swiveled on her boot heels to look down at me. She was tall, and the childlike look of vulnerability was nowhere to be seen. Her brows came together disdainfully, and I felt the loser rising up, the miserable faker, but it was too late. I stuck out my hand. 'Bruno Kleinfeld, your neighbor. I wanted to meet you.'

Harry, the stranger, smiled just a little, and took my hand. 'Good to meet you, Mr Kleinfeld,' she said.

I kid you not, the sun came out from behind a cloud at that very moment and lit up the street, and I grabbed the moment, for that is what we must do if we don't want women to pass us by, and I said, 'A fateful luminosity!'

She looked confused. What had I meant? What did she think I had meant? I could see her struggle to understand. She smiled, embarrassed.

'The gods approve!' I blurted.

She examined me silently. I have rarely known anyone who took such a long time between sentences. Finally, she said, 'Of what, Mr Kleinfeld?'

She reminded me of Mrs Curtis, my ninth-grade biology teacher at Horace Mann. Of what, Mr Kleinfeld? This is America. Who says, 'Of what, Mr Kleinfeld?' except high school teachers?

'Of us,' I said, 'of our fortuitous meeting.'

110

'I thought *fortuitous* meant by accident, by chance. It looks to me as if you've chased me down.'

Harry and I agreed on the dialogue up to that point, word for word. The exchange was branded into what would become our mutual brain. We tussled over the next part of the scene. I still swear up and down and across and under and in every direction that I dove right in and asked her to dinner. She swore that we went round and round with the word *fortuitous* and that I had obviously blocked it out because she got the better of me in the etymology department. Latin, *forte* – by chance. The word does not mean 'fortunate.' I know that! I had merely hoped that she had not noticed my wild pursuit of her post-dump (which she knew nothing about until later when I confessed that she had brightened my bowel movements many a day). Harry had a pedantic side, a persnickety grammar-teacher side that sometimes made me nuts. You thought about *fortuitous*, and you thought you said what you thought about it, but you never did. It happens. It happens. That's what I told her, but she didn't believe me.

I'm not sure which Bruno Kleinfeld showed up at the restaurant three nights later. The character who shaved beforehand was the same old louse of useless recriminations. What woman would want the asshole in the mirror who's been writing the same poem for twenty-five years, who teaches two creative writing classes at Long Island University for twelve thousand dollars a year, who does free-lance copyediting and a book review here and there for next to nothing, who's a failure with a capital *F*? Anxiety cramped my lungs, and I puffed shallow breaths while I ironed my good shirt, the one my daughter Cleo had given me for my birthday the March before. On top of that, I'd borrowed the hundred bucks to take Harry out from Louise, the woman down the hall, who had waggled her finger at me and said in her screeching voice, 'This isn't charity, Bruno, you've got to pay me back!' My heart was running a marathon while I stood stock-still, and I had started to sweat in the clean, pressed shirt. The tension was para-lyzing. I stood in front of my door for about five minutes. The force that pushed me through it was loneliness – the bad, restless, anguished, pulver-izing kind of loneliness I felt I couldn't abide anymore.

And then, after the how-do-ye-do and the glances at the stiff paper menu and the ordering and the waiter who tells you his name is Roy or Ramon, in short after all the awkward pleasantry that goes on whenever two strangers embark on that voyage known as going-out-to-dinner, the gods or the angels or the fairies or the movie stars – any one of those unreal heavenly beings we all half believe in when convenient – smiled down on us as we sailed from salads of baby greens into a chicken dish we both ordered, a bit dry, with mushrooms. But while we were ingesting the desiccated fowl, it happened again: The authorized Bruno came roaring back in triumph to charm the Lady of the Coats, who charmed him back because she was funny and smart and oblique, too, making arcane comments even the full-blown genuine Bruno couldn't really penetrate, but which made him awfully curious; and when the lady breathed, her breasts breathed with her, and he had to shut his eyes a couple of times to keep his head on straight.

I think there were diamonds in her ears, and I know there was perfume in the general atmosphere of the table wafting over and up into my nostrils, a scent she said Napoleon, pipsqueak conqueror of Europe, had concocted for one of his wives, Josephine. He had just two, one fewer than me. The arrogant son of a bitch once said, 'I am the revolution.' Well, that evening the revolution of Bruno Kleinfeld had begun, and I knew it had to be carried through or I would live forever as a state divided.

I listened to her. I am not cynical when I say this is the first rule of seduction. There is no seduction without big listening ears. Call me Harry, she said. I called her Harry. I listened to her tell me about her two grown-up kids, one documentary filmmaker, one prose writer, and the grandchild who could do somersaults and had developed unusual passions for Buster Keaton and Peggy Lee, and about her dead husband, who had been half Thai, half English, the son of a diplomat, a man who had been at home everywhere and nowhere. He sounded like a smoothie to me – a lot of money and a lot of angles – the kind of guy who steals into a smoke-filled bar in one of those Hollywood movies from the forties, wearing a white dinner jacket as he scans the room with his foreigner's eyes.

I couldn't really get a handle on Harry, on who she was, that is. She was frank and forthright, but there was hesitation in her, too. She formed her sentences slowly, as if she were thinking about each word. She spoke at some length about Bosch, about how much she loved his demons and 'mutations.' She loved Goya. She called him 'a world apart.' 'He was not afraid to look,' she said, 'even though there are things that should not be seen.' Sometime around the second glass of wine, she lowered her voice as if she were afraid the couple at the next table would overhear her. There had been a little boy, she said, who lived under her bed in her family's apartment on Riverside Drive. 'He breathed fire.' Her exact words. He breathed fire. Harry did not say 'imaginary boy' or 'imaginary friend.' She placed her long hands on the tablecloth, leaned toward me, inhaled and exhaled. 'I wanted to fly, you see, and breathe fire. Those were my dearest wishes, but it was forbidden, or I felt it was forbidden. It has taken me a very long time, a very long time to give myself permission to fly and breathe fire.'

I did not say I hoped she would breathe fire on me, although the hankering to say it was strong.

I made some other crack, and she laughed. She had good teeth, Harry did, nice even white teeth, and a sonorous laugh, a big fat laugh that gave me amnesia, that wiped out years of my life in the rat hole, that made me feel light and free and, as I said to her, unburdened, unburdened because Harriet Burden's laugh lifted LIU and the poem and the chipped linoleum right up and off of me. I don't know why, but my pun on her name made her serious, and her lips quivered. I thought she might break down on the spot with the weepies and water her half-eaten chicken, so I swooped in. I swooped in with Thomas Traherne. Nothing could have been better than my old friend Tom, dead in 1674, an ecstatic versifier if there ever was one, a poet all but lost until 1896 when some anonymous but curious soul discovered a manuscript in a London bookstall. I had memorized Traherne's poem 'Wonder' years earlier. All at once, the third stanza popped into my head, and I read it straight off some sheet of paper inside my skull as the lady of my heart looked at me all atremble:

> Harsh ragged objects were concealed;
> Oppressions, tears, and cries,
> Sins, griefs, complaints, dissensions,
> weeping eyes
> Were hid, and only things revealed
> Which heavenly spirits and the angels prize.
> The state of innocence

And bliss, not trades and poverties,
Did fill my sense.

It was a wonder that we found each other, Harry and I. It's still a wonder. My Harry was a wonder.

She took me home, and when we walked into her gigantic place with the wall of windows that looked over the water, and the long blue sofas, a space that was still raw but not raw, if you see what I mean, fashionably raw, with art on one wall and floor-to-ceiling bookshelves with a couple of thousand volumes along another, and big old rugs on the floor and a shiny kitchen with pots hanging from a ceiling rack, I said to myself, it's paradise, man, pure paradise, no cracks and crumbs and dust mites and roaches, and it's right across the street! Then Harry showed me the studio floor right below. We walked down a flight of stairs. She flicked on some lights, and I noted the long hallway, lined with doors, one after the other, and I heard somebody snoring behind one of them. I didn't ask. It was all going so well I didn't want to screw it up.

Harry opened up double doors on the other side of the hall, turned on more lights to illuminate her workspace. I will not pretend that Harry's art didn't scare me a little. To be honest, that first night it gave me a voodoo feeling. I walked right under a flying cock, as in penis, not rooster, authentic-looking as hell, and there were several bodies in progress, at least five of the former spouse in

116

miniature, and other figures that were life-size with clothes on, lying around like so many corpses. She had massive machines and racks of tools that reminded me of medieval torture instruments, and in the middle of the floor there was a big glass box with mirrors inside it and a couple of human shapes that gave me the willies. Louise had said there were people in the hood who called her 'the Witch,' and I had said, 'Come on. That's just stupid.' But the place had an infernal quality, no doubt about it. I half expected that fire-breathing brat she had told me about at dinner to come flying out of the beams. The elegant Lady of the Coats was making some weird shit, and I confess that when I looked around that massive factory, I felt the minor character creeping up in me again. He was a shrinker, and I shrank.

Harry was so excited, she didn't notice. She smiled and pointed at her creations and talked more fluently than she had all evening, telling me she was working through certain ideas; she wanted to represent ideas in bodies, embodied minds, and play with perceptual expectations. She liked Husserl, another incomprehensible German she probably read on the F train. I read a lot, but philosophy tires me out fast. Give me Wallace Stevens's version of philosophy any day. She wanted me to understand. She wanted me to get it: operational intentionality. So the shrinker just nodded. Yup, Husserl, yup, good. Aha.

Okay, okay, I was intimidated. It's one thing to

be in a restaurant, in neutral territory; it's another to wind up in the woman's warehouse palace and discover an army of ghoulish dolls and body parts, some of which you could plug in and heat, while she chattered on about abstruse books you'd never read. When I left Harry's studio, I had dwindled to the size of Tom Thumb and wasn't quoting anybody. I was ready to run out of there, but Harry put her hand on my arm and said, 'Bruno, you mustn't mind me. I'm wound up because it's so rare that I meet somebody I can really talk to. And now here you are, and I feel kind of dizzy.' That girlish look was in her face again, not sad this time, but happy.

We walked upstairs, and she put on Sam Cooke singing 'You Send Me,' a song with the sweetest, dumbest lyrics and the nicest melody in the world: 'Darling, you send me / I know you send me / Darling, you send me / Honest you do, honest you do.' And Harry grinned at me with her big white teeth, and she sang along and wiggled her hips and her shoulders and did a little soft-shoe. I grew back to my full stature, and once I was all grown again, I lunged. I threw my arms around her waist and buried my head between her beauteous boobs, and we didn't stop there.

I'll censor the juicy business that transpired between us on that first night of the bodies electric when the sparks flew and we breathed lots of red-hot fire. It had been a long time for both of us, such a long time for Harry that when it was all over, and we lay on our backs, spent and listless in her big bed, she started to cry. She didn't make any noise except for a few sniffs. I looked over at her, and I watched the tears stream down the visible side of her face into her ear. She sat up, hugged her knees, and the tears just kept coming, leaking steadily from her ducts until I guess they finally went dry. I know when to shut up. I didn't comment on those tears. I didn't say a word, because I understood all about it. If she hadn't beaten me to it, it might have been me sitting on the bed, raining tears of relief onto those clean, soft white sheets.

MAISIE LORD
(edited transcript)

No one could have been less like my father than Bruno Kleinfeld. When Mother told me she was seeing someone, I was happy for her, but when I first met Bruno, I was surprised. Bruno knows all this, so I'm not going to upset him. My father was immaculate; Bruno is rumpled. My father never swore; Bruno swears all the time. My father liked tennis; Bruno likes baseball. My father floated; Bruno tromps. It's funny because Bruno is a poet, and my father was an art dealer, and the stereotypes are that poets are cloud people and business types are grounded in the nitty-gritty of trade and money. I could go on and on about their differences, but I won't. All I know is that my mother was different with Bruno. She was freer. She told jokes, teased him, pinched his cheeks, and he gave it back to her. They reminded me of Ernie and Bert or Laurel and Hardy, a wisecracking pair of screwballs. They were embarrassing, to be honest, but you'd have to blind and deaf not to see and hear that they were in love with each other.

I think it was seeing my mother with Bruno that

started me thinking about my parents again, about who they actually were, not who I thought they were. My father made mysteries around him. That was his gift, his charisma. He always made you feel that he had a secret in his pocket or a trick up his sleeve. I was his daughter, and I felt it all the time. I saw the way people were drawn to him. Like me, I think they wanted him to smile, which he did, but only now and then. Sometimes I think he held it back on purpose.

For him, art was the enchanted part of life, the part of life in which anything can happen. He especially loved painting, and he was extremely sensitive to forms and color and feeling, but he always said beauty alone wasn't enough. Beauty could be thin and dry and dull. He looked for 'thought and viscera' in the same work, but he knew that wasn't enough to sell it either. In order to sell art, you had to 'create desire,' and 'desire,' he said, 'cannot be satisfied because then it's no longer desire.' The thing that is truly wanted must always be missing. 'Art dealers have to be magicians of hunger.'

My father called himself a 'rootless cosmopolitan' and said that he had learned how to play the part from the very best teachers – his parents. As a child, they had lived in Jakarta and Paris and Rome and Hong Kong and Bangkok. I never met my English grandfather, but my grandmother was an aristocratic Thai lady, somehow related to the royal family (which isn't too hard, since the king always had many wives). After my grandfather died, she settled in Paris in a big apartment in the Sixteenth, with tall windows and high ceilings, and one of those cage elevators that lurches upward after you push the button. I was four or maybe five before I knew that Khun Ya was Father's mother. I knew about my other grandparents because my mother called them Mother and Father, but Khun Ya was not like them at all. For one thing, she always glittered with jewels. For another, she moved slowly and deliberately and spoke with a British accent and had nothing to do with the grandmother I had in New York.

The winter after I turned ten, we were in Paris for the holidays. It was a day before Christmas, and it was raining, I remember that gray Paris rain. Khun Ya said she had something for me and led me to her bedroom. I had never been inside that room; it was a little scary, actually, to find myself in there, with her big carved wooden bed and all her shining private things and the strong smells. She had lots of powders and unguents in glass bowls and bottles. She opened up a box lined with yellow silk and removed a small ring – two golden hands grasping a small ruby – which she gave to me. I didn't hug her as I would have hugged my other grandmother, but I smiled and thanked her. Then she put her hands on my shoulders, turned me to the long mirror, and told me to look. I did. I felt one of her fingers press me near the top of my spine. She took my shoulders, pulled them back, let go, and stepped away from me. I knew she wanted me to hold the pose. 'Now your chin,' she said. 'Bring it up to lengthen your neck. You must learn, Maisie, how to command attention in a room. Your mother cannot teach you.'

I wore the ring, but I never told anyone what Khun Ya had said, and every time I looked down at those tiny gold hands, I felt disloyal to my mother, and I worried about it. Even though I couldn't see exactly why Khun Ya thought standing up straight would command a room's attention, her words of damnation, 'Your mother cannot teach you,' were clear enough. Khun Ya was stepping in because she felt my mother was inadequate. I should have defended Mother, but I didn't, and I felt like a traitor. I was thirteen when Khun Ya died suddenly on the operating table during surgery for her hip, and I didn't feel much except vague amazement, and then I felt bad because I thought I should have been much, much sadder. She was my grandmother, after all. Ethan was sad. I think he cried in his closet. But then, Khun Ya loved Ethan. He commanded her attention all right, whether he was crumpled over or standing ramrod straight. The funeral was in Paris, and there were lots of strangers and flowers and heavy scents from women in stiff black suits with hard rows of glittering buttons.

After she died, my father showed me an album with photographs of his parents and some clippings he had brought from Paris. I saw how beautiful my grandmother had been. 'She held court,' he said. She was quick with languages and spoke French, Italian, English, some Cantonese, and, of course, Thai. But wherever they went, my father said, she would learn just enough to say something charming and win over a guest. 'She was clever but not thorough. What counted was the effect, not the knowledge, *très mondaine*.' And then he said something I never forgot. 'In that way, I am like my mother. But I fell in love with your mother because she is exactly the opposite. She is deep and thorough and cares only about the questions she keeps trying to answer for herself. The world has little use for people like your mother, but her time will come.'

Children desperately want their parents to love each other. At least I did as a child. His words stayed with me as only a few sentences do over the course of a lifetime. A writer, whose name I can't remember now, called these verbal memories 'brain tattoos.' Mostly, we forget what people say, or we remember the gist of it, but I believe I have retained Father's words exactly. I puzzled over them a lot. He had told me that he loved in my mother what he thought he himself lacked, a kind of depth, I guess. Worse, perhaps, he had said that the world didn't have use for people like my mother. It – the world – preferred people like my father and grandmother. And yet, I felt that he thought my mother's way was superior. Most important, I felt that he loved her for it. But then again, if he was so aware of not having it, I couldn't help wondering if he didn't have more of it than he thought he had. 'Khun Ya didn't like Mother, did she?' I asked him. I remember he looked surprised, but then he answered me. He said they came from different worlds. He said that Harriet had unsettled his mother's expectations, and he smiled his smile and said, 'Maisie, Maisie, Maisie.'

I didn't know my father had lovers then. I didn't know until much later. My mother talked openly about it only near the end of her life. There had been both men and women. She wanted to tell me and Ethan that she had known about the affairs, not all the details, but she had known. It had hurt her, but she never once feared she would lose him, 'not once.' In their last years together, there had been no one but her. 'We found each other again, and then he died.'

I remember a set of keys lying on a table in the hallway of our apartment. I remember looking at the foreign keys, and my father scooping them up swiftly, casually, and stuffing them in his pocket.

I remember standing outside my father's study while he was on the telephone. I remember his low voice. I remember the words *our place*.

I know now that it's easier to be disappointed by a spouse than by your parents. It must be because, at least in early childhood, parents are gods. They slowly become human over time, and it's kind of sad, really, when they diminish into plain old mortals. Ethan says that I have a stupid bone that acts up regularly. He thinks I'm stupid about our parents. When he was fourteen, he says, he realized that our *mère* and our *père* – he says that to be clever and remote – were frozen against each other, two icicles. He didn't like to be at home and stayed away a lot. I don't remember it that way. I think it was much more complicated, and I've come to think that my father needed my mother more than she needed him. And I think she knew it.

Three days before my father died, Oscar and I had dinner with my parents. I was pregnant, and we talked about 'the baby' a lot. Mother had been reading studies about infant development, about newborns and their capacities to imitate the facial expressions of adults, for example. I didn't follow all the details she cited, which had to do with systems in our brains, but I remember I was very excited by something she called amodal perception – the different senses are crossed in babies, touch and hearing and sight and maybe smell, too. (I can't tell you how many times I wrote down the names of books my mother gave me and then never read them. Oh well.) She talked more about visual development and cultural-language influences on perception, too, that we learn to see, and that much of that learning becomes unconscious. I sensed there was an urgent reason for her studies. She was trying to figure out why people see what they see.

Making documentary films means, at least in part, choosing how to see something, so I found the conversation compelling. Editing is the most obvious way of manipulating vision. And yet, the camera sometimes sees what you don't – a person in the background, for example, or an object moving in the wind. I like these accidents. My first full-length film, *Esperanza*, was about a woman I befriended on the Lower East Side when I was a film student at NYU. Esperanza had hoarded nearly all the portable objects she had touched every day for thirty years: the Chock Full O' Nuts paper coffee cups, copies of the *Daily News*, magazines, gum wrappers, price tags, receipts, rubber bands, plastic bags from the 99-cent store where she did most of her shopping, piles of clothes, torn towels, and bric-a-brac she had found in the street. Esperanza's apartment consisted of floor-to-ceiling stacks of stuff. At first sight, the crowded apartment appeared to be pure chaos, but Esperanza explained to me that her piles were not random. Her paper cups had their own corner. These crenellated towers of yellowing, disintegrating waxed cardboard stood next to piles of newspapers. The woman had also gathered bits and pieces of twine, ribbon, string, and wire on her journeys around the city and knotted the pieces together into a gigantic hairy, multicolored ball. She told me she just liked to do it. 'It's my way, that's all.'

One evening, however, while I was watching the footage from a day's filming, I found myself scrutinizing a pile of rags beside Esperanza's mattress. I noticed that there were objects carefully tucked in among the fraying bits of colored cloth: rows of pencils, stones, matchbooks, business cards. It was this sighting that led to the 'explanation.' She was keenly aware that the world at large disapproved of her 'lifestyle,' and that there was little room left for her in the apartment, but when I asked her about the objects among the rags, she said that she wanted to 'keep them safe and sound.' The rags were beds for the things. 'Both the beds and the ones that lay down on them,' she told me, 'are nice and comfy.'

It turned out that Esperanza felt for each and every thing she saved, as if the tags and torn sweaters and dishes and postcards and newspapers and toys and rags were imbued with thoughts and feelings. After she saw the film, my mother said that Esperanza appeared to believe in a form of 'panpsychism.' Mother said this meant that mind is a fundamental feature of the universe and exists in everything, from stones to people. She said Spinoza subscribed to this view, and 'it was a perfectly legitimate philosophical position.' Esperanza didn't know anything about Spinoza. I'm aware that my film is a tangent, but I'm talking about it because I think it's important. My mother believed and I believe in really looking hard at things because, after a while, what you see isn't at all what you thought you were seeing just a short time before. Looking at any person or object carefully means that it will become increasingly strange, and you will see more and more. I wanted my film about this lonely woman to break down visual and cultural clichés, to be an intimate portrait, not a piece of leering voyeurism about a woman's horrible accumulations.

My parents first saw *Esperanza* at a screening in 1991. Father was polite, but I think the images of the woman's squalor pained him. He found the subject matter 'difficult.' He also said he was glad celluloid didn't smell. He had a point. Esperanza's apartment stank. My mother loved the film, and although she routinely cheered on my ventures, I knew her enthusiasm was real. My father's reticence hurt me, and I suppose bringing up *Esperanza* again at the dinner amounted to a challenge. I wanted to show him that I had known what I was doing, that I had an aesthetic point of view. Oscar talked about hoarding, anxiety, and obsessive-compulsive disorder, and my father noted with some amusement that two years after he had seen my film, he saw Anselm Kiefer's *Twenty Years of Solitude*, a work that included stacks of books and papers stained with the artist's semen, and he had thought of my film. Kiefer's masturbatory remnants had been mostly met with embarrassment or silence in the art world. Father offered that the woman's piles of junk were no more disturbing than Keifer's 'private ejaculations.'

My parents disagreed about the semen stains. My mother wondered why the personal theme of

129

the work should be shunned, why a man's masturbation, his loneliness and sadness were somehow outside 'art.' She was emphatic. She said you had to make a distinction between what you saw – stains – and its identification as human waste. My father found the stain business self-indulgent and repugnant. Oscar, who is usually pretty phlegmatic, said the work sounded stupid, really stupid. I said I wasn't sure, I hadn't seen the show. This meant that my mother was alone defending semen against two men, who had been producing it regularly over the years. I remember thinking it was fortunate that their emissions had hit the mark at least a couple of times. Mother worked herself up, becoming both more articulate and more irritated. My father's age-old technique was simply to change the subject, which would further infuriate my mother, who would then cry out, 'Why don't you answer me?'

I was twenty-six years old, married and pregnant, and still I found the tension between my parents intolerable. My mother hung on to her passionate defense while my father, embarrassed, glanced around the room and wished she would stop. A thousand times I had witnessed the same scene, and each one of those times, I had felt my own anxiety mount until it felt as if I would break into pieces. Anselm Kiefer's semen wasn't really the issue, of course. After all the years of their marriage, my parents continued to misread each other. My father didn't like conflict in any form, and so, when my mother came out swinging, he ducked. My mother, in turn, interpreted his avoidance as condescension, and it drove her to punch harder. I understood them both. My father could be maddeningly evasive and my mother annoyingly persistent.

Their verbal brawl ended when I yelled, 'Stop it!' My mother apologized by kissing my cheek and neck, and we all recovered pretty quickly from the dried-semen debate, but I did notice that my father's face was drawn and tired, and that the age difference between my parents had begun to show. Mother looked robust and still young, and Father a bit wizened and white. After dinner, he smoked a cigarette as always and then another and another. I had given up nagging him to quit. The smoking Dunhill was part of his body, his posture, two fingers aloft, smoke circling in the vicinity of his face. It was also the only sign that my father was nervous. Nothing else about him was nervous. He didn't jiggle or tap or tic. He was calm and contained always, but he smoked, as they say, like a chimney.

After dinner, we went into the other room for a brandy, which my mother and I did not drink, but Oscar and my father did. My mother was silent then, as she often was, weary, I think, from her heated defense of sperm art and content to listen. There were candles and a vase with peach-colored roses on the low table and some chocolates. I remember these details because it was the last time

I saw my father alive. Every moment during that evening has become magnified by his death. I didn't expect to lose him. I thought he would be a grandfather to my child, and I believed my parents would fight on, would annoy each other for many more years and grow old and crotchety together. Isn't it funny how we just think things will go on as they are?

I can't remember how we strayed onto ghosts and magic, but it wasn't very far from our earlier themes: my Lower East Side panpsychist's collection and an artist's peculiar habit of saving bodily fluids on paper, as if the marks that remained had some mysterious value or power. My mother said that when she was a girl, she used to look at her dolls in the morning to see if they had moved at night. She had half hoped and half feared they would come alive. Then my father brought up Uncle and his spirits. Uncle had worked for my great-grandparents in Chiang Mai, a skinny but muscular old man, covered from his neck to his feet with tattoos that had wrinkled along with his thin brown skin, and whose teeth had turned black from chewing betel nuts. I had heard about Uncle since I was a child. I had seen pictures of my great-grandparents' beautiful old house, which rose up from stilts with its gabled roof and curving eaves, and the spacious grounds Uncle had tended.

My father's eyes narrowed as he told the story. He was ten years old and living with his grandparents in Chiang Mai while his mother and father 'traveled.' He had never known why they left him. Neither of his parents had ever given him a straight answer, but his childhood had always involved traveling and multiple nannies, all of whom had dropped hints about his mother's 'adventures' and given him pitying looks.

My father's big room had a view of the garden and was visited regularly by small gray lizards, and a boy, Arthit, who worked for the family, had slept on a palette at the foot of my father's bed, for company, because Thais never slept in a room alone. My father had followed Uncle around without being able to converse much with him, but as his Thai improved, he began to understand the old animist's stories. Uncle told him about a beautiful girl whose fiancé had drowned in the Mekong River. Distraught with grief, she hanged herself, and after that her spirit haunted a tree. Uncle had seen her, a floating head only – dangling entrails from the neck. He also told my father about a ghost his mother had heard and seen, a fetal ghost that cried out in the forest from the place where his mother had miscarried him, a half-formed little monster that sought revenge for his early end by harassing the living.

One day, Uncle drove my father home to his village north of Chiang Mai. He remembered that when he arrived, children had come running and that they chattered and laughed about his light hair, which reminded them of *phee*, the spirits.

He said that the people he met had been kind

to him, but he had felt like a curiosity, a thing on display, and that, most disturbingly, Uncle had turned into another man. All his obsequious mannerisms, his smiles and bows, vanished. He retired to a corner of his sister's house, poured himself a glass of whiskey, and waved my father away from him. It was still daylight when Uncle's sister took him to a thatched hut on poles near the river. Men drummed and played instruments, and then the women began to dance, slowly, rhythmically. He was told the ghosts were on their shoulders, riding them like horses. A very old woman with a cigar in her mouth was waving her arms over her head and puffing out smoke as her eyes rolled upward into her head, and then she moved in on my father, her mouth open, and blew smoke right into his face. He had the feeling he couldn't breathe, gasped for air, and after that, his memory went to pieces.

All he was certain of, he said, was that, at some point, he came down with a high fever that lasted two days. He remembered screams, rolling around on a floor, choking terror, and what he thought was a whip hitting him or someone else, and then the sun through a windshield, tires jolting over a road, clouds of ochre dust. He must have hallucinated the body of a child burning next to his bed and dark birds streaming through the window. He thought he remembered a man beside him, and lying in a cold bath. On the third day, he came out of it. He was in his own room in Chiang

Mai. An amulet of the Buddha was hanging around his neck, but he had no idea how it had gotten there.

He never saw Uncle again. When he asked his grandmother what had happened to him, she said he had retired. *Mai pen rai*. It doesn't matter. Father wondered if he had been drugged or whether he had simply fallen ill. He had been suspicious, worried that the grown-ups had hidden something from him. He checked his whole body for signs of a beating, but there was nothing. 'It must all have been a fever dream,' he said, 'but it frightened me. I couldn't decide what was real and what wasn't, and no one would tell me.' Then he said, 'Secrets and silences and more secrets and more silences.'

'You never told me,' my mother said in a low voice. Her face was all squashed with sympathy. Watching her, I realized how that same look, when it was directed at me, drove me crazy. Too much empathy is annoying, but I've never understood why. You'd think it would be nice. Maybe it's just mothers. You don't want them that close. At the same time, I wondered if Khun Ya had ever looked at my father like that. I had the sudden thought that she might have preferred him as a grown-up.

What had he meant about more secrets and more silences? Why didn't I ask him? Have I thought about this more since I've known about my father's erotic life? He had secrets, too, secrets and silences.

135

Why had he never told my mother that story? I sometimes wonder if I really knew him at all.

Oscar thinks my parents were both odd people. Once he used the word *decadent* to describe my father and *neurotic* for my mother. He thinks Ethan is very smart but 'falls into the high autistic spectrum somewhere,' and he likes to call me the 'fairly well-adjusted' one. He married the 'fairly well-adjusted' one in the family. He thinks Father's money protected us from the 'real world,' that if we had been poor, our lives would have been very different. He is right about that. Still, he knows that *real* is not my favorite word. It's all real – wealth, poverty, livers, hearts, thoughts, and art. (My mother used to say: Beware of naïve realism. Who knows what real is?) And then Oscar always looks at me and says, 'Do my job for a day, and you'll see what I mean.' He does his therapy with kids in foster care in a miserable little office in Brooklyn with a broken desk. The kids he sees are not adjusted at all, because their lives have been bollixed up, often from the very beginning. I fell in love with Oscar because he is devoted to his work, and he has lots of stories to tell. Oscar doesn't care much about art. Maybe that's my rebellion. I married a man who doesn't give a hoot about paintings or sculptures and goes to the movies to be entertained.

SWEET AUTUMN PINKNEY
(edited transcript)

I haven't seen Anton for years, and I don't know where he is or what he's up to now, but we had a moment of true balance when I was an assistant working on *History of Art*. My friend Bunny told me that this book was going to happen, and I thought I ought to tell my story. First, I'd like to say that, whatever other people might think, Anton was definitely not a dumb person. He read books, and he thought about big ideas. When I met him, he had this book called *Anti-Octopus* by two French guys that had something to do with how Freud was wrong, and it was very intellectual. But Anton was a spiritual person mostly, striving for the higher consciousness, even though he had just started making baby steps, if you know what I mean. I was at the beginning of my journey then, too. I was a follower of Peter Deunov, or Beinsa Douno, the Bulgarian master, and I was starting my work with chakras and healing crystals, and Anton and I talked a lot about cosmic rhythms, energy, and astrological signs. Not everybody puts all these knowledges together, but I think they're all related in the big universal picture of things.

Anton was kind of doubtful in the beginning, but then I think he realized that I had it – the power to read auras. I've always had it since I was a little kid. I just didn't know what it was. Sometimes the energy fields, sounds, and colors I felt coming from people were so strong, I almost fell over, or I felt blockages in them, like they were in me, and I'd feel sick, kind of dizzy and faint. Training and meditation helped me to get my gift under control and use it for healing others. I have a practice now, and people from all over the greater Northeast come to me for help.

Right from the first day, I felt there was something out of whack in the studio – weird energy. There were already two assistants on the job, Edgar and Steve. The sculpture part was done, so we were helping put all the pictures on the sleeping woman. (I liked her better naked and plain, to tell the truth.) Anton had his plans – great big sheets with all kinds of writing and notes on them. He seemed anxious and was always leaning over and squinting at them. His aura was bluish, yellow, greenish, but some stoppage, too. I could see and feel how tense he was, so I put my hand on his arm and just left it there. In less than a minute, his aura got more and more blue; it was pretty cool. Anton smiled at me, and I remember thinking he might have died as a little child in a previous life – there was something so young in him, so unformed but full of spiritual potential. Probably the second or third day, Harry came in.

I felt her like a red scream. I had to back up. I mean, I wasn't even close to her, and I had to step backwards because she was emitting so much all at once, racing, multicolored, and churning, but too much red and orange. Harry had a lot of power, passion, and ambition, but there was some black in her, something blacked out, blotted out, and I saw that, too. It can be a sign of night – grief, some kind of harshness. Anton wilted a little when he saw her, but I could feel their closeness. It was hard for him to match her energy, but he tried. It might have been good if I had just put my hands on her, too, but I didn't dare. Too much voltage. I didn't really get the Venus sculpture, what its greater meaning was supposed to be, but I caught the vibrations between Anton and Harry like sparks.

I hardly remember Steve now except that his aura was a very light pink, and he had long hair. Edgar radiated green most of the time, a pulsing yellow-green, partly because he had his music on all the time in his ears, so he wasn't responding to much around him, just the techno beats in his ears, while his chin bobbed up and down, up and down, like one of those carnival dolls with its head on springs. I can't remember when the story boxes came in, but I saw Edgar look at them, and he seemed excited for the first time and turned a little orange. Anton said he had done them at home because they were small. They arrived all finished. I don't think I would be upset now, but I was at a much earlier phase of my enlightenment then, and the boxes made me kind of low. They were sad – the little children in there, the man's arm, the lady who couldn't fit in her own bathroom, the writing. They made me think of gloomy colors and whining sounds, and I said to myself, I've got to let Anton know, and that's how the story between us really got started.

I worked late one night and told him about the boxes, and he looked upset. When I put my hands on his, he said, 'What is it about you? You calm me down. I didn't used to be like this. Things used to be cool.' Then he waved his hands around the studio and said, 'Things were good, but now it's changing.' I told him it was something about Harry, and he looked a little funny, but he didn't tell me anything then, so I gave him a back rub, and he told me I was magic, and I said no, just psychic. I had learned some Tantric sexual practices from a teacher, Rami Elderbeer, who was dispensing his personal wisdom in NYC at the time, techniques that lead to higher minglings and ecstatic oneness, the dissolution of our bodily differences into the higher states where there are no boundaries. Rami knew I had the power from the start – he saw the indigo in me – an indigo child, he said.

Some teachers counsel against all sex. Beinsa Douno did not believe in sex: 'Love,' he wrote, 'without falling in love' and 'Stay at a distance so as not to see each other's flaws. While people stay away from each other they only see their positive sides. When they get too close they cannot stand each other.' This is pretty good practical advice most of the time, but not all masters agree on sex. One of the prophet's students, Omraam Mikhael Aivanhov, taught that the sexual act, Tantric, could be a path to higher wisdom. I taught Anton how to breathe and slow down and lose ego. Anton and I blissed out, really blissed out totally for a couple of weeks on this yoga mat in the studio. He got much happier; his aura went really blue with some touches of purple, and when he worked on the art, he was smooth and humming on a low note that just kept going. We talked a lot about the grasping self and how to transcend it, and we went on a ten-day wheat bulgur fast to tone up our nervous systems. The prophet prescribed it. You begin just after the full moon and end just before the new moon. All you eat for meals is the wheat with hot water, walnuts, and some honey if you want to sweeten it up. You can eat apples between meals. After you've had the apple, you must turn to it and say, 'Thank you, apple.' Then you bury the core and the seeds. We had to go outside to do it. We'd pick up the cigarette butts and cans and condoms and clear a nice spot for the little burial. While you're fasting, you're not supposed to think any negative thoughts, so when we were picking up the garbage, I'd concentrate on stars and clover and clear pools. It really works. In fact, it's pretty amazing. No sex during the fast.

We felt really pure and white and clean as fresh snow and new moons.

During the fast, Anton said that he could feel how nothing matters personally, how the personal is the wrong path. Mine and yours are equal. Mine and yours are the same. We don't really own anything in this life, and nobody owns art either. Making art shouldn't be about names or about selling; it should lead you somewhere better on your path to higher understanding. He said Harry knew that, that she didn't want anything for herself. She was unselfish. She's like another mother to me, he said. I didn't tell Anton that Harry was awfully red for a totally unselfish person, because I knew he had to find his own way. On the last day of the fast, we ate potato soup, and Anton started crying, not loud crying or anything, just tears dripping down his face. I remember that really well. I was in the lotus position, and he was in half lotus, face to face, and his shirt was unbuttoned so I could see the little curls on his chest, just a few light brown hairs, almost like an angel's, really. The archangel Raphael is the angel for healing and wholeness and unity, so I called to the angel in my mind. Sadness, Anton, I said, is because of self-grasping. We are all looking for things to satisfy this sense of want that we feel would satisfy our needs. We all know that the next want will appear, and we will chase that and so on, but when we recognize it and put it on the shelf, we can move beyond it. And he felt better, and then after the soup, we went higher than ever before into the non-self upper reaches of Tantric truths.

We all saw it happening. Steve, Edgar, and I knew when that lady walked in, the one from the gallery – I can't remember her name – but it doesn't matter; she had a greedy face with money in it and lots of blockage in her, and Anton was very nervous. He could hardly breathe. And then it was bad to worse. Harry came in a lot, and she had this certain look. I mean, her eyes could do damage to you. She was quiet, really quiet, and stiff like she had just gotten extra starch at the dry cleaners. Anton was calling her Fairy Godmother, and then Edgar started doing it. I'm Cinderella. That's what Anton said, but he was so keyed up, it wasn't funny, if you know what I mean. The bad karma was building and building. So noisy! I had to meditate a lot. I had to cleanse my aura all the time. Auras are like magnets. They pick up all kinds of crap, and mine was getting mucky from the vibrations and negative energies. I was running my hands through my hair all the time and washing up, washing up. Sometimes I'd go outside and walk and let the wind from the water blow over me and clean me. I liked to walk by the water taxis and peek into the warehouse buildings and check out the Statue of Liberty from different angles. She looks so strong and centered. She always makes me feel better.

Then the show happened. Anton's mom and dad

came, which seemed really nice to me, and they were really nice people, too. I talked to them for a while, and his dad said, 'We're very proud.' But Anton freaked. He was drinking red wine and getting drunk. His spleen chakra was completely shut down. Harry wasn't there. He kept saying, 'I thought she'd come even though she said she wouldn't. I can't believe she isn't here.' He was slurring words. He bumped against the wall. The crowd of people were screeching and laughing; their sounds made me really sore in my arms and legs, as if they were beating on me with their energy – bang, bang, bang. I had to run out of there. So I went home and lit a candle and meditated for a while, and then I called my mom, and we talked for about an hour. She was in a good place then, and her voice was like a healing song.

But it didn't really get better with Anton. People were coming to talk to him in the studio. Tell us this and that, and oh, Anton, what were you thinking when you made the big nude? And blah, blah, blah, but the rest of us weren't really doing anything there. Still, we were paid. Harry and Anton whispered together, lots of low conspiracy-type whispering. Harry read the reviews to all of us, laughing really loud, her eyes all glassy with tears. She thought it was so funny, but that didn't make any sense. I could feel her from way across the room. Meanwhile, Anton got slicker and slicker. He talked different, walked different. His vibes went completely weird. He bought these really expensive shiny boots and some Japanese shirts, and he seemed to think they were going to protect him from what was going on with his inner being, which was shriveling up like a hard little peanut. I did a lot of breathing, a lot of aura cleaning, and I hoped things would change.

One day Harry came in while I was there. She seemed sunken, low-energy. I asked her if she was okay, and she looked at me for the first time. I mean actually looked at me. She smiled, and her face wrinkled up, and I realized she was pretty old. I told her I had used abalone shells on people to clear their hearts of sorrow, that they were very good for soothing and working through emotions, that they might help her. She patted my shoulder but didn't say anything. She talked to Anton for a while. Then they were fighting, and he shouted at her, 'This is my life!' Before she left, she came over and talked to me. She asked me about where I grew up and how I got my name. I told her my mother named me after a clematis because her mom, my grandma Lucy, loved the vine more than any other flowers. She seemed to like that. I told her my father didn't want me. He wouldn't even sign the birth certificate. It's funny, I don't tell everybody that. It depends on their aura, you know, but that day, even though Harry was kind of low on the energy scale, it was okay. I told her about my sensing things most people can't see or feel. Before she left, she said something I still remember. I can't say it like she did, but she told me that people have different names for the same things, depending on what interests they have, but the words can also change how we see the things. I don't really get the last part, but I can understand why Anton thought Harry was wise. That day she seemed wise, and when she touched my hand, I felt warm sweet energies coming from her.

Anton sold everything in the show. Steve and Edgar left, and I didn't see Harry after that. Anton took a lot of pictures of me for an artwork he said he wanted to do, but he never did. Every once in a while, he'd bring in a box with a strange little story in it. He'd sell those, too. But I never saw him working on one of them. He used to lie on the floor and stare at the ceiling a lot. He read some books, and he talked about Goya, the Spanish artist from the sixteenth century or something, and he showed me these terrible war pictures he made, and I said, 'Anton, those won't help you.' He talked about Harry. He said everything had gone wrong with her. He felt like a reflection in one of those fun-house mirrors. 'You don't get it,' he said. 'She's me. I'm her.' He was really imbalanced by now, and I tried garnets on him, but he got worse, and I explained that there were toxins in him, and sometimes there can be a healing crisis, and everything comes out all at once like an explosion. Then he started yelling, 'You fucking little bitch with your stones and your energies and your auras. It's garbage. It's all garbage, don't you know that?' I remember every word because what he said was so hurtful, even though I tried to center myself and understand that he was hurting more than I was; honestly, he was. He knocked over some tools, and he kicked the wall. He made a dent in it, and a piece of plaster shaped kind of like Louisiana fell on the floor.

I stood really still and closed my eyes. It reminded me of Mom and Denny when they fought. Denny would yell and hit the wall, and Mom would cry. They broke lots of things in the house. Once, Mom's nose was bleeding all over her shirt and the floor. Denny left us when I was ten, and I was glad. Then Alex came, and he was much more mellow. He would take me to the beach on Sundays, but that was when I was eleven, and then he left, too. I used to press myself against the wall in my room and close my eyes and try not to hear them – Mom and Denny, I mean. After a while, it really worked. I trained myself not to be there, and I wasn't. Sometimes I could see everything from very far away. I was out of myself, looking down. It's pretty easy to do after a while.

Never mind. Never mind. Never mind, Sweet Autumn, I used to say. Float out and over the room and stay very, very quiet. After a while, Denny would leave – he would run out to his car yelling and drive away. I'd go to Mom and pet her head, and she'd cry and hold me for a while. I had to take care of her and not let the sounds she made go inside me, and then we'd sleep in my bed together. You see, when I was a kid, I learned how to wait, so I waited for Anton. He said he was sorry. He said he didn't mean it. Then he told me about Harry and that it was mostly really Harry's work, and he was just the name on it. I think I kind of knew all along even though I didn't have the words for it. Anton said he tried to give Harry the money from selling *History of Art*, to make a clean break, but she wouldn't take it, and so Anton said he was going to travel around the world to look for answers to the big questions.

I explained that it wasn't good for me to be around him anymore. It was throwing me back and forth and bothering me, and I just didn't need all the bad karma. So I walked out and didn't come back.

About a year later, I was visiting my friend Emily in Red Hook, and I was walking around down by the water, chanting to myself and feeling the wind blow on me, so purifying, and I went by Anton's old studio, but there was another name on the door. That's how energies work, you know, because just two days later, I got a postcard. I saved it.

Dear Sweet Autumn,

I'm in Venice sitting in a café. This morning I went to the art museum here and saw some pictures by Giovanni Bellini. There was a Madonna that looked so much like you, I had to write. She had your eyes, the kind of eyes

*that go straight into you. I'm okay. Thinking
of trying California as a place to live. I hope
you are well.*

Love, Anton

I didn't see Harry again until she was very sick.
That's when she gave me the name Clematis, but
she liked to call me Clem and Clemmy, too, and
sometimes Clammy, to tease me. She'd say,
'Clammy, my dear, isn't it strange how things come
around?' And I'd say, 'No, Harry, the wheel keeps
turning.' It does. The wheel keeps turning, round
and round.

ANTON TISH

(interview from Tutti Fruity, *'Just Checking In,' April 24, 1999)*

Anton Tish's first show, *The History of Western Art*, made a splash at the Clark Gallery in New York City when it opened in September, announcing an edgy new voice in the art world. A twenty-four-year-old bad-boy geek with a mystical underside, he got people talking. Toby Bruner met up with the artist in his studio in Red Hook, Brooklyn, to get the dope on where he's going from here.

TB: So what does a guy do after he's become such a hot property?

AT: I'm thinking about photography. You know, a post-Warhol take on the icon. But not with icons, if you see what I mean, just regular people. There's another twist to it that I'm still working on. I got interested in Mannerism. Bronzino is my favorite, and I keep thinking there's something in his work that will help me frame my new direction.

TB: Cool. And the story boxes? I heard you can't make them fast enough.

AT: I might make a couple more. I don't know. The show was kind of a one-time thing, I guess. Cleared my system of the past, you know, and now I'm ready for a new conceptual path. It could take some time figuring it out, but that's okay with me. Once the concept is really tight in my mind, I can move forward. I've been doing a lot of reading, thinking . . .

TB: What are you reading, man?

AT: This book called *Quantum Enigma: Physics Encounters Consciousness*. It's really wild, man. I mean, these guys say that the way you look at something creates what you're seeing. That's quantum, and it links up to the brain and consciousness. They call it spooky, and it is. It weirds me out, actually. I keep looking at things and wondering what I'm seeing.

TB: Heavy stuff, but then, that's what got you where you are, right?

AT: Yeah, that's what they tell me.

Stay tuned for the next spooky installment of Anton Tish, art world phenom gone quantum!

RACHEL BRIEFMAN
(written statement)

O n Sunday, February 28, 1999, Harry told
me about Anton Tish. I remember the date
because, after she left, I recorded the
details of our exchange in my journal. I have edited
those invaluable notes here.

Although it was chilly and gray outside, I had put
on a fire, and we were warm. Harry was wrapped
up in a dramatic hand-knit purple sweater and had
removed her shoes so she could rest her feet on the
sofa cushions. Ray had left the city to give a paper
at a conference in Washington, and the two of us
were alone with Otto, our Yorkie, who was such a
nervous little beast the vet had put him on Prozac,
a drug that had absolutely no effect as far as we
could tell but gave us the comfortable feeling that
he was being 'treated.' Otto rudely and repeatedly
sniffed Harry's crotch as we sat in the living room,
which made Harry joke that Otto, who had been
named after Otto Rank, was merely doing further
research on his 'pet subject, birth trauma.'

Before that afternoon, I knew nothing about the
show at the Clark Gallery or its success. Although
I regularly take in museum shows, I do not follow

contemporary art closely, and a great many battles are fought and banners raised in that insular world without my knowledge. Harry, however, had come armed with reviews and photographs, so I was able to see her illustrated woman, as well as the boxes that were, as she said, the 'real' work, the ones that counted.

Once I had understood exactly what Harry had done, I wondered aloud what good it did to give credit to someone who didn't deserve it. Why? Harry stubbornly insisted that the deceptive game was being played for a reason. It wasn't merely a sleight-of-hand trick; the magic had to unfold slowly and eventually be turned into a fable that could be told and retold in the name of a higher purpose. At some as-yet-undisclosed moment, she would stride forth out of the shadows to expose and humiliate 'them all.'

Their humiliation did not strike me as a higher purpose, and I told her so, but she countered that it was just a small, if inevitable, part of the plan. Harry had long talked about *them*. *They* had persecuted or ignored her for years, but someday *they* would regret it. After her parents and then Felix died, this monolith of adversarial forces seemed to grow rather than diminish. An enemy with a masculine, not a feminine face, it swatted the likes of Harry away like a mosquito. She had fantasized about her revenge for years, and now it had come – sort of. What did it mean that an amorphous *they* had celebrated her work when it arrived in a *twenty-*

four-year-old body with a cock, to borrow Harry's words? What were the enthusiasts actually seeing, I asked, her work or just Anton, the portrait of the artist as a young hunk? How many people really looked at art? And if they did, could they see anything in it? How did people actually judge it? Since my interests ran more in the literary direction, I mentioned to Harry that Beckett's *Murphy* had been rejected forty-three times and pointed to the many stories of literary journalists typing up manuscripts of celebrated novels, sending them off to publishers, and receiving standard rejection letters (or worse) in return. Without the aura of greatness, without the imprimatur of high culture, hipness, or celebrity, what remained? What was taste? Had there ever been a work of art that wasn't laden with the expectations and prejudices of the viewer or reader or listener, however learned and refined?

Harry and I agreed there had never been such a thing. She said that her idea was not just to expose those who fell into her trap but to investigate the complex dynamics of perception itself, how we all create what we see, in order to force people to examine their own modes of looking, and to dismantle their smug assumptions.

After this foray into the ambiguities of vision, Harry fell silent as she often did, her large eyes focused on her inward narrations. I nudged her to tell me what she was thinking about, and she began another disquisition. We are all mirrors and echo chambers of one another. What actually happens between people? In schizophrenia people lose their boundaries. Why? Because I knew Harry well, I understood that this was not a digression but a circling device to home in on a more personal confession. Finally, I said, 'What is it you are really trying to tell me, Harry?'

After another minute or so of not speaking, Harry leaned toward me, put her hand on my arm, and confessed that during their adventure Anton had gone a little crazy. In the beginning, it had been fun, she said, a grand joke the two of them were going to perpetrate on shallow, preening art world types who could make or break reputations, the pompous asses who knew so much about so little. Harry and Anton had worked everything out between them. She had set him up in a studio, had offered him the proceeds from any sales, and had given him a crash course in Western art, an idiosyncratic survey of what really mattered since the Greeks, according to Harriet Burden. In Harry's class, Duccio di Buoninsegna, the Siennese master, gets more space than Michelangelo, and the perfection of Raphael is relegated to a footnote. This was fine with Anton, of course, who knew next to nothing to begin with. As they worked on the Venus, Anton started calling Harry at all hours to ask questions about the work: Why is the graffiti on her elbow again? Tell me about David and the French Revolution again. Which one is Emil Nolde again? Before long, she said, her answers and comments became his. No one owns language. Do we remember the sources of our own ideas, our own words? They have to come from somewhere, don't they? Anton read books and essays Harry gave him, watched films she recommended, and eagerly digested her opinions.

Although he had been sick with anxiety before the show and nearly fell apart at the opening, he had calmed down after its success. He had felt (as so many of us do) not only massaged by the compliments of his admirers, but that he richly deserved their praise, whether he had actually made the works or not. His majesty, the baby, that infant who believes he is the center of the world, still lives somewhere in all of us. Harry began to notice small alterations in Anton's diction when he talked about the project, especially his use of pronouns. He said *we* and *us* and *our* repeatedly. He began to remember insights as his that weren't his. Anton, she said, became half convinced that her art belonged to him. He knew I had done it and he didn't know at the same time. He said to me, 'I'm your mirror.'

Harry admitted that she had encouraged the idea that she and he were true collaborators. She had elevated his status to lure him into the ruse. As her pseudonym, Anton had played a vital role in the theater she had staged for a single viewer: herself. After all, the gallerygoers were not privy to the power behind the scenes. Anton was the performer. But was Anton playing Harry – or was Harry playing Anton? She said that without him there could have been no big Venus, that the hapless young man had kick-started the idea – shockingly ignorant novice makes sophisticated jokes about art history. But then, who actually believes himself to be shockingly ignorant? Least of all, the shockingly ignorant. And the boy had learned a lot during his tutelage with Harry. I couldn't help but think that their story was an interesting reconfiguration of the Pygmalion myth with the sexes reversed. Anton was Harry's creation, one made, to some degree anyway, out of her disenchantment with the world of men and its intractable biases against women. In the Greek myth, Pygmalion grows so disappointed with the opposite sex that he lavishes his love on his perfect sculpture, the ivory statue Galatea, who is granted life only at the very end of the story. Harry's pretty boy had the misfortune to be made of bone and muscle and tissue from the start.

Once the show's glory faded and the journalists had vanished, poor Anton began to fray. He wanted to return to making his own art, but what had seemed vital and alive to him before had turned flat and dull. Everything he touched shriveled in his hands. He meditated and he fasted and he read, but none of it did any good. He had once believed in himself, and now he didn't. It was all Harry's fault.

She told me that the last time she saw him, he buzzed her door at two in the morning, and when she opened it, he staggered inside, drunk and angry. His life as an artist was over, he declared, and it made him sick. 'You have to talk to me!' he yelled at her. 'You have to talk to me.' It was then that Harry had the strange sensation that she was

157

listening to herself howling at Felix. Hadn't she said to him many times, 'You have to talk to me!'?

The two did their talking at Harry's kitchen table after she made him drink three glasses of water. The boy had been teary and red-faced at first, but then he turned cold.

Harry's position was that Anton had known what the deal was; that she hadn't fooled or cheated him; that together they had experimented with a hypothesis about the importance of the artist's persona in relation to the work shown, and that they had succeeded. Anton had been well paid and had gained a foothold in the art world, should he choose to continue to make art.

Anton agreed that he had known what the plan was from the beginning, that he, too, had been interested in the idea, but he couldn't have been expected to understand what it would mean for him suddenly to find himself sought after, even 'kind of famous.' He had posed for an advertisement for sneakers with several other up-and-coming young artists. He had been interviewed by *Bomb* and *Black Book*, had been approached for comments on other shows. He had been invited to countless parties, had slept with girls who wouldn't have looked at him before. And, he told Harry, he was good at it.

'Good at what?' she had burst out. 'Sleeping with girls? What are you talking about?'

'All of it,' he had yelled at her. 'The whole thing. They wanted me. Do you think they would have wanted you? Isn't this what it's all about? Without me, none of this would have happened.'

Harry winced as she reported the conversation to me. Anton was right, she said. He wanted to hurt me with the truth, and he did. And he went on and on, she said, telling her that the art would have had little effect without him, that his image was what counted, a young, with-it kid who made a lot of references to this and that. 'They didn't know what I was talking about!' he had yelled at her. It had been so easy, dropping the names of works of art he had learned from Harry, but the journalists didn't care. And, he had continued, the irony was that the only artist that really mattered in all this was Andy Warhol, who understood everything about celebrity fascination all along. 'And Warhol was the one artist I really knew something about before you came along. It's funny, really, really funny. Don't you get it? All your learning, all your esoteric crap; it's worth nothing out there, less than nothing!'

'That's what he said to me, Rachel. I was sitting there, fat and old in my bathrobe, looking at him, and it made sense. Even drunk and in the middle of the night, he looked good. I had picked him, after all. It wasn't that he was beautiful exactly, but he had an *élan*; he embodied an idea.'

Anton had essentially told Harry the story she had told herself all along, but rather than feel vindicated, she had felt hurt and confused. 'What do you want, then? You have everything, don't you? Why come here demanding to talk to me?'

But Anton, it seemed, did not have everything he wanted. He was miserable. He couldn't work anymore. He had been en route to a grand discovery before he met Harry. He had felt its importance. He had been rich with ideas, fantasies, and thoughts. He had been all set to make his post-Warholian works. He had just needed a bit of time, and he would have burst through into his own solo stardom.

Harry looked at me and rubbed her chin. 'I asked him why he didn't just do it, then.' He couldn't do it because she had gotten in the way; her ideas had intruded upon his. He didn't recognize himself anymore. Who was he? He saw her when he looked in the mirror. He had tried to give her the money from the sales, hadn't he? But now he understood that he was the one who had 'made her.' He had contributed hugely to 'the whole thing.' Celebrity is not what you do; it's being seen. It's making the scene. He had more than earned his commission because he was the boy who had 'sold the goods,' but 'somewhere along the road,' Anton said, he had lost his 'purity.'

His use of the word *purity* had sent Harry into convulsive laughter. Apparently, she had repeated it over and over. She told me Anton had been modest about his own gifts when she first met him. He had talked about commercial art to pay the bills while he worked on his own 'projects.' She had never heard him talk about either stardom or purity.

Harry looked very sad when she told me this. 'I created a monster.'

But sitting with Anton in her kitchen, she had been angry, furious. She told him he had completely rewritten the past, that he seemed to have forgotten that she had made the artworks, that the boxes had come out of her body, out of years of work and thought. She had felt like slapping him. This kid, this infant, who had been asking her questions for a year, whom she had mentored and paid for, this child had turned into a smug, deluded, pompous creep.

And then Harry cried on my shoulder. I held her for a while and asked her what she was going to do. She said the experiment hadn't worked correctly because she wasn't sure what had happened. Maybe nobody had cared about her boxes. Maybe the boxes had sold just because Anton Tish had supposedly made them. It was too early to claim the work as hers. The ads, the hype, Anton's face were smoke screens. She would have to wait. She would have to try again. She had another idea. I told Harry that she should think twice before she repeated her experiment. The psychological toll was too great. Whether Anton was right or wrong was less important than the fact that both he and she had suffered over the project. I also ventured that Harry's problem might be that she had trouble owning her work, that perhaps she felt she didn't deserve acclaim. She told me sharply not to 'psychoanalyze her' and then, instantly regretful, begged me to forgive her.

When I asked how the evening with Anton had ended, she said that although he had clung persistently to the idea that he had been vital to their 'success,' he had sulkily admitted that she had transformed his thinking about art. He had no choice but to take time off and plot his next move. He would take the money because he deserved it, and he would travel for a while, see the world, think, and read.

And then a mischievous smile replaced Harry's formerly anguished expression. Anton, she said, had adopted a high Romantic mode for his farewell, one that required her to leap up from the sofa and demonstrate.

'I will never see you again!'

(Sentence accompanied by Harry enacting sweeping arm gesture from stage melodrama circa 1895, not at all plausible in young man a hundred years later, but I smiled anyway.)

'I am going away, far away, to the Himalayas, to the Sahara, to Paris, to Timbuktu, but first to Queens to get my stuff out of storage.'

(Back of Harry's right hand moves onto her forehead as she tilts her head upward, eyelids fluttering. She sighs loudly. Lets her hand fall, turns to me, opens her arms.)

'I will rediscover my lost purity, my authenticity.'

(Harry rushes around my living room, lifting up cushions and paging through a magazine in eager search. Bursts into laughter.)

'I hope you didn't laugh at him then,' I said to her, and she answered that she had let him have his moment of cinema or whatever it had been.

When they said goodbye, they had both behaved well. I learned later that Anton did not instantly depart for the Himalayas, but stayed around for several months before he disappeared.

But then Harry returned to her fury. She had been so angry at Anton, she said, she could have punched him silly or burned him to a crisp with a single breath.

This was a reference to Bodley, Harry's imaginary fire-breathing friend, whom I had known about for years.

She was silent for a while, and then she launched into a hesitant preamble: 'I don't know if I should tell you. No, I can tell you. Maybe I shouldn't. I will. There's something in me, Rachel, something I don't understand. I felt it when I wanted to kill Anton. I'm not kidding. I hated him when he was sitting there in my apartment. I was afraid of myself. What is that? It's old, Rachel. It's like a memory in me, but it's not. I feel it, and it's been coming up. With Dr F., I mean. It's something horrible inside me.'

I thought of Harry's vomiting. The body can have ideas, too, can use metaphors.

And then, with her hands gripping my wrists, she said that more and more she was haunted by a feeling that there was a hidden story somewhere inside her, something she couldn't articulate because she didn't know what it was, didn't know whether it was real or imagined. 'It scares me to pieces, Rachel. It's fear alone, cold, frozen fear with no image, no pictures, no words. This is how people create false memories, out of fears and wishes, ugly dreamlike thoughts that infect them like a virus.'

Harry's face was white.

I talked about fantasy then, which lies at the heart of my work with patients, but the inner world and the outer world can be difficult to separate, and the place where they conjoin or divide has been a blurry business in psychoanalysis from the beginning. We invent them, I said to Harry, the people we love and hate. We project our feelings onto other people, but there is always a dynamic that creates those inventions. The fantasies are made between people, and the ideas about those people live inside us.

'Yes,' she said, 'and even after they die, they are still there. I am made of the dead.'

I had never heard anyone say it just that way: I am made of the dead.

Over ten years later, I can still see Harry in my living room performing her Anton skit, the parodic gesticulations of her protégé-pseudonym front. Time has thickened it, given it additional meaning because of the events that followed, especially her relationship with Rune. And now, as I recall her gestures in my living room and her grinning face, I feel haunted. Her melodramatic movements do not belong to the youthful hero who bids his lover (or mother) goodbye before he leaves for an adventure. They are the mincingly feminine gestures of the heroine, that creature who starred in countless plays and silent films, the golden-haired darling of heaving breast and rosebud lips, defending herself against the dastardly mustachioed villain who threatens her virtue. That day in my apartment Harry played Anton as a girl, which was in itself a form of revenge.

She projected onto him her vulnerable girl-self, the child that, I suspect, had been roaring back in her work with Adam Fertig. She had said to me that she felt only fear – without pictures or words. But she had already created figures and images from that emotion in her boxes. There is no doubt that Anton was Harry's pawn. She had wanted an empty male vessel to fill with art, but Anton was not hollow. He was a person, and he was the one who had lived the adulation, who had been feted and touted, not Harry. He had come to her and claimed his rights as an agile performer, another kind of artist, to be sure, but an artist nevertheless. And I think Harry envied and despised him for his deftness. She had been naïve. She had imagined she could borrow the husk of a man for her revenge, but human beings aren't disguises. If Anton had found himself caught in the net of Harry's fantasies, she, in turn, had discovered that her protégé had his own dreams.

All thoughts of revenge are born of the pain of helplessness. *I suffer* becomes *You will suffer*. And let us not lie: Vengeance is invigorating. It focuses and enlivens us, and it quashes grief because it turns the emotion outward. In grief we go to pieces. In revenge we come together as a single pointed weapon aimed at a target. However destructive in the long run, it serves a useful purpose for a time.

I told Harry a story that afternoon because it seemed somehow relevant. I once had a patient who had been brutally assaulted when she was eleven years old. The man attacked her while she was walking home from a friend's house on the Upper West Side. It was not a mugging; he leapt at her with a knife, sliced her neck open, and left her bleeding on the sidewalk. She nearly died. My patient reported that she had had no revenge feelings against the perpetrator. But years later, when a boyfriend left her, she couldn't stop fantasizing about her ex-lover. She manufactured car and skiing accidents, terrible falls, illnesses, and sudden explosions, all of which he survived, but disfigured and paralyzed. In this maimed state, he would inevitably come to recognize that she was the great love of his life, that without her nothing he did had any meaning. After a while, images of his broken and bloody body would intrude on her thoughts suddenly and without warning. She had bouts of depersonalization, during which she would leave cruel messages on the man's answering machine: *I hope you get run over on your way home from work*. She frightened herself. We spent session after session unpacking the meanings of the compulsive fantasies.

All Harry said was, 'She must have had a scar.'

Yes, I told her, I had seen my patient's scar: a clean, terrible line that had become a fold in the skin of her neck.

That night I dreamed I was in a long, empty

corridor, and I saw Harry hunched over on the floor. I walked toward her and noticed a thin, deep cut in her neck. I began to worry that her head would fall off, and I gripped her neck to keep her head on. At my feet lay a piece of scrap lumber with a few nails sticking out of it. I must have let go of Harry, because I picked it up. A pair of tiny green eyes blinked and a red mouth began to move quickly, as if it were trying to speak to me. I heard nothing but was overcome by a feeling of pity. The sun from the window shone straight into my eyes, blinding me, and then I woke up.

There are many ways to untangle and interpret the bizarre condensations and displacements of dreams. My patient's scar returned in Harry's sliced neck. I must have been afraid one of us would 'lose her head.' Of course, the dream is more about me than about Harry, although the half-alive piece of wood might have been an image of Harry's work, which expressed deep parts of herself that were difficult to articulate in other ways. I'm not sure. Almost every day I sit with people, and I listen to them. Sometimes, with particular patients, I worry that I don't really hear them. They are all trying to make sense of their stories, after all, just as Harry was; Harry, who had told me she believed there was something 'terrible' hidden inside her.

PHINEAS Q. ELDRIDGE
(written statement)

Oscar Wilde once said, 'Man is least himself when he talks in his own person. Give him a mask, and he will tell you the truth.' I played Harriet Burden's mask briefly, and I do not regret it for a second. From behind my near-sighted, mulatto, queer self she was able to tell a truth. In the gay world, disguise has a long history, which has never been simple, so when Harry asked me to beard for her, it felt as if I were merely tying an extra knot in a very old rope. I am a performer, and I know that my face onstage can often be more intimate and more honest than the one I wear in the wings. But I have also had two identities offstage. In 1995, I slithered out of my first persona, the one I was born with, to become my second self: Phineas Q. Eldridge. The person who preceded P.Q.E., John Whittier, was a good boy, well behaved if a little dreamy, kind to animals, girls, and poor people (in that order), easily frightened, and, to use my mother's word, 'delicate.' I had my first seizure when I was four years old and my last one when I was thirteen. The doctors said I 'outgrew' them. They belonged to my earlier, shorter, prepubescent body, the one we all shed, along with small jackets and pants and shirts and shoes that once fit it perfectly. The tremors came mostly at night, and not often, but the odors I sometimes smelled and the crawling sensations I felt and the tinglings and face-twitching and the drools and the blanks and the bed-wetting every night for years surely shaped my sentimental education.

When I think back on that four-eyed, interracial, epileptic kid dancing the tango with his little sister, Letty, in the recreation room of a split-level, solidly middle-class house outside Richmond, Virginia, I don't find it at all surprising that he took to God even before his mama was reborn. At school I was a pariah, who had never lived down the full-body seizure that took place beside the slide on the playground in the third grade, but at church I shone, a pious little angel with a sacred affliction. Hadn't St Paul, father of Christianity itself, fallen down on the road to Damascus in a fit just like the ones I sometimes had? Harry was fascinated by the delicate, skinny, freckle-faced John with his black mother and white father who read a lot of books, watched movies on TV, and made up his own world called Baaltamar, a name plucked from the Bible (Judges), but which, in its first incarnation, looked like a Hollywood stage lot. In Baaltamar, overdressed villains with supernatural powers tangled with one angelic hero, my alter ego, Levolor (named after the window blind company because Levolor has such a pleasing lilt). I spent a lot of time in that magical country, just as Harry had spent a lot of time in her own head with an imaginary companion and a busload of anxieties. She, however, grew up godless.

It was painful to feel God looking in on me every minute, judging my secret thoughts and rambunctious longings as I lay in my bed dreaming I was Levolor, who had taken up singing and dancing and lived in a big pink movie mansion with ten servants. Fans came by the hundreds of thousands to watch me wail out songs and shake my tail feathers and do slides, stomps, and brushes. I used to close my eyes and listen to the crowd thunder its adoration, and then, because it was a selfish, unholy fantasy, I would shift its direction, turning Levolor into a Jesus character who walked around Tinsel Town laying hands on the sick, raising the dead, and magically multiplying crackers and soup for tragically poor people in tattered clothes and shoes with holes in their bottoms. This fantasy, too, had its problems because it wasn't right to feel too good about being good, and I knew I felt awfully good about my goodness.

Mama's religion has cooled down considerably, and she's way too soft a person ever to have been a self-righteous holy roller, but there was a time when she went at her worship with a lot of zeal. My parents separated when I was three and Letty was one. We had a daddy on weekends. My earliest memories are of sitting on his shoulders and looking way down at the grass, a rabbit named Buster who lived in a cage in Daddy's backyard, the shiny silver watch he let me wear high up on my arm, and pancakes sitting on a blue plate that looked different from Mama's. I remember that his house smelled funny, and I used to dread he'd pick up the football and suggest a little back-and-forth. When the ball came flying toward my head, I'd duck before I knew what I was doing. The hard, whirring ball frightened me. Later, I trained myself to remain upright and worked hard to catch that damned thing and run like mad. I used to pray to God to help me succeed in my efforts to please my father, to become the coordinated, hearty, real boy he wanted. No doubt I was a disappointment to him. I was not made in his image, but I also think I scared him a little or maybe the epilepsy scared him or the idea that something might happen to me when Mama wasn't around. He never scolded or harangued me about my athletic shortcomings. I just felt he would have liked a different kind of boy. And yet, when Letty and I spent the night, he used to come into the room, sit beside me, and stare at me while I pretended to sleep. He must have known I was awake, but he never let on that he knew, and all he did was sit there and watch.

Then one day in the spring after I turned eight, my father had a brain aneurysm. The balloon burst, and he died on his sofa alone. He was thirty-one years old. Even though Mama didn't want him anymore for a husband, his death seemed to paralyze her for a while until the Pentecostal religion of her youth stepped in to take over the blank spot Daddy had created. We changed churches.

They dunked Mama in the baptism pool, and after that she was filled with the Holy Spirit. 'And they were all filled with the Holy Ghost, and began to speak with other tongues, as the Spirit gave them utterance.' Acts, Chapter 2, Verse 4. I know that for outsiders such doings fall into the remote regions of crackpot religiosity, but I loved the hymns and the 'Amens' and 'You tell 'em, brothers and sisters' during the preaching, and the tongues and the interpretations and the testimonies. Letty and I liked to play church at home because we could bounce and skip and rush around like wild animals hollering out nonsense. All I can say is that the people who were suddenly hit by the Holy Ghost and fell to their knees or collapsed onto the floor and began to speak weren't fakers, although I did wonder about Sister Eleanor at times, who often seemed overly uplifted, and the language that ran out of her sounded vaguely like pig Latin.

I prayed harder and harder and wondered why God had done it, taken my father, and why my mother had sent him away before he died, and whether his sadness had something to do with the bubble in his brain, because he had seemed sad, especially when he sat by my bed – a heavy gloom moved from him to me and settled in my chest like guilt. Mama used the word *incompatible*. They hadn't fit together somehow. After my father's death, Baaltamar became more elaborate, more violent, and more secret. Slavery emerged as a theme. Levolor led armies against Prince Hadar to free the slaves, who were a combination of black Americans and the Israelites, and I began to draw up battle plans in an imaginary geography. When I close my eyes, I can still see Lake Ashtarot and the river Jeshmoth and a mountain range I named Mizlah. After a time, the populace of Baaltamar discovered sex and went at with biblical abandon. Hadar's followers often stripped naked and danced to wild music to tantalize Levolor, who had a lot of fun looking on while he nobly resisted their advances. It was inevitable that my hero would give in to temptation, to the sweet jerks and hard rubs under the blanket with a washcloth and the God guilt and the wet wonder and the poetry of it all.

I think it was my stories of Baaltamar that seduced Harry. The imaginary world disappeared about the same time as my seizures, as did the all-seeing God of the Hebrews, but I have kept a tender feeling for people who speak in tongues and for Mama, who never turned away from me, despite the fact that I wandered into a secular wilderness and never returned to the fold. When I arrived at the lodge, Harry was tending to her own characters, a group of stuffed figures – cold, coolish, warm, and hot. I became fond of her 'metamorphs' (as Harry called them), even though

173

a good number of them were injured or deformed. I take that back. I liked the hurt metamorphs most, the ones with missing legs and arms, with braces and slings, humps, or rashes painted on them. They did not look real, but they felt more human than a lot of humans I know, and Harry was gentle with her homemade critters. Sometimes she'd make them talk for little Aven, who was just four at the time and used to visit 'Gran' on weekends and leave wet spots all over the art from her kisses.

My route to the Red Hook lodge was circuitous. After college, I journeyed to New York City along with legions of fellow aspirants to become a thespian and ended up as a waiter. 'Hi, I'm John Whittier. I'll be your waitperson this evening.' That was the era of broken plates, rude customers, auditions, callbacks, rejections, more rejections, and a few measly parts for a freckle-faced, light-skinned black man who can do any and all accents on request. Auditions are one thing. Auditioning for parts in plays and movies that are so badly written, so poorly conceived, they give you indigestion is another. I decided to write my own material and became a performance artist, Phineas Q. Eldridge, an impoverished one, I'm afraid. I had been dumped by my beau Julius and had fallen from the semisplendor of a Chelsea apartment to my friend Dieter's couch (a kind of a gutter, as it turned out, with gum wrappers, toothpicks, dust fuzz, and nickels between the cushions).

It was Ethan Lord who came my rescue. My act

at the Pink Lagoon had been featured in the *Neo-Situationist Bugle*, probably the most obscure publication in all of New York City, but Ethan and his friend Lenny cultivated performances like mine for reasons that only a few people in university graduate departments understand. They did not approve of capitalism. This was well before the 2008 smash-up, and shopping was still the national pastime. Of course, the two subversives didn't appreciate the joys of a brand-new toaster or the feel of a cashmere scarf or what a dab of extremely expensive cologne can do for you *psychologically*. They were strict, strictly secondhand, thrift-store, vintage boys. It was a matter of principle but also of perversity, one that comes more easily to rich people than to the rest of us. Ethan had a trust fund. Lennie did not, but I gathered that his parents sent him monthly checks.

Despite the fact that the boys were straight, they were advocates of 'queer theory,' which was not only for or about homosexuals but could be applied to all manner of persons and things. The point was to 'bend the categories.' I was all for that, of course, and they were an earnest, touching pair. Lenny reminded me of an anarchist from the thirties with his round wire-rims, and Ethan, with his large eyes and dark curly hair, seemed to be hiding a sense of humor somewhere, although I wasn't sure where. When I first met him, he spoke to me about how my act 'embodied disruptions of normativity.' They were disruptions lifted directly

175

from my own life. I played versions of my parents, whom I called Hester and Lester, and I played Letty as Hetty, when she was a wild tot and as her grown-up, serious engineer self who doesn't approve of the fact that I robbed our family story for the theater, and I played my old-soul, epileptic, little-boy self and Sister Eleanor in the grip of her tongues, but always with comic distance, and I did it in costume, cut in half, black and white, man and woman – but the boys were right: By the end of the show all the neat distinctions between one thing and another had gone queer.

Ethan wanted me to meet his mother: waif saver of the universe. I came preapproved because I was technically homeless and because the *Bugle* had turned H/Lester into a 'theoretical construct,' and this had impressed the rag's nine readers, one of whom was Harry herself. A few days before I met Ms Burden for the first time, there had been an uproar at the Red Hook lodge. One of Harry's waifs, named Linda Lee, whose 'art' involved cutting her body and taking photographs of the damage, overcut herself in the hallway of the resident artists' wing and was rushed to Methodist Hospital, where she was patched up, shipped to a psychiatric ward for a week, and then sent home to her mother in Montclair. Apparently, Harry had not understood that the girl's artistic impulses involved real blood. Ethan might have had his head in cumulus formations, but, as he put it, his mother's 'charitable impulses had to be curbed before disaster struck twice.' He also told me that 'one insane person was enough in the place' – a reference to the Barometer, whom I came to know and tolerate.

In short, that is how I assumed the role of master of ceremonies at the Red Hook lodge. Harry had not been paying attention. I told her that she couldn't take in any piece of trash that came begging at the door. This wasn't a crib for impoverished tourists, nutcases, slatterns, and junkies, was it? We needed bona fide artistic types who would stay awhile and do some chores. The Barometer was already dug in, and Harry was stuck on the man, whom she believed to be harmless, which he was, mostly, except that he did not wash. It was Maisie who convinced him that a weekly immersion in the tub with a bar of soap was the price he had to pay for his living quarters. Maisie was a sort of specialist in insane people, and she went on to make a film about him called *Body Weather*, which won a prize at a film festival. I also discovered that the Medeco key to the front door had been copied by a cabal of lost boys and girls who came and went in the night. I changed the lock.

I took over the excommunicated Linda Lee's spaces and, after posting a sign that read NO ROOMS AVAILABLE, I started the informal application process for artists in need. I decided there was space for three to live and work in the building besides Harry, and since the Barometer and I were already

177

there, we had room for one more resident. We settled on Eve, a flamboyant character born and raised in Idaho, twenty-five years old and a seamstress of force. She moved in with her Singer and sewed up a circus of artworks that Harry and I both thought were adorable. Eve didn't stay long. Ulysses, a sculptor in the minimalist tradition, followed, and then came Delia, who worked exclusively in old-shoe instal lations (my favourite. I created the minimal rules and regulations – no littering on-site; excessive noise after eleven p.m. strictly forbidden; love objects welcome but absolutely no sexual business transacted on site (not a problem anymore, but as a prohibition it gave us some chuckles); presence required once every two months to show and discuss finished work or work in progress. We hired a weekly cleaning team to roar through the two floors of the building, divvied up some domestic jobs, and the lodge was civilized.

But you want to know how it happened, the story between Harry and me. Well, it didn't happen fast. It crawled up on us. We rented movies on Sunday afternoons, mostly oldies Harry had never seen: Busby Berkeley extravaganzas for their kaleidoscope visuals – *Footlight Parade*, *Gold Diggers*, *Forty-second Street*; some Rogers and Astaire; and the old films for Negro audiences only: *Cabin in the Sky* and *Look-Out Sister*, and *Harlem Is Heaven* with the Jangler – Bojangles, 'Everything's Copacetic,' the 'Dark Cloud of Joy,' born Luther-in-Richmond-Virginia-Robinson, who danced up on his toes, precise rhythms, perfect tones – and *Stormy Weather* with Robinson again, some faux version of his life with Fats Waller, Cab Calloway, Lena Horne, and the oh-my-god-I-can't-believe-how-well-they-can-dance Nicholas Brothers. I started tap lessons at four and could impress Harry with some shuffle-ball changes and skating moves, but I never had the real stuff. Lester does a little soft shoe in my show, and it always goes over pretty well. Harry called the Sunday movie our 'cozy time,' and she liked to put on what she called 'soft clothes' or 'nearly pajamas' for the occasion and make popcorn. Then we'd sprawl and laze in front of the TV. We were not always alone. Other members of the lodge joined us from time to time. Bruno, Eve, or the Barometer, who wandered in and out or brought his sketchpad to the sofa and drew.

Exactly when our project was hatched I can't remember, but one Saturday I visited Harry's studio and noticed she had painted SUFFOCATION in huge letters on the wall. 'I'm thinking about it,' she said, 'as a theme.' Then she changed the subject, or so I thought at the time. I now believe it was the same subject, not a transition, because it was a story about her father. She told me about her first show in New York, when she was in her early thirties. Her parents came to the opening. Her mother was sweet and proud and full of congratulations. Her father was silent, but then right before he left, he said to her, 'It doesn't resemble much else that's out there, does it?'

I asked her what he had meant. She said she didn't really know. I asked her how she answered back, and she said, 'I didn't say anything.'

He shut her up.

The man wasn't some unsophisticated boob; he knew art. He had a hankering for Frank Stella, she told me. I said to Harry: 'That's pretty cold, don't you think? I mean, it's a cold thing to say to your own daughter.'

'That's what Doctor F. says.'

I told her a medical degree wasn't needed to see cold as cold.

Harry looked as if she might cry.

I pretended to be sorry, but I wasn't.

Harry told me lots of stories about the man, and my opinion on the matter is that her dad, when he was among the living, had a problem with both who Harry was and with what she did. Being and Doing – the big ones. Harry's work was warm: I don't mean electrically heated – I mean it was passionate and sexed-up and scary. Her father was a tight-ass who liked neat, closed systems: the world in a jar. What was he going to make of her stuff? He wouldn't have liked it whoever had done it. Still, I didn't blame Harry for trying. Hadn't I spent my whole goddamned life making up stories about my own heroic father, loving and hating him? And when Daryl came along courting Mama with his big smiles and his shiny shoes, hadn't I wished he would just vanish or drop dead on the spot?

We started our collaboration because Harry wanted a phallic front. I told her she should think twice about taking on a swishy black man, but Harry was undeterred by my status as a member of not one but two minorities. She wanted scenes of suffocation, she said, metaphorical ones, not pillows over a face, but a theater of rooms the spectator had to enter, and she wanted me to help her build it. Hadn't I lived my life mostly as a nancy boy? Hadn't I changed my name in 1995 to celebrate my second self? Hadn't I known what it felt like to be smothered before that, Pentecostal tongues or no tongues? Didn't we live in a country that is perverted by racism? Wasn't I a black man, even though I wasn't much darker than Harry? People still called me 'black,' didn't they? What did skin tone have to do with it? Her mother was Jewish, so she was Jewish. She knew something about anti-Semitism. The Protestant set of her grandparents had been sick with that particular strain of flu. And what about sexism? How many years had women had the vote? Not even a hundred years! Didn't I play a man and a woman, a white man and a black woman in one body? (Harry swooned for Hester and Lester, especially Hester, the whinnying, haranguing spouse of the not-nearly-so-gabby Lester.) Didn't we understand each other? Weren't we alike in many ways? (Harry's identification with me might sound outrageous to some people, but it was sincere.) She didn't truck much with conventional ways of dividing up the world – black/white, male/female, gay/straight, abnormal/normal – none of these boundaries convinced her. These were impositions, defining categories that failed to recognize the muddle that is us, us human beings. 'Reductionism!' She used to shout this every now and then. Her son took after her. Neither of them liked what they saw out there in the big world – received ideas were for peons and huckleberries – and yet, there was tension between them – *bristling* is the word. Maisie was the peacemaker, the sweetie pie waving a white flag.

Back to *The Suffocation Rooms*: I'm proud of what I gave them, my own twists and turns, but it was Harry's work. It was her idea that the viewer should shrink each time he or she opened a door and entered a new room. The rooms were nearly identical, the same grim-looking table and two chairs with vinyl seats, the same breakfast dishes laid out on the table, the same wallpaper made of Harry's and my own handwriting and some doodles (I had free rein here to put in all my secret messages), and the same two metamorphs in each room. At the beginning of the journey, the furniture fit your median-size adult – we decided on five-seven – but with each consecutive room, the table and chairs, the cups and plates and bowls and spoons, the writing on the wallpaper grew that much larger, so that by the time you hit the seventh room, the scale of the furniture had turned you into a toddler. The soft, stuffed metamorphs grew, too, and they got progressively hotter. The seventh room felt like a Finnish sauna. After a discussion we decided that the single divided window in every room should be a mirror – more claustrophobic that way.

And then there was 'the box.' Unlike all the other objects in the rooms, the box did not grow; it stayed the same size. Harry found a beaten-up wooden trunk with a lid and a lock and had six more made for her by some fabricator in Brooklyn. She was finicky as hell about it and sent one of them back five times before she was satisfied with the 'distressing.'

I was the bright boy behind the color changes. I thought each room's palette and its two characters should get a bit darker – moving from creamy white to a dusky caramel. And we decided to age the rooms. Each one should look a little older and worn than the one before, with furniture a bit more dilapidated, so we orchestrated stains, and scratched and ripped the wallpaper until by the last room you find yourself in a soiled, dingy, fraying kitchen parlor. Time had to get to the creatures, too, so Harry wrinkled up their foreheads, sagged their jaws, and pinched their necks.

We had a high time as wrecking crew. I recall the routine with affection. 'Hand me the knife, P., old pal,' she would say. I would bow to her politely and produce the weapon. She would bow back to me and then impale the vinyl seat of one of the big chairs. I would congratulate her, 'Well done, H., my buddy bud.' And she would say, 'Your turn. A touch of dirt, P., chum of mine, should do the trick.' And I'd smear a wall or table with some mud we had prepared. Harry and I were co-stars in our own early talkie, a comedy team, P. and H. We had fun with pH, the sign of our togetherness and camaraderie.

pH: measure of acidity or alkalinity of a solution. We liked to say we leaned toward the acid. $pH = -\log [H+]$: the logarithmic measure of hydrogen ion concentration as defined by the Danish biochemist Søren Sørensen. Many log jokes flew, including that it was short for what we produced: logorreah. We were the two halves of the Ph in PhD: *philosophiae* and *D* as in *Daddy*, and as in *dead*. We made up other initialisms on the spot: *prurient hiccoughs* – let your imagination run wild – *peeping harlot*, *potted harridan*, *puckish hard-on*, *peevish huckster*, et cetera, et cetera, et cetera. Sometimes we worked in costume, as two men, as two women, as a man and a woman, or reversed. The fat poet took a picture of the two of us in drag, but I don't think he liked it. He liked his lady friend as his lady friend. Bruno has a macho streak. Nevertheless, Harry and I made the perfect drag couple. Big Harry and little ol' me.

One day, while we were working on the rooms, she put down the screwdriver she was holding and looked at me with her serious face. 'You know, P.,

184

my dear,' she said, 'I like playing with you. I feel as if I've found the real playmate I wanted all those years ago when I was a kid, not imaginary, but real. I didn't really have anybody until Rachel came along. You're like the friend I dreamed of back then come to life.'

It's not my way to be sticky, so I batted her off with a josh and a jest, and she laughed. But alone in bed, I remembered her words, and I remembered Devereaux Lewis, his hand on my head and his knee in my back, pushing my face in the dirt, moaning *faggot, pansy, fluff*. And Letty, with her big, tearful eyes, staring at me afterward. I should have smashed his head in, but I was too noble and too fearful. And then I saw myself lying in my bed jerking off to those dream boys in my head, and the God guilt, and the loneliness. Harry had been another one, not a homo, just a lonely kid. She had liked her mother and I still liked mine – conflicts notwithstanding. At least she had known her father. Mine was a fantasy man, a row of facts I shuffled around like cards. White boy orphaned at ten; ward of the state; made good, studied accounting in college; fell for Mama, ambitious nursing student, married, divorced, died.

The box had to open, open very slowly, a little more in each room. We discovered later that the bulk of our visitors didn't even notice the change until about the fourth room. Harry knew there had to be a body in there, a being trying to get out. The 'emergence' had humor, but it was dark humor.

We called the being 'it' and 'the demon' and 'the hungry child.' Harry drew and drew, trying to find its face, its body, its look. The metamorphs were big, goofy-looking, lumpy things, who sat at their tables in all seven rooms with only minor changes in their positions, but the little one, according to Harry, had to come from 'another plane of existence.' Wax. She decided on beeswax. She was inspired, she said, by several sources – the bizarre anatomical wax sculptures of La Specola Museum in Florence from the eighteenth century, with its skinned and opened bodies that displayed systems and organs, the *sacro monte* above Varallo with its lifelike figures, and Japanese ghost-scroll images. Because she did not want the person to look like an alien in some 1950s sci-fi film, the model became more and more realistic: skinny, eerily transparent (liver, heart, stomach, and intestines just barely visible), hermaphroditic (small breast buds and not-yet-grown penis), frizzy red human hair. The creature is strangely beautiful, and when you see him/her in the seventh room out of the box, standing on a stool to look out the window, or rather into the mirror, you can't help feeling touched somehow. The really large (by now) metamorphs have finally noticed that the personage is out and have turned their heads to look at it.

What does it mean? That's what they asked me when the rooms were exhibited. It means what you feel, I said, whatever you feel. It means what you think it means. I was cryptic. I put on a mask, not literally, but one of my actor masks, a persona. It was a great role because it mixed me with Harry. I even took on some of her gestures for my gig in the *theatrum mundi*. When Harry waxed philosophical, she fluttered her hands and sometimes curled her right fist and punched the air to give her point zing. With a few borrowed gestures from Harry, a modified accent, less Virginia, and an altogether butchier me, P. Q. Eldridge strode into the art world.

Harry knew whom to schmooze. She knew where to go and where to send me. She introduced me to the right people at 'art' parties, gallery owners and collectors and critics I charmed and chatted with, and I made her connections mine. It isn't a 'nice' world, but then, no world is. I did meet some artists I still see, people who turned into friends; but, all in all, the scene made me think that the Frenchman Honoré de Balzac had it right: the grubby human comedy. Illusion upon illusion upon illusion. It was all names and money, money and names, more money and more names.

I met Oswald Case, now author of the sensational real-life thriller *Martyred for Art*, at several openings, a midget, poor guy, not a true little person, but he topped off at about five-two, I'd say. Full of himself. Bow tie. Every time I met him he told me about Yale, Yale this, and Yale that. And movie stars. Steve Martin. He knew Steve Martin; what an eye he has, so sure. 'He owns a Hopper, did you know that?' *No, I didn't know.* 'The price? Millions.' (I have forgotten how many millions.)

'Yes, my husband and I have been collecting for years now,' a woman in a Chanel suit told me. 'We just bought a Kara Walker.' (The idea here: Tell black artist about another black artist.) 'Her work is soooo powerful, don't you think?' 'Yes,' I said, 'I think so.' 'We're eclectic, you see,' she said, before her head swiveled toward a known person across the room, called to him, 'David, dear! Excuse me, I see a friend, sooo nice talking to you.'

And so it went. I had fun and I had boredom. For Harry, it was more complicated.

It was true they didn't want Harry the artist. I began to see that up close. She was old news, if she had ever been news at all. She was Felix Lord's widow. It all worked against her, but then Harry scared them off. She knew too much, had read too much, was too tall, hated almost everything that was written about art, and she corrected people's errors. Harry told me she never used to set people straight. For years she had sat by, silently listening to people mess up references and dates and artists' names, but by then she had had it. She said she had been released by Dr F., a figure I began to think was an invisible man behind Harry. Harry credited the invisible man with permission. She now permitted herself to say what she had suppressed earlier: 'I think you mean so-and-so,' she would say, and people inevitably

188

gave her that and-who-are-you? glance. Some of them fought back, telling her she was wrong – and then the battle started. Harry had stopped backing down.

But Harriet Burden's status rose, anyway, not as an artist but as a player in the who's-somebody-and-who's-nobody game of New York City. She had hidden from 'all that' since Felix Lord died, had shunned the whosits and whatsits, the dukes and duchesses of moolah, the muckety-mucks with acquired tastes. But now she was back in it, not as Felix Lord's 'hostess by marriage' (Harry's phrase) but on her own. The whosits and whatsits liked Harry as a promoter, liked her as a rich champion of young, talented artists, and as a collector. (No one knew that her first 'discovery,' Anton Tish, had absconded. They guessed he was hard at work on another show.) Harry played the part. She put on her own mask, and once it was on, she got better at the role, more confident. It suited her. In fact, she was more truthful. 'I thought that article was complete rubbish,' she told a woman who had carefully marked her copy of *Art Assembly* with Post-its. And she started buying art, mostly by women. It's brilliant, she said about a canvas by Margaret Bowland, and it's a bargain.

'Hats, Harry,' I said to her one Sunday afternoon at the lodge.

'Hats?'

'That's what you need.' I told her that she should

always make her entrance with a hat. She groaned over this suggestion as too pretentious, too absurd, but then I bought her one, a taupe fedora, and she looked *wunderbar*, as Dieter likes to say, and so H.B.'s signature look was born. She came to like the headwear. 'It covers up my unattractive mind,' she would say; 'all those unpleasant ideas nobody wants to hear me talk about.'

But, you see, Harry was free to comment on her own work as if it belonged to me, and she knew just what to say. She wasn't putting herself forward, after all. She was speaking up for P. Q. Eldridge, that 'highly interesting' performance artist who had branched out into another medium. 'He stages mysterious stories,' she would say, smiling, 'visual elaborations of his work as a performer.' And she could push Ethan. 'You should read the article about Phinny's act in *The Neo-Situationist Bugle* – the cultural construction of race and gender and ambiguity as the ultimate subversion, fascinating.'

As time went on, we made more works, some of them real collaborations. We designed smaller rooms with itsy-bitsy figures and somewhat larger ones. None of them told clear stories. They were all as murky as dreams. I thought up one called *Guns and Cleavage* for a three-by-four-foot room. We used bits and pieces of images from kung fu, blaxploitation, and old Westerns. We added some shots from Japanese pink movies, and Russ Meyer stills to cover the walls, floor, and ceiling. White or black or yellow, tits, ass, and firearms fuel the movies. BANG, BANG, STAB, SLASH, BOOM, CRASH. I cut down the pictures to their essences – six-shooters blazing, automatic weapons cradled like babies in male arms with burgeoning biceps, Elizabeth Taylor's cleavage in *Cleopatra*, but also the built-up boobs or buttocks of starlets. Some of the fragments were cut so small they became abstract. Lying on the floor of this sex-and-violence burlesque are two little brown kids in pajamas with feet, both protectively holding their crotches. (Made me think of me and Letty.)

The Bandage House was another collaboration. We took a small, crooked house with miserable pieces of furniture in it that Harry had built and covered it with torn white gauze, inside and out, but through the material you can see on the walls and floors and the roof discolorations and marks that make you think of bruises, scrapes, wounds, and scars. At first we had some *farblondzhet* little folks inside it, but we took them out. It had to be empty.

Countless cocktail parties and openings later, we landed a show at the Alex Begley Gallery. When *The Suffocation Rooms* were shown, they were read through me – P. Q. Eldridge was exploring his identity in his art. White boys, the Anton Tishes of the world, have no need to explore their identities, of course. What is there to explore? They are the neutral universal entity, the unhyphenated humans. I was pretty much all hyphen.

There was a further reading, however. The show

was mounted the spring after New York was attacked, and the little mutant that crawled out of the box had the haunting look of a damaged survivor or a new being born in the wreckage. It didn't matter that the work had been finished well before 9/11. The increasing heat in the rooms contributed to the interpretation; the last, hot room felt ominous. At the same time, my debut was an insignificant casualty of the falling towers. There were a few articles, mostly good notices, but the show was probably even more marginal than it might have been. By the time the rooms were truly recognized, it was too late for Harry.

But back then, she watched it all. She told me that Anton had called her his fairy godmother, and she was mine, too, I suppose. She stood in the corner wearing a hat and watched the spectacle she had made unfold before her. A white, half-Jewish woman became a black, gay, male artist of some small notice, causing a little stir among sophisticated black and/or gay or both people, but white heterosexual people, too. Without the latter it's back to a ghetto, an art ghetto, but a ghetto nevertheless. I did not give up my job as H/Lester, but I stopped working five days a week and cut down to three. The show's audience had grown because art world types had started to drift in to see the fighting, dancing, dueling duo. It's all a vanity fair.

No one saw it then, but Harry and I recorded our story in full on the wallpaper of *The Suffocation*

Rooms. We mixed in the narrative of P.Q. as Harry's mask with automatic writing, scribbles, doodles, and some palimpsest effects – writing over what we had written – but it's all there. Unread for years. *Phineas Q. Eldridge is really Harriet Burden* was written on the walls in several places. P.Q.E. = H.B. Harry described the phenomenon as 'inattentional blindness.' She read a lot of science papers, but what it meant was simple: People don't see things that are right in front of their eyes unless they pay attention to them. That's how magic works – sleight-of-hand tricks, for example. Harry was ready to tell the world, but nobody was ready for her confession.

One night I heard her crying on Bruno. They were in her bedroom, but her sobs were loud. Then came his hush-hush, it's-okay voice. Bruno didn't like the experiment at all. They had verbal knockdowns over it. But I disagreed. I wasn't an art expert then, and I'm not one now, but I defend our act, if that's what you want to call it. To be really seen, Harry had to be invisible. It's Harry crawling out of that box – thin-skinned, part girl/ part boy little Harriet-Harry. I knew that. It's a self-portrait.

Why some artworks create such a big fuss is a conundrum. First the idea spreads like a cold and then people spend money on it. Mine-is-bigger-than-yours goes a long way among collectors in that world, maybe in every world. I never knew Rune – that one-name-only artist – who agreed to be Harry's third pseudonym. I first saw the art world glamour-puss at the Reim Gallery. I think that's where Harry first ran into him, too, although I've heard several versions of their first meeting, and I could be wrong. I'd read about him on Page Six in the *Post*, knew he had made it big, but the only works I'd seen were the crosses. He churned out one after another. They resembled the Red Cross sign but were multicolored in flat acrylic. A yellow one had sold for a mint because he had made only one. You can say whatever you want about something so simple, build it up or tear it down, but Rune promoted the Christian symbol as pop icon, as another hot commodity on the art market. The congregants back home at Calvary Pentecostal might have cried blasphemy, but it's unlikely they'll ever hear about Rune's paintings. Fame is a relative term.

Rune had *it*. Whatever it is, it's something you can feel in a room, an animal verve, a slink with some sex in it, but it wasn't personal sex. He was not seducing anyone. He was seducing everyone, and there's a big difference. I am a student of personal presentation, and it is wildly important to appear careless if not indifferent to the opinions of other people. Even a hint of desperation is ugly, and we must avoid it at all costs. Misery sucks up energy in the person who feels it and in all those who are forced to look at it, and then we're all stuck in the mud. Desire functions best when it's directed at a beautiful blank – the boys and girls into whom we toss all our pathetic hopes for happiness. In many ways, Rune was a perfect third candidate for Harry. He arrived with ready-made aura, that mysterious quality that infects our eyes so we can't tell what we're looking at anymore. Is the emperor naked or am I a fool? Some hated Rune's work and others loved it, but no one disputed his power to sway. I don't know how Harry talked him into becoming a front. He had all the markers of success, a palace-size apartment on Greenwich Street, a house in the Hamptons, and legions of women running marathons after him. Maybe he was bored. Maybe something happened to him after September 11 that made him want what Harry had – her passion, her seriousness, her capacity for joy. I don't know.

I have a clear memory of Harry and Rune, heads together in the gallery, talking. They were about the same height. I studied him from behind – short blond hair, big shoulders and upper back, narrow hips and a small, hard, slightly flat posterior, long legs in jeans, black boots with heels. And when I moved around to see his face, I noticed he had some wrinkles around his eyes, not so young anymore, but handsome, photogenic. He had a beautiful young woman with him. The two of them looked more like movie stars than movie stars look when you actually see them. She had that slick shine to her that comes from knowing everybody's looking at you all the time, the pose held for a camera that isn't there.

What had they talked about? In the cab on the

way back to the lodge, Harry said their big subject had been Bill Wechsler. Harry loved Wechsler's work. She counted him as an influence, although he was born after her. He had died suddenly a few months earlier. I remember she held my hand in the taxi and kissed it several times in a fit of sudden affection, saying, 'Dear, dear Phinny.' Then, after we got home, we lounged about with a cognac, getting tipsy. Harry confided she found Rune's crosses boring, but she liked some of his earlier works, the plastic-surgery screens, which were genuinely creepy. Maybe she'd buy one – a good investment. If it didn't hold up, she could always turn around and sell it to some hungry collector eager for the name.

After bussing me in the taxi, Harry turned prickly, irritable, and sour. She had drunk too much, and I could feel the self-pity mounting as she rolled off the names of women artists suppressed, dismissed, or forgotten. She jumped up from the sofa and stomped back and forth across the room. Artemisia Gentileschi, treated with contempt by posterity, her best work attributed to her father. Judith Leyster, admired in her day, then erased. Her work handed over to Frans Hals. Camille Claudel's reputation swallowed whole by Rodin's. Dora Maar's big mistake: She screwed Picasso, a fact that had obliterated her brilliant Surrealist photographs. Fathers, teachers, and lovers *suffocate* women's reputations. These are three I remember. Harry had an endless supply. 'With women,' Harry said, 'it's always personal, love and muck, whom they fuck.' And a favorite theme of Harry's, women treated like children by paternal critics, who refer to them by their first names: Artemisia, Judith, Camille, Dora.

I crossed my legs, looked askance at Harry, and began to whistle. It was not the first time I had taken this approach. 'I am not the enemy,' I said. 'Remember me, Mr Feminist Phineas Q., your friend and ally, black gay man or gay black man with *slave* ancestors, hence original name, Whittier? You may recall that black people were both feminized and infantilized by racism, dark bodies and dark continents, honey child. Seventy-year-old men were called *boys* by twenty-year-old white *ladies*.'

Harry sat down. Whistling, along with a few caustic verbal darts, usually brought her up short. She gave me that oh-Phinny-I've-gotten-carried-away-and-am-embarrassed-but-still-fiercely-attached-to-my-opinion look. Much later, I looked back at the evening and saw further ironies. If Harry knew that art history had steadily sunk the reputations of women artists by assigning their work to the dad, the husband, or the mentor, then she should have known that borrowing a big name like Rune might sting her in the end. And yet, what Harry took for granted was that she moved as a collector in circles where money and celebrity mingled, white circles with the rare black and brown face. I know because I had been that face.

Rune was smart, and he was gifted, but I doubt

anyone can actually separate talent from reputation when it comes down to it. Celebrity works its own miracle, and after a while it lights up the art. I am curious about the man's death, but I suspect he was one of those people who could never feel enough, and as time went on he had to push himself to further extremes to get any kind of a rush from life. I don't really know what happened between him and Harry. I know she cared about him. I know he fascinated her. But I had fallen for Marcelo and moved away by the time it went wrong. All the gossip, all the lying and posturing billowing up like smoke around the whole story, have made me bilious. There was plenty of pain to go around.

A small plastic-surgery work popped up at the lodge a couple of months later. Most of 'the collection' Felix Lord had accumulated was in storage, but she had Rune's screen mounted on the wall upstairs, and we could all watch the artist's little film: *The New Me*. It began with multiple versions of 'before and after' ads, including the old drawings of a scrawny wimp on the beach transformed into a muscleman. We saw the fat, sagging, lumpy, and drooping metamorphosed into the slender, tight, smooth, and lifted. Rune, however, included 'during' as well – films from facial surgery with blood-soaked gauze, knives slicing cheeks, skin flayed open, as well as flashes from an instructional video in which a row of practicing physicians bent over heads that had been severed from cadavers.

The movie had a music video feel to it but played in silence, with fast cuts, clever edits that juxtaposed gore and loveliness. After about five minutes, the transformations became fantastical, a visual science fiction journey with animated bits of molded, airbrushed, robotic body-beautifuls. Rune himself was all over it in brief stills, close-ups, and long shots, some flattering, some not.

I liked it.

When Ethan saw it, he told to his mother that the work was a side effect of celebrity culture. He called it 'life in the third person,' a phrase I liked. He said that's what people want, to lose their insides and become pure surfaces. He told Harry she had wasted her money. She could have written out a check for the homeless. (We could always give it to the homeless or the environment or disease research.) Harry defended Rune. Ethan called it a pandering piece of shit for the stupid class. He didn't raise his voice, but he argued steadily. He reminded me of my hero Levolor, that pious adolescent crusader, bumping along on his high horse. Ethan's brand of Puritanism had a left-wing coloring, but that didn't soften it any. Harry muttered that it was all right for the two of them to disagree, but her voice had turned husky. She reached out for him with her long fingers, but hesitated when they neared his shoulders. He stepped backward and blurted out, 'Felix would have hated it.'

Harry flinched. Then she closed her eyes, inhaled

loudly through her nose, and her mouth stretched flat and tight in preparation for tears, which did not come. She nodded as she tried to hold her face still. She put her fingers to her mouth and just kept nodding. I wanted to vanish in a puff of purple smoke. Ethan had a paralyzed look about him. Say something, I thought, come on, say something. He was speechless, but he flushed to his ears, and his eyes had lost their focus. Soon after, Ethan left, and Harry sequestered herself in the studio. The scene had made me sad, and I knew I would be on my way before too long. The lodge was transitional, a temporary hideout, one of the strange turns in a strange life.

There is one other story I have to tell. There are times when I've thought to myself, Phinny, you must have dreamed it, but I didn't. One night, I came home from the club. It was about five in the morning, maybe a little later. The night was cold, and before I went inside, I stood by the water and looked up at a skinny little moon with some thin clouds over it. When I walked into the hallway, I immediately knew something was wrong. I heard a retching sound, a cry, then loud cracks and thuds. The acoustics were strange in that building and tracing noises wasn't easy. I checked on the Barometer, but he was in his sleeping bag. Burglars are quiet, I thought. I heard gasps, more choking sounds. They're coming from Harry's studio, I thought. I rushed to the door, opened it, and at the far end of the room, about twenty-five yards away, I saw Harry kneeling on the floor. She had a big kitchen cleaver in her fist and was ripping open one of her metamorphs. I couldn't tell which one. The huge space was dark except for a single light that shone down on her. She didn't hear me, because she groaned each time she thrust the knife into the padded body. There were also broken fragments of wood around her, and I guessed she had torn apart one of her little rooms or boxes.

I closed the door as quietly as I could and tiptoed to my room. I'm sure there are scads of artists over the centuries who have kicked, beaten, and mangled their own works in despair and frustration – it was no crime. Looking at her through the door frightened me, though. I told myself I was a queasy oaf – oh-so-sensitive Phinny. The figure wasn't a person. It was no more than a stuffed doll. It felt no pain. That was all true. The police were not going to come around and make an arrest for metamorph murder. Later, I realized that, despite all that, what scared me had been real. Harry's rage had been real.

AN ALPHABET TOWARD SEVERAL MEANINGS OF ART AND GENERATION

Ethan Lord

1. Artist A generates artwork B. An idea that is part of the body of A becomes a thing that is B. B is not identical to A. B does not even resemble A. What is the relation between A and B?

2. A does not equal B, but B would be impossible without A, therefore B is dependent on A for its existence, while at the same time B is distinct from A. If A vanishes, B does not necessarily disappear. The object B can outlive the body of A.

3. C is the third element. C is the body that observes B. C is not responsible for B and knows that A is B's creator. When C looks at B, C does not view A. A is not present as a body, but as an idea that is part of the body of C. C can use A as a word to describe B. A has become one of the signs to designate B. A

remains A, a body, but A is also a shared verbal tag that belongs to both A and C. B cannot use symbols.

4. What happens when A makes B, but A vanishes as both body and sign from B? Instead of A, D becomes attached to B. C observes B created by A, but the idea of D has replaced A. Has B changed? Yes. B has changed because the idea in the body of C when observing B is now D rather than A. D does not equal A. They are two different bodies, and they are two different symbols. If the bodies of D and A are no longer there, B, the thing that cannot use signs, is not changed. Nevertheless, B's meaning lives only in the body of C, the third element. Without C, B has no significance in itself. C now understands B through the sign D, all that remains of D after D's body no longer exists.

5. D is not the generator of B, but this ceases to matter. A is lost. A's body is gone, and A does not circulate as a collective sign for B. Where is the idea that was in A's body that created B? Is it in B? Can C observe the idea that was once in the body of A in the object B? Can A's idea be found somewhere in B, despite the fact that C does not know A was there and believes in D?

6. B's value is also an idea, an idea that is transformed into a number. After observing the thing, C wants to own B. A number is attached to B, and those numbers are dependent on the name connected to its genesis, which is D. D = $. C buys B because the idea of D enhances C's idea, not about B or D, but about C. B is now a circulating thing, which also inspires ideas about C and D, but which once was an idea inside the body of A, now burned to a fine powder that was put into a box and buried in the ground.

7. There were many ideas that were part of A's body when it was alive, but they did not begin with A. They were part of other bodies – too many others to be listed. They were in other living bodies that A knew, and they were in signs that had been inscribed by living bodies that had stopped living generations before A was born: E, F, G, H, I, J, K, L, M, N, O, P, Q, R, S, T, U, V, W, X, Y, Z. Had A not taken these other ideas into the body that was A, B would not exist. B now circulates as an object known as D's B. A is underground. A is the sign of ABSENCE.

January 15, 2000

Self-examination results in confabulation.

*Confabulation is the falsification of episodic memory in clear consciousness, often in association with amnesia, in other words, paramnesias related as true events.**

* A standard definition of *confabulation* in neurology. Some brain-damaged patients fill gaps in their memories with stories and explanations that are manufactured unconsciously. Burden extends confabulation beyond pathology to the metamorphosing character of memory in general. In Notebook U, Burden writes at length on the myth that memory is fixed. She quotes William James in Chapter 11 of his *Psychology* (1896), 'A permanently existing "idea" which makes its appearance before the footlights of consciousness at periodic intervals is as mythological an entity as the Jack of Spades.' She cites Henri Bergson on memory, calling him 'the enemy of every static division, threshold, and category,' as well as multiple neuroscience papers. 'The demonstration of the vulnerability of memory when it is in an active state reinforces the idea that memories, reorganized as a function of new experiences, undergo a reconsolidation process.' S. J. Sara, 'Retrieval and

But the neurologists are wrong; we all confabulate, brain lesions or not.

I wonder if I am explaining things away now, remembering my life all wrong. I look at Dr F. I try to remember. I can't remember. So much has disappeared from the past or appears altered to me now. Remembering is like dreaming unless it was yesterday. Dreams are memories, too, anyway, hallucinatory memories. And the doctor is himself and others at the same time.

When you don't remember, you repeat.

*But in reality I would not know that I possess a true idea if my memory did not enable me to relate what is now evident with what was evident a moment ago, and through the medium of words, correlate my evidence with that of others, so that the Spinozist conception of the self-evident presupposes that of memory and perception.**

That is all there is – perception and memory. But it's ragged.

*   *   *

Reconsolidation: Toward a Neurobiology of Remembering,' *Neurobiology of Learning and Memory Journal* 7 (2000), 81.
* Maurice Merleau-Ponty, *Phenomenology of Perception*, trans. Colin Smith (London: Routledge & Kegan Paul, 1962), 39.

Why do you always walk with your head down?

Elsie Feingold said this to me on the telephone.

I didn't know I walked with my head down.

Why do you always say you're sorry? I'm sorry this, I'm sorry that. Why do you do that? It's so annoying. You're so annoying. That's why the other kids don't like you, Harriet. I'm telling you this as your friend.

This happened, words very close to these were spoken. Lung constriction. Pain in vicinity of ribs. I remember I had pulled the telephone into my room and am lying on the floor just inside the door. I say nothing. I listen. A litany of crimes – my clothes, my hair. I use too many big words. I am always answering in class, brown-nosing Harriet. As your friend . . .

You must be quiet. Your father is reading. I am so quiet and so good. I hardly breathe.

What are you doing in here, Harriet?

I am smelling the books, Mother.

She is laughing, letting out her high chiming sounds. She leans over and kisses me. Does she kiss me? I see myself as small. Observer memory.

Do I remember this or is it because Mother told me? Her laughter was a balm, always, but this may be her story of little Harriet smelling her father's books, and she laughs when she tells me the story.

I was four. I may have stolen the little tale from her and given it an image, a memory that is mine by proxy. I see the study with its big desk, and I smell the pipe. Why did all philosophy professors smoke pipes? An affectation. His students, too, all young men, smoked pipes, every single one of them. The graduate students all grew beards, and they smoked pipes on the seventh floor of Philosophy Hall. The Analyticals. Frege. The logic is out there.*

Felix is standing in the doorway. He is looking through me again, as if I am not there. The note to Felix the Cat from the couple in Berlin is in my pocket. I have carried it with me for a week.

* Gottlob Frege (1848–1925), German mathematician, logician, and philosopher, who decisively marked modern mathematical logic and early analytical philosophy, in particular Bertrand Russell and Wittgenstein (the *Tractatus*). 'The logic is out there' probably refers to Frege's contention that logic is an objective reality, not created by the human mind. According to Frege, logic deals with a world of ideal, not physical objects, but these ideal objects have as much objectivity as physical things. In Notebook H, Burden charts her reading of Husserl, who was influenced by Frege. Burden writes: 'The mind is inescapable. How can logic be floating in some ideal reality beyond the human body and beyond human intersubjectivity? And yet, ideas move among us, not as physical objects but as utterances and symbols.'

Practicing what to say, learning it by heart, so simple.

Before you leave, I say, I would like to return this to you, a note from friends. It was in your blue suit, the one you wore to the opening last week.

I can see the surprise in his face, can see his embarrassment, not shame. He has become negligent, flippant about it all.

He takes the note and slips it into his pocket.

But you know, he says, it has nothing to do with you, my love. It has nothing to do with my love for you.

I am erased.

Dr F. says, I don't think you understood how angry you were.

No, I did not understand how angry I was.

Last night. This I remember, don't I? Yes, it is clear still, parts are clear enough, although there are peripheries never seen. Too many voices to distinguish any single voice except now and again – a soprano squeal or squawk. The throng in the well-lit white room, the paintings – so little on them – but a few hazy body parts, underpants, garters, bottles of nail polish and perfume. Mildly interesting. The artist smiling. He has a stiff smile, but who can blame him? Long, convoluted essay in the catalogue, quoting that buffoon Virilio.* Phinny has put his arm around my waist. I can feel his hand. I do remember this warm gesture, this little goodness. In that instant, I worry over Bruno's refusal to come with us. Maybe it is Phinny's hand that makes me think of Bruno, my mauling lover. I am back to life under his hands, his rumbling voice, his jokes, but he said, I hate that art world shit. It's worse than the poetry world, and that's pretty bad, but there's no money in poems. Just egos.

Phinny and I: PH. We make an *F* sound together, as in *phuck you*.

Last night again. James Rukeyser has heard that I am building on Felix's collection. He is interested in me now. Oh, yes, I hold a sudden luminous

---

* Paul Virilio (1932–), French cultural theorist, critic, and urbanist, has written extensively on technology. He argues that modern life is gripped by a never-ending acceleration and that speed and light have now displaced space and time. He has often been referred to as an apocalyptic thinker. Burden is obviously unsympathetic to his views. In Notebook X, which she apparently used as a dumping ground for random thoughts, Burden writes, 'The man is nothing short of hysterical, in the *theatrical* sense. He has gained a following among bone-headed, equally hysterical young men by pushing half-truths to their logical but extreme ends. He is the theoretical incarnation of panic.'

210

charm. Felix's wife has Felix's art and Felix's money. Maybe he will lure me into a purchase. Show me the cabbage. That is what he means as he smiles. I am wearing my blue velvet beret. My affectation, which is not a pipe, courtesy of Phinny. James gives me his card. I have a flash memory – the stiff paper in my right hand, my thumb visible over the name. The business card is beige with black type. Miriam Bush joins us. 'I have not seen you in years, Harriet! Why, what are you up to? Someone mentioned you. Who was it now? Are you still making those little houses?' James looks confused: little houses? He does not know that I have ever made art. When Phinny and I get outside I throw the card away. I see it in the wet gutter, its lettering invisible, just a small rectangle vaguely illuminated by the streetlamp as the ice-cold rain falls.

I am ten in the memory. Am I ten? Maybe I am eleven. I cannot feel ten or eleven anymore, really, can I? No. But I am inside this memory; I am inside my body. I have walked from Riverside Drive to Philosophy Hall on a Saturday to surprise Father. Why have I done it? What possesses me? An idle whim? A plan? No, I am just walking in the spring air, and I decide to walk there. The day is sunny after a rain. Sun over puddles. That seems right, and it comes into my head that I am so close to Father's office, and I walk through the doors and climb into the elevator. But I am nervous, yes, some anxiety is attached to this bold move. I have been to his office before, as he dashes in to pick up papers, while I wait with Mother. There is a smell in the gray hall, a dry smell like erasers; it is never noisy, hushed but with a hum, white noises, I guess, and low voices here and there, as if these are the sounds of mental work, of thoughts. I knock. He must say *Come in,* but this I don't really remember. I see him before me at his desk and the window behind him. The light is hazy; the glass is smudged. His head is down. He looks up. 'Harriet, what are you doing here? You should not be here.'

It has nothing to do with you.

'Harriet, you should not be here.' The ten-or-eleven-year-old is flummoxed. I'm sorry. Do I say I'm sorry? I think so. But this is crucial. What is the tone of his voice? Angry? I doubt it. Strict? Puzzled? Perhaps puzzled, but I can't recall this accurately. What I recall is the drawing in of my breath, the pang, the shame. Why shame? This I know. I am deeply ashamed. In the memory he says nothing more. He looks down at the papers in front of him, and I leave. But is this possible? Maybe he escorted me to the door, and in the shifting eddies of recollection, those steps with Father to the door have disappeared. Maybe he patted my shoulder. He did pat my shoulder sometimes.

★   ★   ★

212

And sometimes, too, I heard a hint of musical softness in his voice. I learned to listen for it – a crack in the tone that lifted a vowel into another register, not fully controlled. And something broke for an instant, as if he had seen me, his child, seen and loved.

Mother is lying in bed. I hold her hand and idly look at the protruding veins in it – the palest of greens. I wouldn't have recalled that if I hadn't said to myself, *Her veins through her skin are the palest of greens.* Words consolidate memories. Emotion consolidates memories. Something has happened to Mother after Father's death, and she is telling now, telling her life, telling me that my father did not want the baby. When she told him she was pregnant he did not speak to her for two weeks. I feel the cramp of emotion, but I don't want her to stop. After I was born, I want to know, was it okay then? It took some time, my mother says, before he got used to you. *Your father loved you, of course.*

Hume couldn't find anything to hold on to, no self in the bundle of perceptions that become memories. Imperfect identity.

He did not want me.

But this is nonsense, Harriet, isn't it nonsense? How many men have not wanted their unborn infants? Millions. How many women, for that matter? And how many have come to want them once the little thing has arrived, is out, is real? Millions. And yet, it took some time, she said, and there is the feeling, as if I'd been kicked, as if it had all become clear, as if a door had opened to a truth. And I look into the room, and there is the thing that has been born. There is something wrong with it. Count the toes.

But I would first ask you to note that I do not attribute to Nature beauty, ugliness, order or confusion. It is only with respect to our imagination that things can be said to be beautiful or ugly, well-ordered or confused.*

But imaginations mingle, Professor. Imaginations merge. When I look at you, I see myself in your face, and what I see is deformed or missing.

But nothing happened, did it?

There is no one story, no perfect answer to the problem of H.B. Until about the age of three or four, every one of us is hidden behind amnesia clouds. The feelings come back, but we don't know what they mean.

★　　★　　★

* From a letter dated November 20, 1665, by Baruch [Bendictus] Spinoza (1632–1667) to his friend Henry Oldenburg. Spinoza, *The Letters*, trans. Samuel Shirley (Indianapolis: Hackett, 1995), 192.

Perhaps I wished for something rather than nothing – a smack of passion to make me believe I was really there for him, not missing. And then the blow rises up from imaginary depths. When there is nothing, the phantoms come up to fill the emptiness. It is not true that nothing comes of nothing. There is always something. I stand on the stool and look out at the street. Stand beside me, Bodley. Here, there is room for you, too. I love you, Bodley. You are my best friend. Breathe now, Bodley, breathe fire.

Your order is my wilderness, Father. I cannot walk between the high rows of hedges and find my way out. I am not out of the maze. Stifled. I am trying to breathe, but I cannot. I am hardly breathing.

Your patterns did not make sense to me, Father, or, rather, the sense they made is shallow. Tidy formulations to clean up the mess. I have read your papers, and I am a little sorry now, sorry for a life spent on true and false, however lean and elegant the logic.

The 'specialist' emerges somewhere – his zeal, his seriousness, his fury, his overestimation of the nook in which he sits and spins – his hunched back, every specialist has a hunched back. Every scholarly book also mirrors a soul that has become crooked . . .

* * *

* Friedrich Nietzsche, *The Gay Science*, section 366.

Felix goes to work. Felix comes home. Felix gets on a plane and flies away. Felix sells and Felix buys, but you should have told me about your secret life, Felix, your secret lives, on the chase. It did have something to do with me. You were wrong, Felix. But you wanted your babies, didn't you? Yes. They were easier to love than me. Maisie rushing to the door, bouncing up and down in her pajamas, panting with excitement. He's here. He's here. Daddy! Daddy! Elusive fathers. How we love them.

I am feeding Ethan, his tiny soft nose smashed against my breast. He pauses, a thin stream of milk bleeds from the edges of his mouth, and he looks around confused, blinks, breathes noisily, and returns to feeding. The curious Maisie is watching, pushing her head into my shoulder, whining at me. Is my Maisie lazy? Do you want to cuddle under my arm, lazy Maisie girl? Yes, Mommy. And I have them both, one hanging from a nipple and the other nudged into the cave made from underarm and elbow – a triple body. A depleted body of three. Tired as I am, I know this is joy. I say to myself: This is joy. Don't forget it. And I don't.

To end there, with the babes. That is good for the sleepy mind grown lazy with writing.

Tomorrow there is work, and there is Bruno at night. I call him the Rehabilitator, because he loves the big body of his big love. He likes to see me spread out on the bed, Harry, an aging, naked Venus no Baroque painter would have chosen, but here I am mooning over my own dive-bomber, Bruno the Bear. Not so young, my Romeo, an old fart if there ever was one, with a gut, too, and most of the hair worn down on his legs and the skin turned smooth, to his surprise! He's not young! What happened? He worries over semen flow, a bit low, the flow, compared to days gone by. You'd think he had walked around with a volcano down there for years, conceited man. But face to face and pubes to pubes, or face to pubes and pubes to face, or straddling and riding or fingers inside delicate orifices here and there, God (why do we call on the supernatural at times like this?), God, I cannot wait to tackle that fat man and kiss his round ass.

And we fight and snarl, too.

> **H:** Finish the poem or flush it!
> **B:** Get your butt out there and show your own work, you coward!

But I'm in love, isn't that mad? Now, to really end here. I am wanted, wanted. In your eyes, Bruno man, I am shining (well, at least part of the time). Sleep now, sleep, as the bard says, sleep, the balm of hurt minds.

January 18, 2000

Maisie reported today that Aven has an imaginary friend who lives in her throat. The person is known as Radish, and is causing upheaval in the household. Maisie has taken to addressing Radish, which means that Aven spends a lot of time with her mouth gaping, so her mother can confront the invisible insurrectionist directly. I am all sympathy because Bodley was with me for years, and I remember him with much love, but Maisie is worried that Radish has made her appearance (it's female) for dark psychological reasons – the child is under stress in nursery school. They are showing her letters and numbers she wants nothing to do with. She has just been given eyeglasses, another worry (for her mother, I believe, more than for Aven). I told Maisie that these friends, wherever they may be lodged, inside or outside, are usually helpful and serve some useful purpose. My own mother was very kind about Bodley. She set a place for him at the table and talked to him politely (when he wasn't misbehaving).

As for the plot, it seems to be working. Phineas has been offered a show of *The Suffocation Rooms* at Begley in the spring of next year. I had a hallelujah moment about my own queer sensibility, about showing my Phinny man. But then a hint of sadness, low thoughts soon after. I have begun to wonder if I could show work by Anonymous.

That might be impossible. There is no orderly vision without context, it seems. Art is not allowed to arrive spontaneously unauthored. Bruno says that turning my pseudonyms into moving pieces in a philosophical game about perception is just a cover for my insecurity. I am masked twice. Phinny disagrees. He has been out and about with me, traveling incognito, so to speak. He says that he has seen it over and over again. He has seen that it matters little what I say; my intelligence is discounted. Piffle and twaddle. Were I to come out with *The Suffocation Rooms*, the powers-that-be would instantly back away.

The work would look different.

Would it look old-womanish all of a sudden?

I insist that this is a question with urgency.

I have often wondered what a Josephine Cornell would have looked like to people? Piffle and twaddle, frippery and sentiment? Soft?

Not the same, surely, as Joseph.

When it's a gay man, it's something else again, right?

Phinny says yes and no. He cites Ethan; it's queered, he says, but there's macho and fey, top and bottom, somehow important.

Is it?

I tell him I like being queered with him, paired and queered.

Eve, with her high heels and her low-cut sweaters and her corsets worn on the outside and her Rube Goldberg machines made out of old dresses, is oblivious to the onus of her sex. Well, she's young.

She knows about me and P.Q. She had to know because she lives here.

Two days ago while we were lounging about before bed, Phinny actually yelled at the big B. 'Don't you get it? It doesn't matter what she does! They see the widow or they see her money. They are blinded by what they think they see!'

Another Goldberg, the Goldberg study, 1968. Women students evaluated an identical essay more poorly when a female name was attached to it than when a male name was attached. The same results were found when they were presented with a work of visual art. Goldberg study revisited, 1983. Men and women students rated the essay with a female name attached more poorly than with a male name attached. And so it goes, but there is a twist as the research progresses in the 1990s. When expert credentials are attached to a woman's name, the bias disappears. For artists, expertise is fame. Sex and color don't disappear; they no longer matter.*

★　★　★

* Philip A. Goldberg, 'Are Women Prejudiced Against Women?' *Transactions* 5 (1968), 28–30. The study was replicated in 1983 by Michelle A. Paludi and William D. Bauer, using male as well as female subjects. 'What's in an Author's Name?' *Sex Roles* 9, no. 3, 387–90. For later studies, see Virginia Valian, *Why So Slow? The Advancement of Women* (Cambridge, Mass.: MIT Press, 1998).

Bruno does not want any part of bias studies or psychological research. I am not just another dame. I am his very own brilliant Harry. Give the jerks a chance. They'll come around. Weirdly, his faith that Phinny and I are wrong makes me happy, and Phinny's insistence that I am right makes me unhappy. I am perverse.

(Phinny is thinking of himself, too. The glare of prejudice is all too familiar.)

Sometimes I think of Anton sadly.

There is something else. I met Rune. I can't say why, but I didn't mention our encounter to Bruno. It was at the opening for some silly work – balloons, faces. Such a handsome man. Anointed, heralded, wearing his laurels. Vain, I think, probably very vain, but aren't we all? And then maybe we attribute more vanity to beautiful people than to the plain, and perhaps it isn't fair. We talked about memory. Mnemosyne is the mother of the Muses. Cicero. One thought led to the next. It was almost as if he knew me, one of those uncanny connections. And what about machine memory? This fascinates him, artificial intelligence, but, I say, they have hit many dead ends. I told him about Thomas Metzinger.* Looked at Rune's work again

* German philosopher, born in 1958, whose work integrates philosophy and neurobiology. Burden took extensive notes

221

– faces in surgery, flaps of skin. I have a catalogue. New surfaces, he was saying, surgically transformed, but also bionic technology for new limbs that respond to the nervous system, computers as extended selves-minds. All true. But what does it mean? He spoke to me about external memory – an odd idea. For him the frenzy for documentation, photos, films, the second lives on the Internet, the simulated wars and games. I pointed out that self-consciousness is not new. But the technology is, he insisted. He said, 'I want my art to be these questions.' We don't agree, but that might be the pleasure, the sharp back-and-forth, the agon with a worthy partner. I recommended papers and books to him, and he wrote them down. Read Varela and Manturana, I said.* He said he would.

---

on a book Metzinger edited, *The Neural Coordinates of Consciousness* (Cambridge, Mass.: MIT Press, 1995).

* Humbert R. Manturana (1928–) and his student Francisco Varela (1946–2001), Chilean neurobiologists and philosophers who coauthored *Autopoiesis and Cognition: The Realization of the Living* (Dordrecht, Netherlands: D. Reidel, 1972), a book Burden mentions repeatedly in her writings. In Notebook P, she quotes from the book: 'Living systems are units of interactions; they exist in an ambience. From a purely biological point of view they cannot be understood independently of that part of the ambience with which they interact; the niche, nor can the niche be defined independently of the living system that specifies it' (9). This embodied, embedded-in-the-environment position stands in opposition to computational theories of mind.

We talked about Wechsler. On him, we agreed. *O's Journey*. When we said goodbye, his handshake was just right, neither limp nor too firm. When his e-mail arrived, I felt giddy with hope, for the end of exile in my own head, for someone who will understand me, someone who will *see* what I know and talk back to me about it. Is this so ridiculous? Isn't it possible?

Recognition. Dr F. Isn't that what we talk about? My greed for recognition. One to one. Tête-à-tête. You and I. I want you to *see* me.

Bruno listens to me, but he doesn't always know what I am talking about. Nobody seems to know what I am talking about.

A year ago, I saw part of his film diary – the man, Rune (once Rune Larsen), at daily tasks, brushing his teeth, flossing his teeth, lying on the sofa, reading, sitting in front of the computer, and then stroking a redheaded woman's hair over and over as she lay with her head on his shoulder in a big rumpled bed. And I thought to myself, this is what we never see because we are inside, not outside, and most of us cannot recall habitual events except as a blur of routine. Is this why he wants the film? The date appears on the screen, and there is a film for each day. The film does not run all day. It is not Warhol's sleeper or the Empire State Building, but he documents one event, often minor, every day.

Do I remember if I took my vitamin this morning or brushed my teeth? Was it this morning or yesterday morning or the day before?

The hair-stroking might remain inside Rune and the young woman as a memory, but most likely from the internal perspective of each of them, each 'I' – but sometimes we remember as observers. It is a kind of false memory. I remember the afternoon I stroked your curls over and over when we were first in love. I remember lying with you in bed and feeling your fingers in my hair as you petted me for minutes on end and how lovely it felt, and I remember the daylight in the room, and I remember our love. What is the memory of love? Do we actually recall the feeling? No. We know it was there, but the manic desire isn't there in the memory. What do we recollect exactly? The sensations are not reproduced. And yet, an emotional tone or color is evoked, something weightless or heavy, pleasant or unpleasant, and I can summon it. I remember lying in bed with Felix. But is it one time or is it many times merged together from the early days of our clutching love, when I ached for his touch? I know I held his head sometimes when we fucked. I know I put my lips to his ear afterward and whispered words long forgotten, probably stupid words. But do I really remember a single time, the once only? Yes, in the Regina in Paris, with the uncomfortable beds we had to push together. Five stars and those beds. I think I remember the line of light between the heavy curtains as I sat on top of him, banging him. Long ago.

I remember coldness, too, his back to me. The distance between us, his eyes dead to me. I remember this: at a dinner. Where was it? The caustic joke about marriage, not ours, of course, but the institution in general. What were his words? I can't remember. I recall I started, looked at him. In my mind I see a plate with a gold rim. He turned his head. Now it returns with the memory, pain, perhaps not as acute, but pain arrives with a recollection so vague it has almost disappeared – there was a joke, a plate, a look, and a cutting pain. Is pain more durable than joy in memory?

What moron said the past was dead? The past is not dead. Its phantoms own us. They own me. They have a stranglehold on me, but I don't know if the revenants can be dispelled. Maybe I will consult with Radish. Maybe she will have some good advice for me. I will just have to keep working – the studio is burgeoning with the unseen works, the myriad monstrosities by someone named Harriet Burden. Maybe when the revelation comes the proverbial scales will fall from their eyes. Maybe when I'm dead some wandering art critic will come to the building where the goods are stored and look, really look, because the person (me) will finally be missing. Yes, nodding wisely, my imaginary critic will stare for a long time and then utter, here is something, something good. Rescued from oblivion like Judith Leyster.* Then

* Judith Leyster (1609–1660), Dutch Baroque painter, a member of the Haarlem Guild of St Luke, celebrated in

225

again, what if it's all crap anyway, despite my precious pseudonyms – the ones they desire, rather than me, not me. I am going to be sixty. Maisie has said she will throw a birthday party, and I have said, yes, but only for the dear hearts – no outlying friends of friends. Phinny wants to shop for a dress for me to wear when I turn the corner of another decade, something 'ravishing,' he says.

Felix in dreams. Another Felix – hateful. He was never hateful in life – cool, closed, but not hateful. Why does he come?

But tonight, as I sit here at my desk and look out at the water – at winter, at the night, at the shining city – I feel a grief that has no object I can name, not Felix or my father or my mother. Just now, it came hard upon me, the grievous ache, but for what? Is it simply that there is so much less in front of me than behind me? Is it for the child called Harriet who walked with her head down? Is it for the old woman I am becoming? Is it because the fury of ambition has not been beaten

---

her time but forgotten after her death. Because her work was similar to Frans Hals, many of her paintings were attributed to him. In 1893, the Louvre purchased what was believed to be a Hals but which turned out to be by Leyster. The discovery helped to restore Leyster's artistic reputation.

out of me, not yet? Is it for the ghosts that have left their tracks inside me?

Yes, Harry, it's the ghosts. But are names ghosts, too, insubstantial? Did you want to see your name in lights, up on the marquee? Vanity of vanities. The letters assigned to you at birth, designation of your paternity. Paternal lights? Is that what you hoped for? But why, Harry? Your father did not want the Burden born, his squalling burdensome little Burden, but there you were.

He came around.

Did he, Harry? Did he, really? Not to your satisfaction, I would say. Didn't he prefer Felix? Didn't even your mother favor Felix? Didn't she say to you, You mustn't be too hard on Felix? Didn't she fuss over him, protect him?

Yes, but she loved me.

Yes, she did. But your work?

She didn't understand my work.

It's coming up, Harry, the blind and boiling, the insane rage that has been building and building since you walked with your head down and didn't even know it. You are not sorry any longer, old girl, or ashamed for knocking at the door. It is not shameful to knock, Harry. You are rising up against the patriarchs and their minions, and you, Harry, you are the image of their fear. Medea, mad with vengeance. That little monster has climbed out of the box, hasn't it? It isn't nearly grown yet, not nearly grown. After Phinny, there will be one more. There will be three, just as in the fairy tales. Three masks of different hues and countenances, so that the story will have its perfect form. Three masks, three wishes, always three. And the story will have bloody teeth.

BRUNO KLEINFELD
(written statement)

Did we settle down the way two fogies ought to settle down in their late-middle-to-old-age, their copious butts in a couple of La-Z-Boy chairs, their feet propped on ottomans, muttering, Did you take out the garbage, dear? Did you remember the milk? No, we did not. Old Man Time screwed us over. He ripped my lady away before we could become the doddering old farts we deserved to be together, sans teeth, squinting through our cataracts, reaching out for the old, soft flesh in the middle of the night. But Bruno, you wax Romantic. Harry was not a settler, and who knows if she ever would have settled in, settled down with her bear. She had been there, done that, in the time before Bruno. The husband – what a strange word – the husband kept coming back, like smoke in the room, stinking up the air between us. Felix Lord and his dough and his art and his sex life still burned like a forgotten cigarette in one of those goddamned crystal ashtrays Harry kept around from her former life on the uppity Upper East Side. God, I hated that effete ghoul who refused to rest, the way decent, normal dead people do. He haunted her. I kid you not. My verbs are not casual. I am a poet, failed, maybe, but a blathering bard, nevertheless, telling tales of those halcyon days of Harry not too long ago and not too far away. I am Bruno Kleinfeld declaiming for all to hear that Felix Lord came to her in dreams, half dead and half alive, a vampire with his fangs fastened in her neck, and my beloved would wake up sweaty and panicked, her eyes roaming the room for him, not because she wanted him back, but because she wanted to make sure he was dead and gone.

Maisie and Ethan, I beg your pardons, but Daddy-o took Mommy for granted. Did he fight for her? No, he did not. Where did it come from – Harry's pseudonymous mania – except from him? How many women artists did Felix Lord show? Three? And over how many years? Harry watched, and Harry learned. She learned that her very own art-hustle mastermind wasn't going to lift a finger for her work and that only art's big boys get satisfaction. 'He couldn't help me, don't you see?' Harry used to wail. 'Sure he could' was my roared retort. After a while, the injustice of it all, the sick, sad misery of being ignored, cracked her heart in two and demented her with anger. I wanted her to fight on, but she decided to walk through the back door and send someone else around the front.

She was a strong woman, my Harry, but not an easy woman. The poem, the project of projects, the anthill that became a mountain, the thing I was eternally climbing and never getting over, my darling work of great verse, the one of Whitmanian proportions, my own American Commedia, that Harry had hugged close during the first year of our passion as my noble quest, became a bugbear once she understood that it wasn't going anywhere. The poem became a nasty goblin that turned the flesh-and-blood darling of my life into a shrew, a carping, screeching, nagging witch who threw flaming daggers at me and the poem. 'It's so neurotic! You've rewritten it five hundred times. What is the matter with you? You're so afraid. Do you think your cock will shrivel up if you're not Dante, for Christ's sake?'

No, it wasn't easy loving Harry and the poem. I would creep off after a showdown about the interminable project and return to the hole across the street to lick my wounds on the scarred linoleum, and then crawl back, like the dog I was, to her big bed and her muscular arms that held me harder than any woman I've ever known. I couldn't say it then, but the old girl was right about the poem. It had taken me into a dark wood all right, and it wasn't ever going to get me to the Paradiso, but to give it up meant to give up me, myself, and I, as the ten-year-old Bruno Kleinfeld used to say as he admired his mug in the mirror after a game, reliving a big one he had blasted over the fence.

I couldn't tell Harry, feminist warrior, that it was worse for a man, worse for a man to fail, to lose the strut in his walk as he feels the power sucked from his guts, the manly fire that had kept him going uphill. Millennia had piled up expectations, stone by stone, brick by brick, word by word, until the stones, bricks, and words weigh so much that the hopeful antihero can't get out from under them – can't see his way into a single line he might call his own, and he writhes under the tonnage, begging for mercy.

Despite her fears about the outside, Harry was free inside. She believed in her steam and fury, and she pushed her art out of her like wet, bloody newborns. When I die, they'll see, she used to crow. The last joke will be mine. When I told her she reminded me of a de Kooning woman, one of those scary mammas with the leering mouths, she grinned with pleasure and rubbed her palms together. She hid *The Heathcliff* from me until she had finished it. The figure had a huge head thrust back, an open mouth, and a half-crushed birdcage between its gigantic hands. In the cage were bits of ripped lace, a book of Shelley's poems, pieces of written-over paper, and a torn white stocking that drooped like a tongue between the bars. At first, the thing felt like a kick in the stomach, all force, but from up close, the person, if it was a person, had cuts and slices in its mottled bronze body and hanging breasts.

'Heathcliff was a man, Harry. This is a woman.'

Harry's eyes ignited as she said, 'He is more myself than I am.'

Catherine says it. The first and wildest Catherine in the great, meaty, diabolical novel that is *Wuthering Heights*. Harry's brain ran hot and fast. I knew the book and its branching sensuous prose, an old favorite of mine, a literary brick, to be sure. But Harry gobbled down other treatises and tracts and obscure works I'd never heard of. She read and read, on top of making her art, and there were days when I said, 'Harry, I don't know what the hell you're jawing on about now.' The woman was chin-deep in the neuroscience of perception, and for some reason, those unreadable papers with their abstracts and discussions justified her second life as a scam artist. Eldridge egged her on, too, but he wasn't responsible for the ruse. Even though I fought *The Suffocation Rooms* and the idea of Harry as a gay guy (which she found hilarious and I found silly), I can now see the damage didn't last. Eldridge set the record straight. I never met that namby-pamby kid Tish, but it seems to me he wasn't worth the anagram *shit*. Ran off to Tibet. No, it was Rune in league with Lord's phantom that made the mess. I blame the two of them. The story isn't simple and it isn't straight, but I'd like to offer up my memories, some foggy, some clear.

Once Harry and I were thick, tight, and coupled up (to the degree that was possible with a dyed-in-the-wool bluestocking), I saw more and more of the vulnerable girl in her. The nightmares were bad, but she also got the sobs or rages at night, especially after she had seen her shrink. 'Why do you go in for that crap?' I asked her. 'He just shakes you up. What good does it do?' But when I wheedled her for the dope on a 'session,' she'd just shake her head and smile, tears still rolling. 'You're jealous of the doctor. That's nice, Bruno. That's really nice.' I wasn't jealous. I didn't like to see her upset, but she knew I didn't have much use for psychoanalysis either. My pal Jerry Weiner got stuck for thirty years with some doctor on Central Park West, and as far as I could tell, Jerry stayed the same cheap, ornery bastard he'd always been. I liked Rachel, but then, Rachel would have brightened up the morgue if she had chosen to work as a coroner. That was just Rachel.

When Rune first popped up into Harry's life is a mystery to me, but one May afternoon in 2001 – I know because it was the spring before the towers fell, and the day was warm and sprouting, and I was close to the end of my semester at LIU – I found the two of them on Harry's sofa, tittering like a couple of teenage girls, drinking chardonnay, eating peanuts. Harry did the introductions, and Rune, bleached teeth bright as an egg, said, 'Oh, the poet.'

I didn't like the way he said it. Oh, the poet. Didn't like the *Oh*, didn't like the way he trailed off on *poet*, didn't like his whitened teeth or his belt buckle or the stupid tight shirt he was wearing or his scuffed boots or the way he had laid his arm over the back of the sofa or the way he talked about his 'films.' Didn't like the man from the start. When he finally waltzed his puny ass out the door, I felt relieved.

I remember Harry accused me of 'glowering.' I said I didn't glower, but that she was 'all aflutter,' and it didn't suit her, a mature woman mincing and giggling like a teenybopper. There was some peckish back-and-forth between us about semantics – *glower*, *flutter*, and *mince* – and then she looked down on me from the imperious heights of Harrydom, as cold and grand as she could be, and announced that she did not need my approval. She would not accommodate my whims. She had moved out of the way once too often, thank you very much, tiptoed around in her old life like a slavey waiting for crumbs to fall. (This self-portrait by Our Lady of the Coats struck me as nothing short of a howler.) I told her Rune looked like a fucking gigolo. Still hoity-toity, enunciating in complete, well-formed paragraphs, the Queen continued – he was a reigning king of the art market, surely I knew, and he just *loved* her work. She had given him the tour, the tour she gave only to friends, highly select friends who knew she didn't show, knew she had finished with dealers and galleries and 'all that.' I said maybe he loved her money, was sniffing around for a sale, and the fireworks went off, whistle, crack, boom. Cash and assets. Felix Lord's cologne stinking aboveground.

After the fire-breathing sparks had been snuffed out between us, I wondered aloud if he didn't strike her as a bit slick and shiny. Mr Surface Rune had mastered the art walk and the art talk, hadn't he? Yes, he had, she admitted, but Harry waved her arms. He had loads of money, and *ideas*: Mr Memory, Mr Artificial Intelligence, Mr Computer. My Harry's face was all sunny and warm with Rune's lofty thoughts. Can robots have consciousness? Is thinking information processing? They had debated the Turing machine, and the Turing test. 'He's dead wrong, Bruno, but it's fun to argue, don't you see?' And the art? I looked him up. I thought he looked like a goddamned male model with his rippling abdomen, popping biceps, films of him scratching his ass, picking his nose. Who is he kidding? I said to Harry, and she said, 'But he *is* kidding, Bruno.'

Who started the idea that every life should be recorded for posterity? Was it that lunatic Rousseau? Look, I'm a liar, a cheat, a masochist. Look, I'm chucking my children into an orphanage! The man sliced himself open for all to see. I have a weakness for Jean-Jacques, it is true, the hero of me-me-me. By the end of his life, Allen Ginsberg had a camera crew with him everywhere he went. Self as myth, self as movie, he droned on to the camera, but at least he wrote a couple of good poems. My hero Walt was pretty big on self-promotion, too. He plastered Emerson's words on *Leaves of Grass*, words he stole from a *private* letter. Whitman was a nobody, and Emerson an *eminence grise*. Emerson's words: 'I salute you at the beginning of a great

236

career.' The book received two anonymous reviews written by young Walt himself: 'An American bard at last!' Maybe we should be glad he had no Internet access. I can see it now: *Be part of it: Whitmania!* And why not me? The Bruno Kleinfeld website: unknown antihero pounding the keys of his Olivetti typewriter for whom?

Who was Rune, né Rune Larsen? The hell if I know. What did she see in him? One night in bed, lying flat and staring up at the ceiling, I blurted out a question. Did she have a hankering for younger bones? Harry played obtuse. 'What? What are you talking about?' 'Him,' I said to her, 'Him, the art star.' Her blast of hilarity almost sent me flying across the room. She loved him for his gift, his talent for manipulation, his persona. He had accomplished his glory with bluster and swagger and drive. This fascinated her. His puffed-up ego had contagious properties, and there was something more to him as well. Maybe Harry had him pegged from the start. Maybe when she was giggling on the sofa with that psychopath, they were already conspirators. She hid the plot from me because she knew I wouldn't approve. I didn't track her comings and goings. Harry was tough. No more Mrs Nice Guy. No more pandering to a Husband or any Man. She was free now, and the Big Bear wasn't going to interfere. I got the message. The days belonged to her. The evenings were ours – drinks at Sunny's, dinner at her place, a DVD – but no settling. The loony residents came and went. The Barometer with his weather signs, 'Humid Harassments Amassing from Infernal Circulars,' Eve with her bizarre outfits, Eldridge trying out new schticks for his show.

I'm not sure Harry really liked the thing she bought by Rune – the video screen with faces cut to bits and put back together again, a movie mishmash of glamour and gore. It was a multiple – which meant 'not that expensive.' One afternoon, I parked myself in front of the screen and gave it a yeoman's try. 'Let me be fair,' I said, 'and not loaded with prejudice just because the artist is an asshole. T. S. Eliot was no paragon, was he? Are these bloody mugs and sliced cheeks any good? Am I interested? Do I care?' To be honest, the darned thing stumped me. I told Harry it made me feel lonely, and she laughed, but then she said it made her lonely, too. 'It's not about communion,' she said. I didn't know at the time that Rune was ripe to be her last stand. In her head, he was vehicle numero uno. If she could harness his star power, she could prove how the machinery worked, how ideas of greatness make greatness, and once she had triumphed, the great unmasking would take place! Harriet Burden, her own woman.

And so we two, Harry and Bruno, duked it out and then made it up in our domains in Red Hook, one grand, one puny, but each domicile reliable in its own way. Around us the city buzzed and screeched, and the foghorns blew, and the clouds moved overhead. It rained and it thundered and then it brightened, and the seasons changed. But every day the sun rose, and the sun set, and when we stepped outside, the street was there, and Harry's truck was there, and the Manhattan skyline was there. And then New York City was slammed from the outside. From blue sky to smoking sky in minutes – we heard the second plane, low and loud, and we saw it hit. We saw it again on television. I tried to understand it, but I couldn't. I knew and I didn't know. Once we had found out that Maisie had retrieved Aven from kindergarten at the Little Red School House on Sixth Avenue in the West Village, that Oscar had not had to travel to Brooklyn that day, that Ethan was in his apartment in Williamsburg, that my daughter Cleo, the only Kleinfeld offspring who lived in New York, was indeed in her office in the Brill Building in Midtown, that Phinny and Ulysses and the Barometer had not yet budged for the day, we watched through the window as the winds carried the diseased dust and debris over Red Hook. We shut the windows against the unspeakable stench, and spent much of the early afternoon tending to the Barometer. The man's cosmological delusions bumped and lurched this way and that in ordinary weather. The smoke, the explosions, the falling papers, pulverized plastic, and flesh tipped him into a state of nonstop gibberish and stiff, machine-like gestures. With his wild hair and beard, his dirty Grateful Dead T-shirt, and his torn khaki pants that hung about his bony, bowed legs, he expounded mechanically about the 'groaning sublimity of transportable tempers and their combustible storm-patriots romping in divine intercourse with God's archangels' (excerpt from P.Q.E.'s tape. The Barometer's language is impossible to remember). I prayed. I prayed he'd shut up. The carnage meant nothing to the Raver. Mass murder didn't touch him. He was lost in his own power fantasies of control, which the day had exploded or confirmed (I'm not sure which). Ulysses produced a Xanax, which we eventually managed to cajole him into taking. We put the nut job to sleep.

Ladder 101. All seven firefighters who answered the call died.

Days later, I remember Harry at the window. She made a low noise that came from her chest, not her mouth. Then she said, 'Human beings are the only animals who kill for ideas.'

When I think back, I realize no one I knew lusted for vengeance. For a period of weeks, it seemed to me that nearly every New Yorker who was still alive became a saint. We spoke to strangers on the subway and asked them, 'Are you okay?' meaning 'Did you lose anyone?' We donated shovels, clothes, flashlights. We lined up to give blood, even though that blood turned out to be useless. You had either died or you had survived. Rune grabbed a camera and filmed guerrilla-style. The area was cordoned off, but he must have wormed in past the cops. I know he called Harry. She worried aloud about his lust for photos. Did the mentally sick get sicker after September 11? There must be some goddamned report on it out there somewhere.

Most New Yorkers comported themselves like angels, but the pundits, commentators, and journalists yapped their pieties, waved their clichés, and brandished their platitudes. And in the years that followed, Bush and his cronies erected one big lie after another over the incinerated corpses in lower Manhattan. Soaring collective goodness can't last. We regressed to our sniping, smart-mouthed, but also intermittently kind and helpful selves and, because one day after another came and went without a subway explosion, bridge collapse, or skyscraper meltdown, we were lulled back to what Warren G. Harding called 'normalcy,' code for just-the-regular-day-to-day-crap-life-offers, thank you very much: work doldrums, adulterous affairs, family squabbles, all manner of neuroses, asthma, stomach ulcers, rheumatisms, and acid reflux.

When Harry told me not long after the attacks that Rune had agreed to take a turn as the last actor in her grand tripartite scheme, I burst out with a big why-the-hell-would-he-want-to-do-that? Harry's reasoning was bollixed up by her wishes, but it had various strands. The subterfuge was right up Rune's alley, a ploy that wowed him because, if it all went as planned, he could become the biggest art world kidder of them all. He would expose the critics (some of whom he hoped to draw and quarter) as clowns. This was the man's vulnerability, Harry claimed. There were those who called him a con artist, a panderer. Plus the market scared him. Up one day, down the next. He didn't want to go the way of Sandro Chia, dumped on the market by Saatchi, never to recover. Rune lived like a pasha, indulged himself; he needed upkeep. He would turn the tables on his naysayers. When they mocked his latest, he could produce Harry to confound them. But she also claimed that she had wrenched the great Rune's thoughts, remade his inner world, and that the horrific event downtown had exploded his plotline. It didn't work out like that. In the end, the simpleton Bruno knew more than the Grande Dame of irony.

What does a woman want? What did Harry want? She did not want to be Rune. She did not want to sell her work for millions of dollars. She knew the art world was mostly a stink hole of vain poseurs who bought names to launder their money. 'I want to be understood,' she would wail at me. Hers was a heady game, a philosophical fairy tale. Oh, Harry had explanations, justifications, arguments. But I ask you, in what world was this understanding going to take place? In Harry's magic kingdom, where the citizens lounged about reading philosophy and science and arguing about perception? It's a crude world, old girl, I used to tell her. 'Look at what's happened to poetry! It's become quaint, cute, and "accessible." ' Harry wanted her pseudonymous tale to be read by illiterates. Obsession is what she had, and obsession is a machine that grinds and clanks and hisses hour after hour, day after day, month after month, year after year. She hated my poem. I hated her fairy tale. She built Rune a magnum opus, a maze of her own private dance of grief, and he stole it. When she told me he wasn't going to go through with her plan, she was flat on her back in her studio ogling a big, fat lady with forceps and a cowbell she had hung from the ceiling. Edgar and two other assistants, Ursula and Carlos, had gone home. It was about six in the evening. She had called me a few minutes before. 'Come over, Brune. Something's happened.' Her voice, hurt and faltering. She didn't look at me once while the story rolled out of her, word by word, slowly, deliberately. Only her mouth moved. The rest of Harry had turned into a rock.

Rune had shown her a video of himself with Felix Lord. It was nothing, she kept saying, nothing at all, just the two of them sitting on a sofa in a nondescript room she had never seen before, not saying a word to each other, thirty, forty seconds of silence and one smile exchanged between them. The dead husband had roared back on film. 'Why didn't you tell me you knew Felix?' Harry had asked him. And he had said, 'Does it matter?'

'Does it matter, Bruno?'

You bet it does, I said. It's sneaky as hell. I told her I'd like to take my bat and smash his brains out.

And Harry said, 'This is not a cartoon, Bruno.'

So much is gone now, of our conversations, I mean. The nights we lay and burbled into the wee hours, we two, my big, warm Harry and me, my pet, my heartsease, all lost, not a word left, but *This is not a cartoon, Bruno* is stamped into the furrows of my brain forever. I have perfect recall for this exchange. I went mum then, mute as a man who'd lost his larynx. She made me feel like some stupid jerk in a gorilla suit, blindly swinging because he can't see out the eyeholes.

When I asked Harry what it meant, she said she didn't know. Rune wouldn't say. 'He said that it's just part of the game.'

I asked, 'What game? What game?' I pressed her. I pressed her hard. 'Blackmail?'

Harry stared at the ceiling and shook her head. She said she thought Rune was playing mind games with her and that the bastard would do anything to win. She said he wanted to worm an idea into her brain, that he had been Lord's lover, maybe, or that he had known all about her from Felix before they met, something, anything. Once there is a secret, Harry said, you can fill up the hole with suspicion. When he was alive, Felix had secrets. Harry set her jaw and her eyes narrowed. She didn't look at me. 'He's going to say *Beneath* is his. But it's too late,' she said. 'He won't get away with it.'

Lord's grave was never quiet. I wanted to shake Harry, force her to end it. Now was her chance to stop the merry-go-round, to jump off. I would help her. Bruno, her hero and protector, would swoop in to save her from herself. 'Let's go away,' I said. 'Let's leave.'

Harry shook her head.

I told her I loved her. I love you to high heaven, I said. I love you. Do you hear me?

She heard me. 'I love you, too,' she said. She was not thinking of me.

Bruno, high on his noble sentiments, Mr Rescue: All I needed was a phone booth where I could change into the suit. There aren't phone booths anymore, old man.

I remember the sun made rectangles of light on the wood floor. I remember Harry's sad face, and I remember the words that popped up to be quoted on that palimpsest in my mind. They came from the book of Ruth, King James version, the words of a woman who trailed after another woman and refused to turn back.

Whither thou goest, I will go, I said to Harry. *Where thou diest, will I die, and there will I be buried.*

Harry smiled a wobbly smile. 'That's nice, Bruno,' she said.

It felt like a kick to the gut.

OSWALD CASE
(written statement)

Rune never gave up on irony. That was his victory. Despite the general nothing-will-ever-be-the-same-again moaning and hand-wringing and great American soul-searching that went on in the aftermath of 9/11, if you ask yourself whether the art world was permanently altered by that day, the answer is an earsplitting no. After all is said and done, three thousand dead downtown ranks as a sneeze in the market, a momentary convulsion of conscience. Yes, artists whined about meaninglessness and a new beginning, but a few months later, it was life *comme d'habitude*. Mea culpa. I am the author of 'Irony Died at Ground Zero,' published in *The Gothamite* the week of September 23. Let me put it this way: When I banished irony, that most necessary of all forms of thought, I meant it. Lower Manhattan was a freshly dug graveyard, and I thought I had been remade as Monsieur Sincère. Furthermore, I have since acknowledged my error. That is more than I can say for any number of my esteemed colleagues who poured their thwarted literary ambitions into cringingly bad articles. They forgot the motto of our noble profession: here today, gone tomorrow. My offering to the end-of-irony moment was not nearly as bathetic as most of the garbage that was published after 9/11. How many times did I read: 'Who could have imagined it?' Every two-bit screenwriter in Hollywood had already imagined it. Rune had it right. He knew the spectacle would be used, exploited, rewritten in a thousand different and, mostly, tawdry ways.

When I interviewed him in 2002, he talked about his struggle with catastrophe as art. How could a slaughter that had already been manipulated into multiple narratives be represented? He talked about the speed of technology, about simulation, and finally, about awe. He said he'd never experienced it – awe. He hadn't felt it before 9/11. He called it 'emotional superconductivity.' He wanted it in the work. I know that Harriet Burden believed she had found a third cover for her this-woman-can-become-a-celebrity-artist-too campaign. The question is, did she intervene enough to rob Larsen of credit for the works, which would be shown a year and a half later? I think not. I think he knew exactly what he was doing. *Beneath* hit the art world like a tornado. The timing was brilliant. He knew that to show the images everyone saw on television on 9/11, and for a few days after, would not do, not in New York City. But if you had to walk through a maze, and look at black-and-white film footage of devastated cars or kiddy shoes covered in dust, along with that weird mask fantasy sequence (which I believe Rune directed), the viewer's experience would increase in intensity. He used Harriet Burden as a muse. I give her credit for that, but mingling the fantasy images with others that were completely banal – Rune with a coffee cup looking out the window or snow falling – directly referenced *Banality*. Also, the robotic motions of the dancers are pure Rune. *Beneath* looks nothing like those squishy Burden works that are being shown now.

Well before my interview with him, Rune had become a bad-boy celebrity, which of course means that he was not nice. He was too complicated to be a nice guy, but then, niceness is not only overrated, it is far less attractive than it's cracked up to be. People love a large, meaty ME. They say they don't, but in the art world a cowardly, shrinking personality is repellent (unless it has been highly cultivated as a type), and narcissism is a magnet. The artist's persona is part of the sell. Picasso was a genius, but look at the mythology. He ate people for breakfast. He had lots of women and loved torturing them. He was King of Confidence, a bloated, swaggering tower of talent whose scribbles on napkins are worth more than I will earn in a lifetime. If you don't seduce people, you don't have a chance. Look at Schnabel in his pajamas. Entitlement works.

In that first interview, Rune revealed his savvy for the ins and outs of the market. When I asked him about his last show, he said, '*The Banality of*

Glamour did well because collectors found it edgy. They liked the reference to Hannah Arendt, even though they'd never read her book. I've never read it either. But the play on glamour and evil is fun because evil is not supposed to be banal but now glamour is.' By then, Rune had recorded himself daily for years: the life of the artist as a young man about town. I shall take this opportunity to correct a tired old truism: 'Beauty is skin deep.' It is not. It is life down deep. Beauty makes you. Six-three, blond, blue-eyed, and fine-featured, Rune's northern European roots blared as loudly as the commercials on TV that run at several decibels higher than the regular shows. His eyes were pale blue. There were times when I looked at him and felt as if I were talking to one of the replicants in *Blade Runner*.

For a while in the nineties, he adopted metrosexual affectations – cologne, manicures, hair mousse, body scrubs, self-tanners – and dutifully filmed all these applications for his diary. Then he stopped. He turned himself into an art cowboy *au naturel* – stiff jeans, boots, sweaty T-shirt. Not long after his Western incarnation, he appeared everywhere in sleek Italian suits and made loud statements about this or that artist, which entered the rumor mill. He understood his image, understood that he was his own object, a body to be sculpted in his work. 'It's fake,' he said. 'The film diary is a big fake. That's the point. It's not that I staged it. It's me waking up. It's me at the parties. The fakeness comes from the fact that you believe you're seeing something when you're not seeing anything except what you put into the picture. That's what celebrity culture is. It's not about anything except your desire that can be bought for a price. I know that if I stick to some story about myself, I'll get boring. Look at Madonna. My reinventions mean that I have no looks, no style. I'm bland, a bland blond. I haven't created anything new. It's been done before, but I've added little twists and turns, and people like it. I actively fight against every trace of originality.'

His stance was a tease, a smart, complicated tease about America as consumer heaven where things are neither original nor real. Whether they knew what he was talking about or not, Rune made people around him feel hip. The colored crosses were so simple, they excited people. They were as easy to read as road signs, but hard to read, too. What did they mean? Modeled on the Red Cross symbol in different colors, they could have been an ironic reference to the whole history of Christianity or to the Crusades. After 9/11 they looked prescient: East-and-West conflict, civilizations at war. Or were they just a shape? Yes, some critics went after him, but I didn't notice that collectors cared. The true irony is that September 11 did change him. He felt he needed a new aesthetic, at least for a while. Maybe this led him to Burden, an artist so obscure she wasn't even a has-been. Personally, I find her work to be little more than neo-Romantic gushing – high-flown, sentimental, and embarrassing – one big agonized groan that reminds me of a half-baked Existentialism. I have yet to penetrate the supposed interest of her 'metamorphs.'

Political correctness and identity politics have infiltrated the visual arts as well as every other aspect of cosmopolitan American culture and account for a good part of the applause that her work now receives. The poor, neglected woman who couldn't find a gallery! Poor Harriet Burden, rich as Croesus in five-hundred-dollar hats, the widow of one of the shrewdest dealers ever to work in New York City. My heart goes out to her. It throbs with sympathy. Art is not a democracy, but this blatant truth must not even be whispered in our prickly, tickly city of do-gooder, liberal, decaffeinated-skim-latte-drinking mediocrities blind to the facts. To suggest, even for an instant, that there might be more men than women in art because men are better artists is to risk being tortured by the thought police. And yet, read *The Blank Slate* by Steven Pinker, distinguished psychologist and a bold prophet of the new frontier – genetics-based sociobiology – and then tell me that men and women are identical, that they have the same strengths, that 'gender' difference is environmental. Test after test in brain science has determined that men score higher on visual/spatial skills and mental rotation tests than women. Might this not, in part at least, be related to the dominant position of men in the visual arts? It's evolutionary. It's in the cards. Men are hunters and fighters, active, not passive, doers and makers. Women have been nurturers, caring for children. They had to stay close to the nest. Has there been discrimination and prejudice against women? Of course there has, but feminism hasn't helped the cause; feminists have screamed about numbers and quotas and turned women artists into political tools. The good ones want nothing to do with feminism. Harriet Burden is the latest craze in a venerable tradition: the woman victimized by a 'phallocentric' world, which stomped on her greatness.

Nevertheless, Rune was looking for a way to mix up his work – to add a retrograde element, to introduce something of the past, some nostalgia for the avant-garde, for Expressionism, for art before Warholian accommodation to the ultimate consumer fantasy – the world before Campbell's soup. I think he found it in Burden. She didn't find him. He found her. Later, he told me as much. The woman was well placed, and he had known her husband. Just for the record, Rune wasn't gay. Women were all over the man. They sidled up to him. They brushed against him, as if by accident. They cooed and babbled at him with silly, dumbstruck expressions on their faces. Young and beautiful women and not-so-young-and-not-so-beautiful women couldn't get enough of him. I recall a pool game Rune and I played together downtown. Afterward, we had a beer at the bar.

A babe in her twenties, a real babe (forgive me if I ruffle any delicate feathers with this mild slang for 'gorgeous female') with dark hair and a tight shirt tied at her waist, so her navel with a little gold ring in it was just visible, walked over and sat down on the stool next to him. She didn't say a word. He didn't say a word. He didn't buy her a drink. *Niente.* He turned to me and said, 'Night, Ozzie.' I watched them leave the bar together and turn right at the corner.

For the profile on Rune I needed the facts. They're sticklers for facts at *The Gothamite*. They check and recheck the facts. The joke on all this fastidious fact-checking is that you're allowed to humiliate anybody, as long as the subject's birth date, hometown, and all numbers connected to him are flawless. And you can quote out-and-out liars, as long as you quote them correctly. It gives roundness to a piece: a bit of positive, a bit of negative. We like balanced reporting. But balance is most important in things serious. Politics is serious. Muckraking is serious, and it must have prose to match. War zones require that all humor and/or irony cease and desist. The arts are not serious, not in the U.S. of A. They do not involve life and death. We are not French. In reviews of the arts, if you spell the guy's name right, you can write whatever you want. You can send hate mail to whichever pompous ass you choose in the form of a review and make a reputation for yourself in the bargain. Do I offend? *Excusez-moi.*

H. L. Mencken once wrote that if a critic 'devotes himself to advocating the transient platitudes in a sonorous manner,' he gets respect. The contemporary platitudes are: Dump on white males, encourage diversity, and destroy the canon; or conversely, wave the flag for the canon and old-fashioned artistic virtues. Of course, Mencken was writing back in the day when college meant literacy. It no longer does. I could regale you for hours with stories of our interns, fresh from the Ivy League, who cannot distinguish between *like* and *as*, who cannot conjugate the verb *to lie* (as in lie down on the floor), whose diction errors give me gooseflesh, but from their semiliterate mouths come one transient 'right-thinking' platitude after the other. How I yearn for the future, when these people who cannot write a cursive hand have taken over the world.

In the visual arts, Clement Greenberg was a successful dictator while his reign lasted, but that world is finished. And yet, the more writing generated around an artist, the better, especially if the arguments for said artist's greatness sound suitably abstruse. I wasn't reviewing Rune, however. For the profile and later for my book, I needed his life story. The facts are these: Born in Clinton, Iowa, in 1965 to Hiram and Sharon Larsen. One younger sibling: Kirsten. Father, owner of car repair shop. Mother takes in sewing. Described by neighbor as 'a quiet, polite boy.' Attends Clinton High School. 1980, wins first at science fair. 1981, mother commits suicide by sleeping pills. 1982, arrest by

254

local police for vandalism (decapitating garden dwarf in neighbor's yard). Attends Beloit College for one year on scholarship. Transfers to University of Minnesota. Takes classes in engineering and media studies. Drops out after six semesters. Erratic transcript. Hitchhikes to New York City. 1987, cast as extra in the movie *City Slaves*. Same year becomes attached to Rena Dewitt, author of the novel *City Slaves*, who is briefly famous. Dewitt, daughter of *the* Percy Dewitt, heiress to pharmaceutical fortune, introduces new boyfriend to joys of big money – Hamptons parties, nightlife, and art world. 1988, begins self-documentary. 1989, declares himself an artist of one name only – Rune – in his *Diary*, ceremoniously amputating family name by holding up sheet of paper and cutting loose *Larsen* with a pair of scissors. 1991, debut in group show at P.S. 1: *Just a Regular Guy* [Diary entry 1556], film of Rune painted blue, à la Yves Klein, narrating his day to a small robot that nods its head up and down. Noted in *New York Times* as show highlight. Befriends and is often seen with model Luisa Fontana. Luisa comes to a bad end. She jumps from the eleventh floor of her apartment on East Sixty-seventh Street in April. Sad death of beautiful girl merits big story in the *New York Post*. Rune is mentioned as one of her coterie of friends.

(No known source of income between 1986 and 1992.) 1992, *Breaking Up Is Hard to Do* [Diary entry 1825] shown at the Zeit Gallery. Two films run simultaneously: (1) Documentary film of Rune and Dewitt's histrionic parting of the ways in huge glamorous apartment on Central Park West owned by Dewitt. Considerable athleticism displayed by both parties in hurling of shoes. (2) Animated 'cybernetic' version of two figures enacting identical gestures. Generates press attention. William Burridge takes notice. Rune leaves Zeit for Burridge Gallery. Several hypocritical articles published by journalists moaning about invasion of privacy. Isn't that what we do? Rune claims Dewitt knew about camera and both versions are 'simulations.' Dewitt claims she forgot the camera was there. October 1995, Hiram Larsen dies in Clinton family house of head wounds sustained after falling down stairs to his basement workshop. Rune attends funeral in Iowa. November 1995, William Burridge attempts to contact Rune in Williamsburg, where he had moved in with Katy Hale, but to no avail. Breaks with her after two months, takes up with India Anand. No film, video, or digital recording. Autobiography stops until 1996, when Rune resurfaces in New York City. No fixed address until November.

October 1997, blockbuster show *The Banality of Glamour* at Burridge Gallery using facial morphing technology to incrementally alter his features in video sequence of himself waking up, walking in streets, and attending an opening at night wearing T-shirt that says *Artificial Man*. Simultaneous films of plastic-surgery patients under the knife (both cosmetic and reconstructive) mixed with images of prosthetic and robotic hands, arms, legs, as well as crucifixes and crosses. Bricks poised at various junctures in gallery with simple inscriptions: *Art, Artificial, Art Man, Man Art, Manart, Artman, Cross, Crosses,* and *Crucifix*. Brisk business in bricks. *Art Assembly* publishes article 'Rune: Constructing the Non-Self.' Shows in Cologne and Tokyo. Cross show in September 1999. Yellow cross sells for three million.

'In heaven,' someone wrote, 'all the interesting people are missing.' Rune was surely an interesting person. He told every journalist a different story about his missing period, not a vague or general narrative but highly specific accounts, which each reporter swallowed whole. A synopsis:

1. He left New York heartbroken after his affair with Dewitt and moved to Newfane, Vermont, where he lived under another name, Peter Granger, and did odd carpentry jobs to make a living.
2. He escaped to Berkeley and, after losing a job as a clerk at Cody's Bookstore, ended up homeless and lived among a roving group of bums in San Francisco.
3. He lived in his car for those months, driving from one place to another, taking work where he could get it but never staying anywhere for more than three weeks.

Nobody I spoke to in Newfane had ever heard of Peter Granger. The people at Cody's knew nothing of Rune, and the on-the-road tale could not be verified one way or another.

Rune fed me a fourth version. After the fiasco with Rena Dewitt and his father's death, he felt not depressed but elated. 'I could do no wrong,' he said. 'I was so up, I never walked; I soared. The feeling was way beyond good. It was ecstasy. I spent money. I had sex, sometimes five women a day. I danced, sang, and jerked off. I had visions, man. No drugs, just wild mirages of big red beasts and women with dog teeth. Scared me shitless. One of my sex partners, who just happened to be a psychiatrist, took me to Psych Emergency at New York Hospital after we had fucked. Well, fucked and fought. Imagine that, one minute you're panting over a sexy shrink, and the next thing you know you're an inpatient in a locked ward.'

Although I tried to check this story, privacy laws for psychiatric patients in New York State impeded me at every turn. I tend to go with number four, not because I was the recipient of this explanation but because it is bizarre and, having made my way into solid middle age, I have heard enough of the world to know that the truth often sounds invented and the invented has the ring of truth. It is at least plausible that Larsen had some kind of breakdown, although it has not been confirmed.

Doing research for my book after Rune's death,

I understood that his sister, Kirsten, knew where her brother had been during much of that unrecorded period of his life. Kirsten Larsen is a craniofacial technician in Minneapolis. She makes facial prostheses for cancer patients and others who have lost noses, ears, cheeks, chins, and jaws, et cetera. Although it is admittedly difficult to imagine this as a life's calling, during our phone conversation she spoke of it as a noble profession, waxing grandiloquent on the challenges of forming just the right proboscis in 'biocompatible materials' for the man who has lost his own, and cheerfully acknowledged that her work had played a role in *The Banality of Glamour*. She was far more reticent when it came to her brother's disappearance, however, and spoke vaguely of his need 'to find himself.' Rune had wanted solitude. She was 'not in a position to say,' et cetera. When asked point-blank about possible mental illness, she said very quietly, 'I think he had to be crazy to die like that, don't you? That's all I'll say.' 'And your father's death? Was it very hard on him?' There was a long silence. I waited patiently. Then I heard sniffling. I lowered my voice and adopted the consoling lilt I have perfected over time; it had not been my intention to upset her. Their father's accident must have been a shock, a terrible shock. Sobs on the other end of the line. 'He found him. Don't you understand how terrible that was? He found him dead.' And then, growling, she said, 'The dead deserve some respect. Don't you get that? Mom, Dad,

259

Rune. They're all dead. But they ought to be respected.'

Investigative reporting can be trying, and one has to get used to the intrusions that are necessary for a story. I had adapted to the tearful faces and choked-up voices long ago, but here was a woman who wasn't willing to talk, and I liked her for it. We live in a world in which those desperate for media attention regularly sell their souls for a turn on TV. The mere mention of my magazine brightens eyes and loosens tongues, but as the ironies pile up, one on top of another, it must be said that Rune lusted after attention. I said this to Kirsten. 'Don't you think your brother would have wanted a book about him? Wasn't his last gesture for art and technology? I believe he made it clear that his death was an aesthetic statement, and that was how he chose to do it.'

Before she hung up the telephone, Kirsten Larsen said, 'I don't think you understand anything.'

Rena Dewitt released a statement articulating her 'shock and sadness' after the death, and then vanished behind the legal wall that inevitably surrounds billions of dollars. I have hours of taped conversations with Katy and India, however, who provided minutiae about their mutual paramour's likes and dislikes, his childhood stories, his eating habits – the real Rune, as it were. There was some agreement. He read a lot, especially science fiction, comics, biographies of artists. He loved Nietzsche and liked to quote Marinetti, the Italian Futurist, who kicked every drippy sentiment in the pants. All the particulars are revealed in my book, but to make a long story pithy: The reports on his personal life did not match. Interview after interview with friends and acquaintances uncovered not one person but several. He loved his mother. He called her a 'cold bitch.' His relations with his mother were 'troubled.' He was alienated from his father, who used to beat him. He admired his father, but found him a bit 'simpleminded and conventional.' He had taken a number of hallucinogens in college. He had never touched drugs but had spontaneous hallucinations. I can confirm that he liked whiskey. One night when we were out, he put his arm around me after four drinks and said, 'You know why I like you, Ozzie, old man?' After I had dutifully said, 'No, Rune, why?' 'Because we get it. The world is shit.'

This may pass for a philosophical statement, I suppose. We were both confirmed atheists, but what fascinated me about the man was that with me, too, he changed from one day to the next. He talked a lot about 'honing his image' and his 'self-presentation,' his need to 'nail down a game plan.' But then he would confess to a desire to make art that would 'slice people open' and 'shake them hard.' According to Katy, he wept regularly over newspaper articles about dead and/or abused children, gave money to a host of animal charities, and professed vegetarianism. It may have been a phase. With me, he ate meat.

Rune was a fabulist. He reinvented himself again and again ceaselessly until the end. In this respect, he was a man of our time, a creature of the media and of virtual realities, an avatar walking the earth, a digitized being. No one knew him. His comment about his autobiography as a 'fake' is at once deep and shallow. And that is the point. There can be no depth in our world, no personality, no true story, only images without substance projected anywhere and everywhere instantaneously. Soon we will have communication devices implanted directly into our brains. The distinctions between reality and image are already fading. People live in their screens. Social media is replacing social life.

I saw Harriet Burden with Rune once at his place not long after *Beneath* had been mounted. I liked to refer to Rune's warehouse conversion as 'Versailles on the Hudson.' The elevator held twenty. The rooms were stupendously large, with monumental sofas and overstuffed chairs covered in brocades, silks, and velvets in brilliant colors, streaming with light. 'I wanted it to look like a Hitchcock movie, a Technicolor extravaganza,' he said. His own gigantic film stills were hanging everywhere. His girlfriend at the time, Fanny-something (former Victoria's Secret model), drifted in and out wearing Ugg boots and cut-off jeans. 'I need a pan for the brownies, Rune.'

Sometime later, Felix Lord's widow was ushered into the room by some underling who had answered the door, and there, in harsh contrast to the lithe and lovely Fanny, stood the enormous Harriet, a shrill presence even before she had opened her mouth. I knew she had been buying and selling art, had spied her at a few openings, but I had not spoken to her since the day I met her at Tish's studio. She greeted me coldly, sat down, and said nothing for a while. Rune and I talked about AI, an interest we shared, when she interrupted us with a harsh comment to the effect that AI scientists couldn't even make a robot that walked like a human being, for God's sake. Then she started in on consciousness, as if she were some kind of expert, and then I mentioned *Beneath*. She called it a big change after the crosses. I was polite. I humored her. I said it was the oscillation in Rune's work that was interesting – the movement from one position to the other – but that his work was always about bodies, technology, and simulation, this time in disaster mode.

She interrupted us. 'I don't see how *Beneath* is about technology.'

I mentioned the robot dance.

'Why do you think those figures are robots?'

Rune took my side. The dancers had robotic movements, he said, sure, in line with his earlier work. Most of the reviews, he said, had described them that way.

I merely echoed this comment, saying that it was obvious to everyone.

This set her off. Her voice rose an octave. She

asked who 'everyone' was, said I was blinded by context and so were the other fools, or something to that effect. She accused me of multiple failings as a writer, most of which I can't remember. I was embarrassed for her, really, and wasn't going to egg her on with a response. This annoyed her further. Women who resort to wailing have always had a chilling effect on me. My admittedly brief marriage ended because I became allergic to my wife's voice. Since then, I only consort with women who keep their tones low and dulcet. The Harriet tirade lasted seven, maybe ten minutes. Rune tried to placate her: 'Harry, Harry, it's not important. Relax. Come on.' The upset ended with her sweeping up her coat and hat and making a grand exit.

I had no sense that the two were collaborators. It was obvious that Rune was calling the shots. I asked him what her problem was, and he said she was overly sensitive, a bit unstable, but a friend. I would like to note here that he defended her: 'People don't understand Harry, but she's highly intelligent. She's stuck on her own view, that's all. I admire her for it.'

After Harriet left, Rune and I strayed onto the meanings of money, that eternal American subject. He had never seen real money before he came to New York. His hometown, Clinton, Iowa, had rolled in the glories of lumber riches in the second half of the nineteenth century, but when the forests were depleted around 1900, the wealth died with the trees. He had grown up with the moldering mansions and ragged parks left by long-dead millionaires, but in New York City those riches had been reborn in the body of Rena Dewitt. 'Her soul was made of money,' he said. My own initiation had come at Yale, where I witnessed firsthand the casual assumptions of class, its ease and smugness, the lawns and paintings and town houses that lurked behind the friendly but distant smile. Of course we need the rich. We always have: to ogle and envy and imitate. They are our spectacle and our joy because in the head of every American lies the thought *That could be me.* (*That could be I,* grammatically correct though it is, does not lurk within our collective heart, not anymore.) The rich constitute our mythos, after all, our fairy tale, our hymn to success: the self-made man, the robber baron, dog-eat-dog, rugged individualism, nice guys finish last, carry your own gun and ride in your own limousine, long-legged babes with enhanced boobs on either side of you as you drive to the premiere and exit the car, flashbulbs exploding around you. There is still old money around, quiet and hidden and stealthy, but it has no grip on the public imagination as it once did. The social register, the 400, the debuts – still around, but there are fewer and fewer Philadelphia stories told in our world of Twitter and Facebook.

Rune and Rena – a gleaming pair. 'Rune, the Rube,' he joked, 'learned fast.' He learned because in the United States there is still a teeny-weeny bit of truth in the myth. Millionaire hairdressers hobnob with heiresses. Cowboy traders, suddenly flush, saunter through the doors of the Metropolitan Museum for a gala. The actress, once the kept paramour of Mr Old Money slumming backstage, is now royalty in her own right. The newly minted artist buys up lofts and houses right and left. I have seen it all. Believe me. They're up. They're down. They soar and they crash. I am nobody's conscience, but I am the man who looks on at the fiascos and the greed and the pills and the booze and the bouts in rehab. And I still have a job. I am still in my comfortable apartment, and I am invited to dinner a couple of times a week with people who count. I own two tuxedos. No one remembers the Crawler, but the techniques I used then are still good, and I have what cannot be faked: wit. It is a commodity in short supply.

The art of conversation has been dwindling steadily until there is nearly no art left, but I do my best to resurrect it when I can. And I understand the power of the compliment, which must always seize upon a truth. I told Rune that day that he was fascinatingly elusive, that he held my interest not only because I admired his work but because he embodied contradictions I felt in myself. I am continually torn between admiration and contempt for the circus of vanity and stupidity I witness every day and on which I dutifully report. I admire the ruthless vigor of the climbers, but I often bemoan their lack of style. I feel the pull to the future, the revolution of the digital age, but I long for the literate niceties of the past, for a touch of romance and courtesy.

He snorted at my comment, but then he made a long, rambling, excited confession of sorts, which I taped. I wasn't going to use it. I just pushed the button through my jacket pocket and, even though the sound wasn't perfect, I got a lot of it. He had always wanted to get out of Clinton, and he attributed this desire to escape to his mother. Not surprisingly, when one examined the son, the mother had been a beauty, a homecoming queen and then Miss Iowa Dairy Farm. Yes, even in Rune's not very distant youth, such traditions continued in the Midwest. The woman had nurtured her own Bovary pipe dreams focused chiefly on Chicago, which came to naught. She had loved Motown music and used to dance wildly to the Supremes, bumping, grinding, and panting with her two children as all three laughed until their sides hurt in the living room, where she kept the framed photographs of the homecoming court – she at center smiling beside the king – as well as several eleven-by-thirteen glossies of herself in full Miss Dairy Farm regalia with a ribbon that crossed her chest and a golden crown on her head. 'That was her glamour, her moment,' he said, 'everyone staring at her.' She never let go of the moment, apparently, to her husband's annoyance. She told the stories of her triumph again and again. 'My poor mother,' Rune said. 'She used to dress up for nobody and sashay around the house. Now I think she was crazy, nuts, certifiable.' And then there were the days when she didn't get out of bed. She'd lie inert in her nightgown, staring at the ceiling, a glass of vodka beside her, disguised as a Coke. 'Or she'd cry.' Brother and sister would try to rouse the listless parent, but nothing worked.

No, it was not a charming family portrait. The woman killed herself with a lethal combination of sleeping pills and alcohol. It was probably intentional, but Rune didn't talk about her actual death, how exactly it had happened, and I didn't ask. He beat his thighs as if they were two bongo drums through most of his tale, his eyes not on me but on the lamp beside his chair. At some point, he wandered onto the story of the cat, and he stopped drumming. He had been eight at the time.

Mrs Sharon Larsen, an orphan of Nordic stock – hence the names of her two progeny – had been feeding a feral or near-feral cat against her husband's wishes, a scraggy tabby, who came around for food late in the afternoon. After a while, the cat settled into the household, but the three familial conspirators would always put the feline out before the Patriarch returned, although the man took to sniffing for the animal and complained bitterly about 'cat stink.' 'No cats! I said no cats!' And then one fateful afternoon, the interloper gave birth in the family's hamper on one of the paternal shirts, a gray work shirt with the name of the business, Hiram's, embroidered on the pocket. A domestic battle ensued, which led to the act Rune then described. His father scooped up the litter of tiny, blind pink bodies in paper napkins and drowned them in a bucket in the garage as his mother screamed 'No!' and the children cowered in the doorway. When Mr Larsen retreated back to the laundry room to grab the tabby and expel her permanently from the household, Mrs Larsen kneeled beside the crime-scene bucket and fished out the corpses as she howled, 'I hate you! You monster!' The neighbors called the police. By then, Mr Larsen had come to regret the massacre, and had apologized to his spouse, but Mrs Larsen would have none of it. The officers managed to frighten her into silence, but there was no reconciliation between the couple, despite the fact that Mr Larsen, according to his son, begged and blubbered and, at one point, kneeled in contrition. In the morning, the children found the cat remains on the garage floor. Rune's descriptive adjective for the poor stiffs was 'gross.' Kirsten orchestrated a proper burial in the garden, complete with prayers, but her brother did not participate. 'I decided,' Rune said, 'right then and there, looking at those disgusting dried-up little pieces of shit, that I wasn't going to be me anymore.'

When I asked him what he meant, he said he knew that he didn't belong to those people, and he never would. They weren't going to see him again. I asked him if he had run away. No, he didn't mean that, he meant that they could see someone, but not him. 'I'd give them Rune Two, Rune Three, or Rune Four, but never Rune One. They couldn't tell the difference. As long as I didn't bother them, what did they care?' He said the cat kept coming around looking for her kittens, meowing outside the door. He used to go out and talk to her, pet her, and give her something to eat. His mother, it seemed, had lost all interest in her former cause. 'She became my cat,' Rune said. 'I had her spayed with money I stole from Sharon's purse. She never noticed the cash was gone, or if she did notice, she probably thought she had spent it on the booze she imagined she was hiding so carefully. I never let my cat into the house. I'd go out to her.'

Rune smiled at me. The ready adjective for that facial expression among many of my colleagues would have been *sphinxlike*, but I work hard to keep my prose unsullied by slack clichés, not that anyone truly notices in our illiterate age. The man's smile was illegible. I put the family cat histrionics into *Martyred for Art* because I admired the idea of numbered Runes, whether he had invented it on the spot for my benefit or not. It captured his aesthetic and a longing for virtual selves: one, two, three, four, and (the coming rhyme is intentional) perhaps more.

THE BAROMETER

(excerpt from Phineas Q. Eldridge's taped conversation, October 15, 2001)

PQE: How did you get interested in the weather?

B: From God. Beginning and end. He is, I proclamate, all weather, the weatherman of all and allness, of all's well that ends well. Windy pressures ride high in his blasted being of beginnings and endings. You understand he is a totalitarian, but also a hotelitarian, who takes in mankind, takes him in to the inn, but then blows him down. The song goes, 'Blow the man down, O give me some time, and give me some rhyme and blow, blow, blow the man down.' Blow that puny little butthead, Man, man and his kind, into ribbons and smithereens. How does he do it? It's a big secret deal of the Potentate, the Reprobate, the Pulverizer and Mercifier, the Big Blue Sky Daddy who dreams on our screens. That's what happened with the World and Trade, the Power towers. God had a nightmare, you see,

271

and it went viral onto every TV and computer and also into the heads of every geek tuned into the net. Divine Head, the godhead storms onto the earth, his curse on our things, but no things we can understand or demand or remand or take in hand. I am blessed with inside scoops of ice cream and then I scream on these matters, these barometric matters that aren't matter, but air issues for fair, fair weather, which should be fair, but often are not fair, in that life is not fair. It all registers, tremors and tickles and rumbles, ups and downs in my organs and my head, in the gray pulp up there with graphs and that little needle wobbling, you know, in there, too. My head has a direct connection to the godhead, two heads, and it can be too much, way too much for me, and some days I can't manage the management of the bandages needed, too many, when the earth and the air are crying outside and inside my head . . .

PQE: You've lived with Harry for quite some time now. I've heard you say you want to leave, but you end up staying.

B: The reasons are demonish.

PQE: Demonish?

B: The bad angel who comes sometimes at the dark hour, stealing around in Harry's things, into her world of the metamorphoses and the changelings. The Barometer can feel him, his omens. I stay as the barrier, the needle speeds when he's here. I can wrestle. I was on the team. I will wrestle. Jacob wrestled him. The sinew of Jacob's thigh shrank.

PQE: Yes, they wrestled all night. I always found it rather homoerotic. But you don't mean Bruno, do you?

B: Bruno is not an angel. Have you no eyes? Are you blind, blind and unkind? He comes when you're gone, Phineas. He hides behind the buildings and the trash cans. He keeps his wings folded in, big, awful, veiny wings. He's fallen, you know, fell from Heaven to here below, to keep us low, to build our ruin, but nothing broke when he fell, and now he roams through wood and waste, over hill and dale to the place where Longitude meets Latitude, you see, don't you, he's fallen down, the Arch-Enemy. If he touches you, you burn and shrivel. Look here on my arm.

PQE: You say the angel left that red mark on you?

273

B: A fiery finger of wrathful fate. He said, 'Don't say a word, you crazy fuck. Not one word.'

PQE: He said that? Not very angelic.

B: He said that, and then he turned around and walked down the hall, dragging his wings like peacock plumes behind him.

MAISIE LORD
(edited transcript)

My mother had to tell me and Ethan that Phinny was her front, because she knew the moment we saw *The Suffocation Rooms* we'd know she was responsible for them. Those lumpy figures, the heat in the rooms: No one but Mother made art like that. She just blurted it out: 'Maisie, Phinny's showing my work for me.' When I gaped at her and asked her if she had gone completely batty, she got that wrinkled, knowing look on her face, which always let me know a big explanation was coming, and she launched into a story about James Tiptree, the science fiction writer. According to Mother, for at least ten years no one actually saw Tiptree in the flesh, not even his editor. His secret identity caused a lot of speculation, and there were some people who thought that hiding behind the pseudonym there might be a woman, not a man. Robert Silverberg, another science fiction writer, wrote an introduction for a book of stories by Tiptree. He weighed in on the sex question and argued that just as no man could have written the novels of Jane Austen, no woman could have produced the stories of Ernest Hemingway or

James Tiptree. Mother loved this part of the Tiptree drama because Silverberg's faith in the writer's unimpeachable masculinity turned out to be misplaced. When the actual person stepped out from behind the pen name, the macho Tiptree turned out to be Alice Bradley Sheldon.

But Mother stressed that nothing was simple. After she had invented Tiptree and before she unveiled herself as Alice Sheldon, the writer took on another persona, a female one she named Raccoona Sheldon, whose work was rejected by a number of publishers and deemed inferior to Tiptree's. The writer, who had been praised as a man who could write feminist science fiction, now had a female mask, too. My mother said the bizarre name Raccoona had surely been inspired, at least on a subliminal level, by the masks raccoons don't wear but simply have – the ones given them by nature. That's the title of my third film, the one I'm working on now about my mother: *The Natural Mask*. The revelation that James Tiptree and Raccoona Sheldon were two sides of the same person didn't make life simpler for Alice Sheldon. Although the women who had been friends with Tiptree by letter, including Ursula Le Guin, greeted the newly revealed Alice Sheldon warmly, a number of the men who had been writing to her vanished abruptly from her life.

Mother told me the whole story with shining eyes. We were sitting across from each other at her kitchen table, and she leaned toward me, lifting

276

her index finger every now and then to make her points. What interested her was not simply substituting a man's name for a woman's. That was boring. No, she pointed out that Le Guin had suspected all along that Raccoona and Tiptree were two authors that came from the same source, but in a letter to Alice she wrote that she preferred Tiptree to Raccoona: 'Raccoona, I think, has less control, thus less wit and power.'

Le Guin, Mother said, had understood something deep. 'When you take on a male persona, something happens.'

When I asked her what that was, she sat back in her chair, waved her arm, and smiled. 'You get to be the father.'

As her daughter, I didn't like hearing my mother talk about being the father. I felt a visceral jolt under my ribs, but I started giggling and said something like 'Oh, Mother, come on, you don't really mean that.' But Mother did mean it. She told me that in 1987 Tiptree shot her husband and then killed herself. Mother said Sheldon couldn't live without her man – not her husband, obviously, but the man inside her – and she believed that's why she exploded into violence.

I retell the Tiptree story in my film. Alice, who was known as Alli to her friends, once said: 'My biography is ambisexual.' Harriet Burden, known as Harry to her friends, could have said the same thing. It did not end there. My mother knew that telling me about her pseudonyms upset me because her father and my father were somehow mixed up in it. I suppose we all like to have people and things in their place, neatly outlined in black, but the world just isn't like that.

We talked about Aven for a while and the death of Radish, who drowned in a glass of orange juice. My daughter had been so cavalier about the death of her noisy, difficult, but also jovial companion who lived in her throat that it had worried me. Mother laughed and said imaginary friends didn't need funerals. They returned to 'from whence they came,' and we both laughed.

And then we covered the Ethan territory. Mother and I always did. He was our shared obsession, the son and brother we couldn't quite figure out so we always had to talk about him. He had just published his first short story in a literary magazine, and Mother was proud. 'The Umbrella' is a curious tale about a man who forms an erotic attachment to his striped umbrella. Whenever it rains, he shudders with excitement at the prospect of opening the umbrella, and he has to work hard to resist pressing the little spring on sunny days, although he spends a lot of time admiring its beauty as it leans casually to one side in its stand. Like my brother, the story's hero has rules for how to behave. Out in the street on rainy days under his umbrella, he doesn't want anyone to see that he's actually quivering with joy. To everyone he passes or meets, the umbrella should be only a thing – a tool for keeping off the rain. And then one day, after he has checked it with his coat at a restaurant and had his meal, the woman who hangs the outerwear retrieves the right coat but the wrong umbrella. A search ensues, but the striped umbrella is not found, and Ethan's nameless hero is devastated, although he keeps up a false front for the obsequious manager, who apologizes profusely for the error. He walks into the street with the wrong umbrella, which he discards in a bin, and proceeds home in a deluge, getting wetter and wetter and colder and colder. The last sentence, which uses the feminine pronoun for the first time, is: 'And no one would understand that she was irreplaceable.'

Mother thought the story was better than anything Ethan had written before, less pretentious, and I agreed, even though being titillated by a gendered umbrella struck me as another oddity in the catalogue of oddities that all together made up my brother. I had always been jealous of Ethan's specialness. He always had to be handled so carefully, our eccentric boy with his stiff movements. He used to remind me of Pinocchio (before he became a real boy, of course). And he'd get so frustrated with stupid little things and throw tantrums. All the pounding on the floor, the howling and the kicking. Mother would hold him tightly in her arms and just let him wail. I was always told to 'make allowances' for his 'peculiarities.' Looking straight at her, I told Mother I had wanted peculiarities, too. I had wanted to get the special, Ethan boy-genius treatment, but I had been good old normal Maisie without a special bone in my body. I remember Mother looked shocked because I was so vociferous. She leaned across the table, took my hand, and said, 'Maisie!'

I suppose I was peevish. I also suppose that my mother's confession had opened the door to more confession, and that I had a perverse need to get some attention myself. I reiterated that it had always been all about Ethan, extra meetings with his teachers, long chats with him in his room before he could get to sleep, his special 'medicine' that wasn't medicine at all but a little concoction of cocoa, sugar, and milk, and that sometimes Mother hadn't even demanded that he brush his teeth afterward. Mother sat back in her chair with wide eyes and said, 'Go ahead, let me have it.' And I did. I went on for quite a while, but my letting-her-have-it reached its apex with a story that still hurt when I remembered it.

Ethan was sick. He was sick a lot with earaches, one earache after another, and Mother had made a bed for him on the living room sofa. She stayed with him all night. I couldn't sleep and crept out of bed to go to her. I remember looking down at Ethan and at his stupid ears and, instead of whispering, I talked loudly, actually, maybe I yelled, and he woke up.

'And you were so angry,' I said, 'you told me to "grow up and cut the crap."' I wailed this sentence at my mother. The old emotion came blasting back, as if I were seven years old again and all hot with misery and a crusading sense of the injustice of it all. 'You sent me away!' I yelled at her. 'You sent me away!'

Mother looked at me sadly. Her face wrinkled up with that look of pained compassion I knew so well, but there was a little smile on her face, too, and she opened up her arms and said, 'Come here, Maisie.'

And I walked around the table, and my mother pulled me onto her lap, and she folded her long arms around me. I closed my eyes and collapsed into her, my face pressed into her neck. She embraced me firmly. She kept a tight hold on me, and she rocked me back and forth for a long time, for several minutes, anyway, and as she rocked me, she stroked my hair and whispered into my ear, 'God, how I love you.' The clutching, hard sensation I had had beneath my ribs loosened up completely, and for the time I sat in her lap, I forgot that I had grown up. I even forgot that I had a child myself, and I certainly forgot that I had a brother. She could do that, Mother could. When you least expected it, she would make some magic. It is ordinary magic, to be sure, but there are many people who do not know how to use it.

The evening of Mother and Phinny's opening – Mother in the wings and Phinny in the spotlight – arrived in windy, blustering blow-your-hat-off weather. The city was in mourning, and everyone was still jumpy. A sudden noise, a plane overhead, a stalled subway train made us all freeze for a moment, and then go on. I left Oscar and Aven at home and grabbed a cab to Chelsea. Bruno didn't come, because he was angry at Mother about the pseudonyms. Rachel came but didn't stay too long. I remember her pointedly kissing both Mother and Phinny and offering them congratulations. Ethan was there with a very tall African woman, pretty, very thin, with narrow glasses. It turned out she was some sort of princess or other, who was getting her PhD in molecular biology, but my first impression was that if any person could resemble an umbrella, she did, a closed one, naturally.

I always notice how little the people who go to openings seem to care about the work. Some of them hardly glance at it. Others stand in front of a piece and stare at it for a while, but with no expression on their faces – blanks. When people came out of the *Rooms*, they were sweating and had slightly twisted expressions on their faces – a smiling discomfort. I had a feeling they were all reminded of what it was like to be a child again, to have to look up to the big people, and that it wasn't the best feeling. I especially liked all the writing on the walls because it made me feel as if I'd gone inside a book, not literally walking on the pages, but as if I were actually moving around in the space between the words and the pictures you create in your mind when you read. I also experienced little puffs of memory rising up and then falling away, a half-known piece of some old place or thought, often a little painful, floating up in my mind for an instant and then vanishing.

Mother stood like a sentry against a wall with her arms folded. I remember she was wearing an elegant gray suit with a green scarf, her eyes narrowed in concentration. You'd think she would have hated giving it all away to Phinny – who was also in gray, a natty charcoal-gray suit with a red tie, and he was charming as all get-out and cracking jokes as usual. It worked because Phinny loved Mother. They were comrades in arms. He believed in the eventual revelation, in payback day, in vindication. She was his 'date' that evening, and he ushered her around and acted the part of a new artist on the scene.

Still, people didn't really know what to make of the work then. After all, Phinny had more or less dropped out of the blue. The question was how to interpret it. My father had been a player before the heroic chapter in American art closed. He had glimpsed 'the Romantic cowboy era' of tragic, drunken glamour boys. My mother adored de Kooning. 'Of all the big boys,' she liked to say, 'I love de Kooning the most,' but it came together for those artists. A contagious hysteria fed their fame and glory. 'Big, bad, and brutal,' Mother said. 'Everyone loved it.' But even de Kooning was dumped on when the weather changed, when Pop Art and cold-and-bold took the stage.

There was no atmosphere for Phinny or for Mother, no art culture to raise them up and anoint the mask. Rune was the one in a position to succeed, to frame my mother's gifts and sell them to the public. I feel sorry for Anton Tish, wherever he is. The flurry around him must have made him feel like a fraud. According to Mother, he had nurtured some notion of authenticity, and he had felt robbed of it. With Rune it was different. I doubt he was bothered by thoughts of originality. It's awfully hard to know if anything is truly original, anyway. An original thing would be so foreign, we wouldn't be able to recognize it, would we?

Rune came to the opening late, scattering his glamour dust around him. I felt it. Everyone felt it – that combination of Mr Handsome and Mr Famous. I had met him only once before, in my mother's studio about a year earlier, and he had impressed me although we had hardly said a word to each other except 'Nice to meet you.' I had walked into the studio with Aven to find my mother looking up at Rune, who was at the top of a ladder examining a sculpture that was hanging from the ceiling. On his way down, he had swung out from the ladder, which he had gripped with one hand, and then he had jumped to the floor, landing very softly. Somehow, he had made it seem as if he were not showing off, and I had found myself grinning in spite of myself. Aven was amazed and wanted to try the trick herself, but we persuaded her it was too dangerous. I had not forgotten either Rune's smile or his handshake, and when he walked into the show, I couldn't help looking at him. I was surprised when he rushed over to me and gave me a real double kiss – lips hit flesh – and planted himself in front of me as if I were the person he wanted to see most in the whole room.

Rune flirted with me. He looked at me intently, which is a form of flirting. I told him about the film I was making on the Barometer and how I had tracked down his brother and father and found out that his mother had died. I explained that psychiatrists no longer paid much attention to what their patients said, but that I had become fascinated by the Barometer's language and cosmology. We talked about different cameras and how wide shots and close-ups create meanings and how hard it was to do black-and-white movies anymore. He loved cinema and was fun to talk to. I can't remember exactly what he said to me then or how we got onto Mother, but he mentioned something about how difficult it must have been for Mother to be known as Felix Lord's wife, and that he really liked her work, and I told him a story I now regret. Mother had run into an acquaintance on Park Avenue, a man who dealt in Old Master drawings. He and she had ducked into a place on Madison Avenue for a cup of tea to catch up. In the course of their conversation, my mother had mentioned that she was rereading Panofsky with great interest. And Larry had casually said, 'Oh yes, Felix introduced you to all that, didn't he? He was a big man for theory.' Mother told him that Father had never read a word of Panofsky, that whatever he had known about his work had come from her. She was livid. I explained to Rune that it had probably happened one too many times, and she couldn't stand it anymore. Still, I told him, I wished she would just relax, just let it go. Although he didn't say much, Rune listened to me with a gentle, sympathetic expression on his face.

At some point we stepped outside and sat on the steps and talked more. He cupped his hands to light a cigarette and smoked. He jittered his knee as he inhaled and exhaled. The wind blew. I had no intention of taking our flirtation anywhere, but it was enjoyable nevertheless. He liked me in navy blue. He approved. I was flattered, a tad nervous, and therefore loquacious. Anxiety makes me talk more, not less. Rune examined my palm and invented a comical future for me with four husbands and many adventures and a very long life, and when he held my hand, he traced the lines with his index finger. He went on to say he read noses, too, and touched mine. And then he brought up Father. He wanted to know what it had been like to be a child in my household, to have all those paintings around, to watch the 'gods' come and go.

I told him kids don't think about that – whatever is just is. He told me he had known Father 'a little' back in the day, when he was first in New York. 'You have his eyes.' I do have my father's eyes, and somehow hearing this made me suddenly sorry for myself. I felt that I was looking at me from the outside. Poor thing, she's tired, I thought. And then I realized I had been tired for years. I was trying to make a film. Aven was six, a demanding oddball of a kid, who took everything too hard. Oscar was feeling neglected by me. My mother was lost in her own world of metamorphs, phenomenology, and pseudonyms, and my dear father, who surely would have helped make the whole situation better, was dead. An involuntary sob escaped me.

'You worshiped your father, didn't you?' Rune looked me straight in the eyes. I told him *worship* was not the right word, but it wasn't the word as much as his intonation that made me feel awkward. He smiled. 'I always had the feeling that Felix was a man who knew what he wanted.' I don't know why, but I felt slightly alarmed. Then he added, 'He had a great eye.' This meant nothing. It was what everyone said, but I felt vaguely distressed. I was wearing a scarf, and Rune picked up the end of it and began to play with the fringe. He had a souvenir, he said, from those days that he carried with him. He reached into his pocket and took out a key. He held it out to me in the palm of his hand.

I remember looking down at it, confused. I asked him what it was for. He said it was the key to a place that no longer existed. I asked him what it had to do with Father, and he said, 'Don't you know, Maisie?' I didn't know, and I was annoyed. I stood up to leave, but he still had a grip on my scarf, and as I pulled away from him, it tightened around my neck. I demanded he let go, but he tugged me down toward him so my face was only inches from his, and he smiled broadly. I pushed him away, and he lifted his hands in the air, a surprised look on his face, as if it had all been an innocent joke. He accused me of being 'touchy.' He was only 'teasing' me. But I was shaken, and he knew it. How I wished later that I had been able to hide my dread, laugh at him, make some cutting remark, but I couldn't.

I have never mentioned this to anyone. I'm telling it now for the first time, and I've wrestled with the fact that something so small could have felt so large. What had happened, after all? He had shown me a key that could have been any old key to any old door, and then he had implied that I should know about it. He had grabbed my scarf to prevent me from leaving. At the same time, he had charmed me, and I had felt attracted to him, more attracted than I had felt to a man in years. I had let him touch me, let him fiddle with my scarf. I had giggled at his jokes and had yattered on about my project. The instant he mentioned my father, however, the conversation had been twisted into another shape. Suddenly, it had turned rife with innuendo, as if this man had shared a story with Father, and the mood had changed. No, *my* mood had changed. He had remained unruffled. But I had felt humiliated, as if all that had gone before had been a prelude to a subtle moment of cruelty, a play on my doubts, doubts he seemed to know I had, doubts I could not talk about, not only because they frightened me but because I did not know what they were. I didn't know what I was afraid of.

I can't really say what went on between us.

Whatever it was seemed to be as much about my father and mother as it was about me. We are always concocting theories about how the world works and why people act in the ways they do. We invent motives for them, as if it's possible for us to know, but more often than not these explanations are like flimsy cardboard stage sets we put up in front of reality because they are simpler and less distracting than what's actually there. I think I became a documentary filmmaker to try to get a truer view. It's not that film can't lie or distort or be used for dastardly purposes, it's that sometimes the camera extracts from the faces and bodies of its subjects what they do not say aloud. I was sixteen when I first saw Marcel Ophüls's *The Sorrow and the Pity*, and after that, I couldn't stop thinking about the expressiveness of people's hands when they are controlling their faces. I have often wondered what I might have seen in Rune if I had had a camera. Maybe nothing. After all, he was an expert at filming himself.

That night, as I lay in bed next to a snoring Oscar, I remembered Rune saying 'Don't you know, Maisie?' It had felt like an accusation. Did I know something? And then I remembered my father's keys, the strange keys he had scooped up that morning when I was just a girl. I remembered standing in Green-Wood Cemetery and the glamorous white angel on a gravestone near Father's plain one, and then I remembered visiting my mother a few months after Father died. I was there

289

often, and the doorman let me up without phoning. When I rang the bell in the hall, Mother didn't come to the door, even though she had to know it was me. The door was open, so I went in, and I heard the sound of retching from the guest bathroom in the hall off the dining room. I ran toward the sound and found my mother hunched over, her arms folded across her chest. Vomit shot from her mouth like a missile, not into the toilet but onto the seat and floor. There were tears in her eyes, and I took her arm. She said, 'No, no, it's okay. Leave me.' But another wave struck, and I was shocked to see the force of the heaving that convulsed her body. I grabbed her around the waist and held her forehead close to the toilet bowl. As a child when I threw up, Mother always held my forehead for comfort. 'I can't keep it down, Maisie.' She was gasping. 'There's something wrong with me. I can't keep it down. I'm sorry. I'm so sorry.'

I cleaned her mouth with a washcloth and walked her to the other end of the apartment and settled her into bed. She lay down. Then I left her and returned to the bathroom and cleaned the vomit with a big roll of paper towels, which one after another I discarded in a garbage bag. I remember the pungent smell that made me hold my breath, the yellow liquid slime with small brightly colored bits of food in it. I remember that I spilled some bleach, too, which left white spots on my jeans. I worked hard to make sure that no trace was left on the floor or walls or behind the toilet bowl. When I moved quietly down the hallway toward the bedroom, I heard the noise of Mother crying. She didn't cry, at least not in front of me. She hadn't cried at Father's funeral or at Grandmother's or Grandfather's. Her sobs were strange, somehow inhuman. She sounded like a dog that makes strangled yelps and yowls when it tries to talk, and then came a long, hoarse shriek that made me stop short in the hall, an extended howl of agony. I felt my face contort as I leaned against the wall outside my parents' bedroom, listening to my mother. I wanted to go to her, but I was afraid to look at her, afraid of her feeling. I waited. I waited for the worst to end. By the time I went in to her, she was calm. Again she apologized. I told her there was nothing to be sorry for.

There are nights when I can't sleep, and I lie awake thinking about *The Natural Mask*, which means that I think about Mother and her story, and how to tell it in the film. I do not want it to be too neat and tidy. I do not want to explain away the mess. She would have hated that. Over and over, I have looked at my film of her just a year before she died. She is sitting in her studio beside the Empathy Box, talking into the camera. At one moment she speaks directly to me. She says my name, and when I hear it, I always feel a quickening inside me.

'We live inside our categories, Maisie, and we believe in them, but they often get scrambled. The scrambling is what interests me. The mess.'

PATRICK DONAN
(review of The Suffocation Rooms,
Art Beats, *NYC, March 27, 2002)*

'I love the heat, don't you?' Phineas Q. Eldridge
smiles as he talks about his installation at the
Alex Begley Gallery. His first solo show consists
of seven enclosed kitchens connected railroad-style
by doors. Each room is a little hotter than the one
before, which means every visitor must get ready
to sweat. The downtown performance artist, known
for his gender-and-race-bending monologues at
the Pink Lagoon, has made a move into visual art.
Each kitchen of *The Suffocation Rooms* features two
large stuffed figures, a chest, and a creepy wax
character that might have popped in from another
galaxy. Theater is part and parcel of installation
art, but Eldridge has brought his overt staginess
to this series of rooms.

According to Eldridge, the piece has no message.
And yet, it is hard not to think of American culture
wars while passing through his otherworldly
kitchens. The eerie intersex person rising out of
the seven chests speaks directly to the LGBT
community. The box (perhaps a little too obviously)
is also 'the closet.' Eldridge came out in 1995 and

has been exploring gay and racial identities in his work ever since he launched himself as part of the underground cabaret scene.

And the two oversized, stuffed humans? Could it be the white America of right-wing 'family values'? Eldridge is noncommittal. Twisting Susan Sontag, he says, 'Interpretation is dangerous.'

After 9/11 a lot of art has just looked irrelevant, but the claustrophobic atmosphere and the gradual decay and destruction of the seven rooms address the smug insulation of most Americans, who were locked in their own materialistic dreams until they were shocked out of their complacency by the terrible events of last September. Alex Begley offers his own take on suffocation. 'This installation has genuine impact. It addresses our situation now.'

ZACHARY DORTMUND
(review of The Suffocation Rooms,
Art Assembly, *March 30, 2001)*

The interest of Phineas Q. Eldridge's installation *The Suffocation Rooms* at Alex Begley lies in its subversion of the clean aesthetic associated with avant-garde modernism, as well as the easy pop consumerism of the Young British Artists. Its invitation to the spectator, however, remains private. Unlike the practice of an artist such as Tiravanija, whose open works invite DIY interaction, Eldridge's closed rooms are walkthroughs. This is not fully relational art, to cite Nicolas Bourriaud. It is not altermodern. Nevertheless, the successive real environments may pack a punch that is ultimately more subversive than the accommodating relationalism advocated by Bourriaud. The transgendered figure that reappears in each room summons the delirious machine subjectivity of Guattari, a self-technology of desire and a body without organs, which echoes Eldridge's life as a queering performer onstage. The chaos of the final room has genuine political bite.

HARRIET BURDEN
Notebook K

April 19, 2001

He is clever, not as Felix was clever. Felix knew how to excite collectors, how to flatter them, how to make them imagine they were the ones who had truly seen and under-stood the work of art in front of them. This man wants all eyes on him all the time. He films himself every day, as if the camera tells him he is alive. He would like to be an escape artist – that, above all, I think. Defy nature or appear to defy nature's limits.

I just want to work and pull off my scheme.

And yet, I like him. He has an almost weightless bounce. I have a feeling he will want to play, because the manipulation of appearances excites him. For him, the pleasure is almost sexual, a form of titillation, yes, of rising. Tumescence. This I can feel. It is not the aging Harriet who attracts him, but my talk. He is not Anton, my green mask, or Phinny, my blue one. Phinny and I were each other or enough of each other to skip along in tandem, a duet, two whistlers out for an adventure or misadventure, P & H. But Phinny is leaving me. He's fallen in love with the Argentinian, and I can see the lights have turned on in his eyes. How I will miss him. It was easy for us to mingle.

Rune, a name made of stone, another pseudonym altogether: gray.

He has a tic. He licks his front teeth as if checking for food.

I want to stage Rune. I want to discover the works that are his works but which I will make. Rune will be my Johannes the Seducer: terrible, sly, brilliant mask. The Kierkegaard commentators have missed the heart of the ogre. They suppress the sadistic thrill.

Peel the onion of personas, from one to the next, moving further and further inside the book.

Listen to this, Harry. You remember when you first read it. The sentence comes right near the end of the first volume. You are still in Part I. It shook you hard. Remember? He was your own being, wasn't he? Not Cordelia.

No, that's a lie. Poor Cordelia. But that *poor* is the something you spit out, reject, cough up, vomit out. Not always, not always, but the seduction is complete, his of you, not as a woman but as a man. I am Johannes. The reader Johannes seduces becomes Johannes – in part. There's the knot. Look at the knot. It is so dull, so familiar, so unjust being treated as a woman first, always as a woman. I rebel. Why womanliness first? Why this trait first? Inescapable.

Dr F. noticed that I was wearing a skirt. He knows. It is only the second time in all these years, he said. It is noteworthy. It was a show of vulnerability. The ones in skirts are vulnerable. This is the history of women in skirts.

Women fall, drop from the skies, one after the other, falling and falling again. Open your thighs, beloved, and I will hurl you over the cliff to your death. Vagina as battleground. Vagina as ruin. But he never says, Let me in. That is the coup. Her only power is in not letting him in. I will cross my legs tightly.

Cross your thighs, Cordelia.

The Seducer writes, 'Everything is a metaphor. I myself am a myth about myself, for is it not a myth that I hasten to this tryst? Who I am is irrelevant; everything finite and temporal is forgotten; only the eternal remains, the power of erotic longing, its bliss.'

The Seducer lives only on the page. He is a phantasm of A, who is a phantasm of Eremita, the editor of *Either/Or*, who is in turn a phantasm of Søren Kierkegaard, long dead and animated by his pages.

Isn't A appalled by his own aesthetic invention?*

---

* Burden compares the role she wants Rune to play to Kierkegaard's use of Johannes, the pseudonymous author of 'A Seducer's Diary,' the final section of *Either/Or*, Part I. In the diary, Johannes writes about his seduction of Cordelia, which he manages with such consummate skill

We are all myths to ourselves.

Johannes is going to fuck Cordelia.

And then he will leave her.

S.K. loved Regina, and he left her. He did not literally screw her, it seems. He left her virginity for another, but he hurt her to the quick.*

---

that she imagines she is pursuing him. Part I is an 'onion' of pseudonymity. The editor, Victor Eremita, writes the preface for Part I. A is the character who occupies the aesthetic point of view in the first volume and declares himself the editor of 'A Seducer's Diary,' but not its author. Following Eremita, Burden understands that Johannes is A's fictional creature, the pseudonym of a pseudonym, a 'metaphor' and a 'myth' that represents an extreme aesthetic position of reflection. A is horrified by his own creation. In the preface Eremita writes, 'It really seems as if A himself has become afraid of his fiction, which, like a troubled dream, continued to make him feel uneasy, also in the telling' (*Kierkegaard's Writings*, vol. III, 9).

* Kierkegaard met Regina Olsen in 1837 when he was twenty-four and she was fourteen. They became engaged in 1840, but a year later he broke the engagement, leaving Regina by all accounts in despair. Kierkegaard writes, 'So, there was nothing else for me to do but to venture to the uttermost, to support her, if possible, by means of a deception, to do everything to repel her from me in order to rekindle her pride.' Quoted in Joachim Garff, *Søren Kierkegaard: A Biography*, trans. Bruce H. Kirmmse (Princeton: Princeton University Press, 2005), 186. Although he repeatedly declares his love for her in his journals, the reason for his withdrawal from his promise has been the subject of endless scholarly speculation. Despite her fascination with Kierkegaard, Burden thought

'I shall not bid her farewell,' writes Johannes, 'nothing is more revolting than the feminine tears and pleas that alter everything and yet are essentially meaningless. I did love her, but from now on she can no longer occupy my soul. If I were a god, I would do for her what Neptune did for the nymph: *transform her into a man.*'

There they are, the last five words: the razor.

I will transform myself into a man through Rune.

Will I become Johannes?

But Johannes was not Søren. He wasn't A. No, he was not. We know S.K. believed in women's tears and women's pleas and women's prayers. And I am not Rune. And yet, and yet, and yet, I am he somewhere else, in the phantasmagoria. Let me whisper in your ear. Let me whisper that the fantasy man with the dialectical whip is Søren, too. A trickster. I will borrow a trickster self.

Look at me, a Prometheus. I am myself a myth about myself. Who I am has nothing to do with it.

S.K.'s relations with Regina were 'perverse.' In Notebook K, she writes, 'Regina occupies the remote space assigned to all female love objects and muses. Poor Regina! Poor Cordelia! I turn the tables!'

HARRIET BURDEN
Notebook A

May 4, 2001

Bruno is writing a memoir. I must not show that I am too happy about it. He's just fooling around, he says, having a little fun. He's waltzing. That's what he should have done all along, the stubborn S.O.B., waltzed, had a little fun instead of bleeding out those verses for the millennium. But I must not gloat or preen or he may stop just to spite me. Dear Bear, what have you done with all those years of your life? I want you to write that caustic, tender, bullish man into a book. Make him up, darling, if you have to. He's there.

A passage he read to me about ice cream on the boardwalk at Coney Island, about his mother pulling her hand away after he had reached for hers – the cold chocolate had run into his palm. So tiny, this moment, but taken as a slap, its sound reverberating over many years. What do they say? A difficult woman. She was a difficult woman. Heads shaking over difficult women. We are all difficult women. Was Bruno's mother more difficult?

No, but she was Bruno's mother. Just now, this word *difficult* looks mad to me, an insane spelling of a word I cannot recognize anymore.

Aven told me that Julie said, 'I won't be your friend anymore.' Aven's mouth stretched into a grimace. 'But then,' she said, 'you wouldn't believe it. The next day she forgot!' Aven doesn't forget. She is one of us.

Mother plays in my body like a tune. Her voice returns, old and hoarse, as she thinks through time. 'He loved me more at the end.' And when I ask her what she means, she says, 'More than he did in the beginning. I loved him. I put your father on a pedestal, but he ran away from me.'

And I see my father running away with long strides over hills and dales.

He punished her with silence.

'I rarely got a word in at a dinner party, you know. I brought in the food and I cleared the table and I listened, but when I began to speak, he would cut me off. Once, after a party, I brought it up. I said that I had felt bad about it, hurt. He didn't answer me, but the next time we had a dinner, he said nothing, not a word.'

'That was cruel,' I said to Mother.

Dr F. has heard it all now. I remember my mother.

'Don't forget,' my mother said in the hospital. 'You're a Jew.'

'I won't forget, Mother.'

The room in the hospital is ugly. My mother is recovering from septicemia. The nurse from Trinidad looks at me. 'We were afraid she might leave us last night, but she's tough.' My mother had roamed the hospital corridors, hallucinating with fever. She was back in Indianapolis in the old house, or rather parts of it, climbing the stairs at home in search of her room. 'But I couldn't find it. I opened door after door, Harriet.'

And I think to myself my father wanted his own kind, not me. His natural kind. No, Harry, sex is not a natural kind in philosophy.* Fish. Fowl. A two-headed calf.

Who would they have been, I wonder, the siblings that were never formed?

'What should I wear?' she asks.

'Wear, Mother?'

She is irritated, looking around. 'To the faculty dinner. Where are my pearls? I will need my pearls. I don't think that sweater suits you, Harriet.'

And I wished I could smile. I rubbed her feet because they were cold. Three pairs of socks and still cold.

* *Natural kind* was first introduced by John Stuart Mill in 1895. *Philosophy of Scientific Method*, ed. Ernest Nagel (New York: Hafner, 1950), 303–4. The term implies that there are groupings in nature independent of human categories. There is considerable debate in analytical philosophy about whether natural kinds exist at all, and the question as to whether sex is a natural kind is part of that debate.

I can see the East River, the gray waves, and the light, and inside the room, the IV drip, and the tape on my mother's discolored arm, the sleeve of her lilac-colored robe pushed up.

Don't die yet, I think.

Time is thick in the present, a distension, not a series of points, subjective time, that is, our inner time. We are forever retaining and projecting, anticipating the next note in the tune, recalling the whole phrase as we listen.*

I remember my protruding navel on my big, hard belly, the skin pulled tight in the last month – the strange push and pull of the life inside. My pink, swollen feet propped up on an ottoman before me. Felix with his ear pressed against the bump. Hey there, little fella, little chiquita. It was Maisie. Yes, I think it was Maisie.

* Burden is paraphrasing Husserl. The philosopher discusses listening to music as a primary example of the subjective experience of time, which includes more than is immediately present. It also includes succession and duration. *The Phenomenology of Internal Time Consciousness* (Bloomington: Indiana University Press, 1966).

HARRIET BURDEN
Notebook M

I am going to build a house-woman. She will have an inside and an outside, so that we can walk in and out of her. I am drawing her, drawing and thinking about her form. She must be large, and she must be a difficult woman, but she cannot be a natural horror or a fantasy creature with a vagina dentata. She cannot be a Picasso or a de Kooning monster or Madonna. No either/or for this woman. No, she must be true. She must have a head as important as her tail. And there will be characters inside that head, little men and women up to various pursuits. Let them write and sing and play instruments and dance and read very long speeches that put us all to sleep. Let her be my Lady Contemplation in honor of Margaret Cavendish, Duchess of Newcastle, that seventeenth-century monstrosity: female intellectual. Author of plays, romances, poems, letters, natural philosophy, and a utopian fiction, *The Blazing World*. I will call my woman *The Blazing World* after the duchess. Anti-Cartesian, in the long run anti-atomist, anti-Hobbesian, an exiled Royalist in France, but she was a hard-bitten monist and a materialist who didn't, couldn't quite leave God out of it. Her ideas overlap with Leibniz. Had my father known about Cavendish and her links to his hero?

Mad Madge was an embarrassment, a flamboyant boil on the face of nature. She made a spectacle of herself. Allowed once as a visitor to the Royal Society to watch experiments in 1666, the duchess in all her eccentric glory was duly recorded by Samuel Pepys, who recorded everything. He called her a 'mad, conceited, ridiculous woman.' It was easy. It's still easy. You simply refuse to answer the woman. You don't engage in a dialogue. You let her words or her pictures die. You turn your head away. Centuries pass. The year the first woman was admitted to the Royal Society? 1945.

The duchess sometimes wore men's clothes, vests and cavalier hats. She bowed rather than curtsied. She was a beardless astonishment, a confusion of roles. She staged herself as mask or masque. Cavalier hat off to you, Duchess. May its plumage wave.*

---

* On the occasion of Cavendish's visit to the Royal Society, John Evelyn, a diarist of the period and a friend of Samuel Pepys, composed a ballad: 'God bless us! / When I first did see her: / She looked so like a Cavalier, / But that she had no beard.' Quoted in Emma L. E. Rees, *Margaret Cavendish: Gender, Genre, Exile* (Manchester: Manchester University Press, 2003), 13.

Cross-dressers run rampant in Cavendish. How else can a lady gallop into the world? How else can she be heard? She must become a man or she must leave this world or she must leave her body, her mean-born body, and blaze. The duchess is a dreamer. Her characters wield their contradictory words like banners. She cannot decide. Polyphony is the only route to understanding. Hermaphroditic polyphony. 'What noble mind can suffer a base servitude without rebellious passions?' asked Lady Ward. But the ladies always win in her worlds. Through marriage, beauty, argument, and rank wishful fantasy. Lord Courtship is thunderstruck by the woman's lucidity and feeling. He is reborn instantly.

Is this not what I want? Look at my work. Look and see.

How to live? A life in the world or a world in the head? To be seen and recognized outside, or to hide and think inside? Actor or hermit? Which is it? She wanted both – to be inside and outside, to ponder and to leap. She was painfully shy and suffered from melancholia, a drag on her gait. She bragged. She adored her husband. A few sages called her a genius.

I am a Riot. An Opera. A Menace! I am Mad Madge, Mad Hatter Harriet, a hideous anomaly who lives at the Heartbreak Hotel near Sunny's Bar on the water in Brooklyn with people straight from the funny papers. Bruno says there are those in the neighborhood who call me the Witch. I take it on, then, the enchantment of magic and the power of night, which is procreative, fertile, wet. Isn't that where their fear lies? Don't women give birth? Don't we push those squalling babes into the world, suckle them, and sing to them? Are we not the makers and shakers of generations?

Tiny Gulliver in Brobdingnag looks up at the giant nurse who gives suck to an infant. 'No sight disgusted me so much as her monstrous breast. Its size is alarming, and every imperfection of the skin visible.' A Swiftian conflation of microscope and misogyny. But isn't every infant a dwarf at the breast?

Mother said, 'He ran away from me.'

I want to blaze and rumble and roar.
I want to hide and weep and hold on to my mother.
But so do we all.

HARRIET BURDEN
Notebook T

May 24, 2001

We have made the pact, or at least I think we have made it. He looked into my eyes and he said it would be fun.

I have bought a Rune multiple – a video work. *The New Me*. I am curious to see how it holds up over time.

His apartment: a plumber's dream of Baroque splendor. I didn't dare ask him if the gold tassels were tongue in cheek or not, but he is too smart *not* to know. He indulges himself in contradictions and expects everyone to go along with him; and this is paradoxically charming because it is child-like. Look at my toys. Aren't they cool? He strutted through the rooms, giving me the tour, as his arm shot out in the direction of each object, but he did not pause to examine a single trophy: 'pot from Cambodia, 2000 B.C., Diane Arbus photo – killed herself in '71, – the shoes Marlene Dietrich wore in *Morocco*.' When a girl with a pixie cut suddenly appeared in a doorway, he flung out his arm and barked 'Jeannie,' after which he grinned at me to make sure I understood he was joking. An 'assistant,' one of a team of 'helpers' roaming about, mostly competent-looking young women with telephones.

Robot photos in heroic display, taken in various labs around the United States and in Geneva, but also 'filmbots,' imaginary machines, a movie still of Hal from *2001* and Woody Allen as the robotic waiter in *Sleeper*. Give me Woody Allen's bumbler any day, I said, but Rune did not smile.

He has ideas, but they are jumbled. He never read a single page of the books I recommended. But a demon called the Singularity has possessed him, the grandiose offspring of one Verne Vinge, mathematics professor and science fiction writer, who in 1993 predicted a monumental, revolutionary shift in time, the moment we poor mortals will manufacture machine intelligences greater than our own. Our technical devices will race ahead of us, and a post-human, postbiological world will dawn. We will all be machine-organic hybrids. We will 'upload' ourselves and become immortals, although the trick remains elusive. Vinge, a techno-Frankenstein, writes: 'Large computer networks may "wake up" as a superhumanly intelligent entity.'*

* Vernor Vinge first presented his views on the Singularity at the Vision-21 Symposium sponsored by NASA, March

Wake up?

I grunted and guffawed and waggled my finger,
but Rune tells me with a straight face that it will
all happen by 2030. How I would love to bet on
it, but I'll be dead. Harriet Burden will be dust,
bones ground to ashes. Does Rune really believe
it? Has he really embraced this article of faith
founded on a false theoretical model: computational theory of mind?* The boys in the labs and
some of their cohorts in analytical philosophy have
been kneeling in obeisance to the sacred machine
that processes information at ever-increasing
speeds, that plays chess well but translates from

30–31, 1993. For a review of the continuing discussion,
see 'The Singularity: Ongoing Debate, Part II' in *Journal
of Consciousness Studies* 19 (2012), nos. 7–8.

* Computational theory of mind (CTM) advances the
idea that the mind works like a computer through rule-
based symbol manipulation. Hilary Putnam, 'Brains and
Behavior' (1961), in *Readings in Philosophy of Psychology*,
vol. 1, ed. Ned Block (Cambridge, Mass.: Harvard
University Press, 1980), 24–36, and Jerry Fodor, *The
Language of Thought* (New York: Thomas Cromwell,
1975). In Notebook T, Burden criticizes the scientists
and philosophers who have adopted the model, because
it doesn't account for 'the brain as a wet organ of the
whole body' and it 'leaves out guiding emotional knowledge.' She also calls CTM 'a surreptitious form of
Cartesian dualism' and cites Hubert Dreyfus's critique
of the theory in *What Computers Still Can't Do* (Cambridge,
Mass.: MIT, 1992).

one language to another so badly it hurts, and which doesn't feel anything at all. Don't you know that others are writing about paradigm change, that information processing as a model for brain function fails at many levels? Rune wants to believe. It is a form of salvation.

The Singularity is at once an escape and a birth fantasy. I said to him: A Zeus dream that avoids the organic body altogether. Brand-new creatures burst forth from men's heads. Presto! The mother and her evil vagina disappears.

I pointed out that his crosses are fertility symbols.
I don't know how much of what I say goes in. Deafness is part of his being. And it helps him, helps him assert himself as the young Wonder Man.

But there is an undertow, and it is personal. He is trying to leap out of his biography. Maybe this is where we overlap. I would like to leap out of my story, too.

Today, after my tirade on CTM and its fatal flaws, he told me a story about his mother, now dead and buried. I see the woman in my mind in baby-doll pajamas teetering around in backless slippers with high heels and a puff of feathers at the toes. He did not include a description of what she was wearing, but from his stories I have invented a vain, troubled, pathetic creature. I have made her the seductive mother, a crazed and scary beloved for the boy child, a woman who lunges between tearful clinging and crushing rage. She is a cliché, a feminine mess from a 1950s movie, one of those Technicolor tarts, drunk and disorderly with lots of cleavage. We are all guilty of types. But the story is grim, and as he tells it, his eyes are cool and empty. Rune's sad, mad mother takes in a stray cat and feeds it. One day, the pregnant cat gives birth in the family's hamper, a warm, soft, dirty, smelly bed. But his mother becomes deranged when she discovers the kittens and wails, No babies, no babies. She drowns the newborn kittens in a bucket in the garage as Rune and his sister watch.

The father was passive. I see him, too, sitting in a chair, a long, pale, beleaguered face. I could draw him. Where do these pictures come from?

'I'm happy to be you,' Rune said, 'or rather happy to be you as me or me as you.' He stood on his hands and walked across the floor, only a few steps, but I was impressed. As I looked on, I had a moment of flight, a sense of losing me and looking at the world as if it had just been made, then and there in all its strangeness. It used to happen to me when I was a child. I would discover noses all at once and find myself fascinated – nostrils, for example, some with hairs, pale and waving or coarse, black wires. What were these two holes in a face of multiple openings? Some tight and narrow – mere slits that hid the channel that led up into the unknown; still others flared and round or great and gaping or inflamed and moist with mucus.

It might have been his upside-down posture that brought on the thought. I used to dream of turning over my room and walking on the ceiling. When I told him, he stared at me. Kirsten and I used to do that, he said. Kirsten is his sister.

HARRIET BURDEN
Notebook O. The Fifth Circle (discovered
by Maisie Lord, June 20, 2012)

June 5, 2001

On Nantucket alone, and I miss Bruno. He is with his 'girls.' The wary Jenny, the pregnant Liza (bearing first grandchild), and the adoring Cleo. They keep their distance from their father's lover, and I realized a few weeks ago I don't care. They do not have to like me. Maisie and Oscar and Aven will come next week. Ethan may come. My son: Mr Maybe. I long for signs of affection from my buttoned-up boy. I imagine the great long hug, a sudden blurting of love and admiration for me, his ma, but that is not his way. I cannot remake Ethan. Like me, he reads. He reads all the time, and he reads women these days, Simone Weil, Suzanne Langer, Frances Yates. Hope for the earth. But he is severe, an avenger of the downtrodden, an enemy of the system. Sell the Nantucket house! Sell the art! Divest and scatter the funds for redistribution. Ethan Lord in sackcloth and ashes. There are days when he reminds me of a Jesuit priest performing the spiritual exercises over and over as purification. And I founder and fall, unclean and guilty. Mercifully, today on the phone, he hopped off the track and asked me if I'd ever read Bachelard's *The Poetics of Reverie*, and I quoted a line to him: 'Then words take on other meanings as if they had the right to be young.' And Ethan chuckled and said, But I think you have to be old to know that. And I received the chuckle as love.

Little Ethan marches into the house after a day at kindergarten. I see him carry a stack of puzzles into his closet, turn on the light, sit down, and close the door behind him. I know what he is doing. He begins one, finishes it, and starts the next. After half an hour, I knock gently on the door and call out to him in my cartoon voice, Any reports from the closet? Twelve, he sings back at me, or fourteen, or sixteen.

Felix speaks in the darkness of the bedroom: 'Do you think the child is normal?'

Yes, yes, yes, I would say. He just has a different pattern of mind.

Many shades of Felix in the house: both caresses and slaps. His wellies stand in the hallway, and I conjure his ghost heading for the beach in an icy rain, and I remember how it aroused me to see the Felix of suits and ties in an old sweater and blue jeans, that here on Nantucket he was nearly another man when he was not on the telephone. Today I touched the stones that are still piled in the wide, shallow crystal bowl on the dresser, a little dusty. He gathered them one by one over the years. He liked to cover them with water to bring out their color. Last year, I did not even notice them, did not think of them. This year I am all wounded feeling as I look down at the stones. I remember throwing a magazine at him and his surprised look. Pay attention! I yelled. It's time you paid attention. The collage of photographs in the kitchen: Ethan and fish – the terrified six-year-old hoists a small bluefish in the air. A radiant Maisie in her father's arms, her upper lip a little moist with dirt and snot. Felix is turned to her, reflective, soft, the corner of his mouth raised. This house. I am wading in the ruins of was.

Rune arrives tomorrow. It would have been silly to keep the visit from Bruno, so I didn't. A long weekend. Thursday to Sunday. Project talk. I want to study him further. He is right for the part, but I must discover the work.

Remember: Straight Wharf tomorrow for swordfish, bluefish pâté, those little crackers.

I've been watching *The Diary*. It goes on and on. There is too much to see. The visual glut of too much.

A moment when I stopped the movie: a lackey is filming Rune at a party. That means there are two cameras. One seen. One invisible. Rune is smiling, gesticulating. His eyes narrow in interest as he chats up a woman with a magenta bob and narrow green glasses. He laughs, a big cackle, waves goodbye, and turns toward the unseen camera. But in his face there is no sign of the animation immediately past. The transition is too violent. Our feelings usually linger for a few seconds anyway. I ask myself what lies under his conviviality.

Thursday, June 7, 2001

I picked him up at the airport at 1:30, and his big smile and broad wave made me feel instantly guilty about the thoughts I had last night. He teased me about my truck, my beloved junk heap, but it runs and runs.

Praise for the house – a real beach house, not a McMansion, not an overblown summer place like some of those horrors in the Hamptons. I showed him the studio. Showed him some of my little people in the chorus for *Blazing*. All their mouths are open in song.

Ate the swordfish with relish and drank wine. We looked out onto the beach and the tall moving grasses that grew nearly black against the night sky, a cobalt blue – straight from the tube. Only a few moments of strangeness when I thought, What is he doing here? What am I doing? Maybe I am the mad scientist.

I watched Rune move. I remarked silently on his grace. This is helpful in the world – grace. His left hand (I understood today that he is left-handed) flies out open-palmed for emphasis, and his speech rolls out of him, not too fast, and with little emotion. His voice is low and soothing, and he smiles only at long intervals, but when he does, it feels as if I am being rewarded. He is curious and has read all kinds of books, but it is not what he says that seduces. It is his belief in his own power to seduce.

After dinner, we lay on the two red sofas in the living room. He smoked, and I inhaled the smell of cigarettes, an odor reminiscent of my marriage. I have learned that there is no debate of ideas with Rune, no point for a rational point to be made between us. He is a man of the scattershot and sporadic, of apt quotations, remembered dates, unlikely pairings, and non sequiturs. April 1938: Eight days after Austria voted for the German Anschluss, Superman made his first appearance on the American stage. The Marquis de Sade, he informed me, was born on June 2, 1740. The very next day, June 3, King Frederick the Great of Prussia ascended the throne and, as one of his first decrees, abolished torture. I am not surprised that Rune takes a fashionable interest in Sade, in desire as repetition, in bodies as machines, in the man's bleak extension of Enlightenment clockwork to sexuality. Do you fancy yourself a libertine? I asked him. And he said no, just an information-processing machine with inputs and outputs attached to a potent sex drive. He quoted Nietzsche: 'Man is something to be overcome.' (He is loose and fast with Nietzsche.)

318

In a single beat, he jumped to J. G. Ballard and the man's 1970 exhibition of crashed cars at the New Arts Lab. Better than Duchamp, better than Warhol, he said. *Crashed Cars* is the art exhibit *par excellence*. Ballard's book *Crash* heralded 'the new sublime,' an erotic explosion of metal and glass and dismemberment. But more than the glories of the smash-up, Ballard was a soothsayer, a juggernaut, a harbinger of what was still to come. Hadn't art museums become Disney palaces, just as he had predicted? Hadn't the oracle said, 'Sooner or later, everything turns into television'?* Hadn't he said, 'In the post-Warhol era a single gesture such as uncrossing one's legs will have more significance than all the pages in *War and Peace*'?† When I wondered what the latter statement meant, Rune said, Isn't it obvious? I said, Not at all, not at all, but he had moved on to Philip K. Dick and all things Phildickian, and how he loved him, too, another great shaman of our age, born in 1928, dead in 1982, still young, only fifty-four – a paranoid, addicted, five times married, hallucinating, quasi-religious maniac, but oh so wonderful. Hadn't Dick said, 'Everybody knows that Aristotelian two-value logic is fucked'?

I asked him if Dick had advocated a three-value

* J. G. Ballard, *The Day of Creation* (New York: W. W. Norton, 1987), 64.
† J. G. Ballard, *The Atrocity Exhibition* (London: Fourth Estate, 1990), 27.

logic. Boolean logic has two values, too, I said, essential to computing. Three values includes true, false, and the unknown or ambiguous. Was that what he had proposed? Was he thinking larger? About Gödel's incompleteness theory? Does he really understand it?*

Rune is used to impressing people with such statements but unused to defending them. Despite his ignorance, he just grins, extends his open palm, and tells me I'm too serious.

What if I were like that? What if I just waved contradictions aside? It would be pleasant to play the blasé hero, bloated with himself, collecting admiring glances for the half-baked and the ill-conceived.

I see my father in my mind. Your logic, Father,

---

* The popular quote about Aristotelian logic is from a character in Dick's novel *VALIS*, not from Dick himself. In her notebooks, Burden frequently returns to what she calls 'the limits of logic.' Her attempt to engage Rune in a discussion of various forms of logic fails. Boolean logic, named after the nineteenth-century mathematician George Boole, is an algebraic binary system in which all values can be reduced to true or false, a logic fundamental to the design of computer hardware. Paraconsistent three-valued logic systems are designed to retain forms of traditional logic but also tolerate inconsistencies: 'the unknown or the ambiguous.' In 1931, Kurt Gödel's incompleteness theorem demonstrated that any system of mathematics or logic cannot be both consistent and complete because it must rely on unproven assumptions that lie outside the system.

was about the consistency of relations, not the murk of so-called real life. It was bounded logic. That was its problem. Your true and false propositions function perfectly in their own hermetic sphere.

It is a mistake to apply logic to human life as a whole, to think logic will 'wake up' machines.

But then Rune relates that once upon a time there were two Dicks, Philip K. and his twin, Jane Charlotte, who died when she was six weeks old, and the little girl ghost haunted the brother's writing. Philip K., it seems, blamed his mother for Jane's death. The foul womb killed his sister? He had been in there with her, after all. The mother had neglected her for him? Alas, I didn't get the details. Rune was on a roll.

The dead girl child led us to mirrors and doubles and ghosts that never leave us, and the old story about the two sexes as the cleaved halves of a single whole being. He told me about his sister Kirsten, to whom he had always told his secrets. They had invented a code when they were children to send messages to each other their parents couldn't read, and they called the code Runsten. They had built a fort from boxes and scrap lumber, and inside their fort they had dissected the body of a dead baby bird. And I told him about my mother's miscarriages and that I had always wondered if my father hadn't wanted a boy. Maybe one of those who had died had been a boy.

Later, he rattled on about artists I'd never heard

of, and I understood he had an encyclopedic knowledge of the now – what's in the Chelsea galleries this minute. It was impressive, but after a while my mind left his words for my own silent ones, the ones who think they have a right to be young and wander off to look for new meanings, and I interrupted him at one point to bring up our work. I said the project would have to disguise the line of suture, the incision between his art and mine. I had to know more about him. It was a question of becoming.

Becoming me?

No, I said to him, double consciousness. You and I together. I am hoping you will goad me into something else. My voice rose. Goad me into the dizziness of exile.

His face went dead, blank, as I had seen him on the film. No answer.

With your name on my work, I said, it will *be* different. Art lives in its perception only. You are the last of three, and you are the pinnacle. I could hear the cracking passion in my voice. I altered my tone to one of calm deliberation.

He liked the idea of pulling a fast one, but my ideas felt outdated, a little lame to him. We live in a postfeminist age of gender freedom, transsexuality. Who cares which is which? There are lots of women in art now. Where is the battle?

No, I said to him, it's more than sex. It's an experiment, a whole story I am making. Two down, one to go. After that, I retire from the game. We

322

will find a project, I said. Hadn't his work *The Banality of Glamour* focused mostly on women's faces and bodies? Surely he knew that women face pressures men don't. I had suffered from the cruelty of the beauty culture. I knew what I was talking about.

He smiled a gentle smile, and he said, Harry, you have your own style, your own elegance, your own femininity. He wanted to be kind, but I boiled – fists clenched, fury rising. He had offered me condescension, compensation. Don't worry, Harry, you count, too, he was saying, even if you are funny-looking. I bristled at him and growled, But that's not the point. The point is the trap, the suffocation. I turned away.

No pique from him: You want to wear me for one exhibition. It was a good phrase, 'wear me.'

I told him yes, that was it exactly, except that by 'wearing' him I might find something else in myself. This is what I was trying to explain.

He licked his teeth and asked me what that something might be.

I don't know. I don't know. I don't know.

Little talk after that. I'm tired now, very tired.

Tomorrow the masks come out.

Friday, June 8, 2001

Hid all day without speaking to him. I had notified him of the house rules: He had to find his own breakfast and lunch. I watched him through the studio window, loping toward the beach, book in hand, saw him lean over and brush sand from his heel, then light a cigarette. I have already dug out a couple of Felix's ashtrays for Rune. I kept thinking of his surgical videos while I worked on a head for a sculpture. The controlled mutilations made me think of his beloved crashes – a bloody aesthetic.

Faces. The face. Locus of identity. What the world sees. My old face.

What happened today in the studio, Harry? Think it through.

Harry, you were worried. You were anxious. Be honest. When you unwrapped the masks, you were a little frightened, weren't you? But why?

Because you weren't sure he would play. Is that it?

But when he saw them, your man face and your woman face, when he saw your face masks, he smiled, and then he ran his finger over the woman and took her up and put the face over his own.

He took it off and examined it. They're both so blank, he said.

I made them blank.

Like Noh masks, he said, and I said, a little like Noh masks, but light and flexible. The difference between the two is very slight, in the chin.

I want to use them, I said, as part of the experiment for our work together. We'll change sex and

324

play a game, a theater game. It'll be fun, I said. Are you up for it?

Are there rules? he said.

No rules, I said. He would find a woman, and I would find a man.

He wanted to film it with a stationary camera. He could set it up quickly. He would add it to the Diary.

Loss of air in your chest, Harry. Increased heartbeat, a feeling of danger. Why? Were you frightened by that machine's eye? Will I look bad? Will I look ridiculous? I insisted he give me a copy. He agreed. But there's more, Harry. Examine yourself. Weren't you afraid you were opening a door you might not be able to close?

It is almost midnight, but I must write it down now, or I will lose the immediacy, lose the force of it, because whatever is on that damned film, it's not my insides, not my perceptions, not the magic of transformation.

It moved slowly at first. We were awkward, silly. I told him I was John. He hated John. Why John? Such a bland name. I had to explain that I had played John as a girl. John's adventures. Captain John on the ship in a hurricane, Soldier John killing Nazis, John in the caves. I did not say that I alternated between being John and being Mary, Mary who was rescued by John, swooning, delicate Mary who loved being saved. I agreed to give up John. Dumb name, okay. As soon as Rune had put the mask on, he began to wriggle and mince and roll his shoulders up and down. I told him sharply he was a woman, not a drag queen. No woman moves like that, for Christ's sake, and he shot back, Wanna bet? But he stopped the ridiculous parody after a few minutes. He told me he was Ruina.

A nutty name, I said, but Ruina is kind of funny. A ruined woman. Poor ruined Ruina/Rune.

The mask changes everything.

It changes far more than I had imagined when we began the game.

Rune began to vanish.

I looked at that empty face with its soft, pink, expressionless mouth, arched brows, and narrow chin with the thick elastic band that held it in place over his ears. Rune lifted his voice to a higher pitch and spoke more softly. He said he liked to draw. Then he looked down at his lap, then upward again. His eyes through the holes held mine for a moment before he looked away. I must try to explain this to myself. Why did this series of movements feel like a blow to my skull? He was making a character, wasn't he? I took a breath. Under the mask, I felt my skin grow hot. Masks do not move, but when I looked at him/her, it was as if I saw the fixed lips tremble, as if in this act of looking down, up, and away he had captured something feminine, and I found it terrible.

Richard, I said, Richard Brickman. The name appeared in my mouth, and I spoke it. Looking at it now, written on the page, I am smiling.

Richard, as in Lionhearted, as in the Third, as in Tricky Dick, as in dicks and pricks, more pricks than kicks. What's in a name? The choice is hilarious. And bricks? Need we go into it? Hard, of course. Stable, of course. The three little pigs, of course. Remember, Harry, whose house stands? And he blew and he blew and he blew, but he couldn't blow the house down. And the *man* in Brickman? Harry, you're Mr Overdetermined himself.* But he came, Richard Brickman came, coming like a wind blown from old Harry's blue lungs into the purple space between him and Ruina, that shrinking pinky of a girl. She had a story. She had dreams, big, little, pathetic dreams of grandeur. Rune was making her up for me, for Richard. She was not an artist, no, just an illustrator. Her grand ambitions were to draw and paint for children's books. Where had he found this shy, hopeful creature? I wonder now, but I didn't wonder then. In his mother, his sister? I was too caught up in Richard and Ruina, in the miracle of their talk.

I sat across from the mask, Ruina, with the brilliant

* 'Overdetermined: The fact that formations of the unconscious (symptoms, dreams, etc.) can be attributed to a plurality of determining factors.' J. Laplanche and J.-B. Pontalis, *The Language of Psychoanalysis*, trans. Donald Nicholson-Smith (New York: W. W. Norton, 1973), 292. Burden suggests that her sudden coming upon the name Brickman is derived from multiple unconscious sources.

light of the afternoon sun behind her. The faded red of the sofa's cotton at her back, I watched her play with a cushion in her lap. My posture changed. I sat with my legs open, and I leaned forward, my elbows on my knees. But can you draw? I demanded. Can you draw?

She didn't want to brag, you see, but she could draw some, and she was getting better, and she was hoping for a break, an introduction, perhaps. I might be able to help her. The masked head went up and down and back and forth. She was in motion, our Ruina, a bobbling head of hesitation and nervous laughter. It was so hard for her to ask. She didn't like to do it, and a new high note of pleading entered her voice.

As she wheedled and sighed, I began to find her contemptible. Pull yourself together. If you want something, ask for it straight out.

And then, horribly, Ruina began to whisper. I could hardly hear her. Was she asking for a favor? Her head fell forward, and she spoke so softly under her breath that the words ran together in a murmur of sounds.

Speak up! I, Richard, was telling her to speak up. I didn't shout. I ordered her to speak clearly so that I could hear her. What was the point of a conversation with a person who could not be understood, who could not get a sentence out of her mouth without mumbling? We would get nowhere.

She whined. The sound of her whining made me

close my eyes, made me wince. You disgust me. You sound like a kicked dog. Who said that? Richard said it, cruel bastard that he is.

High protestations from Ruina followed. She is suddenly enlivened. In her feeble way, she fights back. Her voice rises into new registers, high, splitting sounds of pain. That's mean. You're a mean, horrible man. Blubbering follows.

I am not mean. I am reasonable. You hear me. I am just speaking rationally. You, on the other hand, are acting like a hysterical child. I ask you to stop right now, immediately.

Ruina is crying. She is holding the pillow to the masked face. I imagine that the mask moves. I see the corners of the mouth move downward, and I feel the wrinkling of the forehead. I feel invigorated by my anger. Richard stands up and walks to the sofa in three swift strides. He grabs her by the shoulders and begins to shake her. She is loose as a rag doll. I lift my hand to smack her hard. The masked head is thrown back, and Rune is laughing. The laugh enrages me. The laugh storms inside me. I lift my hands from Rune's shoulders. I make a noise, a hollow grunt. The game is over.

We take off the masks.

I feel shaken, a bit shocked. Rune is jovial. He repeats this sentence: We have it on film.

But Richard and Ruina have unsettled me. I told him so as he snipped the rubber bands off the steamed lobsters. Why had it gone in that direction? Who had led the way? Why had he made

Ruina so wimpy? Is that his idea of what women are? I wanted to talk about it, but he said that I always wanted to interpret everything, and enough was enough. It had been fun, hadn't it? And I felt both oddly relieved by his humor and still troubled. Our conspiracy, he said, was interesting, damned interesting, and he sure as hell wasn't going to let it go yet.

He talked about an artist friend who had hanged himself last year. A woman he loved had left him.

It must be terrible for her, I said.

And he said that some deaths are more beautiful than others.

I said I didn't find death beautiful, except maybe the perfect death, dying in one's sleep at a hundred.

God, that's boring, he said.

I must think it through now. I must find some distance. Harry is trying to understand what has happened.

Saturday, June 9, 2001

I called Rachel this morning. We talked for almost an hour. I wanted to tell her about Richard Brickman, but something stopped me: shame. I am ashamed of both Richard and Ruina.

Ray has had a stent put in his artery.

Who are you, anyway, Harry, a wimp? Who cares about this little theatrical event? Isn't the world in thrall to actors, especially to those who press themselves to extremes, who starve themselves for authenticity, who rage and gnash their teeth and turn themselves into demented patients or idiots savants or leering, cannibal psychopaths? Are we not all malleable beings made of putty, who can be pulled and pressed and reconfigured? Doesn't all art partake of this extension into others? What's the big deal? This was next to nothing, no violence at all – just a shaking of shoulders – a little anger, a laugh. Why worry?

Because Brickman was there, fully formed. Who is that man?

And yet, consider this, too: He may be the avenue to the project. Didn't I say it: the dizziness of exile? Exile into the other.

I called Bruno, too. (I will never tell him about the masks.)

Cleo is his salvation, but I knew that. Jenny needles him. Liza is taciturn but much sweeter to her old dad. He tells me, in a typical soaring moment of hyperbole, that he has botched fatherhood, and I tut-tut the comment because it isn't true. They want to see him, after all. They leave their spouses to come to Papa. And Liza has let him feel the movements of the fetal boy under her skin, the first grandchild, and he wonders why this unborn child is so much more exciting for him than the first time around. And I tell him he was afraid then, and he isn't afraid now. He doesn't have to take care of it, and we laugh, and soon he makes some comments about my clit, 'ever on alert,' he says, and how his tongue longs for it, the clit, and I make a few false moans on the telephone, and he yuks it up. Laughter is a boon. He asks me about my gigolo, the slithering pretty boy, but his tone is not cruel, and so I take it. I tell him the project is coming along and that it's 'interesting,' borrowing Rune's word. Yes, it's interesting. And then we can't wait to see each other, and he hopes Francis, Liza's lawyer husband, whom I've never met, will not insist they call the baby Brandon – so sissy, so meatless. How could Bruno tolerate a grandson named Brandon? He plans to write here on the island. We do not mention the bloody poem. He knows what I think – write the memoir!

It wasn't easy to work today with the resonant anxiety beneath my ribs.

At four, I found him lying on the sofa reading a book on Houdini. He waved it in the air and delivered facts – the man's father had been a rabbi in Appleton, Wisconsin; Houdini loved his wife, Bess. Twenty years before Kafka published his *Metamorphosis*, the two Houdinis, husband and wife, traded places in a locked trunk and called the act *Metamorphosis*. (The German word is *Verwandlung*, but Rune lives entirely in English.) The master magician could regurgitate small keys at will, dislocate and relocate his shoulders at will, and had learned by practicing in an oversized bathtub to hold his breath for three minutes. Rune said he, too, was practicing not to breathe, and when I asked him why, he said he had his own projects.

He wanted to play again, change masks. I'll be Richard, he said. I thought to myself, that's impossible, you can't be Richard, you don't know him, but I didn't say it. I said, no, another time. I wasn't up to it. We talked some more, but just blather, and then he said, I think Ruina should get her revenge on the bastard, don't you? I must have looked confused. If we keep the game going, he said, she'll have to fight back, won't she? I had to think about it. I understood I had cut myself off from the ongoing story out of dread.

Rune thought the film sequence could be used outside the Diary. We'll put it into a piece, he said, maybe your piece for me. I felt him watching me. I tried to be blasé. But what if it's bad? I said. He had already watched it several times, and he wanted to see it on a larger screen. He could hook it up to the television.

We watched the masked aliens in silence. I noticed that I had forgotten large chunks of our dialogue and that the game had lasted longer than I had thought. As a spectator, I saw immediately that without the masks the exchange would have lost its power. As it was, I felt startled by the vapid dialogue. The authoritarian Richard and the cringing Ruina were types lifted straight from melodrama or soap opera, but their immobile, artificial faces – my empty creations – enhanced the archetypal character of their struggle, and their gestures took on a quality of pathos.

Pathosformel?*

Master and slave locked in their contest for recognition?†

Role-playing gone mad?

Cultural parody written in capital letters?

Was this TV show the objective view? I noted that my green sweater had lost its shape and hung loosely over my substantial breasts, that beneath the man mask, my own flaccid chin fell into a neck with no Adam's apple, and that my hair floated out around the false face in a frizzed halo, but somehow these physical details did not feminize Richard. They were overpowered by the mask and its, or his, decisive movements. And despite Rune's rounded biceps, broad shoulders, and flat chest,

---

* The art historian Aby Warburg (1866–1929) developed the term *Pathosformel* to describe the emotive formula of visual representations. For Warburg, works of art were charged with psychic energies expressed in a gestural language. See Warburg's *The Renewal of Pagan Antiquity: Contributions to the Cultural History of the European Renaissance*, trans. David Britt (Los Angeles, Calif.: Getty Research Institute, 1999).

† Burden is referring to the master/slave chapter in Hegel's *Phenomenology of Mind*, in which the philosopher argues that self-consciousness is achieved only through an agonistic battle with the other.

his quivering Ruina, crunched up in a ball and crying by the end, read as womanly. Performativity.* The particulars of the room, with its fireplace, big conch on the mantel, and Calder print on the wall, were submerged by the raw emotion that passed between the two players. Was it pretend? We watched it again.

Rune leaned forward. His elbows rested on his knees, his chin cupped in his hands – his body tense with concentration. What had he seen? I asked him. I think we were good, he said. We plunged right in. You believe it. It's so fake, but you believe it.

I told him to run it again without sound.

He did it automatically, which surprised me a little. He seemed to understand. We watched. Without the voices, the film became all masks and movement. I didn't look at Rune beside me on the sofa, but I felt him. I may have heard him breathing. I don't know, but he did not stir, and neither did I. The two people on the screen had been changed again. The two had spoken from behind the motionless lips of the masks, but this

* Judith Butler coined the term *performativity*: 'Gender proves to be performance, that is, constituting an identity it is purported to be. In this sense gender is always a doing, though not a doing by the subject who might be said to pre-exist the deed.' In *Gender Trouble: Feminism and the Subversion of Identity* (New York: Routledge, 1990), 25.

time we listened to nothing. The static faces appeared to speak because they nodded and lifted their hands, but without words, and I watched the two of them perform a dance that in silence had become alarmingly erotic. Ruina's gestures had a seductive quality that inflamed Richard's brutality and the pleasure he took in it.

I felt Richard again, felt his desire to smack the cowering girl silly. Without his pedestrian speeches, my figment seemed to grow in stature. But as the final seconds rolled around again, I wondered who exactly was laughing at the end. Was it Rune or Ruina? I had thought that Rune had burst out of character, that he had broken the fourth wall, but now I wasn't sure. It seemed to me that she, Ruina, was laughing inside the game, which added another layer of pretense or, at the very least, complicated the imaginary realm. I felt disoriented.

I said to him, Who was laughing?

Rune gave me a puzzled look.

I pressed him. I said again, Who was laughing? You or Ruina? He just stared at me. I spoke to him sharply. I said, Tell me.

He leaned back in the sofa and folded his arms. Are you being Richard now?

No, I said, I'm Harry. I could feel anger tighten my chest and throat.

Tom, Dick, and . . . he said to me.

I lowered my voice and said I was serious.

He joked and said, 'The mask made me do it. The mask made me do it.' Then he accused me of being too serious. I had started it, hadn't I? Games were meant to be fun. Was I worried about which of us had won, for Christ's sake? It hadn't been scripted. What came out of us had come out. Who cared? Where was my sense of humor?

Where was your sense of humor, Harry, that glorious feeling for the ridiculous? Who was that masked man galloping across the television screen? Wasn't it you? Laugh loudly! Do not turn back now, Harry. You two are partners in the masked dance, and its steps will mean nothing if they are danced alone. Are you not double in the game? Johannes and Cordelia, John and Mary, Richard and Ruina? And why did you drone on about Dora Maar to Rune if you weren't doubling yourself yet again without even knowing it?

There you were, Harry, on the red sofa beside Rune, telling him about Picasso sighting Maar at a café in Paris, her fingers splayed on the table in front of her as she stabbed the spaces between her fingers with a knife. When she missed, she bled. Five-fingered fillet. Picasso saved her gloves as a trophy.

Picasso painted Maar as the crying woman, as Spain in mourning, but the he-goat loved to make women cry. As the tears tumbled, the goat's penis stiffened. What a buoyant, energetic little misogynist Picasso was! And you told Rune the whole

337

story, about Maar's Surrealist photos, the sublime *Ubu* that won a prize in 1936 among them, and her not-as-wonderful paintings. You told him about how she broke down after Picasso left her, about her analysis with Jacques Lacan, about the hideous chair with steel bars and hairy ropes Picasso wrapped up and sent her as a present and the rusty shovel blade she mailed to him, a game of gifts they played together. And then the package that was found in 1983 among Picasso's possessions: a signet ring he had designed and engraved with the letters *P D, pour Dora*. Inside the circlet was a spike.

The man who unwrapped the ring was horrified, but, I said to Rune, it must have been meant as an allusion to Maar's knife game, don't you think? To look at the ring is to see a bleeding finger.

No one can play alone, I said. Even when there is no one else in the room, there must be an imaginary other.

I found the quote from Cocteau for Rune: 'Picasso is a man and a woman deeply entwined. He is a living ménage. Dora is a living concubine with whom he is unfaithful to himself. From this ménage marvelous monsters are born.'

We are all a ménage, I said to him.
And then Rune said, A long time ago someone told me you were brilliant, just brilliant.

Who? I said, but he couldn't remember. It was someone who knew me or had known me. It might have been at a party. It's true, he said. You are.

I was so pleased. Slathered up with the compliment, I felt yielding, pliable, happy. Shine a warm light on poor old Harry and she turns into melted butter.

We were silent then and listened to the ocean. Let's go down to the beach, I said. And we did. The moon was a crack of light only, a gleaming pale space in the sky briefly uncovered by the thick moving clouds, and we looked up at those cumulus depths with their illuminated grays, and I suppose we saw the same thing, because he whistled. We trotted down to the water and let the surf wash over our feet and felt its drag on our ankles as it withdrew. I felt we were friends.

It was only an hour ago, but in memory I have already changed the view. I find that odd. I am no longer inside myself. I see the two of us from behind, standing on the beach, two tall, dim silhouettes in the compromised moonlight. At some point, we turn and walk up the beach and down the path of gray wooden planks that leads to the house. When he bids me good night, he smiles. He says that it has been a great day, a banal phrase, but that is what we say, don't we? It's been a great day.

Then he kissed me lightly on both sides of my face and said good night again.

Sunday, June 10, 2001

Coda:

Tonight I luxuriated in the empty house, ate pasta with heaps of vegetables, read Emily Dickinson. She blazes.

> Mine – by the Right of the White Election!
> Mine – by the Royal Seal!
> Mine – by the Sign in the Scarlet prison—
> Bars – cannot conceal!

Rune, on the other hand, is a lowly jingle that has dug a trench in my mind and plays again and again. He lingers as a song of doubt. I see his tanned face at dinner as I listen again to his talk about AI, facile and adolescent, but somehow alive: 'Machine and human libido.' I have invented new pictures for him: a towheaded boy with his head in sci-fi novels. I see him build a machine in his backyard. I see him in a darkened movie theater, his eyes lit by the screen as he watches an alien invasion. He must have felt like an alien out there in Iowa with his sister. I see cornfields and red barns. I have never been to Iowa. I am painting by the numbers.

Yesterday – I think it was yesterday – he inscribed a quote in the sand with a shell as we sat on the beach. It was from Marinetti's 'Futurist Manifesto,' 1909: 'We are going to be present at the birth of

the centaur and we shall soon see the angels fly.'
When I told him Marinetti was mad and repulsive,
he said he loved the mad and the repulsive. He
loved fire, hatred, and speed. There is beauty in
violence, he said. No one wants to acknowledge
that, but it is true. I looked at his lower arm, brown
under the white linen shirt he was wearing, the
sleeves rolled to his elbows, a baseball cap on his
head. I argued with him. It was a fascist aesthetic,
I said, and in order to see beauty in maiming and
bloodshed, one had to be far removed from those
involved. But Rune has learned that the swift
verbal or visual kick will prod strong reactions,
which he can then lie back and enjoy. He falls into
easy insurrection, the kind for which no one pays
a price. But this persona is perfect for my plan.
They will sit up and notice.

It is the dark thing, the inexplicable lump of a thing
that gives you real doubts, Harry. And the dark
thing is not in Rune but in you, isn't it? It is in you
as Richard Brickman. And Rune knows this. He is
sensitive to undercurrents, just as you are. I see him
pick up the mask and put it on. That is what you
wanted, isn't it? You wanted to play. But there is the
fear of the burning arousal between your legs born
of the game, out of control. The secret: I am not
attracted to Rune, except when I'm Richard and
he's Ruina, but in order to play one has to take both
parts. There's a confession. Do I dare tell Dr F.?

*   *   *

I am responsible for the drama (or whatever it was). I, Mistress of the Masks, have created the whole shebang. Rune played along with it, nothing more. He played well. He was game, but it was my show, wasn't it? Where is the boundary between the two inventions, Harry, the absurd masked beings on the screen? Can you draw the line? Have you given too much away? Are you vulnerable? That is the melody of your doubt.

And now, as you write these words, you see your not-yet-old father sitting in silence at the end of the table in the Riverside Drive apartment, a speechless statue. Then you see your old mother many years later wearing her lilac robe in the hospital. She is telling you the story of how he punished her for wanting to speak. He punished her by saying nothing, and you, Harry, blurt out the words, That was cruel! He was cruel! Your mother agrees. It was cruel.

Of this I am certain: There has been more than one turn of the screw.

RACHEL BRIEFMAN
(written statement)

I confess there were times when I found Harry's intensity about her pseudonymous project rather exhausting. At our weekly teas, her eyes shone as she reported on her voluminous reading and how it fit into her larger schema. She showed me drawings and charts, handed me books of philosophy, science papers on mirror systems in the brain, and she wanted my opinions on all of them. Every once in a while, an article or book caught my attention, but often I had to tell her that I didn't have time to work my way through it. I never met Rune or witnessed Harry designing or building the project, but she discussed it regularly with me and worried continually about the risks they were taking by introducing elements he had never used in his work before. I know she imagined a great victory waiting for her at the end of the tunnel, redemption for her years of toil and oblivion, and I admit that this fantasy had an irrational coloring to it; but to those who believe that Harry lied about her work with Rune, I say it is not possible, and to others who have argued that she lost her hold on reality altogether and no longer knew whether she was coming or going, I can say firmly as a psychiatrist that Harry was not psychotic. She was not delusional. Her friend the Barometer was psychotic and delusional. Harry was no more deluded than the average neurotic.

In fact, she was hell-bent on understanding the psychology of belief and delusion, which, let us be frank, are often one and the same thing. How do preposterous, even impossible ideas take hold of whole populations? The art world was Harry's laboratory – her microcosm of human interaction – in which buzz and rumor literally alter the appearances of paintings and sculptures. But no one can prove that one work of art is truly superior to another or that the art market runs mostly on such blinkered notions. As Harry pointed out to me repeatedly, there is not even agreement on a definition of árt.

In some cases, however, delusions become apparent. Harry and I were both fascinated by what have been called 'moral panics,' outbreaks of spreading terror, often directed at one supposedly 'deviant' group or another – Jews, homosexuals, blacks, hippies, and, last but not least, witches and devils. During the 1980s and early 1990s, satanic cults popped up all over the United States, and their gruesome rites were all soberly reported in the newspapers. Countless arrests, trials, imprisonments, and wrecked lives resulted from that hysterical contagion. Social workers, psychotherapists, law enforcement officials, and the courts were all swept up in the panic. In the end, there was no evidence

344

of a single accusation having been true. One conviction after another has been overturned. Caught in an epidemic of traveling thoughts, hundreds of people were eager to believe that the woman or man at the day-care center, the sheriff, the coach, the neighbor down the street were monsters who raped and mutilated children, who drank their blood and ate their feces for breakfast. Gruesome memories sprouted from the minds of grown-ups and children, accounts of Black Sabbath masses, of sodomy and untold numbers of murders, but no one ever found a dead body or any marks of torture on a single person. And yet people believed. There are those who still believe.

Think of the stories that bloomed and circulated after 9/11, that no Jews were killed at the World Trade Center and that the U.S. government had manufactured the atrocity. This nonsense had adamant followers, as, of course, did the Bush administration's big lie about the same carnage and Iraq. It is easy to claim that those who are swept up in these beliefs are ignorant, but belief is a complex mixture of suggestion, mimicry, desire, and projection. We all like to believe we are resistant to the words and actions of others. We believe that *their* imaginings do not become ours, but we are wrong. Some beliefs are so patently wrong – the proclamations of the Flat Earth Society, for example – that dismissing them is simple for most of us. But many others reside in ambiguous territory, where the personal and the interpersonal are not easily separated.

345

It should not be forgotten that Harry had been rewriting her own life in psychoanalysis for years, that what she called a slowly developing 'revisionist text' of her life had begun to replace an earlier 'mythical' one. People and events had taken on new significance for her. Her memories had changed. Harry had not recovered any dubious memories from her childhood, but on February 19, 2003, only a month before *Beneath* was shown, she told me that when she looked back on her life, vast stretches of it had vanished. With a little prompting, she could easily fill in those blanks with fictions. Weren't most memories a form of fiction anyway? She remembered what I had forgotten, and I remembered what she had forgotten, and when we remembered the same story, didn't we remember it differently? But neither of us was prevaricating. The scenes of the past were continually being shifted and reshuffled and seen again from the vantage point of the present, that's all, and the changes take place without our awareness. Harry had reinterpreted any number of memories. Her whole life looked different.

And, Harry asked, where does it begin? The thoughts, words, joys, and fears of other people enter us and become ours. They live in us from the start. Moral panic, the multiple-personality epidemic, and recovered-memory mania ran wild in the eighties and early nineties as a wave of suggestion passed from one person to another, a kind of mass hypnosis or spreading unconscious permission that allowed countless people to suddenly become many, a Pandora's box. Therapists reported on patients with dozens of personalities. Whole populations housed inside a single body – men, women, and children coming out as alters. What did it mean? And then when the name of the illness was changed to Dissociated Identity Disorder and skepticism reasserted itself, the numbers of people diagnosed with the illness diminished to a few cases here and there. What Harry wanted to know was: Were we just one person or were we all many? Didn't actors and authors invent characters for a living? Where did those people come from?

I argued that however passionate artists were, they knew the difference between creator and creation, that the illness, under whatever name, was connected to trauma and that, without question, the epidemic had been encouraged by eager and often ill-informed therapists.

Harry sat across from me, her gray hair curling out from under her beret, waving at me with her right hand, with which she knocked over her teacup and sent the pale brown liquid seeping across the tablecloth. Yes, yes, she said, but aren't creatures and alters manufactured from the same subliminal material? Aren't these others inside us like dream figures? She shooed away our solicitous waiter who had come running, placed her napkin over the stain, and continued. She had been working with Rune for some time, and for *Beneath* the two of them had been playing games and staging them on film, games with masks, costumes, and props. And when they played, things began to happen. Harry held me with her eyes. I asked her, What things?

What excited and sometimes frightened her, she said, was what Rune brought out in her, and whatever it was, she believed it had been in her for a long time but had never been let out. I recorded her words in my journal the same evening, or at least her words as I remembered them. *The whole project is almost over now, Rachel. Soon the trilogy of my personas will be finished.* She stressed that Rune had been embedded in *Beneath* as a 'personified possibility.' She had borrowed the words from Kierkegaard. It was the idea of Rune she wanted to exploit, far more than Rune himself, but the idea of him had given her mobility, had opened doors inside herself. Harry's voice grew louder, and I noticed that a man and a woman at the table next to us had stopped talking and turned to glare at us. I put my finger to my lips to indicate that she should lower her voice, and Harry's mood turned dark. *That's what I mean*, she hissed at me. *Don't be loud, Harry. Don't make waves, Harry. Keep your knees together, Harry. It's not polite, Harry.*

Irritated, I said to her, Good grief, what have I done? I noticed you were talking too loudly to keep our conversation private, and I sent you a discreet signal. Harry leaned toward me and growled in my direction. *That's what I'm trying to tell you. The thing, the person – whatever it is – is ruthless, cocky, loud, cold, superior, cruel, dismissive, and untouchable. The thing is not polite. It has never been polite.*

Sounds like a real charmer, I said to Harry. I was smiling, but Harry did not find my characterization funny. She looked at me gravely. I suggested that different personalities bring out various aspects of our own, and I explained that I often feel loud with soft-spoken people or retiring and shy with someone who bellows at me. It all depends on the interaction. Harry insisted that she was talking about something far more dramatic. She had never been able to resist what she called 'the pull of the other.' As a child she had always obeyed the rules. She had rarely been punished, because she couldn't bear the idea of disappointing her parents. Neither one of them had been strict or severe, but for some reason, she had always felt wrong, not right. *I worked so hard to turn myself into the right kind of child, but I never succeeded.* It pained me to listen to her, but I knew I was hearing her revised story.

Harry leaned forward, both hands in front of her over the soggy napkin. I covered her right hand with my own and felt grateful that we had been seated in a corner and that she was now speaking in a voice so soft I had to lean close to her to hear what she was saying. She wanted to know if I remembered the grand plans we had had for our futures. *We were both going to be famous women, remember?* I remembered. Harry smiled at me. *We raised our consciousnesses. Do you remember?* I remembered. *It didn't do any good,* Harry said. *What I raised turned out to be false consciousness.* She had become an artist, all right, but no one can be an artist when her work always comes second to everyone and everything else. She had never been first in anything. Ever. Harry pulled her hand away from under mine and looked at me with tears in her eyes.

I pointed out to Harry that she had actually been first in our Hunter class, to which she said, *A lot of good it did me.* Harry's grievances rolled out of her. She had adored Felix, she said, something Bruno could not accept because he was jealous of her dead husband, but it was her mad love for Felix that had made it so hard for her to oppose him. He had made her feel interesting and beautiful, and she had tried hard to be what she thought he had wanted her to be. *This is what I mean, Rachel. What are we? What was Felix and what was me? He was in me.* She had always read Felix for his wishes, had always bent herself to him, and it hadn't been so hard, because deep inside her she hadn't believed that it should be the other way around. Why should he bend to her wishes? Who was she to ask that? *Bend, bend, bend,* Harry said, *always bending and swaying, bending and swaying.* Then Harry remembered her mother bending over to pick up her father's socks and shorts, remembered her mother serving her father at the table, remembered her mother kneeling on the floor with a toothbrush to clean the grout between the tiles, remembered her small mother smiling anxiously up at her father to read his eyes. Did he approve? Was he happy? Harry said she had found herself tiptoeing past Felix's study so as not to disturb him on the days when he had worked at home, had squelched her opinions at dinners because Felix hated conflict, but he would march into her studio without knocking to ask her some trivial question. He would criticize an artist at a dinner party, and everyone would listen rapt to the great man's opinion. Sometimes he'd regurgitate Harry's own words, words she had spoken earlier at the very same dinner, but to which no one had listened. This was true. I remembered several occasions when I had been an uncomfortable witness to those unfortunate repetitions. I did not say to Harry that Felix inspired confidence because he combined authority with a cool, unflappable demeanor. He didn't need people to listen to him. Harry did.

For years, Harry said, Felix had interrupted her mid-sentence, and she would go silent. That's just how it was. Felix had always said that he admired and supported her work, but he had flown here and there for his own work, and he had called to say he'd be late or had changed his flight, and Harry had stayed home with Maisie and Ethan. Yes, yes, yes, she said, she had had help, all she wanted, but you can't farm out your children's souls to others. And although Maisie had been a relatively easy child, Ethan had been difficult, hypersensitive and prone to explosions. His voracious needs had sometimes swallowed her whole. He had grown up all

351

right, she said. He had become a strong, functioning person, but what if she hadn't sat up with him at night, holding his hand, singing the odd, repetitive Philip Glass–like songs she had discovered were the only ones that soothed him. Harry sang a few bars under her breath: *Bleep, bang, rum, rum, rum. Drum, drum, drum. Thrum, thrum, thrum.* And the *guilt, guilt, guilt,* she said wryly to me, the *guilt, guilt, guilt* that she was to blame for his problems. I knew most of this, but I recognized that Harry needed to tell me, needed to explain. And, she said, she had never felt the money belonged to her. She hadn't made it. Felix had started out with money and made much more. Over the years, she'd sold a few pieces of her art, nothing more. And the exhibitions she had had. Harry's lips trembled. *They were ignored or trashed.*

I told her this wasn't actually true. There had been some good reviews. There had. I remembered.

Harry's face was a reproof. *Money is power,* she said. *Men with money. Men with money make the art world go round. Men with money decide who wins and who loses, what's good and what's bad.*

I offered the comment that this was changing, slowly perhaps, but changing nevertheless; that more and more women were getting their due. I had just read something about it . . .

Harry's expression turned bitter. *Even the most famous woman artist is a bargain compared to the most famous man – dirt cheap in comparison. Look at the divine Louise Bourgeois. What does that tell you?*

Harry's voice cracked. *Money talks. It tells you about what is valued, what matters. It sure as hell isn't women.*

She had all the answers. I didn't reply. I looked down at the tablecloth and wondered what time it was, but I was too alert to Harry's feelings to look at my watch. Maybe Harry had an inkling of what I was thinking, because she apologized to me. She said that she was selfish and obsessed and carried away and that she loved me. She asked me about Ray's health, and I told her he was doing well, still bicycling in the park three times a week with his doctor's approval, and he seemed sanguine about his retirement from NYU in the spring. He had hated the idea of forced retirement, but now his whole attitude had changed. She even asked me about Otto, and I said our nutty pooch had turned twelve and had to take both an antidepressant and an anti-inflammatory drug for arthritis. Harry smiled. *We're all getting old,* she said, *old and older.*

I nodded. We talked about Maisie's film *Body Weather,* about the psychotherapist who was seeing the Barometer and about the antipsychotics the man refused to take. I thought they might help him. Harry did not. Before we parted, Harry brought up Felix again, this time his love life, or rather the part of it that did not include her. Felix's bisexuality has now become a public fact. The book *The Days of the Felix Lord Gallery,* which was published only a few months ago (in which the author, James Moore, treats Harry's work with great respect and seriousness, I am happy to say), discussed the subject openly. A number of his lovers stepped into the open to talk about him, so however secret his adventures may have been while he was alive, they are not secret anymore. Nevertheless, it is fair to say that Felix's sex life remains a mystery in the sense that the inside story cannot really be known. If one gains anything over the years working as I do, it is an overwhelming sympathy for the variations of human desire. Sexual arousal is surely not under our control, although acting upon it may be. And the notion that we live in an age of sexual freedom is a half-truth. I have had many patients whose shame and misery about their sexual thoughts has made them ill. And it can take a long time to discover the forces that lie beneath a particular fantasy, whether the desire is for boys or girls or older men or women, the thin or the obese, whether it involves tenderness or cruelty, or whether it is aided by all manner of paraphernalia, standard or idiosyncratic. Is it not anathema in our culture to express even a hint of compassion for the man with pedophilic yearnings, or to acknowledge the simple truth that there are sexual encounters between adults and children that do not leave lasting scars on the latter?

I mention this because intolerance about sexual life is everywhere. Not long ago, a woman whom I know only a little made a coarse comment about Harry after she had read the book about Felix. 'Any woman who would put up with that shit,' she said to me, 'had to have been a rank fool.' I told her that Harry had been 'a dear friend of mine' and that she had been 'no fool.' It was an awkward moment, but the woman said nothing more about it.

At first, I didn't know where Harry was going. She began the next turn in our conversation by saying that sometimes when Felix had been out very late at night, at an opening or a dinner with collectors she had not attended, she would hear him when he came home. He was always very careful not to make much noise, but she would hear his light footsteps in the hall anyway. She explained that when their children were young, she would wake to a sigh or a squeak or a cough and lie in bed listening to hear if that small sound would be followed by a wail or a call for her. There had been two parallel worlds at the time, she said, of sleep and of wakefulness, each held in perfect balance with the other. It was as if she had lived in both states at once, and so the creak of the door opening, followed by her husband's steps, never failed to rouse her. She said that on some nights he would come directly in to her, pull open the bed and crawl inside with her, always facing away from her. Then she would pull him close to her and stroke his back, which he liked. But on other nights, particularly the ones when he returned in the wee morning hours, she would hear him undress in the bathroom and step into the shower. And Harry would lie awake listening to the noise of the rushing water and say to herself, *He is washing off the others.*

Harry did not confront him. She said she had simply known what those nocturnal ablutions meant. He had wanted to keep his worlds separate. He had cleaned off one to enter the other. And, she confided, she had pitied him. *I would lie there, Rachel, and think to myself, Poor Felix. What if it were me? What if I had desires that overwhelmed me? How would I want to be treated? Would I want meanness and rejection?*

I said I thought sainthood usually had a price.

Harry agreed with me. She said she had paid dearly. He had hurt her, and she had pushed down her rage at him, but a part of her couldn't help feeling sorry for him anyway. *That's why I need the cold mask, you see.* Harry looked at me so earnestly and in such a big-eyed, childlike way, I found her face comic.

Cold mask? I asked her.

Yes, she answered me, *a cold, hard, indifferent mask, an imperious persona that will rise up and smash the stupids. He comes out when I'm with Rune.* That's why she was interested in multiple personalities, because she thought plurality was human, she explained. She didn't get dizzy, black out, or lose people inside her. She knew perfectly well that she was Harry, but she had discovered new forms of her self, forms she said that most men take for granted, forms of resistance to others. *Why do you suppose,* she said, *that over ninety percent of all the reported cases of multiple personality have been women? Bend and sway,* Harry said triumphantly.

356

Bend and sway. The pull of the other. Girls learn, she said. *Girls learn to read power, to make their way, to play the game, to be nice.*

I said that she was making it a bit too simple, that there were cold, imperious women, too, tough and entitled, who cared little about those in their way.

Oh, Rachel, Harry said to me. *You're so reasonable. Don't you ever want to scream and yell and punch someone in the face? Don't you ever want to breathe fire?*

Of course I do, I said to Harry. Of course I do, but we have different stories, you know. She knew. When we left the restaurant, Harry took my hand. It was cold that day as we walked down Madison Avenue, and we were both dressed warmly. Harry was wearing a beautiful scarf of woven blue and green yarns wrapped around her neck several times. I remember that I admired it. *We used to hold hands,* she said to me, *when we were girls, do you remember?* I remembered well. *We used to swing our arms back and forth as we walked,* she said. *Do you remember?* I remembered. *Now we're two old ladies together,* Harry said, and I told her to speak for herself, and Harry grabbed my hand and began to swing my arm back and forth, and we walked at least a block holding hands and swinging our arms, and because it was New York City, no one gave us a second glance.

PHINEAS Q. ELDRIDGE
(written statement)

I said goodbye to the lodge and its residents in the summer of 2002 and flew off to winter and financial crack-up in Buenos Aires with Marcelo. My beloved's money was mostly elsewhere, fortunately. Harry had her fairy tale. I had and still have mine, most of the time, anyway, in the land of Borges and psychoanalysis and taxi-driving poets. Marcelo and I were back in NYC when *Beneath* opened, and I was deeply curious about Harry's grand phallic finale. Convincing Rune must have been quite a task, I said to Harry, and when she told me it hadn't been all that hard, I felt a few flutters because it didn't really make much sense to me. Then again, the human heart (as metaphor for desire, not as pumping organ) is an unknowable thing. I thought maybe after those crosses, Rune felt it was time for a grand hoax to up the ante.

When Marcelo and I arrived at the opening, there were throngs of arty types on the street waiting to enter the maze. High circus excitement in the air. We lined up with the predictably over-dressed girls, teetering in their high shoes, and the

358

young, mostly white slacker boys, disheveled and slouching, eager to convey their indifference to fashion, but they gave themselves away with their cool hats and their T-shirts, adorned with skulls and parrots or clever little sayings: *We strive for games of great seriousness.* We were parked in line right behind an aging diva with red-framed owl glasses, dressed head to toe in chic black Yamamoto. Two sweet-and-expensive gallerinas, one in black and white and the other in red, stood watch at the entrance, ushering in ten people at a time, so as not to overcrowd the twisting, turning corridors of the maze. 'Don't worry, if you can't get out, we have maps. All you have to do is holler,' said Miss Red, straight out of Georgia. I never miss an accent. Harry was nowhere to be seen. She had not wanted us to go with her, and she had given me strict orders not to look for her – much, much too nervous.

The moment we stepped through the door, Marcelo and I found ourselves enclosed on both sides by thick white walls I guessed were Plexiglas or Lucite. Harry loved to use milky-colored walls in her work, and these were about eight feet tall, not high enough to see over, but not towering either. What I noticed first was their translucence. I could just make out the shadows of three people walking down the adjacent passageway as flickering rectangles of light appeared and disappeared behind their moving figures. The maze was claustrophobic and disorienting, as mazes should be, and after a few wrong turns I felt that dreamy, hallucinatory, life-really-is-awfully-strange atmosphere asserting itself before I knew why I was feeling it. Slowly, I understood that the corridors of the maze were not of uniform size. Their widths grew narrower and then wider. The walls lengthened and shrank, too, but always gradually, gradually, never abruptly. At one juncture, I was able to stand on tiptoe and peer over the wall. Getting out of there wasn't easy. Marcelo and I kept bumping into what we took to be the same corner or the same turn with the same window. The corner, turn, or window looked like the last one, but when we continued walking, we ran smack into a dead end that could not have been the one we had run into minutes earlier. A new dead end signified progress, I suppose, but the 'windows' we used as landmarks, which had been cut into the walls or into the floor under our feet, were forever misleading us. Unless we perused each window box, with its collection of objects inside it or its film sequence, carefully, we inevitably believed we were looking into the same old box or at the same old movie. Of course, sometimes we were and sometimes we weren't. Marcelo kept muttering *diabólico, diabólico* until I told him to can it. *Can* it? he said. How interesting. *Can* it? I was giving him hard lessons in American slang. Unless you slowed down, looked hard at the space around you, and noted the changes in windows, walls, and proportions, you could not know

360

whether you had come farther in that 'diabolical' space or not. Harry had cleverly designed an art object that forced people to pay attention to it because if they didn't, they'd never get out of the blasted thing.

A few notes on the windows. The first one we saw was an illuminated box underneath the floor. When you crouched down and looked through the glass, you saw two full-face caramel-colored masks with big empty eyes, a roll of cotton gauze – the kind one finds in every basic first-aid kit – a black crayon, and a piece of white paper with two vertical lines drawn on it. This window returned throughout the maze, both on the floor and on walls, a visual mantra. Sometimes we ran into an exact replica of that first box, but at other times we noted slight and not-so-slight variations on the theme, which Marcelo and I began to track once we had settled into the game: The masks had been placed closer to each other or a little farther apart. The crayon was a deep gray, not black. The two lines on the paper were at an angle rather than vertical. The two lines crossed. The lines lay on their sides horizontally. The gauze had been partially unrolled. The gauze was stained with rusty brown spots. A pair of scissors now lay beside one of the masks. A mask had been sliced through the cheek and eye. The pair of scissors had disappeared, and the paper was blank.

There were window films, too, inset in the walls, that reappeared throughout the maze without any noticeable differences, at least none that we could see.

1. Rune sits motionless at a table with a cup of coffee on the table in front of him as he looks out the window at a cloudless blue sky. I watched this boring movie for a while. The man breathes, of course. His chest expands and contracts, his nostrils wiggle a little, and at one point he moves his left hand about half an inch.

2. A camera moves slowly past one charred, mutilated car body after another on Church Street, vehicles incinerated in the catastrophic heat. It must have been filmed only days later.

3. A camera pans the window of a shoe store. Through the unbroken glass, we looked at rows of children's shoes that had been neatly paired on graduated steps for display: Mary Janes, sneakers with Velcro straps, sturdy little oxfords and boots. Not a single shoe or boot had been disarranged, but they were all thickly covered in the pale dust of 9/11. Footwear for ghosts.

4. Large snowflakes fall slowly onto a wet sidewalk.

I didn't notice the cracks in the walls until we had been losing ourselves inside the maze for about twenty minutes. They were clues. The closer one came to the exit, the more cracks there were. They were not obvious. The texture of the walls changed by increments. Tiny cracks like spiderwebs or broken blood vessels began to mottle the white walls, becoming denser and denser as one neared the exit. Marcelo didn't notice these veins at all. They were, as the saying goes, hiding in plain sight.

Finally, there were peepholes drilled into three of the maze's dead ends. These were my favorites. I love peeping. Maybe we all do. When I peeked into the first one we happened upon, I saw a small TV screen deep inside the wall, maybe fifteen inches away from my eyeball. Two tiny figures wearing black masks over their faces, identical caps that concealed their heads, loose dark tunics, and pants stood face to face in a blank room. After a couple of seconds, the two began to waltz, step-two-three, step-two-three, and then they fell into the lilting turns of the dance. It was pleasing and I danced along a little, to Marcelo's embarrassment, but then the rhythm sped up and went wrong. Like a pair of automatons, the couple's motion became rigid and mechanical but also out of whack with each other. They danced faster and faster, circling madly and stumbling into each other, until I felt dizzy just watching them, and then the figure I took to be the woman – I think because the other person had rested his hand on her back – tripped and fell. With a violent tug, the man yanked her back to her feet, pulled her body close to him and back into the dance, which began to resemble an upright wrestling match. She twisted and squirmed. She hammered at his arms and tried to release herself from his grasp. They bumped blindly into the wall, but the man held on tightly, and then, without warning, the woman went limp. Her head fell backward, her knees buckled, and her arms fell to her sides. Then the little narrative began again.

This sequence couldn't have lasted more than a couple of minutes. In the two other peephole films, this sequence was repeated exactly but given another ending. After the woman has collapsed, the man continues his lunatic waltz, but his once-solid human partner has been replaced by a spineless rag doll. The man shakes the doll hard, throws off its mask and cap to reveal an airy nothing, a Ms Nobody. He lets the bundle fall to the floor, kicks the withered, unoccupied rags in disgust, and walks offscreen. In the third peep show, the one that was just around the corner from the exit, the sequence repeats itself up to this point; but once the man has left the stage, the heap of rags reconfigures by some movie magic into the living dancer, who then spreads her arms and begins to levitate toward the ceiling, slowly rising until only her feet are visible at the top of the screen, and then they, too, disappear. A fairy-tale ending.

Marcelo and I emerged a little dazed from our wanderings. The open space of the gallery beyond the maze came as a relief. I spotted Rune in the noisy crowd, dressed down in jeans, black T-shirt, and a sports jacket, chatting away, a cool customer. I've loved that phrase since I was a kid because I've always wanted to be one, and I've always wondered where the expression came from – a person in a store pretending he doesn't like the goods, driving the salesperson mad? I told Marcelo that I wanted to scout out the cool customer and so we moved closer to the art star and gossiped about him from our corner. Marcelo thought Rune had a John Wayne–ish feel to him, and I agreed. Wayne's gunslinger had a touch of swish to him, a bit of the girl in his walk, hips swaying under his holster, with those cute little steps of his. Rune had it, too, that give in his hips. We like our movie stars androgynous, whether we know it or not, both boys and girls.

I looked for Harry, but my dear giantess wasn't in the room. We spotted an actress from a TV show but couldn't remember her name, and after a few minutes, Marcelo pronounced the party more bruising than festive, and we made our retreat. From what I could tell it looked like a hit, a big deal, not the little deal our *Suffocation Rooms* had been, although I have to say I love those heated-up rooms as much as the maze – no, more. When we left the gallery, the line extended all the way down the block. Marcelo and I strolled over to Tenth Avenue to look for a restaurant, and there, standing alone on the corner, in a Burberry trench coat and a green cloche, was Harry. After the three-way multiple-kissing ritual, I told her the maze was great and congrats, et cetera, et cetera, but she didn't reply. It was dark on the street, but not so dark that I couldn't see she looked stunned. I gathered that she hadn't been to the show yet, and I asked her why. She shook her head slowly, her forehead wrinkling. I asked her to join us for a bite, but she refused. After a few more bids to convince her met with no success, Marcelo and I left her.

The parting from Harry tugged at me all evening, and I talked too much about it over my angel hair pasta, which annoyed Marcelo, and we had a spat. Of course, Marcelo had never lived with Harry. She'd never rubbed *his* back during a Bette Davis movie. He'd never seen her sit and talk quietly to the Barometer about his drawings to calm him down when he needed it or seen her quietly checking on the skinny madman at night to make sure he put Neosporin on his scratches. And Marcelo hadn't seen Harry twirling around the room in the long violet shantung dress I helped her pick out at Bergdorf's, singing 'Zip-a-Dee-Doo-Dah' at the top of her lungs before her sixtieth-birthday party. I couldn't blame Marcelo for what he didn't know.

RICHARD BRICKMAN
(letter to the editor in The Open Eye:
An Interdisciplinary Journal of Art and
Perception Studies, *Fall 2003)*

To the Editor,

Ten days ago, I received a sixty-five-page letter delivered to me the old-fashioned way, through the U.S. Post Office. Why Harriet Burden, the author of the letter, entitled 'Missive from the Realm of Fictional Being,' chose me as her confessor, I don't quite know, but she said that she had read my paper published in the pages of this journal and thought my interest in the philosophy of self and the dynamics of perception made me a good recipient for her 'revelation.' After verifying that a person named Harriet Burden does, in fact, exist, that she is an artist who a number of years ago exhibited her work in New York City, and that the three artists featured in her letter are also actual persons, I decided to accept her invitation to write my own letter about her letter in these pages. Burden's 'missive' is far too long to be published in full. Its style, at once peculiar and various, includes circumlocutions, elaborate tangents, extravagant quotation, as well as terse philosophical sentences and argumentative leaps which distance it from every standard readers have come to expect from an academic journal. Although I cannot agree with her conclusions, or with her mode of expression (which occasionally veers toward the fervid, exclamatory, and vulgar), I find Burden's artistic experiment an interesting one, and I believe the readers of *The Open Eye* will find the material broadly relevant to their concerns.

Although this journal is committed to ongoing conversations among various disciplines, its pages have underscored the difficulties involved in such dialogues because epistemological approaches vary. The burgeoning research on perception in the neurosciences, Anglo-American analytical philosophy, a more unorthodox strain of thought that has emerged out of European phenomenology, as well as poststructuralist theory offer different answers to the question: How do we see?

Studies on change blindness (subjects missing blatant alterations in their visual field) and inattentional blindness (subjects who fail to notice an intrusive presence when attending to a task) suggest that, at the very least, there is much around us that we simply do not perceive. The role of learning in perception has also been crucial to understanding predictive visual schemas, which lend some support to constructionist theories of perception.* Most of the time we see what we expect to see; it is the surprise of novelty that forces us to adjust those schemas. Blindsight studies and masking studies have further illustrated how unconscious perceptions can and do shape our attitudes, thoughts, and emotions.†

* Burden as Brickman is referring to poststructuralist, continental theory, which maintains that perception of things in the world is socially created (constructed) and maintained in cultural tradition. If, as some recent science suggests, human perception is shaped by expectation, then the constructionists, Brickman argues, have a point.
† Blindsight is the name given to a condition in patients who, despite lesions in their primary visual cortex, retain visual capacities but insist they can see nothing. When presented with an object and asked to identify it, these patients guess correctly at a much higher level than chance, which implies that what they are missing is the awareness of an object they have registered implicitly. See Lawrence Weiskrantz, 'Blindsight Revisited,' *Current Opinion in Neurobiology* 6 (1996): 215–20. In visual masking studies, a visual stimulus, 'the target,' becomes less visible due to interactions with other stimuli that are called 'masks.' For example, when a target stimulus is presented to a viewer and then immediately followed by a mask, the target is

Burden appears to have closely followed the debates on perception and taken inspiration from various writers and researchers, some of whose papers have appeared in *The Open Eye*. On the second page of her letter, she asks what happens when a person looks at a work of art and produces the following sober formulations:

'I' and 'you' hide in 'it.' In this view, subject and object cannot be easily separated.

If we had no past visual experiences, we could not make sense of the visible world. Without repetition, the seen world is nonsense.

Every visible object is an emotional object. It attracts or repels. If it does neither, the thing cannot last in the mind, and it has no meaning. Emotionally charged objects stay alive in memory.

But the subliminal forces of an invisible underground also exercise a pull on us. More often than not, we do not know why we feel what we feel when we look at an art object.

---

rendered invisible. Nevertheless, research has demonstrated that the content of the target image can have a subliminal effect on the subject. See Hannula et al., 'Masking and Implicit Perception,' *Nature Reviews Neuroscience* 6 (2005), 247–55.

In the letter, Harriet Burden claims responsibility for creating the works that appeared in three solo exhibitions in New York City: *The History of Western Art* by Anton Tish, *The Suffocation Rooms* by Phineas Q. Eldridge, and, most recently, *Beneath* by the artist known as Rune. Her articulated motive is simple: 'I wanted to see how the reception of my art changed, depending on the persona of each mask.' She pointedly maintains that when she showed work under her own name in the past, few were interested, but her pseudonymous art, presented behind three 'living male masks,' piqued the interest of both dealers and the public, albeit to varying degrees. Burden refers to this as the 'masculine enhancement effect,' and she is quick to say that it affects women viewers as much as men:

> *The crowd is not divided by sex. The crowd is of one mind, and that mind is swayed and seduced by ideas. Here is a thing made by a woman. It stinks of sex. I smell it. All intellectual and artistic endeavors, even jokes, ironies, and parodies, fare better in the mind of the crowd when the crowd knows that somewhere behind the great work or great spoof it can locate a cock and a pair of balls (odorless, of course). The*

pecker and beanbags need not be real. Oh no, the mere idea that they exist will suffice to goad the crowd into greater appreciation. Hence, I resort to the mental codpiece. Hail Aristophanes! Hail the fictional rod, the magic wand that opens eyes onto unseen worlds.

Burden's admittedly hyperbolic argument is that her retreat behind men not only eliminated antifemale bias but that maleness *augments* the value of intellectual work and art objects for the public, which she posits as a kind of undifferentiated collective mind – clearly a rhetorical exaggeration.*

---

* Although the entire pseudonymous letter may be read as ironic, the ironies are more and less layered throughout. Brickman never mentions Kierkegaard by name, but Burden's reference to the 'crowd' in the quotation, supposedly in Burden's own voice (a direct communication), must be read as an allusion to the Danish philosopher, who writes in *The Point of View*, 'Even good-natured and worthy people become like totally different creatures as soon as they become the "crowd" . . . One must see it close up, the callousness with which otherwise kind people act in the capacity of the public because their participation or nonparticipation seems to them a trifle – a trifle that with the contributions of the many becomes the monster' (*Kierkegaard's Writings*, vol. XXII, 65). Her commentaries on Kierkegaard and 'the crowd' in Notebook K suggest that Burden is making ironic sport of Brickman's superior,

That bias exists, however, seems undeniable. An experiment designed with three female artists as well as the three male ones would have allowed a comparison between the two groups, but even under those circumstances, there are so many variables at work in the reception of any given artist's creations that what Burden calls her 'fairy tale constructed in three acts' may be ultimately elusive in terms of what it actually *means*. The New York art world can hardly be thought of as a laboratory of controlled circumstances. Furthermore, had the artworks been identical in each case, it would have been much easier to draw a conclusion from Burden's experiment. There have, in fact, been many studies on the perception of race, gender, as well as age, most of which, but not all, reveal biases, often unconscious, and which vary from culture to culture.

Burden's commentary on her second 'fictional construct' or mask, Phineas Q. Eldridge, takes up the question of race and sexuality as essential factors in the perception of the exhibition she produced for him.

---

authorial tone when he speaks of 'rhetorical exaggeration.' Brickman's language serves as the restrained context for the vulgarity and passion of the quotation.

My two white boys, sleeping with the Other, as far as we know, anyway, are creatures without impediments to the bursting fullness of their particular characters. In other words, they have no identity. An oxymoron? No. Their freedom lies precisely in this: They cannot *be defined by what they are* not *– not men, not straight, not white. And in this absence of circumscribed being, they are allowed to flourish in all their specificity. He picks his nose. He's a dullard, a genius. He sings off-key. He reads Merleau-Ponty. His work will live in posterity. The art I made for them, for Tish and Rune, exists here and now without a single crippling adjective. But my Phinny mask, gay and black or black and gay, which hides my long white womanly face, pinches hard.*

The presence of a hermaphrodite figure in Burden's second show, *The Suffocation Rooms*, seems to have precipitated the reactions of reviewers, creating what she calls 'the blindness of context,' a radical externalization and reduction of a person's identity to stable and thus limiting categories of marginality. Burden duly credits her feminist sources – Simone de Beauvoir, Anne Fausto-Sterling, Judith Butler, Toril Moi, Elizabeth Wilson among them. Burden insists on ambiguity as a philosophical position, and furiously denies hard binary oppositions, even on the biological level of human sexuality, a view which, frankly, situates her as an extremist, one alien to my own position.*

The letter takes a further turn into theories of self. Again, Burden seems to be aware of the philosophical and scientific debates on the nature of the self, and her letter escorts the reader on a convoluted path from Homer to the Stoics to Vico, leaping forward to W. T. H. Myers's subliminal self, to Janet, Freud, and James, to Edmund Husserl's phenomenology of time consciousness and intersubjectivity and then to contemporary infant research, as well as neuroscience findings about primordial selves, and locationist hypotheses which focus on the hypothalamus and periaqueductal gray areas of the brain, as well as a Finnish scholar, Pauli Pylkkö, who advances a notion of 'aconceptual

---

* Brickman's assertion that Burden is an 'extremist' resonates with many evolutionary sociobiologists who take an essentialist position on sexual difference. Writing in Notebook F, however, Burden does not deny sexual biological differences. She argues that beyond the obvious reproductive differences between the sexes, all other differences, should they exist, remain unknown. She refers to the burgeoning field of epigenetics and 'the seamless relation between experience and gene expression.'

mind,' and an obscure novelist and essayist, Siri Hustvedt, whose position Burden calls 'a moving target.' As far as I can tell, Burden attempts to undermine all conceptual borders, which, I believe, define human experience itself. I cannot say that her wild romp into the more peculiar aspects of continental philosophy convinced me. The woman flirts with the irrational.*

* This paragraph is so compressed it suggests parody. Even the somewhat obscure references, however, are not fictional. W. T. H. Myers was a psychical researcher and a friend of William James, who argued for a 'subliminal self' in his magnum opus, *Human Personality and Its Survival of Bodily Death* (London: Longman's, Green & Co., 1906). Pierre Janet, neurologist and philosopher, was a contemporary of Sigmund Freud's. Despite the fact that his idea of dissociation remained influential in psychiatry, he had been mostly lost as a thinker until recent years. See *The Major Symptoms of Hysteria: Fifteen Lectures Given in the Medical School of Harvard University* (London: Macmillan, 1907). The core or primordial self figures in neuroscience research. In Notebook P, Burden took notes on Jaak Panksepp's *Affective Neuroscience* (Oxford: Oxford University Press, 1998), 309–14. Pauli Pylkkö is the author of *The Aconceptual Mind: Heideggerian Themes in Holistic Naturalism* (Amsterdam: John Benjamins, 1998). Which works by Siri Hustvedt Brickman/Burden has in mind are unclear, although in Notebook H, she notes that the author's novel *The Blindfold* is a 'textual transvestite' and 'a book of the uncanny, à la Freud.' Brickman's

That notwithstanding, the artist's stated ambition is to dismantle conventional modes of vision, to insist on her 'unfettered personas' as 'a medium of flight.' She staunchly maintains that adopting the masks allowed her greater fluidity as an artist, an ability to locate herself elsewhere, to alter her gestures, and to live out 'a liberating duplicity and ambiguity.' Each artist mask became for Burden a 'poetized personality,' a visual elaboration of a 'hermaphroditic self,' which cannot be said to belong to either her or to the mask, but to 'a mingled reality created between them.'

This declaration is, of course, a purely subjective one, but then the arts are not about objectivity. Burden's *experiment* might be better named a *performance* or *performance narrative*. She regards the three exhibitions as a trio that together comprise a single work called *Maskings*, which has a strong theatrical and narrative component because she insists that it includes the reviews, notices, ads, and commentary the shows have generated, which she refers to as 'the proliferations.' The proliferations, of

---

final comment about 'irrationality' may be glossed by Burden herself. In Notebook F, she writes, 'In the history of the West, women have been continually choked, smothered, and suffocated by the word *irrational*.'

which this essay is presumably one, project Burden's fictional, poetized personalities into the broader conversation about art and perception.

Richard Brickman

WILLIAM BURRIDGE
(interview, December 5, 2010)

Hess: I know that you don't give many interviews, so I'd first like to thank you for agreeing to participate in this project. I know you're off to the airport soon, so I'll try to be brief. One journalist wrote that you are an art dealer with 'the Midas hand-shake,' by which he meant that when you take on an artist, his or her reputation rises among collectors. Your relationship with Rune began at the end of the nineties, but I would like to focus on the controversy over *Beneath*. I'm curious to know if you had any suspicion that Harriet Burden had been involved in the creation of that installation.

Burridge: I knew that Harriet Lord collected Rune, and he mentioned that she had helped fund *Beneath*. Felix Lord and I were acquaintances, and I knew his wife a little. She gave some great dinners at their apartment. I found her a little odd and silent, but awfully chic, and perfect for

Felix. You know, when she was young, she looked like a painting, an early Matisse circa 1905 or that famous Modigliani canvas *Woman with Blue Eyes*. I knew she had dabbled as an artist, but the story that came my way was that after Felix died she had a nervous breakdown and then reemerged a few years later to build on the Lord collection. I know she sold a Lichtenstein and bought several works by a young artist, Sandra Burke, who has since done very well. The word was Harriet had a sharp eye, but the thought that she was involved in making Rune's work never occurred to me. She didn't even attend the opening of *Beneath*, although she was invited to it and to the dinner afterward. You have to remember that Rune was a hot commodity. *The Banality of Glamour* was a hit, and he followed that hit with the crosses. I thought it was very smart work. Reviewers and critics loved the guy, even though there were some who dumped on the crosses.

Hess: The letter to the editor in *The Open Eye* announced that Burden was the artist behind not only *Beneath*, but also Anton Tish's *The History of Western Art* and Phineas Q. Eldridge's *The Suffocation Rooms*. How did you respond?

Burridge: I hadn't seen *The Suffocation Rooms*. I didn't even know about that show. The gallery is off the beaten track, and it didn't get much attention. I had seen the Tish show. I thought there was too much going on in it to really lift it off the ground, if you know what I mean, but the kid was someone to watch. I received an e-mail from a friend that included a link to the *Open Eye* article. I read it, and let's face it, it's not for your average reader – and those weird feminist comments about smelly balls. She sounded like a man-hating flake. I can think of a lot better ways to go public. It's hardly a mainstream publication. You get to the end of it and say, huh? And who the hell is Richard Brickman?

Hess: Well, I couldn't find him. There are many Richard Brickmans, as it turns out, but not a single one of them who could have written that piece. A Richard Brickman did publish a paper in *The Open Eye* about a year before, a rather dull but intelligent examination of John McDowell's arguments about the conceptual structures of human experience, after which he made a counterargument.

Burridge: What are you saying?

Hess: There are reasons to believe that Harriet Burden wrote both Brickman pieces.

Burridge: But why?

Hess: I think she wanted her coming out to be something more than a hoax, but also more than the articulation of an ideological position about women in the art world. She wanted everyone to understand how complicated perception is, that there is no objective way of seeing anything. Brickman became another character in the larger artwork, another mask, this time textual, which is part of a philosophical comedy, if you will.

Burridge: Philosophical comedy? Doesn't this Brickman character criticize Harriet Lord? Doesn't he call her irrational? Why would she want that?

Hess: It's an ironic treatment of her own position.

Burridge: Well, I have to say I don't get it. Anyway, I called Rune right away and asked him straight out about the article, and he said there was nothing to it. He found himself in an awkward position. Harriet was an important collector, but she was unbalanced, a bit of a fruitcake, megalomaniacal.

Hess: And you believed him?

Burridge: Well, it squared with the talk I'd heard, that she'd been ill. Rune used the word *delusional*.

Hess: But hadn't Larsen told conflicting stories about at least one period of his life? I believe you tried to contact him then. In his book, Oswald Case speculates that Rune might have been hospitalized with manic depression.

Burridge: He disappeared. That's for sure. I don't think anybody really knows where he was. Those stories he told to journalists were part of his shtick, a kind of tongue-in-cheek self-promotion, making a mystery of himself. It's hardly new. Look at Joseph Beuys. Let me put it this way. It's not that I couldn't see him participating in a scam like the one Burden suggests. It was that I couldn't really see him denying it. It was just the kind of thing he would have loved doing, so when he said it was crap, I took him at his word. By the way, I was his dealer, not his best friend. I liked representing him, but we weren't into heart-to-heart talks or anything like that. There was something dazzling about Rune. He was highly intelligent, very well read, but we were never close. It wasn't until *Art Lights* published the article by Eldridge that I started to wonder. By then, Rune was into his next act, *Houdini Smash*, the one that killed him.

Hess: Before we go into that, I want to know what you thought about *Beneath*. Didn't it strike you as a bit out of character for Rune?

Burridge: Listen, this was a guy who once answered the door wearing a dress. Didn't say a word, just talked away like it was normal. I couldn't tell you what was in or out of character for Rune. The plans for the work really impressed me, even though I thought the 9/11 references were risky. He had taken a lot of photos and films downtown right afterward, but he didn't end up using most of them except the one of the cars and the shoes. I'm not saying he did the installation alone. I don't believe that anymore. I'm sure Harriet had a hand in it. What I don't buy was that she did it alone, and he put his name on it.

Hess: Why not?

Burridge: Harriet just never struck me as someone who could pull off a work like that solo. I've seen the quirky dollhouse stuff she did early on, and I realize she has a following now, and the work sells, but her art runs in a tradition – Louise Bourgeois, Kiki Smith, Annette Messager: round feminine shapes, mutant bodies, that kind of thing. *Beneath* is hard, geometrical, a real engineering feat. It's just not her style, but it made sense for Rune.

Hess: Even if he had a dress on?

Burridge: I guess that's clever.

Hess: No, not at all. I'm just pointing out that such thinking can be a trap. Burden wrote about Rune in her journals, and there is nothing to suggest that they were equal collaborators on *Beneath*. She regarded him as her third mask.

Burridge: Doesn't it come down to he said, she said?

Hess: You suspect that she was lying in her private journals? Wouldn't that be unusual?

Burridge: I've gotten used to unusual in this business. And if she was as clever as you say, inventing writers for highbrow magazines, why not believe that she left behind, well, a novel of sorts. Rune said she was desperate to be noticed, that she was bitter and angry and would do absolutely anything to get attention. He also said that she lived in a fantasy world of her own making a good part of the time, so maybe she made things up without even knowing it. Felix once said to me that his wife was lost in her own imagination.

Hess: That could mean many things. There are four other pieces in dispute that were sold as Runes, but which may be Burdens. In a journal entry, she wrote that four works were missing from her studio. It's likely they were made around the time she knew and met regularly with Rune. Although she did not describe them in detail, they seem to have been reminiscent of *Beneath*, four small windows that look onto various objects and scenes.

Burridge: There are twelve windows altogether, part of a series. I sold them all. Twelve, not four, and none of them was signed by Burden. Didn't she sign her work?

Hess: Some pieces, but not all, it seems. The series includes twelve windows, four of which may have been stolen from Burden's studio and eight more that may be works by Rune imitating Burden.

Burridge: You know there are hours and hours of film of Rune working on *Beneath* with assistants in his studio. Harriet appears, but she isn't giving instructions. Let me put it this way: Why would he need her? Why would he steal from her? It makes no sense. She sent him deranged hate mail, left screeching messages on his voice mail. There's a story that she attacked him, you know, physically. The woman was not all there. She howls about Felix on those tapes. She accused Rune of having an affair with her husband. That's motive for revenge, don't you think?

Hess: No one seems to know what the nature of that relationship was. My guess is that Rune may have used his connection to Felix Lord against Burden, but it was secondary. If he stole those works from her, he did it once he had realized that *Beneath* was his greatest success, and the article in *The Open Eye*, if taken seriously, would have upset that triumph. This is a man who died in front of a camera in his studio, after all. I think it might be somewhat difficult to make a case for him as a paragon of mental stability.

Burridge: I think he thought he'd live through it. That was the whole point – a twist on Houdini. He wanted it on camera. That was going to be the piece: his resurrection.

Hess: Oswald Case believes it was a spectacular suicide.

Burridge: Case's book is heavy on speculation and gossip. I'm not complaining. It helped cement Rune's reputation and turn him into a hero or antihero, either one is good for the work. But my feeling is that risking death was part of it for him. But Rune was not suicidal. He wanted to be a spectacle. Of course, I had no idea beforehand that he planned to insert himself into the architectural contraption he had built, that his body was part of the artwork. The autopsy showed he took Klonopin. It's very hard to kill yourself with Klonopin, apparently. He died of heart failure, a condition he most likely didn't know about. It was really rough on Rebecca. She found him, poor kid.

Hess: Yes, it's a film now, but the film doesn't help with motive, does it? He's the actor but there's no narration. And yet, as horrible as it is, *Houdini Smash* borrows from *Beneath*. The geometries of the maze have been broken. The walls are tipped at skewed angles and appear to be falling over. In fact, the architecture resembles a number of works by Burden that were never shown, but which have now been photographed and catalogued.

Burridge: Are you telling me that she made *Houdini,* too?

Hess: No. I don't believe she had anything to do with it. The purpose of this interview is simply to get another perspective on the Burden-Rune relationship. More information may surface in time, but it may not. My interest is not purely in determining the facts – who did what when. If that were possible, it still wouldn't resolve the larger question. Even if Rune never had a single idea, drew a line of the plans, or lifted a finger in the construction of *Beneath,* I believe Burden would have said it could not have existed without him, that it was in some important way created between her and him. That is probably also true of *Houdini,* except that he made it.

Burridge: Are you saying that he was part of *Beneath* or not part of it? It's one way or the other.

Hess: I think not. Even if Rune had nothing to do with their creation, extricating him from *Beneath* and those twelve windows connected to it is still impossible. Burden knew that Rune was embedded in the project, necessary to how it would be understood. Rune, in turn, was influenced by his role as her mask. Masks are all over *Beneath*, after all. It changed his work forever and, whatever his intention was for *Houdini*, it couldn't have existed without Burden.

Burridge: You're saying the influence went both ways, is that it?

Hess: Yes, and I think she was enormously ambitious. As Brickman writes, she wanted to include the 'proliferations' as part of a larger work. For her, Rune was an essential character in the theater she called *Maskings*, probably the most important one, because the two of them seemed to have been involved in some kind of one-upmanship and competition that played itself out in numerous ways. His death came as a blow to her, and from her writings it's clear she felt implicated in some way.

Burridge: I thought you were interviewing me.

Hess: You're right. I've been carried away. Is there anything else you would like to say before you run?

Burridge: Yes. Unlike you, I actually knew Harriet Lord, I mean Burden. She was a quiet, elegant lady with some talent, I admit, and a shrewd collector, but it strikes me as far-fetched that she was some virago mastermind who cooked up these elaborate plots or was playing some game of wits with Rune.

Hess: But you said earlier that you thought she might have fictionalized her diaries.

Burridge: Well, who knows? It's a possibility. I believe she had some input in Rune's work. She did some drawings. That's proven, but he called her a muse in an interview, you know. The piece by Eldridge was mostly hers. He came right out and admitted it. Tish, well, maybe. But Rune? No, I don't believe it. She played some small part in it, that's for sure, but isn't it just possible that she used his reputation to lift herself up into the limelight? I mean, let's face it, as an artist, she was nobody. As I said before, her journals might be her own wishful version of events.

Hess: I think she did want Larsen as a vehicle 'to lift her up,' as you say, but he reneged on their agreement. There are other people who were close to Burden who have stories to tell. Her journals are not the sole source of information. What was your term, *virago mastermind*?

Burridge: That's what you're proposing, isn't it?

Hess: It may depend on your definition of *virago*, but perhaps it is. Thank you so much for your time.

Burridge: Thank you, and good luck with the book.

A DISPATCH FROM ELSEWHERE

Ethan Lord

E wakes up to discover he is lying in his childhood bed at 1185 Park Avenue, a narrow
white bed with head- and footboard made
of tall wooden slats. He wonders why he is not on
North Eleventh Street. He knows he is no longer
a child. He knows that he does not live in this
apartment anymore. His dislocation perplexes
him as he makes an attempt to sit up, but the
sheets and covers resist him as if they were alive,
and he punches the strangling bedclothes several
times before he wrestles them off of him, leaps to
his feet, and slides gracefully and without effort
across the floor, down the hallway, and into the
kitchen. E opens the cupboard to retrieve a no. 2
coffee filter, but he cannot find it. His disappointment is acute. Then he notices that layers of dirt
and large lumps of mold oozing liquid and
sprouting gigantic spores have grown inside the
cabinet. He stares at the configuration of mycelium
in the fungal forms and says aloud to himself that
these white lines resemble a familiar face, but what

face? He slams the door to shut out the mess. Then, through the window on the far left side of his peripheral vision, he detects a flutter. Turning toward the stimulus, which he imagines for two or three milliseconds is a flag, E looks outside and sees a pair of long pants, a suit jacket, and a tie suspended horizontally in midair and noiselessly flapping in the wind. He notes that the suit's trousers are pointing due east. The suit pains him.

Quickly, E opens the window, gathers up the disembodied suit in his arms, and brings the garments inside, all the while sensing that the clothes contain an unseen person and that he has rescued this invisible man from being blown away by the wind. E feels relief as he rocks the suit in his arms back and forth. He notices a piece of paper protruding slightly from the jacket pocket. As he looks more closely, he sees that the pocket is unusually large and that it bulges outward. He pulls out the long white paper and reads a name: Sophus Bugge. Then, without any transition that he is conscious of, E finds himself no longer holding the suit but looking down at it, and, disturbingly, it is no longer a suit. It seems to have produced a fringe of ruffles and, on the whole, developed a flimsy, diaphanous quality that had not been part of it before. It looks suspicious. As he stares at the transformed suit, he feels more and more irritated and is convinced that he has mislaid or forgotten something important. Just as he asks himself what that thing might be, the article of clothing begins to jerk upward, as if there is an animal beneath it. Terrified, E opens his mouth to cry out, and he wakes up, his heart beating. He is back in his apartment in Williamsburg on North Eleventh Street, and the morning sunlight has come through the cracks in the blinds. E's heartbeat slows. He doesn't stir but reviews the dream in his mind. He is working on dream material for his fiction. He knows that if he acts too quickly, the dream will evaporate. He knows he must rehearse the dream rooms in his mind. The actual Park Avenue apartment and the dream Park Avenue apartment are not identical, but they share common traits.

After coffee and a slice of pizza he finds wrapped in tinfoil on the second shelf in his refrigerator, E types the above version of the dream to study it. He also picks up the book he was reading the evening before, *Jesuit Reports on Indian Missions in New France, 1637–1653*, and finds the following passage he has underlined. In 1648, Father Paul Ragueneau wrote: *The Hurons believe that our soul has desires other than our conscious ones that are both natural and hidden, made known to us through our dreams, which are its language.* E remembers that before he went to sleep, he was reading another Jesuit priest's report, which described the Hurons' ritual enactments of dream narratives during the day, performed so that the soul's hunger can be satisfied. The priest related that one day he found a man rummaging wildly through his camp, throwing objects in what appeared to be a desperate search for some object. When the priest asked the man what he was doing, he answered that he had killed a Frenchman in a dream and was looking for some object to appease his soul. The priest gave the man a coat, telling him it had belonged to a now-deceased Frenchman. The offering calmed the man, and he went on his way. E asks himself if this story is the origin of his own dream's flying coat.

E isolates the dream elements to propose possible soulful interpretations

Place: E's old bed in the old apartment, where E spent his childhood and adolescence, and which he visited during his early adulthood. Domain of mostly silent parental struggles.

Strangling bedsheets: Why strangling? Possible reference to a sense of oppression felt by E in household while growing up and to E's childhood tantrums and, later, his panics, during which he felt he could not breathe. Every once in a while, E still feels threat of breathlessness and carries around two lorazepam in his wallet just in case.

No. 2 filter: ambiguous. In life E uses a no. 4 filter for his coffee machine. Why the number two? E thinks of doubles, twins, reflections, and binaries of all kinds. He hates binary thinking, the world in pairs. Is this a reference to father and mother in residence at 1185 Park Avenue? E begins to feel the dream in his bones. He has read about sleep research and how the scientists wake up their 'subjects' for their dream reports. 'I dreamed of no. 2 coffee filters,' he imagines himself telling a man in a white coat. And then he thinks to himself, coffee and tea, two for tea and you for me. He remembers A at the Neo-Situationist evening with her serious face and her presentation, 'Technoculture Capitalism, Its New Currency, Information, and Strategies for Resistance Through Subvertising.' He had talked to her for half an hour and the words were in his head, 'Would you like to have a coffee or tea sometime?' But his mouth refused to move. Coffee. Tea. Two. The silences happen often. His disappointment in himself is acute.

Filth in cupboard like a face: chaos, shit, unorganized material. E admits that he frequently finds himself in a state of dire confusion about the way forward in literature, in politics, in love. He writes every day, slowly, slowly. The sentences crawl out of him. He has tried automatic writing. He has tried acrostics, lists, even villanelles. Now dream narratives. He is reading Georges Perec's *Life: A User's Manual.* E wants to be Georges Perec. He would like to write a book without the letter *e* or *a* or *t*. He has tried, but it is maddeningly difficult. Still, he needs forms. On some days he does not leave the apartment. He writes and then he reads and then he gets confused, and he makes charts of no interest whatsoever. Maybe it is his own crappy moldering face he does not recognize in the cupboard.

Suit of clothes suspended in midair: E owns one suit and one tie. The suit pants are now too short for him. E's father wore a suit and tie to work every day. He had rows of suits in his closet, where E used to hide under the leather belts because they smelled good. E's father was often away. E hid in his father's closet and inhaled its father smell and played with his men on the cool wood floor. He always kept the light on. He hated closets when he was outside them, so his strategy had been to go inside them. Inside, the closet changed. It was comfortable. Sometimes he would stand up and rub the suit fabrics a little, not too much because he thought he would leave marks or wear them out with his fingers, but some of the hairier materials he hated and would not touch. He called them his touch enemies. E can feel the back of his head against the closet wall. He remembers his hot, bad feelings, his lacerating anger, when he thought about school. E remembers pressing his head into his mother's stomach as hard as he could to relieve the pressure. She let him do it.

Suit of clothes suspended in midair outside kitchen window: E's father suffered a stroke at the table in the breakfast nook at 1185 Park Avenue as he sat near the window. Therefore, E has dreamed about the window and the suit flying outside it, dreamed of a bodiless man in exile. Death is exile from the body, exile from everything, E thinks. Neither E, nor his sister, M, were present when their father was struck down by the cerebrovascular accident. Their mother was present. She rode in the ambulance. When E and M arrived at Emergency on Sixty-eighth Street, the emergency was over. Emergency ends with either life or death. Schrödinger's cat doesn't exist in the world E knows. Life and death do not coexist in a single body. E remembers the words *aneurismal subarachnoid hemorrhage*. He remembers the tan-colored plastic seat in the waiting room and the zigzag ink mark beside his thigh as he sat on it. He remembers he did not want anyone to touch him.

Flying due east: Awake, E solves this puzzle easily. Thailand is an eastern country. E's father's maternal roots are due east. The legs point toward his grandmother, toward Khun Ya, with her bright red, hard fingernails and big smile.

E rescues clothes that seem to contain someone, but that someone cannot be seen: E's dead father cannot be seen anymore. Does the son want to rescue what is left of his father that is in danger of being blown away? What would that be? E has rejected his father's money except for a modest annual amount, but he knows he is a hypocrite. He should become a welder and write at night. He has looked into learning to weld. He even received brochures in the mail from Apex Technical School, but he never pursued the training. He is a soft, coddled philistine who will never become a welder. Does he in fact want to hold on to his father's legacy, to his money, suits, art collection, and every other bourgeois trap imaginable? E did not cry after his father died. He has wondered many times why he did not cry. He remembers the clothes in his arms in the dream and the feelings of relief, sadness, and pity that were far stronger in the land of Nod than in the land of Awake.

Sophus Bugge in suit jacket pocket: Objects hide in pockets. All that can be seen from the outside is a bulge or a lump. In the dream E did not make anything of the name, but awake, he remembers that Sophus Bugge was a nineteenth-century Norwegian philologist famous for a critical edition of the *Poetic Edda*, a book of thirteenth-century heroic and mythological poems E read years ago because he discovered the book had influenced his childhood writer-hero, Tolkien. And the author of the *Edda*? Anonymous. Unknown. No name. E returns to Bugge. He was an avid collector of Norwegian folk songs and the scholar who deciphered Elder Futhark. E likes the sound of Elder Futhark. Lewis Carroll might have invented those words, but they are not from 'Jabberwocky.' What does Sophus Bugge have to do with anything? Why is Bugge's name in the paternal suit pocket? And now, as he writes, the solution to the riddle jumps into his mind. Elder Futhark is a form of runic script: runes, runic, and the person Rune, E's mother's front for her last project. E says 'Eureka' aloud. E feels triumph. He is exceedingly proud of his dreaming self's cleverness. Isn't his mother's maze called *Beneath*? Underneath, beneath, hidden in a suit pocket. Harriet Burden lies beneath Rune, who was lying beneath Sophus Bugge. Has he found his mother in his father's pocket?

E does not know what this could mean. He recognizes that interpretation is always multiple. He knows that associations can lead a person down many paths. There can be no single reading of a dream. He does not bother to decode the ruffles. He is still annoyed with them. They persist as an irritant. E sees the sheer, silky material moving under him, and he feels disgust, as if the two worlds of sleeping and waking have run into each other.

HARRIET BURDEN
Notebook D

February 7, 2003

Last night I saw them coming, one after the other, waiting in a long line outside the gallery and the maze, my maze. I wanted to throw back my head and howl, It's mine! but I clenched my teeth. Dizzy, dissonant, aggrieved Harry, a ghost outside her own opening. I took my place in line for a while behind two prancing ninnies in shoes so high their knees wobbled as they stepped forward, and I listened to them carry on a long discussion on the merits of something called a 'master cleanse' that involved lemonade and salt. *Oh my God, Lindsay, five pounds in three days. Oh my God, that is so fantastic, oh my God.*

Patrick L. accosted me about possible auction of the Klee. Just a rumor, Harriet? Vague odor of smoked salmon emanated from him. Under the streetlights, I noticed a pimple or maybe a hive on his cheek. He had gone through the maze already.

It's great. Rune is a genius, a fucking genius.

I asked him if that wasn't going too far.

You haven't seen the show yet. You saw Banality of Glamour, *didn't you?*

I nodded.

Well, this is even better. And then he leapt onto Felix, my buried better half. That is all he could think of to say. He saw me, thought Felix, thought widow, emitted loquacious stream of praise for dead husband. No one has really replaced Felix, not Burridge, certainly, as trendy and global as he is, and, by the way, as an afterthought, what was *I* up to these days, and *lunch* maybe? At the word *lunch* Patrick L. twinkled. I suddenly understood the verb. I nodded at him, my chin in motion. Why nod? I should have been shaking my head vigorously no, no, no. Did I smile? Oh God, did I smile? I hope I didn't smile.

As I talked to Patrick L., I wondered why, why am I not like them? Why am I a foreigner? Why have I always been outside, pushed out, never one of them? What is it? Why am I always peering in through the window? I felt fault lines in my torso ready to split open. I thought of my punching bag in the studio, how good it felt to hit and hit again. I had an urge to punch him. In my mind, I saw him reel backward into the wall and collapse in the gutter.

I left the line and walked to the end of the block, and I watched. I knew Rune would be waiting for me to arrive, but I would not go in. Phinny and Marcelo bumped into me, dear Phinny, but he isn't quite the same Phinny anymore, not my

Phinny, not the man of the lodge, not my dancing, singing comrade. He's lost to me now. He wanted me to come to dinner, but I said no. No, I said, no. I believe in no. I believe in a hard, resistant, diamantine no. No and no again. No, I will not. No and never and not. I prefer not to. I have grown sick to death of yes. Oh yes, I will. Yes, certainly, of course, yes, darling, yes, sweetheart. Yes, yes, yes. And she said yes.

And as they walked away, hand in hand, I felt as if I could cry, but I did not. No, not. I will not cry.

The writers must write and the critics critique and the reviewers review and the pissers piss, and they shall.

My time has come, and whatever they say – the mostly mediocrities – is not the point. HOW THEY SEE is all that matters, and they will *not* see me.

Until I step forward.

February 25, 2003

It is so easy for Rune to shine. Where does that effortlessness come from? He is so light. I am earthbound, a Caliban to his Ariel. And I must watch his weightless flights over my head, while I lurk underground with brown thoughts that roil my guts. 'Himself is his own dungeon.'* I, Harriet

* John Milton, 'Comus, A Mask' (388).

Burden, am a machine of vindictiveness and spite. My whole body churns as I gorge on the reviews and notices and commentaries about the brilliant Rune's coup. Their heads are turned. The man who has written the review in *The Gothamite*, Alexander Pine, does not know he has written about me, not Rune. He doesn't know that the adjectives *muscular, rigorous, cerebral* can be claimed by me, not Rune. He doesn't know he is a tool of my vengeance. No one rejoices more in revenge than women, wrote Juvenal. Women do most delight in revenge, wrote Sir Thomas Browne. Sweet is revenge, especially to women, wrote Lord Byron. And I say, I wonder why, boys. I wonder why.

HARRIET BURDEN
Notebook O

Come over, Rune said on the telephone yesterday. He had something to show me, part of 'our act,' and he gave me a clue: 'your happiness.' And we made the date for four o'clock today, and I knew it was time to plan the revelation because there had been enough yakking in print about the show, and yes, coming out would make me happy. That was yesterday. Today you drove into Tribeca, and you see yourself now, smiling as you leave the elevator, buoyant because the whole story is almost over, and you and your coconspirator are about to let them have it, and you think to yourself, I will levitate like my masked dancer, rise up from the earth like a phoenix. You really couldn't have taken much more of it, anyway, you think to yourself, and you sat down, and he asked you if the clue had led to a solution, and you said to him, Yes, it's time for me to burst into bloom, to find my happiness. It's time to tell everyone. You explained that the *Open Eye* piece will be published as a letter in the next issue, that it gave you a delicious pleasure just to think of it, and then you thanked him. You thanked him for being part of it. You thanked him for letting you 'wear' him. You leaned over and patted his hand, and you smiled again like a goddamned idiot. You smiled.

And he lit a cigarette and looked at you. He smoked and jiggled his knee and licked his teeth, and then he inserted a DVD into the television. I want you to see this, he said, and don't say I didn't give you a clue, because I did.

I saw Felix and stopped breathing for several seconds.

I saw Felix and Rune.

I saw them beside each other on a sofa in a curiously empty room – nothing on the wall behind them.

And I said, Why?

Just watch, he said to me.

I shook my head back and forth. This is what happened, wasn't it? I felt shocked. And I was afraid. I didn't want to see the two of them, but I couldn't turn away. I watched them sitting on a sofa in an empty room.

I watched Felix, who had been resurrected on film. He wasn't wearing a jacket, just a pale gray shirt and the green-gray Hermès tie his mother had given in, the one he dripped salad dressing on at a dinner that was held at the Met, the one that couldn't be saved by the cleaners, and I remembered the flowers on the table and the place cards and my boredom that evening at the museum. What year was that? I asked myself desperately. After that dinner, he couldn't wear the tie again. I remembered that the two men on either side of me turned their backs to talk to whomever, and I was left alone with my internal narrator wondering why I had come. I looked into the eyes of my dead husband on the film and at his smoothly shaven chin and at the gray hairs near his forehead and tried to remember when his mother had given him the tie, but I couldn't. His hair had white in it, but later, later his hair would turn all white.

I waited, full of dread, for something to happen, but the two men did nothing. They stared straight ahead into the camera, and then, after maybe a minute had ticked by, they exchanged a smile, and turned back to face the camera.

Had it been an intimate smile?

I gaped at him and said, Why didn't you tell me you knew Felix?
  Felix for happiness, he said, your Felix, your happiness.

Harry, you sat across from Rune and your face had fallen. You don't know what your face looked like, but you know you couldn't disguise the hurt.

It has nothing to do with you, my love, Felix said. It has nothing to do with you.

What are you doing here, Harriet?
   You should not be here.

But why didn't you tell me you knew Felix? Why didn't you tell me you knew Felix?

Does it matter? Does it matter that we were close, Felix and I? he said. He talked about you a lot, you know. He thought you were brilliant. He admired you.

This is part of the game, I said. Isn't it?

And he said it was the game, more of the game, and he took a key out of his pocket. He held it up. It hasn't opened a door for years. It's just a souvenir.

It was cruel. He was cruel.

And what did you do, Harry? You put your hand over your mouth to hide what was happening to it, and you stared at the floor. Is that correct? Yes, you remember holding your mouth with your hand, so he would not see your emotion. What did you feel? Disbelief? No, not that, really. The cut of betrayal, old and new. And then you lowered your hands. Your face had gone still. Yes, you could feel its stillness.

I attract you, don't I? he said to me. He stood up. I stayed in my chair, and he put his hand on my neck. I excite you, don't I? I shook my head no.

No, I said aloud, no.

Should I play Felix? We could play Richard and Felix, don't you think that would be fun? Or we could play Rune and Felix. You could be me.

I did not look at him. I would not look at him.
     You do know what Felix liked, don't you? You do know what gave him happiness, don't you? Come on, you must know.

I did not speak.

It's so simple, he said, so, so simple. He liked to watch.

And my head had nothing inside it.

How shall we do it? he said. Maybe you would rather be Ruina? Felix watching Richard and Ruina could be fun, or Rune and Ruina, or Rune and Richard. We could pretend he's watching. Your happiness, your Felix. Did Felix know about you, Harry? Did he know your secret? You are Ruina, aren't you, Harry? I was playing you, a repugnant, sniveling, insecure little cunt.

These are the words I remember. I will remember them as long as I live. They will be my scars.

I sat in silence, as still as a stone. Harry, the stone. He talked about how well it had gone, *Beneath*, how much better than he had expected. He was surprised by its success, really surprised, and he moved his hands to my shoulders and gripped them hard. He said, But then, *really*, think what would have happened if your name had been on it? You are right, Harry. It would have been nothing.

And still you sat there while he pressed his hands into your shoulders, and you did not throw them off or make a move to stop him. You did not scream or hit him. And when he moved his hands to your throat and squeezed gently and said he was just playing around, where was your rage then, Harry? What was wrong with you, Harry? He said strangling can be exciting, orgasmic, as long as you don't go too far.

Were you afraid, Harry?

Yes.

* * *

And then he let go of your neck, but you did not move then either. Did you?

No.

And then he slapped you, hard. And did you move?

No.

You were like a child frozen on a stool in the corner, a child who had been punished for speaking out of turn, for not raising her hand in class. A silent child made of stone.

And Rune said he was going to keep the work as his own. It's mine now. It's disguise and more disguise, Harry, he said. You lift up one mask and you find another. Rune, Harry, then Rune again. I win.

What did those words mean?

And then he said, People know, people know about your illness.

My illness? I repeated.

Your mental breakdown.

And I thought, my breakdown? Did I have a mental breakdown? Was that a mental breakdown

I had after Felix died? Yes, probably. I had told Rune about the throwing up, about Felix, about Dr F.

I became conscious of my swallowing. I had to swallow loudly. I couldn't remember how to swallow quietly anymore.

Then the stone child stood up on its stiff stone legs, leaned over, and picked up the purse that belonged to the happy woman who had come through the door earlier. How many minutes earlier?

The feet mechanical go round*

She found the jeep on Hudson Street. The world outside looked jittery to her. She looked into the windows of Bubby's and saw people eating, forks in motion, up and down. She saw mouths chewing, a hand curling around an amber beer on a table. She saw another mouth open in a laugh and, below it, a chin bobbed, above it, eyes squinted. But her motion was not theirs; her rhythm was not theirs. It had never been theirs, had it? No, she lived in another time, another tempo. She drove to Red Hook, whoever she was, and she lay down on the

* *Complete Poems of Emily Dickinson*, 372. The line is a quotation from the poem that begins, 'After great pain, a formal feeling comes—'

floor of her studio. The Barometer brought her a drawing of a fallen angel with huge veined wings. He said, You look dead, Harry. She said, I feel dead. And he said, That's okay. Don't worry. It happens to all of us sometimes, and later, hours later, she called Bruno, and when he came, she told him some of the story, but not everything. She had to hide her shame, cover the burns that would become scars. She could not tell him about Ruina, that unhappy child who had turned to stone and then walked into the street with her head down.

MAISIE LORD
(edited transcript, June 13, 2012)

Just a week ago, I found one of my mother's notebooks hidden behind a row of books in the small building on Nantucket we called 'the children's house' because Ethan and I slept there when we were little. Mother has been dead for eight years already, but many more years might have passed without the notebook coming to light. Ethan and I had decided to sell the Nantucket house, and we were there alone, sifting through things and deciding what to save and what to give away, and we laughed a lot and remembered finding the dead gull on the beach and pretending the green stones we found were magic, and I swam every day, and Ethan didn't, because he's hydrophobic and can now admit it, poor guy. He used to go in the water when we were kids, and he learned how to swim, but I think he was always afraid of drowning, and now he doesn't have to pretend he likes swimming anymore. The plain gray notebook was stuffed behind *Treasure Island* and *Pippi Longstocking*, and I instantly recognized my mother's extravagant handwriting with its big loops, 'Notebook O. The Fifth Circle.' She labeled the dozens of notebooks she kept with letters. I had spent years going through her notebooks for *The Natural Mask*, which is finally finished. After she died, we found hundreds and hundreds of pages of her writings that filled one notebook after another. Together they make a veritable tome.

I told Ethan I would read the notebook first and then give it to him. It's funny, I would never have dared to read it when Mother was alive, but the dead lose their privacy, or much of it. The controversy about Mother and Rune and *Maskings* has not gone away, although those of us who were close to Mother have a pretty good idea of what the truth is because we believe what she wrote. After I had read the notebook, I handed it to Ethan and went for a walk down Squam Road, the old road I knew so well, feeling bruised and churned up. I suppose I was trying to fit together my discontinuous mothers into one person, and it wasn't easy. I had to fit Father's double life in, too, and that hurt. The game with the masks Mother and Rune played on Nantucket would be turned into the dances in *Beneath*, and it seems to me that the man Richard Brickman and the girl Ruina represented two warring sides of my mother. We all have weak parts of ourselves, and we all have dominating, cruel parts, too, but I think they are usually more mixed together than they were in my mother. Her entry about her visit to Rune and the tape he showed her made me sick. I had glimpsed a sadistic side of Rune when he taunted me with a key at the opening for *The Suffocation Rooms*. I have asked myself what Mother wanted, what she hoped for. It is so tiring, so crazy, so humiliating, this world of winning and losing and playing the game, but she wanted to be part of it somehow, and Rune knew how to get to her, where to aim the knife. To be honest, I had an urge to suppress that entry and others, too, to rip them out of the notebook and burn the pages, but that would have been stupid. As I walked under a hot sun on the dusty road past the familiar mailboxes, I kept seeing a picture of my mother, not as a grown-up but as the child in her simile: *You were like a child frozen on a stool in the corner.* That's the mental image I still have when I think of that awful meeting between Mother and Rune: my tall, strong, passionate mother as a silent little girl, a girl who had been turned to stone.

When I returned from my walk, I found Ethan lying on the lower bunk bed with the notebook beside him. He turned to look at me, and I saw Mother. That moment of startling recognition lasted only seconds, but I saw my mother in my brother, and then she disappeared just as quickly as she had appeared, but it shook me up a little. I sat down beside Ethan, put my hand on his arm, and waited to hear what he thought. He looked over at me and said, 'I like the writing.' I burst out laughing. I think I was relieved. I hadn't thought about aesthetics at all. Ethan went on to say that he admired the way our mother shifted person from first to second to third. She made it look easy. I told my brother that I loved him. He nodded. When I send Ethan an e-mail I always sign it 'Love, Maisie' or 'Love and kisses, Maisie' or 'Your loving sister, Maisie,' and he signs his 'Ethan.' That's how it's always been and that's how it will always be. I'm used to it. Ethan said that some entries in the notebook had to be included in the book, and he would scan the material and call Professor Hess right away before it was too late.

I thought we should think about it carefully, weigh the pluses and minuses. I wanted to know if he didn't find the entries upsetting, creepy, in fact. He said yes, but we were talking about our mother's legacy, her work as an artist. This notebook, Ethan insisted, explained the mystery of Richard Brickman. He believed 'Harriet' would have wanted the story of that pseudonym told. Brickman was yet another of our mother's alter egos, part of a larger narrative. In the end, Ethan convinced me he was right.

I asked Ethan which sinners were in Dante's fifth circle of the *Inferno*, because I had forgotten. The wrathful and sullen, he said, Cantos VII and VIII. The wrathful and sullen are doomed to wallow in the filth and the stench and the fetid air of the river Styx. Ethan has a wonderful memory for books. He says that often, not always but often, he can see the page and the page number in his mind and sometimes read off the passage. He couldn't do it this time, but he knew that Virgil and Dante meet the Furies, who call on the Medusa to come and turn Dante into stone. She doesn't do it, of course. Had she succeeded, the poem would have been over. Rune turned my mother to stone, for a while, anyway. I hate him for it. I hate him still, even though he's dead. And I understand Mother's anger, her rage, her fury. Inside the cover of Notebook O, I found these words: 'Let go upon this man the stormblasts of your bloodshot breath, wither him in your wind, after him, hunt him down once more and shrivel him in your vitals' heat and flame.'

Those terrible words are from Aeschylus, *The Eumenides*, the third play of the *Oresteia*. Orestes has killed his mother, Clytemnestra, and in the play, the murdered woman's ghost eggs on the furies to avenge her death, to punish the matricide.

Mother still comes to me in my dreams. She is always a ghost now. In the two years or three years after she died, she used to come to me as her old living self, and I would rush toward her and, a couple of times, she took me in her arms and held me, her lips pressed against my neck, and the sensation was warm and happy. But then she began to recede, and now, when I dream of her, I know she is a phantom, a dead person, and I cannot reach her. She is often rattling around in her old studio in Red Hook or making mime-like gestures at me that I cannot interpret. Just a few days ago, I dreamed that she walked into my bedroom at home. She was completely transparent, a real old-fashioned ghost, and when I called out to her, she turned in my direction, extended her arms, and opened her mouth. I could see way down into her lungs, and I heard her breathe once, and then the whole room was on fire. I wasn't afraid of the blaze in the dream, and I didn't try to speak to her. I just stood by quietly and watched the room burn.

BRUNO KLEINFELD
(written statement)

My epic poem. Harry's grand experiment. Neither one of us could heave the darlings overboard. I sequestered the Meisterwerk over in my slummy digs, which I had retained for the sake of my manly independence, and brought out the twenty-pound MS. (stored in the closet on the shelf above three retired baseball mitts) for brush-ups, revisions, cuts, and additions, unbeknown to Harry, who listened joyfully to MS. #2, the ever-growing *Confessions of a Minor Poet*, the mostly true tale of one Bruno Kleinfeld, a moody Jewish fornicator from the Bronx, whose adventures hewed closely to mine but were blessed with the gap that inevitably arrives between present-self scribbler and his various tawdry or gallant past selves, a chasm also known as humor, irony, or forgetfulness. I salute Harry for kicking my ass, which in turn loosened up my old knuckles for work on the Olivetti's sleek keyboard, a machine inherited from dear old Uncle Samuel Kleinfeld in 1958. The story of my life, such as it was, seemed to arrive easily and breezily, a saga of, among other things, cream sodas, gefilte fish, and

Doris McKinny's maddeningly distracting breasts, which were allowed three pages to themselves once I arrived at puberty on page 101.

I am not alone in observing that autobiographies lose interest when the hero leaves his youth, so I decided to give my middle age short shrift: twenty-five pages devoted to my all-around failures as poet, husband, and father delivered in a mock-heroic tone to relieve the reader of realism or maybe naturalism – whatever that grubby genre of rusty sinks and honest squalor is called. After that truncated interim, I arrived at my three grown-up girls, and the noblest of all my seminal offshoots, my grandson, Bran. Yes, my *Confessions* are shaped like an hourglass. The form of my time on earth eschews the middle for its fat ends, early and late. Bran came squalling into my life as an ugly red-faced little bruiser, but as I write these words, he is running around the diamond and kicking a soccer ball and explicating the ins and outs of avatars to me, and has become, I must say, the shining light of his granddad's dotage.

The very day after Harry lay on her back and told me the tale of her visit to Rune in a voice as cold as steel in winter, I noticed that her thoughts had been tinted by or maybe sprinkled with paranoia. Harry knew she had struck a Faustian bargain, had made a soul-killing exchange, which had been fraught with risk from the beginning. Rune, once the great white hope, had turned into Beelzebub. She worried that the dead spouse had shared intimate stories with his young 'friend.' Hadn't Rune seemed possessed of an uncanny knowledge of her from the start? Rune's cleverness began to look paranormal. When Harry loudly proclaimed that four of her works were missing from her studio, my guess was that one of the assistants had mislaid them under a mountain of ready-mades. Between her stints of depth cleaning, Harry let congenial chaos reign in the studio. Arms, legs, heads, wigs, and hairpieces littered the floor. Stacks of lumber, sheets of glass, coils of rope, wire, cable, tools, and mystery machines lined the walls. In one corner, Harry stockpiled 'notable dross,' an unsavory collection she had hauled inside from the general vicinity of the docks, various thingamabobs and whatsits that had moldered, withered, languished, or rusted into states so crumbled, mottled, decayed, or lumpish their former identities were no longer with us. Keep looking, I said. Maybe they're hidden under the notable dross.

But Harry blamed Rune for the missing works. She insisted he had broken through multiple locks and an alarm system to snatch her art. I jokingly asked Harry if she hadn't mixed up Rune with the Barometer's fallen angel, a tall man with wings who flew in and out of the lodge as he pleased. It's just not possible, Harry, I said, but she wouldn't believe me. One night, her face quashed with misery, she whispered to me, 'He's climbed inside me, Bruno. He's seen the fear. He knows more than I know.' I hated the S.O.B., but I knew he was human.

Harry hooked her hopes on the letter in *The Open Eye*. When it's out, she said, everyone will know. I will be free. But, Harry, I said, it's a yawner journal, arcane, abstruse. How many people read it? I don't think Harry had a choice. She had to believe in her imminent triumph. When the magazine finally arrived, she read the letter aloud to me, chortling and crowing, chewing on the quotations that belonged to her, her face as hot as one of her electrified metamorphs. I scolded her for the testicle joke – *beanbags*, Harry, I said, really. And who is this character Brickman? He's doing his job, she said. That's what matters.

I told you so is a phrase for assholes, and since I happen to intermittently find myself in that category, I used it on Harry when Rune screwed her over in the pages of *Art Assembly* in an interview, in which he was questioned outright about the Brickman letter in *The Open Eye*. Rune had guts. I have to hand it to him.

Harriet Lord has been really great to me, not only as a collector of my work, but as a true supporter. And I think of her as a muse for the project. Beneath *could never have happened without the long talks we had together and her generous backing. What I can't understand is that she seems to claim she is responsible for my work. She seems to believe that she actually created it. I simply can't understand why she would say that. You know, she had a really hard time after her husband died, and she's been in psychiatric treatment for years. For the record, let's just say she's a kind lady, but a little confused from time to time, and leave it at that.*

I was on-site in the kitchen when the kind but a little confused lady in long-term psychiatric treatment hurled the offending magazine at the pot rack. I was there when she cursed, roared, went cross-eyed and then blind with rage. Head down, arms flailing, she attacked an open shelf, batting mugs, dishes, and bowls to the floor, where they met their spectacular ends in smithereens. After the crash, I knelt on the floor, wielding brush and dustpan to collect thousands of shards, while Harry sat on the floor and said over and over, 'I'll kill him.' The fact that the man had called her Harriet *Lord*, not Harriet *Burden*, had shaken extra salt on Harry's already open wound.

And my refrain was: I told you so. I couldn't help myself. I had told her so. Harry penned a flaming letter to *Art Assembly*, which was never published. She phoned Rune and screeched at his voice mail: Liar, thief, horrible, horrible man, traitor. Her vituperation didn't budge him. Harry contacted Anton Tish's parents. His mother politely but firmly told her, 'My son wants nothing to do with you.' Harry hired a shamus named Paille, a

425

hazy-faced, laconic character with a Maine accent who specialized in blackmail and extortion. Paille tracked the kid to an ashram in India, to Thailand, and then to Malaysia, but after that, the boy's path ended with his airline records. Paille promised to keep up the quest.

Methodically, deliberately, Harry compiled every shred, morsel, sliver, and dust mote of evidence to prove her case. As she dug into piles, riffled through papers, and hunted for signs of her creative ownership, it dawned on her – a rainy, bleak, gray illumination, to be sure – it dawned on Harry how carefully she had hidden her involvement. She unearthed early drawings in sketchbooks and some plans on her computer, but other drawings and further designs were in Rune's possession. Her e-mails to him read like cryptograms, as did his to her. No slips. And the assistants, whom she assumed were in the know, were not. Even Edgar Holloway III, old studio hand, Friday to Harry's Crusoe, had to admit that this time around he hadn't suspected a thing. All he knew was that Harry had written a check for the work she had purchased from Rune as well as checks for the production of *Beneath*, but a benefactor is not a creator, and Rune had thanked her in print for her 'support.'

Eldridge came through for her. *Art Lights* published the story of their work, but his page of eloquence touched very few people at the time. Harry's experiment had been gutted and crushed, and she ranted in protest. Once the gears of despair began to turn, they banged and clinked with the same compulsive music. She had been robbed. No one understood her. No one paid attention to her. They were all blockheads, dupes of creeping sexism and phallus worship. Rune should be drawn and quartered, his eyes scooped out with razor-sharp grapefruit spoons and smashed into jelly with a hammer. Her life's work had been ruined, the ambitious project carefully constructed from the blocks of her radiant intellect, one beautiful irony on top of another – which would prove once and for all her theories about sex bias and perception and God-knows-what-else had exploded in her face.

I begged her to give it up. Show your work now, I said. Take it to the cooperative here in Red Hook. Forget about pseudonyms and figments, your ironies and philosophies. Who cares about the incestuous art world of dupes and phonies. But Harry couldn't give it up. Drowning, she clung fiercely to that small, splintered piece of mast bobbing in the ocean we call justice. There is no justice, of course, or very little of it, and counting on it as a life raft is a big mistake.

I wanted to cuddle her in my arms. I wanted to send her to those sweet, high places we had visited a couple hundred times already, but she pushed me away. She barked, sneered, and hissed. I am not the bad guy, I said to her, but somehow that's what I'd become. One night she sat on the big bed, ferocious in her pain, and she taunted me. Who was I to say a word to her? I had ruined myself, hadn't I? I had had everything – my Whitmanian gifts, my cock, the powers-that-be on my side – and I had thrown it away. She, on the other hand, had fought, worked and worked and worked like hell, and now she was betrayed. I was pathetic, yellow, a leech that lived off her good graces. (Read, her dough, or rather Lord's dough.) Words had flown fast and cruel between us before, but this time her voice smacked me to the ground. My jolly, kind beloved had turned hard, sad, and mean. From my metaphorical position, laid out on my back in figurative dust, I called her a castrating bitch.

She stalked out of the room and did not return. After waiting up for her until three in the morning, I walked across the street to my hole and stayed there. We did not see each other or speak to each other for three long months. Most evenings after our breakup, I'd saunter over to Sunny's with anxious thoughts of spotting Harry, but she was never there. I'd buttonhole some schlemiel at the bar and offer up the rousing but oh-so-sentimental tale of the great Bruno Kleinfeld's decline and subsequent fall, the story of how it came to pass that the literary hero, K., in a far less glorious incarnation than the one who had preceded him, now drank away his evenings at the local bar, the very same hours of the day he had once spent with Our Lady of the Coats, the last great love of his life. When sufficiently doused and soused, K. moved into lachrymose mode, sniffling over his whiskey and swaying to music that came from the speaker over his head, only a foot above his darling's drawing of Sunny's motley regulars, a work of art that caused his heart to cleave in two.

Harry had fled to Nantucket. It's nice to have houses to mope inside, large and empty, with the beds made up in advance. It was Maisie who called to tell me where Harry had gone. She said she wished we could patch it up, make it square, redo whatever it was that had gone wrong between us. Mother shouldn't lose you, she said. You must forgive her, she said, as if I were the bad guy again, instead of the pining Romantic, for Christ's sake. Both leech and castrator held their ground, however. It was a waste, a waste of time, a wasted time. I know that now, but then the world looked different to both of us. What can I say? My pride had been used as a snot rag, or that's how it felt, so I knotted it up even more tightly, just to make sure it hurt keenly enough to justify my life as a suffering scrivener.

And then one early evening in spring, I was taking a leak with two lines from the divine Emily in my head – *This slow day moved along –* / *I heard its axles go –* and from the window I saw Harry striding on the street below, looking thin, too thin, ten pounds gone, at least, maybe more. The un-Harry, I said to myself, not my Harry. And for the second time in the course of our romantic

429

entanglement, I galloped down the stairs and into the street after her, but I didn't hail her. I hastened after her in the cold air and trotted along the water. Like a private dick tailing a suspect, I held my distance at about thirty yards, but then I thought, Run after her. Go get her, man. Hadn't I done it once before? I was about to yell her name when I saw Rune loping toward her from the opposite direction, and I stopped in my tracks.

As I watched the two of them, their figures stood out against the expanses of gray sky and gray water – and above them were halos of yellow light on the low clouds. A wind blew Harry's trench coat up behind her and pushed around her hair. A pair of gulls flapped, flapped and sailed, flapped, flapped, flapped and sailed again high over their heads. The scene is vivid, a hard, clear picture in my mental space, even though in hindsight the memory has an unreal, dreamlike feeling. I watched Harry plead with her hands. She shook them in his face. He leaned toward her. He must have been talking to her, but they were too far away for me to hear anything. Then he opened his arms, palms up, and shrugged his indifference at her. I didn't really need to hear them. Their bodies spoke for them. Harry stepped forward, gripped him by the shoulders, and pushed. He stumbled backward, danced to regain his balance, and, once upright, he wiggled his hips and shoulders, swishing like a fairy, but why? He was taunting her, but what was it all about? The man continued his effeminate gestures, mincing and prancing and limp-wristing her, and I realized they were more mixed up in each other than I had known. God Almighty, had they been lovers? I thought. She was more than twenty years older than Rune. Sick confusion in the general vicinity of my lungs and then a piercing anxiety. I began to trot toward them, my protective instinct rising by the second.

And then, as I neared them, I saw Harry ball up her fist and hit him in the face hard. He stumbled backward, his mouth open as he yelled in pain. I started to run toward them, but so did everybody else within shouting distance. When I reached them, I saw Rune with his hand to his mouth, blood pouring over his fingers. But Harry hadn't finished. She threw herself at him again and punched him in the stomach. He cried out as he held his gut, but he recovered, grabbed her by the shoulders, and heaved her away from him. She lost her footing and sailed backward onto the ground. A woman wearing owl glasses and a red-and-black-checked jacket ran over to Harry and crouched beside her. I noticed that Harry's coat was bloody, probably Rune's blood. She saw me, her old lover come to witness the fracas, and looked up with a surprised face, but no anger, not a trace of anger. Two men had grabbed Rune by the arms to restrain him from further violence. He was saying, She attacked me, for Christ's sake. She attacked me. This was in fact the God's honest truth, but who is going to defend a man standing over an unarmed woman whom he has just thrown to the ground?

Rune avoided my eyes, and this pleased me. He knew that I knew. 'Oh-the-poet' knew he, Rune, was a goddamned liar and thief. There were questions in that citizen huddle about whether to call the police, about whether to press charges, but it was determined that neither combatant wanted the law involved, and while the discussions went on, Rune fished out a pack of cigarettes from his breast pocket and, cupping his hand around a lighter, carefully dragged in the smoke to avoid his fat, bloody lip, and looked casually around him. I'm going to leave now. This is absurd. She's nuts. Anyone who saw her hit me knows she's nuts.

And after the committee had all agreed to it, Rune left. He turned on his heels and strode down the walk beside the water.

Harry hadn't moved. The owl woman gave her a kindly pat and, understanding that the emotional bomb had been defused, she and the other concerned folk who had intervened wandered off to their lives, a few of them turning to look at us to make sure the felled lady was in good hands.

Oh, Harry, I said.

She started to nod at me. Her chin moved mechanically up and down. Her mouth stretched into a grimace, and she squinted to shut out the tears, grabbed her head with her hands, and rocked back and forth. Oh, Bruno, she cried. I'm so lost.

And then I said the right thing for once. I said, That was a nice right hook, Harry.

I practiced, Bruno, she said. I practiced on the bag. And then she lifted up her swollen right hand to show me, and I saw the bruises forming already. The injured warrior slumped toward me, and I gathered her up, as the saying goes. I gathered up Harry in my arms, and we walked haltingly back to the lodge together, bandaged her hand, and celebrated our reunion.

Your body / has not become yours only nor left my body mine only. Capacious, he was, Whitman, and greedy, greedy for people. He wanted to see, hear, smell, taste, and touch people. He rolled around in their humanness. He sucked in the city and its crowds as tactile realities. We went to sleep that night in Harry's big bed folded in each other, and before we slept, I thought of the bard sailing over the world as he surveyed his sleepers in the great democracy that is sleep. All of us creatures have to sleep.

After her first and what would be her last fist-fight, Harry didn't speak of Rune or the project or her resentments much anymore, not to me, anyway. I have been thrown back on myself, she liked to say. I have taken the Kierkegaardian position. The Kierkegaardian mingled with tragic queen. Harry quoted Margaret Cavendish regularly, that colorful lady philosopher, whose most fervent hope was that she would find readers after she was dead. The Duchess of Newcastle had dreamed of a glorious posthumous life when she would finally be appreciated. I had never heard of Cavendish before I met Harry, patriarchal dupe that I am, but Harry loved her. Dead in 1673, her work had been dismissed, ignored, or denigrated for more than three hundred years until she rose again and people began to take notice. Harry embraced the duchess as a battered and rejected sister striver in a man's world.

Harry returned to her Margaret, her Blazing World Mother creature she had begun much earlier and had nearly finished, but which she had abandoned because this monster had never satisfied her. When I first saw the huge, grinning, naked, heated-up, pregnant mama with her hanging boobs squatting in the studio, she gave me a start. This was no sweet, dreaming, oversized odalisque like the one Harry made for that kid, Tish. This woman had worlds inside her. When you looked up and into her bald, see-through cranium, you saw little people, hoards of busy wax Lilliputians going about their business. They ran and jumped. They danced and sang. They sat at miniature desks facing computers, typewriters, or pages. When you looked closely, you could see they were making musical scores, drawings, mathematical formulas, poems, and stories. One dumpy old guy was writing *Confessions of a Minor Poet*. There were seven lascivious couples going at it upstairs in the female Gulliver's head – men and women, men and men, women and women – a regular orgy.

There was a bloody sword fight and a murderer with a gun, looking down at his victim's corpse. There was a unicorn and a minotaur and a satyr and a fat angel woman with wings and lots of chubby babies in all colors. Downstairs – that is, from between the labial folds of her enormous vagina – the fertile matriarch popped out another city of little humanoids. Harry worked hard with her suspension wires in order to achieve the effect: Some of the teeny ones were suspended in midair between the giant doll's birth canal and the ground. Others had already landed and were seen crawling, walking, running, or skipping away from their giant originator in several directions.

Harry didn't believe the piece was finished. It's wrong, she said, too comic. She added letters and numbers in many colors. She added more figures. It wouldn't matter, she said, whether anyone saw them or not. She needed to make them, and she did, small, perfectly formed wax persons. She sewed clothes for some and left others naked. She could work on them almost anywhere, and more than once I sat down on a hard little body on the sofa, smothering some man or woman or child under my colossal ass. After these accidents, Harry would take the poor rumpled critter from me, rearrange its hair or limbs, and generally fuss over it. Why, it's you, Cornelius, she would say, or: Keisha, I wondered what had happened to you. In Harrydom, nobody went nameless.

She wrote and read as well. She punched her

punching bag (good exercise and cathartic release of perpetual anger) and visited her shrink cum usual. Maisie's film *Body Weather* about our own household lunatic came out in September. Harry was red-faced with pride at the opening in New York at the Quad Cinema on Thirteenth Street. Maisie has a gift for making insanity look, if not normal, at least comprehensible. Halfway through the film, the Barometer's father, Rufus Dudek, a tired man with bloodshot eyes, who still lives in the godforsaken Nebraska town where he raised his sons, holds up the prodigious drawings his youngest boy, Alan (later the Barometer), made when he was seven years old, and proceeds to tell the off-camera Maisie about the tornado that killed his wife. A wall of the family's trailer caved in and crushed her while he and his boys were out 'visiting.' Alan Dudek's mother died of weather. Alan made his way to New York and the Studio School, but while he was in a life-drawing class he cracked up and was hauled off to the first of many psychiatric wards. He was twenty-two when he became the Barometer, a man who quiets the winds and stirs them up, a man who feels the motion of the spheres via his high-tech, super-duper, but ever-so-fragile nervous system.

After *Body Weather*, Maisie launched her film on Harry. She trailed after her mother in the studio, set up shots by the water, and held the camera tightly on Harry as she told the story of her life or expounded on ideas, in which the words *preconceptual* and *embodied* came up frequently. I credit Maisie with propping up Harry's sacked dignity. I underscore this: I don't know what we would have done without Maisie. The hours of footage mounted. The daughter was going to tell the mother's story, come hell or high water or hurricane or typhoon, and this made Harry happy, at least intermittently.

I wrapped up my own autobiography-hyphen-memoir, had it typed up on a computer by a woman named Edith Klinkhammer (no fooling), mailed it out to agents, and, after several rejections, found myself a willing representative and then, hail holy light, a New York publisher, after which Harry could gloat at me with her own 'I told you so.' Those are rosy days now when I look back on them – that stretch of freedom we had together after we found each other again. The artists in residence had left us, all except the Barometer, whose existence had become more orderly because he had a doctor and a little lithium and a new diagnosis – schizoaffective. All in all, I have to call those days rosy, just plain old rosy, cozy days of coffee and bagels and goodbye-I'm-off-to-work-now-my-love kisses in the morning and a whole lot of chitchat after work about not all that much as we chopped vegetables for or cleaned up after dinner. We yelled at the evil president in unison and had a few royal fights about men and women and what's innate in one sex or the other and what's not. Yes, to be honest: We fought. We fought, but we also rolled in the hay, and, to be honest again, there were plenty of nights we were too tired to do any rolling because we weren't young anymore, and we talked instead, long sessions of thinking aloud about art and poems and our youngest ones, Aven and Bran, the children who would brave a future we would never see.

When Rune died in his own contraption, he made the cover of the *New York Post* and the *Daily News*, and page 9 of *The New York Times*. Innumerable other 'outlets' opined on his tragic exit from the planet as well. Tributes to Rune spewed from the media maw, accompanied by photos of still-youthful brooding artist decoratively slouched beside his works, including *Beneath*, no, especially *Beneath*. Art magazines devoted issues to his legacy, speculating on what might have been, had the remarkable bad boy only lived. He suffered from depression, it seemed. He had, in fact, a whole drugstore of pharmaceuticals in his bathroom to treat the condition. Sympathy for the down-in-the-dumps artist oozed from journalistic pores. Depression is a chemical imbalance, they wrote. The poor guy was a victim of his own cracked brain chemistry.

Not a word about Harry. Her obliteration was total. *The Open Eye* and the Eldridge letter were meant to cast a spotlight on Harry, but somebody forgot to hit the switch. One night over a nice piece of hake and broccoli, Harry declared in that creepy cold voice I had heard on the day she saw

Rune that she had wanted to hurt him, but now that he was dead, she felt nothing. He was dead, but she was dead to him, too, dead to the story, dead to the pseudonyms. Her shining vehicle had crashed before it reached its destination, just as his had. Harry did not believe he had wanted to kill himself. There was nothing to be done. She had been more right than she had even known. The powers-that-be would never accept her art, because it was hers. Harriet Burden was nobody, a big, fat, unrecognized nobody.

I had prayed for Harry to end her obsession, but the stiff, bitter, defeated woman on the other side of the table unnerved me. I longed for some old vigor and bite. I longed for the dragon lady to return, if only for an hour or so. In this spirit, I asked the lady pugilist if the two hard punches that bastard had taken from her hadn't felt pretty good. But Harry just stared at me, frost in her eyes. The punches, she said, had meant nothing. They had meant nothing because they had not had the desired effect. She had wanted to humiliate and shame him, to make him grovel before her – or something to that effect. It hadn't worked. I wondered about Harry then. I wondered about who she was and if I really understood her at all. She could be so hard.

When she said the story was dead, she must have believed what she was saying, but later I discovered that she hadn't let go of it completely. One after- noon, I interrupted her in the studio to tell her about a starred review I had received in *Publishers Weekly*, which included the words *uproarious* and *tender*. I had let myself in to surprise her with it. I tiptoed in the door with review in hand and saw that she was sitting at her long wooden desk with a pair of scissors in her hands, hunched over a large book with a concentrated look on her face. When I approached her, I looked down to see what she was doing.

The book she had in front of her was called *The Book of Runes*. It turned out that Harry had read and clipped every article that had been written about *Beneath* and the now-deceased traitor to her cause and had pasted them carefully into a fat, old fashioned scrapbook, as if she were a 1950s housewife saving recipes. She did not need to explain. They were documents of the struggle – texts Harry called 'proliferations.'

After that day, we had a little less than a year left, but seven months of it passed before Harry's diagnosis. Every once in a while she complained of bloating and constipation, but show me someone over sixty who doesn't complain of bloating and constipation. She grew a little thinner because she often felt full and couldn't eat more, but her weight loss wasn't extreme. She didn't feel 'quite right,' just 'a little off,' that's all. She would check it out with her doctor.

When she told me what the scan had found, she was standing, white-faced in the kitchen: I can't die now. How can I die now, Bruno?

Harry did not want to die.

I learned new terms: *epithelial-stromal tumor*, *debulking* surgery, and *adjuvant* chemotherapy. They debulked her, all right, scooped out as much of the cancer as they could, but it had gone to her liver. She was in stage four of ovarian cancer, for Christ's sake, a death sentence, but the doctors murmured about procedures that just might possibly extend life expectancy and exceptional cases, although they were rare, very rare, it was true, their eyes averted or looking directly at you to show they weren't wimps. The chemo made her pale, sick, weak, and dizzy. But the tumors didn't shrink enough, not enough to save her.

With her fingers dug into her belly or pressed into her temples, Harry thrashed in her hospital bed, the pain blinding her, pain the morphine didn't dent, and she howled against the fates. Her hollow face, her red eyes leaking tears, her mouth contorted, she cursed the doctors and the nurses and she cursed me, and she cursed whoever else happened to be around, in a voice that blasted like a siren through the ward. My dragon lady came back. Why are you torturing me? And the white and blue coats came running and those in them scolded her about the other patients: They have a right to some peace, too, don't they? Harry was not the only sick person, after all. Look at Mrs P., missing a leg, lost to a tumor. She was sicker than Harry, by God! Look at Mrs P. She behaved herself. Mrs P. was dying fast. Chastened momentarily and sorry for poor Mrs P., Harry snuffled in her bed. I don't want to die.

Harry had let them cut her open. She had let them gut her of all her reproductive organs plus more pieces of herself, had allowed them to sew her up and let her languish in the bed with mostly kind nurses, except one (Thelma). She had let them poison her with chemo and truss her up to IVs and talk down to her as if she were a five-year-old, because she wanted to live. She wanted them to save her, to work miracles on her, to bring her back to her old self. They shouldn't have laid a goddamned hand on her. That's what I say, not a goddamned hand. They should have sent her home with a truckload of narcotics and left her alone. Maisie and I disagreed. Maisie and I bickered. Maisie bustled and cleaned up and wiped her mother's head and cleaned her thighs of errant urine and brought her sandwiches from Zabar's she couldn't eat. Let her be, I snapped at her once. Just let her be. Maisie cried. I apologized, and we made it up. Ethan had shell shock, the big-eyed, silent version. He leaned against the wall and watched. Every once in a while he would cross his arms on his chest, grab his upper arms, and rock back and forth.

We set up a hospice at the lodge, but Harry was worse, too weak to put up much of a fight, except now and again – a piercing wail or a gob of spit sent across the room. Sweet Autumn tiptoed in one day with a weird little mutt and a bag of her healing stones and shells and a lot of New Age craziness swirling in her head, and stayed until the end. We would have kicked her out, but Harry liked her. Harry liked her little heart-shaped face with her bright red lips and fairy princess blond curls and her chatter.

This is hard for me to write. These words come hard to me; each one begins as a stone in my mouth. Harry's pain arrived in bolts that made her limbs stiffen. We turned up the drip. She whimpered as she lay stiffly flat on her back, and she allowed me to stroke her head, her neck, and her shoulders. I'll be good, she whispered. I promise to be good, Bruno. Don't leave me. I'm afraid. I told her I wouldn't leave her, and I didn't. She left me. Her last word was *no*. She said it several times, and before she died, she rattled. The noise came from deep in her lungs, shuddering, dry, and loud, and we watched. Harry died at three o'clock in the afternoon on April 18, 2004, with the window wide open in the room so the spring air and sunlight could reach her face.

Damn you, Harry. Damn you, for leaving me too soon.

TIMOTHY HARDWICK

*('Rune's Ego Machine: Harbinger of
the New Aesthetics' in* Visibility: A Magazine
of the Arts, *February 2009)*

Rune's final work, *Houdini Smash*, which now exists as both a film and as an architectural relic of the 'performance,' calls upon the critic to examine, yet again, questions about the nature of art itself. Arthur Danto persuasively argued that the dominant narrative of Western art came to its end at the moment Warhol created art that was indistinguishable from objects in the supermarket. In the post-Warhol era, Rune's *Houdini Smash* figures as a meditation on the idea of beginnings and endings, not only of art, but of the breakdown between the biological and the artificial, categories that are swiftly becoming indistinguishable. We have entered an era of the hybrid bio-robot, an age when scientists are building computational models of the meta-representational structures of consciousness itself. There are many who believe it is a matter of two, perhaps three, decades before the neural correlates of consciousness will be discovered and replicated artificially. The mystery, one long viewed as impossible to penetrate, will be solved. The hard problem of consciousness will go the way of the double helix.

Rune's *Houdini Smash* anticipates the birth of the ego machine, a humanly created *artistic product* that is itself conscious, the arrival of a technology that will radically transform the meaning of creativity because artists will generate art objects that have self-models, that is, they will be able to make aesthetic creatures or robotic offspring who think and act. In an interview he gave in *Art Assembly*, Rune discussed his fascination with artificial intelligence and its radical potentiality. Citing Vernor Vinge and Ray Kurzweil, he said, 'AI is the cutting edge in art, whether people know it or not. It will revolutionize artistic practice by providing artists with tools for works that are animate and intelligent.' Kurzweil articulated his utopian view in the following statement: 'As we gradually learn to harness the optimal computing capacity of matter, our intelligence will spread through the universe at (or exceeding) the speed of light, eventually leading to a sublime, universe-wide awakening.' It seems unlikely that Rune endorsed the optimism of a futurist such as Kurzweil.

Although there are those who maintain that Rune *intended* to die from the drug he ceremoniously ingests in the film, this critic suspects the opposite. Rune planned for his hours of sleep and eventual reawakening to be recorded by multiple cameras as part of the work's cycle as a homage to his own version of Futurism. In the construction, the artist's body functions merely as one section, organ, or member of what must be regarded as a larger anatomical machine. The biological body cannot be regarded as distinct from the artificial limbs, digital screens, and collapsing walls and pathways in which that body is enclosed. Borrowing heavily on the work that preceded it – the complex, grand-scale maze installation, *Beneath* – Rune built a far more compact maze structure that looks as if it has fallen in on itself, has become essentially a ruined fragment of the former work. In the highly praised *Beneath*, he used the repetition of objects and films, some of which were pointed allusions to the devastation of September 11, to introduce a mournful, lyrical quality to his art for the first time. *Houdini Smash*, on the other hand, evokes mechanistic delirium, not dissimilar to the effects he garnered in *The Banality of Glamour*. Rune's sublime is not Kurzweil's utopia, but a darker vision of ecstatic metamorphosis, which he articulated in the same *Art Assembly* interview: 'The artist will no longer control his art. It will function independently of the designer, and therefore create exciting and dangerous new zones of interaction.'

In *Houdini*, the viewer sees the artist crawl into the coffinlike space at the center of the piece, outfitted with plush pink satin lining and a pillow covered with red crosses, yet another allusion to his earlier work. The viewer sees Rune slowly smoke a cigarette, extinguish it, reach into his pocket, hold out a fist to the camera, then open his left palm to reveal a handful of white pills, which he then swallows with a glass of water. He inserts the empty glass into a cup holder beside him and, like a shaman performing a ritual, covers his face with a soft mask, identical to the masks displayed in the windows of *Beneath*, lies back, and stares at one of the cameras, which is filming him from above. Once he is settled inside his container, the viewer witnesses the transformation of Rune's body from the human to the posthuman. An immense helmetlike form is fitted over his head, and the multiple gleaming aluminum limbs that protrude from the box slowly begin to move. Although the allusions to sci-fi movies from the fifties are immediately obvious, the startling character of the film is only produced over time. The limbs move more and more quickly, and the views of multiple cameras picked up by multiple screens refract and fragment the hybrid anatomy from multiple angles. The eyes close. The ego machine sleeps, but its limbs and the multiple digital images continue for hours and then slowly come to a halt.

When Rebecca Daniels entered the studio the following day, Rune had died, and his body had gone into rigor mortis. The cameras that recorded the work also filmed her discovery, but the Burridge Gallery suppressed the latter portions of the film to protect Daniels's privacy. While this is entirely understandable, it may be argued that although the beginning of the film is determined, the ending of the film is arbitrary. Whether intentional or not, the artwork itself becomes a 'container' for death, a coffin machine for the artist's corpse, but the machine 'survives' its biological part. *Houdini* is not, as Elizabeth Cooper claimed in *Art Digest*, 'a snuff film' or 'horror narrative, in which doctor and monster merge.' It is a spectacle of simulacra. In his essay 'Simulacra and Science Fiction,' Baudrillard writes, 'The stage is now set for simulation, in the cybernetics sense of the word – that is to say, for all kinds of manipulation of these models (hypothetical scenarios, the creation of simulated situations, etc.) but now *nothing distinguishes this management-manipulation from the real itself: There is no more fiction.*' The real and the imaginary, animate and inanimate, artist and product, have entered the zone of the hyperreal, the zone in which these antiquated distinctions will soon be wholly erased.

KIRSTEN LARSEN SMITH
(interview, November 2011)

Hess: You have not wanted to speak publicly about your brother since his death in 2003. Can you tell me why you decided to talk to me?

Smith: Ever since I read the book by Oswald Case on Rune, I've been thinking about setting a few things straight about my brother. It's been eight years since he passed away, and after I spoke to you on the phone, I knew I was ready to say my piece. It's been building up for years.

Hess: You feel the book misrepresented your brother?

Smith: You bet I do. First of all, he turns Rune into some underprivileged child. The way he writes it, you'd think he had grown up as a dirty little piece of white trash running around in the woods behind our trailer, wiping snot from his nose with his arm and eating dinner out of a can. Dad

449

owned and operated the biggest garage in Clinton. Our mom had two years of college, and she was an excellent seamstress. She could have been a clothing designer in some other city. We were *not* poor. We lived in a nice house and drove two cars. Case never talked to anybody who really knew us, except Mrs Huggenvik, who was senile by then and had always been a persnickety woman anyway.

Rune was older than me by four years. Dad said that from the day I could walk, I followed my brother around, and most of the time Rune was pretty nice to his little shadow. I know it's hard to believe, considering how much he grew, but Rune was a short, fat kid. He loved candy, comics, Lego, and the movies. He used to read the newspaper every morning and take notes on the articles he liked in a little book he carried around with him in the back pocket of his jeans. If he had been a good athlete, that little book he kept with current events in it might not have mattered, but he stank at sports, so the other kids picked on him at school. Then he grew seven inches the year after he turned fourteen and, all of a sudden, he was this tall, handsome guy with girls calling him up on the phone and sending him love notes.

I'm sure Rune talked Case's ear off about

his life, but my brother stretched the truth. It became a habit with him. Even when he wasn't lying straight out, he could pull the facts every which way, and sometimes, after all the pulling, there wasn't much truth left.

Hess: But if I remember correctly, Case writes that Rune cultivated myths about himself. I don't think he believed everything Rune told him.

Smith: No, he didn't believe everything Rune told him by a long shot, but he made Rune's fibs and exaggerations into some fabulous achievement. You know, his position was that Rune was so creative he told this story and that one, and isn't it great that he lied and kept secrets from everybody? I think that's perverted, don't you? Case seems to think that if you're a famous artist, you don't need to be a moral person like the rest of us. And then, Case paints a portrait of Mom that is so crude, so nasty – it really upset me.

Hess: You felt your mother was portrayed inaccurately?

Smith: Mom drank. Case had that right. I don't think we ever knew how much she really drank every day. She hid it, and the problem must have gotten worse and worse, but for years she coped pretty well. She was not a 'pathetic, weepy, female boozehound.' That's a quote from the book. My great-aunt Susie used to call Mom 'Sunshine' because she had such a magical smile. Mom knew how to play with us kids better than any grown-up we knew. She could run and do cartwheels and swing upside down on the jungle gym we had behind the house. She worked hard at hemming skirts and pants and doing other alterations for her clients, and she liked to make fancy dress-up clothes and costumes for me and Rune. You should have seen us on Halloween. I think she liked my sparkly, frou-frou princess outfits even more than I did. You see, Mom had been one of those drop-dead beautiful girls. Every time she walked down the street, heads swiveled to look at her. She liked to tell us about the day she was walking down the street in Clinton, just minding her own business, when a man stopped her on the street and said, 'You are the most beautiful woman I have ever seen in my life.' That was all. He went on his way, but Mom's eyes would get bright and glassy every time she told the story. When being beautiful is the best thing you've got, it's bound to be disappointing because you have to get older. She called herself a dreamer. She used to say to me,

'You're the practical one, Kirsten. Rune's the dreamer. You're like your father. Rune's like me.'

She was a fragile person. Sometimes I thought she'd break like glass, just shatter one day, and I guess she finally did. We worried about her all the time. We used to listen at her door in the morning to see if she was getting up. If we heard her walking around in the bedroom, we knew everything would be okay because she'd be at breakfast before school. On days when she was sick – that's what Rune and I called it when she drank too much, being *sick* (alcoholism is a disease, so the word pretty much sums it up) – on the days when she was sick and couldn't get up, Rune used to forge an excuse for school to stay home with her because Dad had to go to the garage. Rune would make her lunch and watch her eat it to make sure it went down. I know because I stayed home sometimes, too. He'd vacuum and pick up in the living room and clean the bathrooms. I mean, by the time he was nine or ten he was an expert. Yes, Mom was a sentimental drunk. It made her 'lovey-dovey,' as Rune used to say. If we found a bottle of vodka we'd pour it down the toilet, but she was clever and obviously we never found all of them. She drank vodka because it doesn't smell and she could mix it with anything. Sometimes she cried, and Rune would sit beside her, pat her, and give her Kleenex. 'I'm so sorry, kids,' she'd say over and over, and then she'd hug us really hard.

Because Rune was older, he felt responsible for Mom and, although he didn't show it, I think it made him angry underneath. He used to snitch things and hide them in his room: a couple of dollars from Mom's purse or a new box of potato chips or cookies from the cupboard. I suspect he nabbed things from stores just for the thrill of it. He had key rings and flashlights and doodads you see hanging near the cash register at the grocery store in his 'stash.' He needed to hide things, and he needed to have secrets. Rune invented a special code for the two of us. It wasn't too complicated. For each letter in a word, we'd count two letters that came after it, and we'd have a secret message. We left Y and Z the way they were, so sometimes I'd come home after my clarinet lesson and see a note on the table: OQO KU UKEM. 'Mom is sick.' We got good at that one. Not long before he died, Rune called me MKTUVGP on the phone, pronounced Mik-tuvga-pa. That's how Kirsten came out. He hadn't called me that for years. We had to put in vowels just to pronounce those crazy words, but you get the idea.

Rune used to tell me he remembered

when our parents got along. All I could remember was fighting, not physical fighting, but yelling, crying, and door-slamming, or silence – the two of them hardly talking at all, ships in the night. I'd climb into bed beside my brother and ask him to tell me about 'before,' and Rune would put me to sleep by telling me that Dad used to come home with big bunches of flowers and valentines on Valentine's Day for Mom, and back in those days, he said, Mom didn't drink at all. He said they danced together in the living room like a couple of lovebirds, smooching and hugging. When I got older, I realized he was making it all up, but my point is that he was making it up for me. Case makes fun of my job in the book, too. It's unbelievable. Everything's a joke to that guy. He writes that my work probably influenced Rune's art, but he says nothing about the accident.

Hess: The accident?

Smith: The accident when I was eleven. I was on my way to ballet class with three of my friends. Jessica's mother was driving, and I was in the passenger seat because that day the girls decided I smelled bad. Honestly, girls can be so stupid and mean. I pretended I was too good for them. They all hopped into the back, said there was no room for me, and I ended up in the front seat, which is a highly important detail because a few minutes later a car sped through the light at an intersection and smashed into the side of the car where I was sitting. The last thing I remember was the sight of the dirty gray bottoms of my ballet slippers lying in my lap. When I woke up, I was in the hospital with cracked ribs, torn ligaments in my back, a dislocated shoulder, a broken jaw, and a sliced-up face. I could easily have died, so everyone said I was lucky. They sewed my face together, but I had to have six plastic surgeries over the years to repair the keloids and scar tissue.

You know, what's funny is that right after the accident, things were better, in the family, I mean. Mom stayed with me, and she seemed pretty sober, and after Dad left work he came straight to the hospital. He didn't talk much, and my jaw was wired shut so I couldn't say a word to him. Even nodding hurt me in the beginning, but he held my hand and he'd tighten his grip and loosen it and then tighten it again, and he smiled at me with a pitiful look on his face. Rune made me little houses from Popsicle sticks, which I liked, and Jessica, Gina, and Ellen, who had walked out of the smashed car without a scratch, were so guilty they brought me cards and flowers, and that felt good.

The doctors did a great job on me, and as you can see, I only have a few minor souvenirs, but it was hard losing my old face. When Mom first saw me, she sobbed and sobbed. I'm sure she thought my life was over. I mean, what was a girl going to do with a face like that? I became a craniofacial technician because I understand what it means to lose your face, to look different and have to live with distorted features. It is extremely interesting work, and believe me, there are people much worse off than I ever was, and whatever I can do to help restore a person's identity is positive. I don't think that's so comical, do you? When Rune made *The Banality of Glamour*, I know he was thinking about me in the hospital. He was thinking about my surgeries and how tough they were. That work was personal, you see. In the book, Case makes it seem as if nothing Rune did was personal. He makes him into a robot, not a person, but that was not my brother at all. His problems, and he certainly had them, were personal. And now that I'm on a roll, I want to say Dad did not drown those kittens.

Hess: But kittens drowned?

Smith: It happened before the accident. When I was seven and Rune was eleven, we sneaked a stray cat into the house, Joe, who turned into Josephine when she gave birth to a litter in our hamper. We were not allowed to have pets, and we were scared Dad would find out. It didn't happen often, but every once in a while Dad blew his top, and when that happened we'd both run like the wind because you didn't want to be in his way. He didn't hit us, but he threw things. Mom and Dad were both out, and that's when Rune grabbed the six pink, blind kittens and drowned them in a big bucket in the garage while I scratched, kicked, pounded on him, and screamed bloody murder. They died right away. Rune stood there looking down at them with a sad and surprised look on his face. I don't think he knew himself why he had done it. I buried them in the dirt under the holly bush in the backyard.

I should mention that there were people in Clinton and on the farms around town who drowned kittens routinely. I thought and still think it's inhumane, but animal rights wasn't such a big concern then as it is today. I didn't speak to my brother for two days, but then he came crying to me because he felt so bad, and I forgave him. And Case was right about one part of the story. Rune took good care of Josephine after that. She never became a house cat. She was a roamer, but Rune had her spayed and fed her every time she came around for food.

Hess: Are you saying that Rune regretted what he had done?

Smith: Yes, he seemed really sorry, and I think he was. Rune played perfect, if you know what I mean, the model citizen, the all-around nice American boy, but it was partly an act, a put-on. I used to see it happening when he talked to Mom and Dad or other grown-ups. He'd get this special hidden look on his face, a disguise, really. With his friends he was different, tougher and cooler, but was that really him? I don't think so. It was lonely for him. That's why he needed me. If you hide yourself too much, you get isolated and sad. We had fun together, even during the really bad time after my accident and Mom was sick, and Dad was pretty much useless except for going to work and coming home. Rune used to help me with my makeup to cover up some of the scarring, but he'd do my eyes and mouth, too. The artist in him was hard at work with sponges and brushes, and he'd say, 'Look at you, glamour girl.' He'd be really proud, and sometimes he'd turn me into a witch, and we'd laugh so hard we had to lie down on the bathroom floor and hold our stomachs.

Mom passed only a year later. I had turned twelve and Rune was sixteen. Rune and I were home. We'd been in the house for an hour, but I peeked in the door and I thought Mom was sleeping. When Dad came home, he went in to get her up and then he saw that she wasn't breathing. It was pretty bad for all of us. After she was gone, we felt lost. We had all spent so much time worrying about her and taking care of her and loving her and hating her, we didn't know how to organize ourselves anymore, how to be together. Before Rune left home, he had black moods, days when he'd go into his room and stay there, lying on his bed with a towel over his face. Once he broke the mirror with a baseball bat. Dad and I heard the crash, we ran into Rune's room, and he was just standing there, grinning. I helped him clean it up. Dad turned around, walked out, and never said a word about it.

After Rune left home, Dad and I were alone in the house. He had his Thursday poker game and we went to church every Sunday. Dad was a sort of quiet believer, I think, and he liked the church suppers and the company. I was glad when he went out, period. Then I left home for college and worried about him because I could see him shuffling around the house, fixing himself hot dogs and beans or a Swanson's frozen dinner in the evening, and it depressed me. I called home every week but Rune didn't. I sometimes felt my brother had departed for another dimension Dad and I couldn't have entered if we'd wanted to. I think I was partly right.

He came back, though. That's another thing. Rune lived with me in Minneapolis when he supposedly dropped out of sight and couldn't be found. He had come home to visit Dad, and while he was staying with him, Dad fell down the stairs. Rune called 911 and a little later he called me. The doctors told us he'd had a stroke. They guessed it happened while he was on his way down to the basement, and that he fell and then injured himself more. He never regained consciousness, but he lasted a week, and then he passed away. Rune took it so hard. Dad and Rune never got along too well, and after Mom died, I think Rune reminded him of her – too much of her, if you see what I mean. They looked a lot alike. Dad also thought it was absolutely nuts to be an artist, but that's a pretty typical attitude. Our father was not some strange bird in that regard. Dad recognized the *Mona Lisa*, knew that Van Gogh had cut off his ear, and that Picasso made pictures of people with scrambled faces. That was about it, but so what? I was closer to Dad because we under-. stood each other, I guess. I used to work to try and cheer him up when he was down. I'd do little dances for him, play him something on the clarinet, show him my good report cards, rub his shoulders, whatever. Sometimes my little schemes worked. He used to call me 'his brave, hardworking girl.' After Dad's funeral, all the air went out of Rune. He was so depressed he could hardly move, so I said I'd put him up for a while. I had graduated from college, done my training, and had my first job.

Rune would lie in my den on the sofa, staring at the ceiling for days on end. I finally got him to a doctor, who prescribed medication. Whether it was the drug he was taking or something else that got him going again, I don't know, but he started moving around, eating a lot more, and fiddling with his sketchbooks, but he turned nasty. He complained about my cooking, my clothes, the way I talked – that nasal Midwestern accent, ugh. One morning he was actually out of bed before I went to work, and he started criticizing my apartment and the convertible sofa he had been sleeping on for months. 'Do you have any idea how cheap and tacky this thing is?' He started kicking it with his foot. He called the furniture vulgar and crass. It was unbelievable. 'This is what you want?' he said. He kept saying that. 'You want Jim and shag carpeting and some middle-class shithole ranch house for the rest of your life?' Jim is my husband. He was my fiancé then. We met at work. I said, yeah I wanted Jim and a house and my work, and I wanted children, and what the hell was his problem? He told me he'd 'severed' the name Larsen from his existence. Did I know that? He and I were no longer related. He hated Mom and he hated Dad and he hated me. I told him not to bad-mouth the dead. You have to understand I had been supporting Rune. He didn't have much money then, and it wasn't any fun to have Jim over with Rune moping around, but he was my brother, and I stuck with him. I did what I had to do. I took care of Rune. He had taken care of me when I was little, after all.

And then he told me that he was having a fight with Dad before he fell. I felt sorry for Rune. It made sense that he fell apart. I said it must be awfully hard to live with that, and he said, 'How do you know I didn't push him?' I screamed at him that Dad had a stroke. He just stood there smiling and said, 'But we don't know when he had it.' I was stunned, literally. I mean, if someone had bonked me on the head with a bowling ball, I couldn't have been more amazed. He must have let a minute go by, seriously, a whole minute. Then he started laughing and said, 'Oh my God, you believed me, didn't you? You must think I'm the devil. You think I could kill my own father? What kind of a sister are you?' And then he said he had another one for me to try on. He said Mom had climbed into bed with him when he was little and touched him sexually, more than once. 'Do you believe that one?' he said to me. He said that and just kept on smiling. I didn't believe it. 'You're crazy,' I said. I told him he had to be out by the time I came home from work.

When I came home that day, Rune was gone, but my apartment had been trashed. He had broken all the glasses and plates in the cupboards and turned over chairs and burned the sofa bed with cigarettes and cut my rug into pieces and left his turds smeared on the toilet seat.

You know, a normal person doesn't do those things. A normal person doesn't say, 'Maybe I pushed my father to his death,' and then, 'Maybe my mother molested me,' and then destroy his sister's apartment. I kept saying to myself, *My brother must be out of his mind.* Without Jim, I don't know what I would have done. Jim and I got married sooner than we had thought we would because I didn't want to stay in that place anymore. We didn't tell Rune, and he didn't call or write to apologize or anything. My own brother scared me. Of course, I found out that he had gone back to New York and plunged into his art again. Things went really well for him, but without the Internet I wouldn't have known. My friends here in Minneapolis aren't keeping track of artists in New York City. I know he was famous, but he wasn't famous out here.

Hess: You weren't in touch with Rune?

Smith: No, not for years, not until September 11, when I panicked. I called his gallery, that's how I was finally able to reach him. Nothing really mattered to me then, except knowing that he was all right. He was the only family I had in the world, except Jim and the kids. We started calling each other once in a while, and eventually I asked him about the awful things he had said. It's hard to explain how terrible it is to have those ideas in your mind, even if you don't believe them. It pollutes your thinking. Someone comes along and throws dirt into your head, and you can't clean it out. He said he had lied to hurt me and that sometimes he just couldn't help himself. He liked to be outrageous just for the heck of it.

Hess: But you didn't visit each other?

Smith: No, Jim didn't want him near the kids. I had to respect that, and the truth is, after that terrible day, Rune made me nervous, too. I wasn't sure of him anymore.

Hess: I have to ask if he ever mentioned Harriet Burden to you.

Smith: Yes, a couple of times. At first I thought he was talking about a man, but then I realized Harry was a woman. He told me he was cooking up something with her.

Hess: Those were his exact words?

Smith: Well, I don't know if those were his exact words; something like that.

Hess: Anything else?

Smith: He seemed to be enjoying himself, and he thought she was refined. *Refined* was a big word in Rune's vocabulary. He said she was really smart and had read a lot and they had things in common. I don't think there was anything else.

Hess: He didn't say what they had in common?

Smith: No. You explained to me that he might have stolen her work. It sounds awfully complicated to me, and she sounds fairly nutty herself, using those guys to show art that was actually hers, but I just don't know. He didn't talk about *Beneath* at all until after the show, and then he sent me some clippings. Listen, I wish I could tell you he confessed everything to me, but I can't.

Rune and I loved each other as kids and then we grew apart. It wasn't easy for either of us at home, but was it that bad? I don't understand what happened to him, why he turned out the way he did. His death was just plain sad, and I don't really care if he wanted to kill himself or not. He must have known that taking those pills was dangerous, that he might kill himself if it went wrong. After all, that's how Mom did it. There are days when the whole story comes rushing over me, and I get pretty low. I try to keep a positive attitude, but it isn't always easy, and then I just feel like crying. But that's not every day. And I say to myself, Rune will send my kids to college. The money from his estate will pay for Edward and Kathleen, who never even knew him. Something good will come out of all the sadness.

HARRIET BURDEN
Notebook U

April 9, 2003

My anger is returning, a sweet fury.
He will not get away with this. I have made a vow.
I am leaving messages, sending e-mails. He will not get away with this.

Bruno says: Your philosophies will bury you alive. No one knows what you're talking about, Harry.

You are all alone with your thoughts.

Today, you accused Dr F. of not listening. Why? Why did you accuse him? Fierce and caustic you were. Then we talked about it. He is listening. He is always listening to you, and you felt bad, bad again.

April 20, 2003

Four works have vanished from the studio overnight. I am desperate. My windows. It seems impossible, but they are gone. I will look again tomorrow. Perhaps one of the assistants has moved them. No one can get into this building without using supernatural powers. Bruno tells me to remain calm. I must.

(Undated)

I wait for redemption from R.B. And before I sleep, a few notes on the beloveds:

Bruno's *Confessions* are getting fatter. He himself is growing fatter. Fat old granddad.

Ethan's story is called 'Less Than Me.' I have been wondering what he means by it. His character S wakes up one morning and is somehow different. Some crucial aspect of herself has gone missing, her me-ness, her essence, her soul has fled her body. She doesn't look any different in the mirror. Her apartment is the same. Her clothes are hanging in the closet. Her cat knows her, and yet, she is certain she is not the same. She begins to behave differently. She is a vegan but finds herself ordering meat dumplings from a Chinese restaurant. She takes a cab to work. She never splurges on cabs. She speaks her mind to a colleague at work. She never speaks her mind, and so forth. She begins to suspect her upstairs neighbor O, whom she has never met, a loose and merry girl with a bright wardrobe and a slew of boyfriends she bangs loudly enough for S to hear the couplings through the ceiling. Ethan doesn't explain the suspicion. It just happens as it might in a dream, or in a fit of paranoia or a delusion. S spies on O. She keeps tabs on her comings and goings. She follows her in the street. She finds out everything she can about O, her favorite movies, books, shopping habits, but every new clue tells her nothing. Then S decides to build a monument to her lost self, an object that will be all that she is not anymore. She works hard every night after work and finally she finishes 'the Thing.' We don't really know what the Thing looks like, but it is some kind of body with writing and images on it. S invites O for dinner. O arrives, looks at the Thing, and says, Oh, it's me.*

I called up Ethan. I was excited, pleased, wanted to tell him what I thought. We are more than the accumulation of empirical data, I said, more than a heap of recorded trivia, more than our wanderings and our meetings and our jobs, but what is that moreness? Is it what we create between us? Is it a neurological business? Is it the product of narrative, of the imaginary? It's so interesting, I said. But Ethan was sullen, monosyllabic, said I had no idea what he had meant to say. S and O were signs in an arbitrary game of exchange. I said nothing to that. Then I said we artists mostly don't know what we're

* Ethan Lord, 'Less Than Me,' *The Paradoxical Review* 28 (Spring/Summer 2003).

doing, and he told me not to tell him what he knows or doesn't know. He never takes off that horrible wool hat. He's worn it for about a year now, a helmet, really, to hide under. When I said we two seemed to have a headwear theme going in the family, he looked horrified. He does not want to be like his mother. I believe he wanted to rip the hat off immediately, but he is too proud. I don't know how to reach across the chasm. I do everything wrong.

I did not say a word about it to him. But is it possible Ethan doesn't know that his 'Thing' resembles nothing so much as some of his mother's artworks?

Aven is my number girl. She is seven, and she tells me her sevens are green. Her threes are yellow. She is my mathematical child, a child for whom the equations glow. The Radish is long forgotten. Maybe I am the only one who thinks of her anymore. My granddaughter has had her hair cut very short – a compromise. She wanted a Mohawk, but her father and mother refused. Hair grows, I, the indulgent grandmother, said to Maisie, but she said, Oscar is afraid she'll be teased. She's already strange. And I remembered my girlish strangeness.

You're still strange, Harry, strange and estranged.

I eagerly await my coming out. It will happen. I am tense with excitement. It shall work. I bid you good night, whoever you are.

I believe Rune is the Barometer's angel. The Barometer has drawn me another image of the intruder he claims he has seen coming and going at night. He likes the phrase *the dead of night*. And then he plays, *Dire night, wee hours, hours of wee and woe, our wee, woeful hours. Wee Willie Winkie goes through the town. Upstairs and downstairs in his nightgown.* We chanted it together. His drawing is of a huge muscular man with wings. When I looked into the Barometer's eyes as he held out the paper to me, I imagined I was seeing Alan Dudek, the Barometer before he was the Barometer. I thought it was Alan for a moment because his gaze looked unclouded. He has moments of clarity, of a consciousness undiluted by madness. He is part theater, not all theater, but there is a piece of his illness he plays and plays with. This must be acknowledged. After all, we all play parts. We shouldn't be so naïve as to believe that insane people are incapable of dissimulation. My mad friend has his masks, too, his games and subterfuges to avoid the all-important weekly bath or shower. But he also has access to the rumblings underground, a psychotic gift. He feels what we have suppressed, what we fear but cannot say. Isn't this a kind of weather we make among us? I have studied the drawing. The longer I look at it, the more it looks like Rune to me. Bruno thinks I have joined the ranks of the mentally ill, that I'm in the grip of a paranoid fantasy.

I used his old name. Alan, I said, did you let him in? Did you let the angel in?

He looked surprised. He dug his nails into the skin above his wrist. I told him to stop scratching and repeated the question. He shook his head and said, He will cut out my brain and boil it for a stew.

Did Rune threaten him? *If you tell, I'll boil your brain and eat it.* The idea is too vivid for Rune and its expression too precise. Rune's diction rarely moves beyond the borrowed and the banal because Rune uses words to create a public being that hides what others would hate if they could see it. His language must socialize the treachery beneath. Beneath! The Barometer, on the other hand, is an ambulatory high tide of verbiage, but those waves of words include the occasional oracular insight. The problem is how to extract the prophesy from the verbal flood.

You must complete your *Maskings* without anyone to help you. There is R.B., after all. And there are the others, your several secret other ones.* The game is not over.

* R.B. must refer to Richard Brickman. The question of 'others' remains open, but it seems possible, even likely, that Burden published articles under other names in various journals.

473

HARRIET BURDEN
Notebook O

September 23, 2003

The summer people are gone, and the island is chill and brown with patches of burning reds. The surf frightens me these days, and I keep my distance, staying close to where the beach meets the grasses that bow down in the hard wind. Today it made a noise that made me think of a great hoarse animal calling out to no one in particular. I am alone. I have lost Bruno now, too, lost him to my schemes and my rage and my failure. I wanted to bite the world bloody, but I have bitten myself, made my own poor tragedy of things.

And I feel even older alone. My belly is always bloated, even though I am thin. I eat alone, and the food doesn't look as good as when he is with me. I have pains, vague abdominal aches that I wonder about. Sometimes at night they scare me, but in the morning I chide myself for hypochondria. My wrinkled face surprises me. I don't know why. I know it is wrinkled. Knowing is not seeing. I have tried to work here, but I cannot. It is as if all the worlds in my head are dying now, my blazing worlds, which I have clung to with my whole being, are slowly being snuffed out. And I sit in front of the fire wrapped in blankets reading *Paradise Lost* again, slowly, slowly, taking in the dense language I know so well. This afternoon I arrived at Eve's dreadful meal, the big turn in the old story. The flawed, stupid, vain woman has eaten the damned fruit. 'Greedily she ingorg'd without restraint.' She has done it for knowledge, to know more, to be illuminated. How I understand it. Yes, light up my head. I will do anything to know, to know more. Adam is horrified, but he cannot leave her. 'Flesh of flesh, / Bone of my bone, and from thy State / Mine shall never be parted, bliss or woe.' And it was like my own fat man speaking to me, and I cried on the old paperback edition I've had here in the house for all these years. No one has loved me better than Bruno, and yet, it cannot work between us.

I have become hard.

HARRIET BURDEN
Notebook D

Rune is inundated with my messages. He has agreed to see me. He wants me to stop 'the harassment.' He refused to see me in Manhattan. He wouldn't meet me in a restaurant. No, he wants to collide here in Red Hook in the open air where no art world types will see us, no tongues will wag. Fine, I said. Fine.

I have lost. Rune will never let go. He will never tell, and without him it is over. I can hold tight to Phinny's words in *Art Lights*, to the Brickman piece, but I see how little people care. Somehow my story doesn't interest them. I wanted to turn Rune back into a whining Ruina, to ruin him, to make him pay; but he owns the game now and makes the rules, if there are any rules anymore, if there ever were any rules. My hand is a swollen, purple mess. I hit him so hard. And I found Bruno. No, that's a lie. Bruno found me. There he was, as if by magic, to pick me up off the ground. Today he made me chicken soup and watched my face closely as I spooned it into my mouth, and I made all the right sounds to please him.

October 18. I read it in the paper. Rune is dead.

He has made the last move, and he has done it in a contraption that steals from *Beneath*, and now he is sanctified. How the world loves the artist suicide, not old artists, of course, not old bags like me. No, they must be young or youngish. Thirty-eight is the perfect age to die if you want to cement your fame, to summon the throngs to feast on your beautiful corpse, to chew on your luminous legacy, made more poignant by the now-impossible future. Ah, Rune. Checkmate. And if he didn't mean to do it? He would have gotten around to killing himself sooner or later. He wanted a beautiful death, didn't he? And such a death must be planned. *It don't come natur'l.* Celebrity is life in the third person. Ethan is right. Some people are better at living the third person than others.

But I sabotaged myself without knowing it, didn't I? It was as if I had to follow the game to its end, to wind up in that room with Rune and the dead Felix to be threatened, slapped, and humiliated, to be turned back into a cowering, ashamed child who cannot speak up. I was pulled toward it, as if time were nothing, and the past had become both present and future, and the dead could walk again. They tramp through the furrows of your mind, Harry, in that rumpled wilderness of gray matter, the two men you wanted but couldn't have, your father and your husband. It was not just love. That's where you went wrong. You know that now. It wasn't just about love and wanting to be loved. You were not that eternal plaintive female bleating over the ages, I love you, and I want you to love me, and I will wait for you, my love, with my hands folded and my head down. I am not that paragon of virtue, Penelope, waiting for Odysseus and turning away the suitors.

I am Odysseus.

But I found out too late.

I hate you, Father. I hate you, Felix. I hate you both for not seeing that truth, for not recognizing that I am the clever hero.

And Mother, you bent your head and you took his punishment. He shut you out and he shut you down. He did not speak to you. He acted as if you did not exist, because you wanted to speak.

And you, Harry, you bent your head and you took his punishment, and you cannot bear it, can you?

And didn't you wait at home like Penelope, without any suitors, sadly, just two children? And were you not faithful? And were you not kind? And were you not long-suffering? So are you not Penelope? No, because she did not want to be Odysseus, at least as far as we know she didn't, but who would want to be Penelope? You did not want to wait, and yet you nearly went mad waiting. And now your son, too, keeps his distance from you, as if you are contaminated. If he identifies with you, he is emasculated, such an old drama; my feminist son is terrified of maternal stench.

I am Odysseus, but I have been Penelope.

But how he loved you back in the day, little, intense, hypersensitive Ethan, whatever he says, whatever he has forgotten. You have that passionate story in your memory fields. And your daughter is with you still. You have Maisie. And you have Aven.

And Rune? He is the sign of your hatred, your envy, your fury, isn't he?

Did he start it, Harry? Or did you? What did he want from you? Did he only want the pleasure of hurting you through Felix?

'He liked to watch.' That's what Rune said, that Felix was a voyeur. Does it matter that he rubbed his cock to ecstasy while he looked at others humping on the floor in front of him? No. And does it matter that when you imagine it you feel sad? But why sad, Harry? Didn't you enjoy tormenting Ruina in the game? Didn't Rune know it filled you with sadistic joy? Isn't that why he turned the tables on you? *He knew that you played both parts.* There's the rub. And knowing is power. Elementary Freud, dear Watson. A child is being beaten.*

But I didn't know about Felix. All I knew is that there were secrets and that some of the secrets had names. I wondered what was in his head when we

* 'A Child Is Being Beaten' (1919), *The Standard Edition of the Complete Psychological Works of Sigmund Freud,* vol. XVII (London: Hogarth Press, 1955), 179–204.

grappled in bed. I wonder if it was Harriet Burden. Was it ever Harriet Burden, wife and helpmeet? Sure it was. In the beginning it was. Rune might have lied about Felix, but even if he were lying, it wouldn't make much difference now. Rune became the sign of all the boys who studied their Quine and mastered their logic and smoked their pipes and looked at your father with worshipful eyes, the boy you might have been, Harry. But for a twist of fate in the womb, you might have pleased him and triumphed. And Rune became the sign of all the boys Felix showed and Felix loved and Felix made famous and Felix bought and Felix sold. That gets close to the heart of the matter, doesn't it? What do you say, Dr F.? Am I getting close to the heart of the matter? Rune, Mr Third Person, Mr Swagger, Mr Glib – the one who counts, the one who wins. And isn't it just that quality of knowing, of assurance, of entitlement that you detest, Harry, that you find so hard to imitate, the quality they all had? And did they not all condescend to you, Harry? Did they not regard you as an inferior, you who could out-think, out-work, out-do every single one of them?

Yes. They did. And they are all dead. I cannot believe that they are all dead.

November 1, 2003

I am back to my blazing mother Margaret. Margaret, the anti-Milton. She gives birth to worlds. It is not God who speaks here, but Nature:

All paines I can take,
Will do no good, *Matter* a *Braine* must make;
Figure must draw a Circle, round, and small,
Where in the midst must stand a Glassy Ball,
Without Convexe, the inside a *Concave*,
And in the midst a round small hole must have,
That *Species* may passe, and repasse through,
Life the *Prospective* every thing to view.*

Mad Madge had no children of her own, no babies to raise up into adults. She had her 'Paper Bodies,' her breathing works, and she loved them dearly.†

★　　★　　★

* Quoted in Lisa T. Sarasohn, *The Natural Philosophy of Margaret Cavendish: Reason and Fancy During the Scientific Revolution* (Baltimore: Johns Hopkins University Press, 2010), 41.
† In *Sociable Letters*, published in 1664, Cavendish writes to an imaginary lady friend. In letter CXLIII, she tells her correspondent about her habit of keeping copies of her manuscripts until they are safely printed, after which she burns them: 'But howsoever their Paper Bodies are Consumed, like as the Roman Emperours, in Funeral Flames, I cannot say, an eagle flies out of them, or that they turn into a Blazing Star, although they make a great Blazing Light when they Burn; And so leaving them to your Approbation or Condemnation, I rest, Madam, Your faithful Friend and Servant, CL.' Sylvia Bowerbank and Sara Mendelson, eds., *Paper Bodies: A Margaret Cavendish Reader* (Toronto: Broadview, 2000), 81–82.

'So do I likewise not persuade myself, that my philosophy being new, and but lately brought forth, will at first sight prove master of understanding, it may be, not in this age, but if God favour her, she may attain to it in after times: And if she be slighted now and buried in silence, she may perhaps rise more gloriously hereafter; for her ground being sense and reason, she may meet with an age where she will be more regarded than she is in this.'*

I will leave my bodies behind me, too. I am making them for hereafter, not for the bruising present with its cold, dismissive eyes.

The witch hides herself in her castle by the sea with the bear, her friend and lover. That is how the fairy tale has ended. The old witch and the old bear live happily and sadly together ever after.

December 1. *The Natural Mask*. That's me. I am the natural mask. It's Maisie's idea. I used the words for Raccoona once, and she's adopted it for the film about her mother and now she's letting me explain myself to the camera, me, H.B., in all my pseudonymous mania, and I'm explicating and expounding and pontificating and we're having

---

* Margaret Cavendish, *Observations upon Experimental Philosophy* (1668), ed. Eileen O'Neill (Cambridge, U.K.: Cambridge University Press, 2001), 12–13.

good fun together. Now you've got a hoarder, a schizophrenic, and your mother, I said to Maisie, a perfect trio. And my Maisie smiles. I can't tell all. I must keep some secrets, of course, but the telling has almost made me feel that I might be understood. Is it such a vain hope?

Aven looked long and tall and thin today. She has entered what I call 'high middle childhood.' She examined my mischievous little people, turned red when she saw my copulating pairs, and laughed wildly at my Ursula who's taking a shit. She let me draw her into my lap today, let her grand-mother revel in the tactile pleasure of holding her young body close to my ribs. I put my nose into her short brown hair. Today, it smelled vaguely of apples.

HARRIET BURDEN
Notebook T

January 15, 2004

When he told me about the CT scan, I watched his mouth move. I remember his teeth had a gray tinge to them in the afternoon light from the window behind him and that the photograph on his desk faced away from me and there was a small price sticker on the back, peeling away from the wood. The words came methodically, but now I recall only their effect – a breathless paralysis. He made sure I understood there was no cure, and that it had spread, that complete surgical resection was unlikely, and even if it were, ninety-eight percent of those patients also experienced a recurrence. Still, he wanted me to check into the hospital immediately for surgery.

They do not protect you. Dr P. did not shake his head sadly. He did not meet my eyes. I suppose that's how they do it. They do it all the time, after all. I am one of thousands. This was his method, delivering information for me to process.

★　　★　　★

When I asked him if there was a stage five, his eyebrows went up. No, he said.

Sure there is, I said. When you hit stage five, you're dead. That's what you're telling me, right? I'm dead.

He did not like my impudence. He did not like it at all, and I was glad he did not like it. I was going home to see Bruno, to discuss it, to register it. When I stood in the street with my hand in the air to hail a cab, I was still frozen, terror high in my throat as I looked around me amazed at what I was losing, city and sky and pavement, the swift and slow-moving pedestrians, and the color of things. It will vanish with you, every color, even the ones that have never had names but are perceived plainly enough. Incalculable losses.

In the cab, I looked at the back of the driver's head and at his photo plastered on the window between us. I guessed he was from Somalia, a Somalian driver, and I thought to myself, He does not know he is carrying a dead woman in his backseat, taking her to Red Hook, just a stop away from hell.

January 27, 2004

I read what I wrote before the knife cut me open and they rearranged my innards for five hours. My naïveté makes me howl with silent laughter. Hell is here now, and its name is medicine. I have been gutted like a fish: uterus, ovaries, fallopian tubes, appendix, and a part of my bowel have disappeared. They threw my diseased organs into a pail in surgery, and someone must have come along with gloves and a mask and removed them to a special diseased organs disposal area. Where do they go? I am trussed up with tape, cut vertically from my navel down. I cannot shift my position in bed without gasping in pain. I cannot sit. My ankles and feet have ballooned to three times their size, and, along with my arms and hands, they have turned to ice. I cannot eat. I am terrified of every evacuation. Every excretion brings fresh agony. And the operation was 'suboptimal.' This euphemism would be hilarious if it weren't so grotesque.

This afternoon I dozed in bed, and when I woke it seemed to me that my bed and the night table and the shining brass lamps and the pale green armchair in the corner of the room had been replaced with exact replicas. The room I know so well had somehow become a fake room. I wasn't myself and I wasn't at home. My fear and pain have infected everything. I want to go home. Please, lift this enchantment and let me go home.

In four weeks they will begin the poisoning, a poisoning that may not do me much good. But I hope, no, I pray for the magic of remission.

I wait now. Penelope, the patient, waits patiently. The robotic Dr P. is gone and now I wait to see

486

the somewhat kinder doctor, Dr R., and I wait to see Dr F. to talk to him about Dr R. and to tell him about my fear and my trembling. I wait in dread for Dr R. to call to tell me about tumor blood markers, CA-125. I wait for her to discover what shrinks or grows in the abdominal disaster area, my very own corporeal ground zero, debulked, but not divested of horrors. I have been attacked from within, and I live in a state of continual envy of people with cells that haven't multiplied into killer legions. I watch them stroll down Madison Avenue or disappear into the Eighty-Sixth Street subway near Dr R.'s office. I see them amble hand in hand along the waterfront, go in to have a drink at Sunny's. I marvel at their casual wellness, their hale, tumor-free bodies, and their complete indifference to the fact that they are alive.

Over and over, I remember giving birth to Maisie and then to Ethan. It must be the memory of the good body, the fertile body before it began to eat itself alive. The now-vanished ovaries that gnawed me unto death – a crueler punishment for H.B. could not have been devised. Have you been ambivalent about your sex, Harry? You bet you have. Well, lady, here is your fitting chastisement, the ironical twist on a life lived partly behind male masks.

Memories of birth pains. I squat for Ethan. A speedy labor. Push. Push down. The head stuck and then push, push, and the long, wet body with black hair slides out of me, still attached by a bloody purple cord. Alive.

Birth, like illness, and like death, is not willed. It simply happens. The 'I' has nothing to do with it.

February 10, 2004

I am desperate to work, but it is so hard. I teeter on knees that shake. My extremities are electrified, and I panic about time. I am so tired. In Bruno's worried face I see my own dread. Often, I cannot believe I will not live.
   Why would anyone want to die?

Maskings is remote now, but I wish that my work had a home and that the pseudonyms might be understood as a complete project – unfinished business.

I am having all the work catalogued.
   A. C. Robinson. Lester Bone.★
   For Felix: *The Book of Disquiet*.

★ A. C. Robinson could not be traced to any likely text. An article by Lester Bone, 'A Philosophical Inquiry into the Emotional Origins of Creativity' appeared in *Science and Philosophy Forum* 9 (2001). Tracking Bone proved unsuccessful because his affiliation turned out to be fictional. The work was probably written by Burden, as it cites scholars and scientists in several fields.

O prince of better days, I was once your princess, and we loved each other with another kind of love. [*]

February 26, 2004

There are mornings when I wake up and it takes an instant to remember. For a few hours sleep snuffs out the terrible real. I am sick, bald, disemboweled, and nauseated. I have a rash all over my body, an effect of the Taxol. Not unusual. The itching is so terrible I have taken to slapping myself. I have spasms of diarrhea and then constipation, and my mind is not working well, because chemotherapy makes you stupid.

I can't remember the date. I've lost the day, too. Panic. Then calm. Then panic again.

I dreamed this afternoon that the tumors had popped out through the skin of my belly above my pubic hair, which looked like bristling foliage. The tumors shook with life, and I eagerly began to pull at them, to tug them out of me, to save myself. They bloodied my hands. I was able to draw out one long, trembling snake. The triumphant joy I felt. Unspeakable joy. We who are leaving the world can still wish to stay.

★   ★   ★

[*] Fernando Pessoa, *The Book of Disquiet*, trans. Richard Zenith (New York: Penguin, 2002). The heteronym Pessoa used for this book is Bernardo Soares.

I have more to do. There are undiscovered worlds inside me, but I will never see them.

It's a Wednesday and the weather is cold and cloudy.

Every dying person is a cartoon version of the Cartesian dualist, a person made of two substances, *res cogitans* and *res extensa*. The thinking substance moves along on its own above the insurrectionist body formed of vile, gross matter, a traitor to the spirit, to that airy *cogito* that keeps on thinking and talking. Descartes was far more subtle about mind-and-body interactions than many crude commentators admit, but he was right that thoughts don't seem to take up any room, not even in one's head. What are they? No one knows. No one really knows what a thought is. It must involve the synapses and the chemicals, of course, but how do the words and pictures come into it? I am still here narrating my own ending. I, Harriet Burden, know I am going to die, and yet a piece of me refuses this truth. I rage against it. I would like to spit and scream and howl and punch the bedclothes, but these demonstrations would hurt this frail skeleton with its few putrid remaining organs far too much. I have laughed, too, laughed carefully so as not to wound same-said bag of bones and sorry scrap of flesh, but I have laughed nevertheless at my imminent death. I have told corpse jokes and carried on about plans for my own funeral.

March 5, 2004

I have come home to die, but dying is not so simple in this our twenty-first-century world. It takes a team. It takes 'pain management.' It takes hospice at home. But I have been strict with them. This is my death, not yours, I said to the goddamned social worker who oozed compassion when we planned the final step, how to die 'well.' An oxymoron, you idiot. I said NO to the grief counselors with their sympathetic faces peddling denial and anger and bargaining and depression and acceptance. I said NO to professional mourners of all kinds and their goddamned clichés. I will have NO simpering crap uttered within ten miles of my deathbed. I boomed these words. I mustered up a boom. I was magnificent.

The boom has left me. I am a leaky vessel – urine and feces and tears ooze from me without permission. I have diapers that must be changed. My bowels ruined by surgery are twisted again with tumors. My hair has grown back straight. The frizzy hair I detested and then learned to love is gone and in its place lank, gray straw has grown. I am truly a monster now, ashamed of its hideous body. I smell piss, shit, and some other unknown odor no one else admits to smelling, but it must be the stench of dying. I smell it as I write this, wafting up from the war zone below the sheets. I should be bathed in bleach. I am lying in my special bed that goes up and down at the press of a button, parked by the window so I can look onto the water and gaze at Manhattan across the way. I miss the world I am leaving, but I have not forgiven it. Its bitter taste remains, a hard crust in my mouth I can't spit out.

Pearl is looking over my shoulder to see what I am writing. She is all efficiency, a sharp one. Born in Trinidad, lived in Sweden, now in NYC. Private nurse. Speak to me in Swedish, I say, and she does.

I would like to retrieve the mind I had – the one that leapt and did jigs and somersaults in the air. I used to want them to see it, to recognize my gifts. Now I would settle for just having it back.

April 2, 2004

I told Bruno today that I am the dying beast, and he is Beauty. He shook his head and his lips trembled. You are so beautiful, I said. You are robust and hearty and my own darling Beauty. Come to the beast, I said. And he laid his head on my chest and squashed my breasts, and the weight of his skull hurt me. Everything hurts me now. Nausea comes. The morphine makes me hazy. The pain rises. I want so much to write, to tell, but it is harder and harder.

April 13, 2004

The clematis is here. The clammy little vine curling around me.

Maisie does not like her.

Ethan likes her. I see him looking at her steadily. He was here today. It is hard for him. It was hard for him when Felix died, too, but Felix died fast. I have spoken to him and his sister in the strange voice that now belongs to me, a rasp just above a whisper. I am glad I have told them about Felix and his lovers so that they will not be surprised if they pop up with old keys. I have told it all to them kindly. I am pleased with myself. If I weren't an ugly, self-soiling creature from the black lagoon, I might pass as a Romantic figure, the wasted mother on her deathbed speaking nobly to her children about their difficult father. The roles are there, ready to be played.

Oh, if I could take away the suffering in Maisie's face. You are too good, Maisie. I told her that. She said, No, I'm not. I'm not. But only the good feel that they aren't good. I want her to live and work and soar.

And Maisie leaned over and kissed my head. I admire you so much, Mommy, she said. She has not called me Mommy since she was six.

I speak to Dr F. on the phone. I can hear sorrow in his voice. It is love. I am grateful for that strange form of intimacy, for the one-way telling. He has known me better than anyone. Strange, but true.

I often return to the Riverside Drive apartment. I walk through the rooms and inspect them. I am in my father's study and have lifted one of the pipes to my nose to inhale that special smell without being seen. I am worried he will come in. My mother interrupts me. She tells me not to touch the pipes or the pens. No, no, no, he doesn't like them to be disturbed. His voice comes from the next room. Mother quickly straightens the pipes. I am looking up at her face and in it I see fear and hope. It is terrible to see. It is terrible to see because her expression is a mirror of my own.

She was afraid of him.
I was afraid of him.
He never hit her. He never hit me.
He didn't have to. We were in thrall.

You did not know how angry you were.
I did not know how angry I was.
How I have raged. I think I cannot rage anymore. I think I am too feeble and then the spite comes up again, a bit weaker, a bit thinner, but there. If only I could feel that I had done my work, that it was finished, that it would not vanish entirely.

Father, you did not know how much I wanted your face to shine when you looked at me. But you were crippled. It helps me to know you were crippled.

★   ★   ★

I would like the ghost of my mother to come and rock me.

Phinny is coming. I hope he is not too late.

Rachel was here. She reminded me of the Beast with Five Fingers. Another Beast. I had forgotten. I asked her to stroke my hand. Her fingers on my fingers – I feel them now as I write. I told Maisie to take her to look at blazing mother Margaret.

Ethan has talked to me. Ethan has told my own fervid stories back to me. His memory is much better than mine.

I used to remember everything – citations, page numbers, names, papers and the year of their publication – and now it is blur.

Clemmy's red mouth. Her radiant touch. Those silly stones. Why do I tolerate it?

I am in love with a holy fool.

I have frightened Aven. I am so sorry.

When was he here? Today? Was it today? The Barometer has sent me on my way with an opulent speech. His is an angry God, who bellows from heaven and sends down lightning bolts and brutal winds.

I remember I am a Jew.

★   ★   ★

I am multitudes.

This earth a spot, a grain, an atom.*

I am made of the dead.

Even my thoughts are not my own anymore.

* John Milton, *Paradise Lost*, Book VIII, 17–18.

SWEET AUTUMN PINKNEY
(edited transcript)

I heard a voice say 'Harry.' The man's voice was pretty loud, and I heard him talking right into my left ear even though nobody was standing anywhere close to me, because it was one thirteen in the morning and only a couple of people were out walking so late at night. I know what time it was because I looked at my cell phone right when it happened outside the Siri Pharmacy on Flatbush Avenue. Kali (she's the little dog I adopted from S.O.S. – Save Our Strays – half poodle, half terrier, half Chihuahua) was having a pee and a sniff before I took her home. Right away I knew the voice was a sign. If you don't pay attention to signs they pass on by, and you might miss being called to your rightful fate. No question the voice took me by surprise. I hadn't even thought about Harry for a long time, and I hadn't heard from Anton since the postcard, and I'd been concentrating on my spiritual becoming and development and healing gifts and helping people in my practice, Sweet Indigo Spiritual Healing, and I'd been making real progress with some backsliding, mostly in the form of guys I'd fall for who turned out to have bad karma that I would somehow miss. But then, backsliding is part of the progress to enlightenment, too. You have to recognize it and move on. In one of his lectures, the master, Peter Deunov, said, 'Your consciousness can travel at the speed of slow trains, it can travel at the speed of light, and it can travel even faster.' I guess my consciousness was catching up to some airplanes by then.

The next morning while I was fixing my blooming green tea, I knew I had to answer the angelic voice by finding Harry, and I looked down at that blossom opening up in my tea and felt the expansion in my sacral plexus chakra, and the feeling of orange drifting up in the room. I remembered Harry's red, smudgy auras. I found her name in the Brooklyn phone book, and I called her up. I had a speech ready in case she didn't remember me. I was going to explain about the voice in the street, even though I know Harry wasn't into the master's teachings and astrology and chakras or anything like that, but it wasn't Harry on the phone. The person on the phone said, 'I am her daughter and my mother is very sick right now, and she isn't seeing anyone except her family and closest friends,' and her voice made a little quaver that came right through the phone and into my body as a tremble. I asked her what her name was, and she said, 'Maisie,' and I said, 'Maisie, this is Sweet Autumn Pinkney. I used to know your mother on account of my relationship with Anton

Tish, and I was an assistant for the artworks, and I think I can be useful to her now. You see,' and I spoke the next words slow and clear, 'I have been called.' Maisie said, 'But *you* called *me*,' because she didn't understand my greater meaning, but that didn't matter. I put on my vintage paisley purple dress with the full skirt, the best color for emergency healing, and packed up Kali in her carrying case and grabbed my bag of stones and called a car service because Red Hook is the absolute worst for subways. You just can't get there underground, so I called up Legends, the trusty service I use in times of need.

I had the address written down, but I couldn't find the exact building, and I saw some kids standing around, and I asked them if they knew where Harry Burden lived, and one boy with a tattoo on his neck and a black baseball cap said, 'Oh, you mean the rich witch.' After we talked a little more it was pretty clear we were talking about the same person, and I asked him why he called her that, and he said he didn't know except there were lots of rumors about 'creepy shit' in her studio and crazy noises and yelling about Satan and God that sometimes came from the building. They petted Kali a little bit and then showed me the door, and I rang the bell. I explained to Maisie and to Bruno, who was Harry's boyfriend, that I had come to see Harry, and he had to go in to Harry and ask her if it was okay to see me, and she said yes, and so I went up the stairs and into a great big room with windows all over the place and light coming in all over and a super beautiful view, and Harry was lying in a hospital bed with the railings, you know, the kind that lift up on both sides, and an IV drip in her arm. I could see her elbow sticking out from under the floppy sleeve of her T-shirt, and sure enough she was just bones, and then I knew she wasn't going to get well at all. It made me hushed inside.

I saw the aura sludge around her and the dull colors – whites, grays, some ochre – and the toxins from the losses and the traumas built up over the years. My mission was not healing but cleaning the chakras so the luminous body would not be earthbound. I had to spin Harry's luminous anatomy free. But she needed to give me permission. You can't just run in and start cleaning and spinning without permission. Kali started barking, so I put her in the hall in her case. I knew she would whine a little but then probably go to sleep.

I approached Harry with my soft walk. It's a toe-heel walk like a dancer. I do it to show respect and not make noise, and I stood beside her. She was propped up in the bed. Her hair was short and stringy, not curly the way I remembered it, and her cheekbones stuck out over her hollow cheeks. The skin under her eyes was dark gray, but her green eyes were clear and hard. She looked straight at me and said in a husky voice full of the disease, 'It's the little mystic, isn't it? The clematis?' And I smiled and put my hand on her arm. Then she squinted at me. I knew she was feeling the warm flow from my fingers. She closed her eyes. And I said, 'Harry, can I pray for you?' Before she could answer, Maisie was standing right behind me and asking me what I was doing, and she said they weren't a praying kind of family. Harry hated praying and on and on. Maisie had a blue aura but a little smoky because she was sad, clinging to her mom, so understandable. But I said in a firm tone that I wanted to know from Harry because she was the person I had been called to see.

Harry said, 'Clematis, I'm a Jew.'

I said it didn't matter and that every religion had its own ways, but God was the same everywhere. I told her that Peter Deunov's Christianity was renewed by the principles of karma and reincarnation. He liked phrenology, too, head-bump reading that was popular all over the world when the master was young. And then, while I was staring into Harry's sunken face, I saw pain in it, and her mouth stretched out, and I felt pains in my solar plexus, such hard strikes I had to put my hand down there to steady me. And after the pains, I had the revelation. The calling, the higher planes. Sweet Autumn, I said to myself. (I talk to myself like that when something is really important.) Sweet Autumn, I said, that was the message the voice was trying to deliver to you on Atlantic Avenue! A master is someone who has taken at least five initiations and completed the human stage of evolution and gone beyond it. Didn't the master say, 'A new earth will soon see day.' Didn't he say that fire would come to 'rejuvenate, purify, and reconstruct everything'? And some of the masters are artists – Michelangelo is one, an artist like Harry. He's moved on to a higher planetary system called Sirius. The Siri Pharmacy! The voice! It was an angelic master, maybe it was Michelangelo, speaking to me from Sirius. I was pretty excited, and I told Harry. I could see Maisie's face getting all screwed up and angry. And Bruno was looking funny at me, but Harry was listening with her eyes closed and then she said in a whisper, 'I remember Deunov now. Clem, he helped save the Bulgarian Jews.'

And I said yes, yes, and I was really happy because Harry knew the story, and that was another sign. Forty-eight thousand people were saved because Master Deunov sent his messenger, Loulchev, to look for the king of Bulgaria, who was hiding out somewhere, to get him to save the people who were going to be deported. The king's name was Boris the Third or the Fourth or something. Well, Loulchev looked and looked, but he couldn't find the king, so he had to go back to the master and say he had searched every nook and cranny but no luck. So the master meditated, and the name of the town was sent to him, and lo and behold, the king was in that town, and the king respected the master, and the Bulgarians were behind both of them, and the king made a law that saved the Jews from being killed.

'I remember,' Harry said to me, 'Tsar, not king.'

And I said I thought they were the same thing, and she said I was right; they were pretty close.

The signs were coming faster and faster, and it was almost too much for me. I felt dizzy, which sometimes happens when I'm feeling a lot in the atmosphere around me, but all the threads were coming together. That's how I think of it, the threads were binding together to form circles, and Harry gave me permission. I could pray for her and clean up her luminous anatomy for its passage on to the next stage. The shamans in Brazil say you walk into mountains and see everything around you with new eyes – a sacred vision.

I came every day for five days. On the fifth day, Harry died.

I want to say that I knew the others didn't really accept me and that they don't believe in what I believe in. Maisie called me an 'interpolator,' which means an uninvited guest coming in from the outside, and, on the first day especially, Bruno and Pearl, who was Harry's day nurse, sent me nasty looks from across the room while I was cleaning up the auras, spinning them first counterclockwise and then clockwise. It's slow work, and they were rolling their eyes at me. Don't think I didn't see them. I've taught myself not to care, that's all. People have been making fun of my gift since I was little, so it's an ancient story. I wasn't like the other kids, not ever. I was always seeing and feeling stuff they didn't see and feel, colors and waves and electricity in my arms and legs, and they used to wait for me after school and yell 'ugly albino' and 'moron' and 'retard' at me. Sometimes they'd trip me or knock against my backpack or rip it off me and throw all my stuff on the sidewalk. Not too original when you think about it. You just have to learn to walk with your chin up and let them scream their heads off. It doesn't come easy. It took me a long time not to care about it.

Anyway, after the first day with the eye rolling and the interpolator business, things got better. Maisie had her little girl, Aven, who had to go to school, and she had her husband, Oscar, who was a really sweet man with a deep voice that made you feel warm when you listened to it, and she couldn't just forget about them, after all. On the second day, I told Maisie I would cover for her because she couldn't keep her eyes open anymore. They kept fluttering shut. I said I'd sit with Harry and that she should try to nap or she wouldn't be much good for anything. Maisie could see Harry liked the feel of my hands and the comfort of the crystals on her belly, and she liked my singing – I sang some old ballads to her that my grandma Lucy used to sing to me. Harry especially liked 'Leaving Nancy.' 'The parting has come and my weary soul aches / I'm leaving my Nancy, oh.' Harry liked Kali, too. And Kali liked Harry. She licked her face and sniffed her, and after that, she stayed with us in the room and it was easier.

Harry said to Maisie, 'Go and rest, love. I'm not dead yet. I've still got some kick in me.' Maisie told me she was sorry about being mad at me, and I said it was really okay and not to worry.

Bruno could get upset at all of us and furious at the hospice doctor, Dr Gupta, who was actually a pretty decent man. He had a green aura, just right for healers. Dr Gupta came and went to check on things because the meds didn't always work the way they were supposed to. I remember Bruno in the hallway with the doctor, getting all excited but trying to keep his voice low so Harry wouldn't hear him, and he kept saying over and over in his gruff way, 'She's not going to suffer. You hear me. She's not going to suffer. You have to make the pain go away.' After the doctor left, Bruno sat down on a chair and covered his face with his hands and cried hard but not loud. I tiptoed over and put my hand on his shoulder. He looked up at me and said, 'Who are you?' He didn't say it in a nice way, and I didn't answer him. I didn't think it would help. Then I thought he said, 'She called you *untimely*.' And I said, '*Untimely*?' And he said, no, not untimely, a word in German: *un-hime-lick*. It means uncanny, freaky, weird. I told him that was okay with me. I don't mind, I said. Bruno shook his head at me, but he smiled just a teeny bit at the corners of his mouth, so I felt better with him after that, and, oh, I have to say, he loved Harry. I'd say he had a gift. He knew how to love her. It was a strong, pure, radiant beam, and he'd sit with her and kiss her hand and pet her head and whisper to her. I heard them laughing, too. I realized I'd like to laugh before I die. I hope I can. But I could tell Harry had been hurt, probably at home somewhere along the line like lots of us. Sometimes I could see and feel the anger burning out of her and into the room, the old red flames dark with smoke and negative energies, the ones I saw when I knew Anton. And I realized Harry had to get clear with everyone she loved before she went on, and that is awfully important no matter what you believe. Then I realized some of those people were already on the other side, and some of them were ghosts with their dim white bones still bound to this side. Poor Harry.

I didn't meet Ethan until the second day. He had this warm hat pulled down to his eyebrows even though it wasn't cold outside, and he looked scared and alone. As soon as he came in, I could see he was all blocked up with fears. I had to concentrate and walk around him, but then I saw a hole, a kind of tear or sore spot in his rear heart chakra. And I could feel the wishes flying out of Harry toward him. He sat down in a chair by the bed and he talked to her. He knew a lot. Right away I could tell he was a very intellectual person like Harry. I really didn't know what they were talking about, but I could tell they were not saying the authentic words they needed to say, and it made me anxious. I started to feel pressure in my chest, so it got a little hard to breathe, and I had to take a break, go into the hall, and clean my own aura. I lay down on the floor and meditated for about half an hour. Winsome, the night nurse, was coming on duty. Isn't that a pretty name, Winsome? Anyway, she went into the room and Ethan came out, and he sat down on the floor and we talked.

Gosh, I can't remember everything we said to each other. Ethan petted Kali for a while and asked about her, but then we somehow got onto the subject of being a kid and how hard it can be just because you're little. Well, I ended up telling him about the time Denny broke my arm. He was having one of his big fights with Mom at the dinner table, and I was just trying to get out of the way because I knew what could happen if I didn't, but he grabbed me by my arm to get to Mom and threw me against the wall, and then I fell on the floor hard, and a bone broke and my arm was sticking out in a crazy direction. It hurt so much and it looked so different from before, I started screaming. That stopped their fight, anyway. They both looked so surprised. Then Denny came over to me, and I was scared of him and backed away, but he grabbed my arm and set the break. It hurt like the dickens, but right after, it felt much better, like a miracle, really. He did that for me, even though he was the one who smashed my arm to begin with. We all went to the emergency room in the car. Denny and Mom lied about how it happened. They said I fell out of a tree, and the doctor congratulated Denny on his great job, and Denny was proud. Jeez, I could see it in his face. It was like he forgot about hurting me. All he could remember was fixing my arm, not breaking it. Ethan said that was pretty ironic. I said, yeah, it was. We were quiet for a while and then I told him he had aura blockage, and he said, 'Really.'

Anyway, I talked to him about Harry and Anton. He wanted me to write something that said I knew it was Harry's work, and Anton had told me so. I said I would for sure. I asked him why he was talking to his mom about some book when she was about to go over to the other side. After a while, Ethan mentioned this world Harry made up about the Fervidlies, and Ethan said he thought about the bedtime stories she told him and Maisie all the time, and that's why he became a writer, but he had never told her that. 'You ought to tell her,' I said, 'because your mom is not going to be here. She's going on, and for her sake and yours you ought to tell her.' Ethan said he didn't know why but it was awfully hard for him. He let me put my hands on him then, on his face and shoulders. The laying-on of hands is the oldest healing method and goes back to the Bible. 'Then after fasting and praying they laid their hands on them and sent them off.' It gave him energy. I could feel it. And then we kissed a couple of times. I know this is for the book, and Ethan will probably read it, but that's okay. The kissing made him feel better, and the colors around him got brighter, and I could see how handsome he was, and I took off his hat. He had nice hair, curly but not as curly as Harry's used to be, kind of silky curly, and I asked him if I could touch it and he said yes and so I did. I stayed at the lodge, that's what they call the place. Ethan, Kali, and I slept together in one bed, no sex or anything. In the middle of the night I heard someone talking loudly down the hall about angels. Ethan said not to worry, it was someone called Barometer. He'd explain in the morning.

The third day, Harry looked whiter and weaker. She had to squeeze the drip for more morphine, too. Still, she had a black-and-white checkered notebook on the table beside her and a pen, and even though her hand was shaking badly, she managed to scribble down some words into it. It took a long time, and when she had finished, all her energy was gone. Big pains. I dabbed away her tears with a Kleenex. We put lip balm on her mouth because it was cracking. I put a new crystal on her stomach under her shirt, and we had to adjust the sheets. For the first time I saw the scar with puckered skin around it down there where they had to cut her open. Her whole belly looked funny, really white and soft, but you could almost see through the skin. I kept cleaning the chakras, making the circling motions to clean and comfort. It was working all right, and it made me feel good that I was making progress. I wanted Harry's last dreams on this side to be good ones, and I knew the purifying would make for peaceful dream pictures.

Sometime in the afternoon, a short, trim older woman came into the room with Maisie. Her gray-and-white hair was cut short and straight at her chin, and she was wearing a long, light green skirt that went all the way down to her ankles, and swished a little when she walked with fast, small steps. Ethan told me she was Harry's oldest friend, Rachel Briefman. You could feel how wise and confident she was right away. She sat beside Harry for a long time, stroking her cheek and talking to her in a low voice. I think they were remembering when they were girls or maybe Rachel was remembering for Harry. Actually, I had to turn my back for a little while. I pretended to play with Kali because I could feel Rachel missing Harry already, missing her before she was dead, if you see what I mean, and I felt like crying all of a sudden. Harry's doctor came, too, her shrink doctor, not Dr Gupta. He was a white guy, pretty old, with thin hair, bald spots, brown horn-rimmed glasses, and a potbelly, not too big, though, just well-fed and comfortable. I liked his eyes. We all left the room, even Bruno and Pearl left. They must have been in there alone for close to an hour. Bruno was pacing back and forth, pushing his hair back with both his hands over and over again. When the doctor came out, I could see on his face that he was sad. He shook my hand in such a polite, respectful way. He let Maisie hug him. Bruno walked him downstairs and outside. I don't know what they said to each other but the mood around us was changing fast because of time, the time here on earth, not the other time of forever. I prayed and meditated and prayed and meditated for strength to finish the job. Nobody had to know about my praying. Kali knew. She put her head in my lap and looked up at me so tenderly. Sometimes the purest energies come from animals.

Harry wasn't eating anything. Maisie tried to feed her broth, but she couldn't do it. I could see that Harry wasn't going to take any more food, but Maisie wanted to keep her mom alive, keep her going. Harry said she couldn't feel her feet anymore, so Maisie and I rubbed them, and while we rubbed them, Ethan sat down beside her and started in on the Fervid stories. There was this girl named Nobisa, who wasn't very clean or very pretty. I liked that because usually, you know, it's the beautiful princess and blah, blah, blah. Nobisa had adventures with some pretty strange types, an ogre named Burnt because he was once almost killed in a fire and was all scar tissue, and there was a fairy named Fat for the good reason that she was obese and it made flying hard for her. She was so weighted down, but she couldn't get thin because she had a gigantic hunger for bacon and eggs. She ate her way through all the pigs in the kingdom and the chickens couldn't lay enough eggs for her appetite, and a war started with the neighbor kingdom because of it. Ethan kept on telling, and Harry lay there with her eyes closed and her fingers holding the morphine drip control, but she smiled now and again.

Then Harry threw up slime with blood in it. She gagged, and I put my hand on her chest and breathed out to her. She moaned. Then she said, 'You know, they chopped me up for no reason, Clemmy. They took me apart and poisoned me, but it just made it worse.' Bruno looked so upset. Tears spurted from his eyes.

Right at that moment a wiry man, with long hair and a beard, wearing a T-shirt with a skull on it, came skipping into the room – I mean skipping the way kids skip, step-hop, step-hop – and he started talking real loud and waving his arms like a windmill. To be honest, for a second I thought one of those crazy characters from Harry's stories had come to life. He bowed down to us like a man who was going to play the piano for a whole hall full of people, and then he shook his fist at the ceiling. But he was winding himself up into a sermon. The words came out fast and furious. The way he talked reminded me of this inspirational preacher Grandma Lucy took me to once, but that guy had his hair all slicked down with grease, and he wore a navy blue suit. The wiry man talked about faith and zeal and tribulation and the blood of the cross and lambs and angels and storms and lightning crashing in the sky and September 11 and even the Internet, although I wasn't sure how that fit into it. I kept trying to read his aura, but he was hopping around the room on his bowed legs, all jerky and nervous, and it was hard to tell what he was sending off. Harry was moaning, and Bruno looked very angry, and I thought he was going to hit the little man.

Suddenly, the preaching man turned quiet. He said, 'Break thou the arm of the evil and wicked man.' It's from one of the Psalms. I learned most of them when I was younger. It's not one of the comforting ones, though, not like lying down in green pastures. Then he hopped right over to Psalm 22, another scary passage: 'I am poured out like water, / and all my bones are out of joint; / my heart is like wax; / it is melted in the midst of my bowels. / My strength is dried up like a potsherd; / and my tongue cleaveth to my jaws; / and thou hast brought me into the dust of death.' I never knew what a potsherd was.

I still had my hands on Harry, and I was breathing in rhythm, and she breathed with me. She said, 'I am like a broken vessel.' So Harry must have known her Bible too. I wouldn't have supposed it, but later Ethan told me Harry had read so many books and of course she knew the Bible because it was 'great literature.' He was a little snobby about it. Oh well.

We took her outside because Harry said she wanted to see the water and the sky. Pearl thought this might be too much. But Harry really wanted it, and Bruno said we were going to do it no matter what. His face was all red, and he said, 'Goddamn it, if that's what she wants, that's what she's getting.'

It was a big production. We took the IV with us because it rolled, but we had to get her into the wheelchair, which wasn't easy because she was so tender everywhere; and she was so cold, we had to bundle her up in a big sweater and scarf and wrap two blankets around her. Maisie found a nice green hat with a brim for her head, even though it was spring and the air was warm. Harry looked pretty funny, I have to say. When she was all ready to go out, it was awfully hard to find the person inside all the wrappings. It looked like we were wheeling out a long sleeping bag in a hat. We took her down in the building's freight elevator. I hadn't even noticed it before. Bruno said he was the one who had to steer the chair because he knew how to handle it, but he bumped Harry a couple of times anyway, and she would squawk 'Ow' every time, but just for a second. Pearl came along with us, all calm and clear with her straight-up-and-down posture, very dignified, and the skinny man, too, who seemed tuckered out from his sermon, was walking with a limp all of a sudden. I wondered if he wasn't feeling sympathy for Harry and it made him lame for a while.

Ethan whispered to me that the wiry person was the Barometer. His mother was killed by a tornado, and he had spent time, a lot of time, in mental hospitals, but he lived with Harry and Bruno now.

We wheeled Harry down by the water so she could take a look at it. I think she wanted to feel the sun on her face, because she lifted it up to the sky. Kali was prancing on the leash and pulling me here and there to get in the smells. How she loves her smells.

I pulled Kali back from the others and walked a few yards away. I thought they should have Harry to themselves – Bruno and Maisie and Ethan should, anyway. I watched the gulls and looked over at Lady Liberty. I thought about what Harry must be feeling because she wouldn't see her again, not like this, anyway. I wanted her to know it would be better, more beautiful on the other side, but it was sad because we can't help loving what's around us even if it is grasping and attachment to the things that don't really matter when you take a higher spiritual perspective. The trip didn't last long. Harry couldn't take it. Her hat fell into her face, and Maisie had to straighten it out because Harry was too feeble to do it. She fixed her mom's scarf, too, and I heard Harry whisper, 'I'm the baby now.' And Maisie smiled, but when she walked along beside Bruno and Harry couldn't see, Maisie's face was wet as wet could be with all the tears.

Aven, Harry's granddaughter, arrived after her school was over. She was a tall kid for her age, with short hair, big eyes, and a serious face. She looked like a tomboy. Ethan said, 'She hates pink. Won't wear it.' He said she was a math whiz, too:

'Calculates like that.' He snapped his fingers. I think she knew she was going to say goodbye to Harry. She called her Grandmother. I kind of wish she could have seen Harry a little earlier in the day, because Harry was so exhausted from the trip down to the water that she couldn't really say much. Maisie brought Aven up to Harry, and Aven looked at her grandmother's white wrinkled skin with a big vein standing out in her temple and at her eyes, which were all caved in, and at her flaky chapped lips, and she was afraid. She held back, didn't want to touch her grandma. Maisie gave her a little punch in her back to push her toward Harry, and I could see Aven's face crumple up, and she sucked her lips into her mouth. She was only eight years old. Maybe nine. I knew Aven was about to burst out crying, so I picked up Kali and brought her over to the two of them. Kali whimpered a little, and she sniffed Harry. Kali knew. My little dog knew just what was going on. So I took Aven's hand in mine, and we petted Kali together, and then I put our hands on Harry's shoulder very gently, and we petted Harry together for a while, but I kept my other arm around Aven's shoulder. Then I felt Maisie's hand on my back. That was nice. Maisie thought it was okay. Harry's eyes were teary, and I thought she was going to start bawling with her granddaughter standing there in front of her; but she looked at Aven, and her bleary eyes didn't look so bleary for a second, and she made a noise in her throat and then, as loudly as she could, which wasn't very loud, she croaked out, 'Fight for yourself. Don't let anybody push you around. You hear me?'

Aven bit her bottom lip, and I could see her white teeth. She looked at her mother because she didn't know what to say. Maisie nodded at her. It was the smallest nod I ever saw in my whole life, and Aven said, 'I won't, Grandmother. I promise.' To be honest, I said a long 'Whew' to myself. I felt glad we had gotten through that one without some big emotional disaster.

Well, after that, we waited mostly. Bruno didn't leave Harry. He had a bed set up right beside her. There was room for all of us. Maisie, Oscar, and Aven slept in one of the rooms, and they gave me and Kali a little study room down the hall, where Harry had done her bills for her foundation and stuff. Ethan kissed me again but he went into a room by himself. Winsome arrived for her shift. Harry was still alive in the morning but restless, talking and moaning. Dr Gupta came to look at her, and he talked to Bruno in the corner. Bruno was nodding. I didn't understand the medical stuff, but they weren't going to let the pain get the better of Harry, so they gave her drugs and Harry got really quiet. She lay there as still as could be, so still it made me think about how all the leaves stop moving right before a big storm. I kept cleaning even though Bruno yelled at me, 'I still don't know what the hell you're doing here!' Ethan told him to leave me alone. 'Mother wanted her here. You know it and I know it,' he said. 'Let her stay.' Ethan was a hero to me right then.

Well, late in the morning, around eleven thirty, we were all sitting around, just waiting for Harry to die. I had done what I could, and I felt pretty confident the chakras were as clean as they were ever going to be. I had put my purple agate on her belly to open the spiritual flood when the time came, because it works on the upper chakra. Then, all of sudden, we saw Harry jolt in the bed, and in a voice that woke us all up, she said, 'No.' Then she said it again, and then a third time just for good measure. And after that, she said nothing at all.

A man named Phineas arrived that afternoon. He was a slender black guy, medium height, actually he was very light brown if you want me to describe him right. He had lots of freckles on his face and thin, arched eyebrows, and a soft mouth with a bottom lip that stuck out a little. I liked his clothes, skinny pants, boots, and a nice-looking sports jacket. They all knew him. Harry couldn't talk to him and that was too bad, because he'd come all the way from Argentina. Ethan informed me that he was one of Harry's covers. He had played a part for her, like Anton, but he hadn't been upset about it the way Anton was. Phineas sat beside Harry and talked to her even though she couldn't hear him, at least not in the ordinary way, because she was not awake anymore. He talked for a long time and he held her hand.

I remember he called her 'pal' and 'my pal, old pal.'

Later, Phinny – that was his nickname – ran out to get sandwiches for us, and we all sat and ate them and talked about this and that. Ethan read the newspaper that was lying on the table, and Maisie got upset and said we were all forgetting Harry, who was lying over there almost dead, and what were we doing? But I told her that's how it is. We aren't dying now. We will all die later. We have to eat. Harry would want us to eat, wouldn't she? It was raining outside, raining hard outside the windows, which were covered with little droplets that ran down the glass like tears. I remember thinking that.

That night I slept with Kali curled up next to me, and I wondered if Winsome or Bruno would come in and say that Harry had died, but she was alive in the morning. Dr Gupta told us her body was shutting down. But Harry was still breathing. And the rain stopped, and the sun came out, and Bruno opened the window to let in some air. I took Kali out for a walk and ran with her past the water taxis and the big warehouse where they show art, and I thought maybe Harry should have had her works in there. When I came back in we waited some more. I studied Harry's aura – so much cleaner. The colors were pure. Some red, but lots of greens and blues. It made me happy because I had answered my destiny. I daydreamed about my apartment and my teas all lined up in my kitchenette and the clients I had canceled to be with Harry, and I was a little bored while I was waiting, to tell the truth, but I didn't want to leave her yet. I wanted to be there for the transition, for the time when Harry would leave our world for higher realms of consciousness.

Before she left, Harry made a strange sound, a deep, dark shaking noise, and when I heard it, the sound bounced around in my own head, an announcement of an end and a new beginning. We were so quiet. I did not go to Harry, but I saw the light leap up and out around her. Dr Gupta, solemn and straight, told us she was dead. Harry looked so still and her skin was kind of see-through, but I didn't see a shred of pain in her face. I knew it was time for me to step away. Bruno was holding her, and Maisie and Ethan were standing by the bed, so just a few minutes later, I picked up Kali and my bag of stones and toe-heeled my way out of the room as quiet as a mouse and called Legends from the kitchen to come and pick me up. I left the purple agate, and I hoped they would remember to rinse it.

I have only one thing left to say. I stayed in touch with Ethan and, about eight months later, he asked me if I wanted to come and see some of Harry's work while it was still in the studio. They were organizing it or something. I said yes. Maisie and Ethan took me in. I'd left Kali with Deborah, my neighbor in the building, because Deb just loves babysitting her. Ethan unlocked a door, opened it, and flicked on the lights that came on above me. It was late fall, and the sky through the windows was gray with some brown and white in it. They told me Bruno and the Barometer were still living there in the building, and that they didn't get along too well, so there were problems, but they were trying to sort them out and there was something about Harry's will and that she had provided for them; but I wasn't listening, because I was looking around me at all the things in the room, the big soft dolls and the rooms and the houses. There were some small sculptures hanging from the ceiling. One was of a penis, and I just had to laugh at it. And then I felt that funny lifting feeling I get sometimes, as if I'm getting pulled up toward the ceiling. It was a sign, maybe it was coming from Harry. I could feel something important was happening to me and then I saw a woman squatting on the floor, not a real person, but a great big statue with no hair. And she had lots of people inside her head, but also numbers and letters, and she was raining numbers and letters and little people from her private parts, her vagina, anyway, and I felt a big grin come over my face, and I walked over to her to get a close look. There's a lot of art I don't understand. To be honest, it's kind of boring to me, but this was different. I got down on my hands and knees and started looking around at the tiny ones, and I had the sacred feeling. I told Ethan I had it. I opened up my arms and said, 'Wow,' and then I saw her.

'Look,' I said to them. 'Look, it's Harry. Can I touch her?' They didn't know that Harry had put herself into the art, so it was exciting. I pointed at the little person, and Ethan and Maisie got down on their knees. They saw her right away. Maisie said, 'It's Mother, all right.' 'Look,' I said, 'she's just walking along, all happy and healthy, just minding her own business, looking up at the sky.' I guess there were too many little sculptures for them to have noticed their teeny-weeny mom among all those other little people.

They told me about the lady philosopher who was almost forgotten, whose name I can't remember, but who inspired the big woman and all her little people. She lived a long, long time ago, in the medieval times, I think. Margot, maybe. I'm awfully bad at remembering names. I'll have to ask Ethan about her when I see him again. But the important fact is this: While I was down on my knees looking at the little figure of Harry, it started to glow. I swear. It glowed purple. I was seeing its energy. It had an electromagnetic field – that little thing did. I was very quiet then. We walked around and looked at some of the other pieces of art, and then, when we were just about to go through the door, I turned around to take one last look at Harry's artworks, and then I saw their auras blazing out all around them. I took a big breath in and held it for a few seconds. They weren't people, after all. They were just things a person had made. For the first time, I really had the understanding of why the master taught that there were artists on the higher plane living on Sirius. It was because they had given their spirits and energies into what they made. They must have had a lot of extra energy to give away. Anyway, I swear the whole room was lit by those shivering rainbows.

Ethan and Maisie must have seen that something had happened to me, because they asked me what the matter was, but I said nothing was the matter. I said I was fine, which I was. If I had told them about the lights and the colors, they would've given me more funny looks, even though they meant well and were really kindhearted. Both of them were. I closed my eyes. I opened them again, and I just stood there smiling because the colors were still there – reds and oranges and yellows and greens and blues and violets – blazing hot and bright in that big room where Harry used to work, and I knew for certain that each and every one of those wild, nutty, sad things Harry had made was alive with the spirit. For a second there, I could almost hear them breathing.